VIVA MODERN CRITICAL INTERPRETATIONS

Bram Stoker's

Dracula

VIVA MODERN CRITICAL INTERPRETATIONS

Bram Stoker's
Dracula

Edited and with an Introduction by
HAROLD BLOOM
Sterling Professor of the Humanities
Yale University

Viva Books

New Delhi | Mumbai | Chennai | Kolkata | Bangalore | Hyderabad | Kochi | Guwahati

First Indian Edition 2010

VIVA BOOKS PRIVATE LIMITED

- 4737/23 Ansari Road, Daryaganj, New Delhi 110 002
  E-mail: vivadelhi@vivagroupindia.net, Tel. 42242200
- 76, Service Industries, Shirvane, Sector 1, Nerul, Navi Mumbai 400 706
  E-mail: vivamumbai@vivagroupindia.net, Tel. 27721273, 27721274
- Jamals Fazal Chambers, 26 Greams Road, Chennai 600 006
  E-mail: vivachennai@vivagroupindia.net, Tel. 28290304, 28294241
- B-103, Jindal Towers, 21/1A/3 Darga Road, Kolkata 700 017
  E-mail: vivakolkata@vivagroupindia.net, Tel. 22836381, 22816713
- 7, Sovereign Park Apartments, 56-58, K. R. Road, Basavanagudi, Bangalore 560 004
  E-mail: vivabangalore@vivagroupindia.net, Tel. 26607409, 26607410
- 101-102 Mughal Marc Apartments, 3-4-637 to 641, Narayanguda, Hyderabad 500 029
  E-mail: vivahyderabad@vivagroupindia.net, Tel. 27564481, 27564482
- First Floor, Beevi Towers, SRM Road, Kaloor, Kochi 682 018, Kerala
  E-mail: vivakochi@vivagroupindia.net, Tel: 0484-2403055, 2403056
- 232, GNB Road, Beside UCO Bank, Silpukhuri, Guwahati 781 003
  E-mail: vivaguwahati@vivagroupindia.net, Tel: 0361-2666386

www.vivagroupindia.com

Published by arrangement with

Facts on File, Inc.
132 West 31st Street
New York 10001
USA

ISBN 978-81-309-0643-0

All links and web addresses were checked and verified to be correct at the time of publications. Because of the dynamic nature of the web, some addresses and links may have changed since publication and may no longer be valid.

Every effort has been made to trace the owners of copyrighted materialand secure copyright permission. Articles appearing in this volume generally appear much as they did in their original publication with little to no editorial changes. Those interested in locating the original source will find bibliographic information on the first page of each article as well as in the bibliography and acknowledgments sections of this volume.

Published by Vinod Vasishtha for Viva Books Private Limited, 4737/23, Ansari Road, Daryaganj, New Delhi-110 002. Printed and bound by Anand Sons, Delhi - 110092.

Contents

Editor's Note

My Introduction meditates upon sexuality and violence, both preternatural and human, in Bram Stoker's *Dracula*.

Phyllis A. Roth, in a psychoanalytical reading, regards *Dracula* as yet one more version of the Oedipal fantasy, while Carol A. Senf conflates Dracula and his human male opponents so that any opposition between good and evil vanishes from the tale.

In a Marxist interpretation, Geoffrey Wall gives us a *Dracula* that secretly "discourses" on the family, sexuality, race and empire, after which Christopher Craft finds a secret or repressed "homoerotic union" that binds together Count Dracula's hunters and destroyers.

John Allen Stevenson views *Dracula* as a "meditation upon foreignness," and so as a racist book, while Daniel Pick, in another kind of Freudian reading, historicizes the novel in the Age of Charcot, Nordau, and Lombroso, forerunners of Freud.

The late-Victorian/Edwardian fantastic is invoked as historical context by Kathleen L. Spencer, after which Jennifer Wicke focuses upon *Dracula* in terms of technology and consumption, so that her version of the book might be entitled *Dracula Typewriter*.

Laura Sagolla Croley offers us a *Dracula* in which the threat of vampirism "stands in for the late-century threat of the Lumpenproletariat," while Nina Auerbach concludes this cavalcade of our academy with a feminist reading, in which women scholars at last may possess a vampire of their own.

Introduction

Rereading the original *Dracula* on the verge of turning seventy-two is a curious and charming experience. Though the tale is rather clumsily organized, and quite without any eloquence in expressive style, it is decidedly not a Period Piece. Or, if it is, then we are still in Bram Stoker's era, after one hundred and five years. By this, I do not mean that our cinematic and popular novel versions of vampirism greatly resemble his. Ours are distinctly more vulgar, gory, and pathologically disturbed, and no better visualized or phrased than Stoker's. No, Stoker is our contemporary because his union of sexuality and violence is endemic among us.

I myself long have believed that in some sense *all* movies are vampire films, so that those explicitly vampiric merely expose all the implications of the medium. Our relation to those enlarged, colored representations upon the screen has something in it of Count Dracula's potential for enjoying his victims. Attending a stage drama, you are aware that you and the players ultimately share the one reality, but projections upon a screen release you from some of the inhibitions of a common humanity. How many movie actresses and actors are raped or vamped, in fantasy, every day everywhere!

As an archaic reader, I differ from all the essayists assembled in this volume, who employ lenses made available by psychoanalysis, Marxism, Foucault's historicism, feminism, deconstruction, queer theory, and the other fashions now prevalent in our institutions of higher learning. These essays are the best of what is now available, and doubtless they will help many seeking approaches to *Dracula*.

Stoker has a fascinated horror of all sexuality, perhaps because of the frustrations of his own marriage. He lived until 1912, fifteen years beyond

---

From *How to Read and Why*. ©2000 by Harold Bloom.

the publication of his one successful book, but evidently suffered terribly from the effects of syphillis, which I think hover in the undersong of *Dracula*.

Are we to think of *Dracula* as an exemplification of the violence of sexuality, or rather of the sexuality of violence? The difference is more than verbal, though any distinction disappears in our vampire movies and Anne Rice's potboilers. Bram Stoker is unhealthy enough, though positively restrained in comparison to our entertainments.

Dracula, such as it is, owes a great deal to Mary Shelley's *Frankenstein* (1818) and to Robert Louis Stevenson's *The Strange Case of Dr. Jekyll and Mr. Hyde* (1886). Poor Stoker cannot sustain comparison with either, as both of them thought clearly and wrote superbly. What *Dracula* takes from them is lessons in the intrusion of the uncanny into the everyday. Mrs. Shelley and the superb Stevenson can terrify the reader very subtly; Stoker is hopelessly crude in his assaults, and yet effective enough.

Stoker's Count Dracula in some respects could be Rohmer's Fu Manchu; the two villains have varying culinary tastes, but the same power-drive, and one is no more deftly characterized than the other. As for the female protagonists, Stoker hasn't a clue as to how to distinguish inwardly between the feckless Lucy and the fortunate Mina. That leaves Van Helsing, as a kind of monster of righteousness, and Jonathan Harker, slow to learn but fierce once instructed, and the amiably violent "band of brothers" who decimate Dracula's gypsies, with a savage gusto both exemplary and a touch disconcerting. I answer my former question by hazarding that the true subject of Stoker's tale is the sexuality of violence. Compared to that, the murderous sexuality of Dracula and his three red-lipped huri dwindles into relative ineffectuality.

Dracula is far more interesting for its influence upon us than it can be in itself, given Stoker's inferior gifts as a writer. Rather like some of Poe's dreadfully stylized stories, *Dracula* verges upon myth because it has contaminated our nightmares. Stoker inaugurates our sordid dilemma, by suggesting that there are two choices only: become a vampire, or transform yourself into a sublimely violent murderer of vampires.

PHYLLIS A. ROTH

Suddenly Sexual Women in Bram Stoker's Dracula

Criticism of Bram Stoker's *Dracula*, though not extensive, yet not insubstantial, points primarily in a single direction: the few articles published perceive *Dracula* as the consistent success it has been because, in the words of Royce MacGillwray, "Such a myth lives not merely because it has been skillfully marketed by entrepreneurs [primarily the movie industry] but because it expresses something that large numbers of readers feel to be true about their own lives."[1] In other words, *Dracula* successfully manages a fantasy which is congruent with a fundamental fantasy shared by many others. Several of the interpretations of *Dracula* either explicitly or implicitly indicate that this "core fantasy"[2] derives from the Oedipus complex—indeed, Maurice Richardson calls *Dracula* "a quite blatant demonstration of the Oedipus complex ... a kind of incestuous, necrophilous, oral-anal-sadistic all-in wrestling match"[3] and this reading would seem to be valid.

Nevertheless, the Oedipus complex and the critics' use of it does not go far enough in explaining the novel: in explaining what I see to be the primary focus of the fantasy content and in explaining what allows Stoker and, vicariously, his readers, to act out what are essentially threatening, even horrifying wishes which must engage the most polarized of ambivalences. I propose, in the following, to summarize the interpretations to date, to indicate the pre-Oedipal focus of the fantasies, specifically the child's relation

From *Literature and Psychology* 27, no. 3 (1977): 113-121.

with and hostility toward the mother, and to indicate how the novel's fantasies are managed in such a way as to transform horror into pleasure. Moreover, I would emphasize that for both the Victorians and twentieth century readers, much of the novel's great appeal derives from its hostility toward female sexuality. In "Fictional Convention and Sex in *Dracula*," Carrol Fry observes that the female vampires are equivalent to the fallen women of eighteenth and nineteenth century fiction.[4]

The facile and stereotypical dichtomy between the dark woman and the fair, the fallen and the idealized, is obvious in *Dracula*. Indeed, among the more gratuitous passages in the novel are those in which the "New Woman" who is sexually aggressive is verbally assaulted. Mina Harker remarks that such a woman, whom she holds in contempt, "will do the proposing herself."[5] Additionally, we must compare Van Helsing's hope "that there are good women still left to make life happy" (207) with Mina's assertion that "the world seems full of good men—even if there *are* monsters in it" (250). A remarkable contrast![6]

Perhaps nowhere is the dichotomy of sensual and sexless woman more dramatic than it is in *Dracula* and nowhere is the suddenly sexual woman more violently and self-righteously persecuted than in Stoker's "thriller." The equation of vampirism with sexuality is well established in the criticism. Richardson refers to Freud's observation that "morbid dread always signifies repressed sexual wishes."[7] We must agree that *Dracula* is permeated by "morbid dread." However, another tone interrupts the dread of impending doom throughout the novel; that note is one of lustful anticipation, certainly anticipation of catching and destroying forever the master vampire, Count Dracula, but additionally, lustful anticipation of a consummation one can only describe as sexual. One thinks, for example, of the candle's "sperm" which "dropped in white patches" on Lucy's coffin as Van Helsing opens it for the first time (220). Together the critics have enumerated the most striking instances of this tone and its attendant imagery, but to recall: first, the scene in which Jonathan Harker searches the Castle Dracula, in a state of fascinated and morbid dread, for proof of his host's nature. Harker meets with three vampire women (whose relation to Dracula is incestuous[8]) whose appeal is described almost pornographically:

> All three had brilliant white teeth that shone like pearls against the ruby of their voluptuous lips. There was something about them that made me uneasy, some longing and at the same time deadly fear. I felt in my heart a wicked, burning desire that they would kiss me with those red lips.

The three debate who has the right to feast on Jonathan first, but they conclude, "He is young and strong; there are kisses for us all" (47). While this discussion takes place, Jonathan is "in an agony of delightful anticipation" (48). At the very end of the novel, Van Helsing falls prey to the same attempted seduction by, and the same ambivalence toward, the three vampires.

Two more scenes of relatively explicit and uninhibited sexuality mark the novel about one-half, then two-thirds, through. First the scene in which Lucy Westenra is laid to her final rest by her fiance, Arthur Holmwood, later Lord Godalming, which is worth quoting from at length:

> Arthur placed the point [of the stake] over the heart, and as I looked I could see its dint in the white flesh. Then he struck with all his might.
>
> The thing in the coffin writhed; and a hideous, blood-curdling screech came from the opened red lips. The body shook and quivered and twisted in wild contortions; the sharp white teeth champed together till the lips were cut, and the mouth was smeared with a crimson foam. But Arthur never faltered. He looked like a figure of Thor as his untrembling arm rose and fell, driving deeper and deeper the mercy-bearing stake, whilst the blood from the pierced heart welled and spurted up around it (241).

Such a description needs no comment here, though we will return to it in another context. Finally, the scene which Joseph Bierman has described quite correctly as a "primal scene in oral terms,"[9] the scene in which Dracula slits open his breast and forces Mina Harker to drink his blood:

> With his left hand he held both Mrs. Harker's hands, keeping them away with her arms at full tension; his right hand gripped her by the back of the neck, forcing her face down on his bosom. Her white nightdress was smeared with blood, and a thin stream trickled down the man's bare chest which was shown by his torn-open dress. The attitude of the two had a terrible resemblance to a child forcing a kitten's nose into a saucer of milk to compel it to drink (313).

Two major points are to be made here, in addition to marking the clearly errotic nature of the descriptions. These are, in the main, the only sexual scenes and descriptions in the novel; and, not only are the scenes heterosexual,[10] they are incestuous, especially when taken together, as we shall see.

To consider the first point, only relations with vampires are sexualized in this novel; indeed, a deliberate attempt is made to make sexuality seem unthinkable in "normal relations" between the sexes. All the close relationships, including those between Lucy and her three suitors and Mina and her husband, are spiritualized beyond credibility. Only when Lucy becomes a vampire is she allowed to be "voluptuous," yet she must have been so long before, judging from her effect on men and from Mina's descriptions of her. (Mina, herself, never suffers the fate of voluptuousness before or after being bitten, for reasons which will become apparent later.) Clearly, then, vampirism is associated not only with death, immortality and orality; it is equivalent to sexuality.[11]

Moreover, in psychoanalytic terms, the vampirism is a disguise for greatly desired and equally strongly feared fantasies. These fantasies, as stated have encouraged critics to point to the Oedipus complex at the center of the novel. Dracula, for example, is seen, as the "father-figure of huge potency."[12] Royce MacGillwray remarks that:

> Dracula even aspires to be, in a sense, the father of the band that is pursuing him. Because he intends, as he tells them, to turn them all into vampires, he will be their creator and therefore "father."[13]

The major focus of the novel, in this analysis, is the battle of the sons against the father to release the desired woman, the mother, she whom it is felt originally belonged to the son till the father seduced her away. Richardson comments:

> the set-up reminds one rather of the primal horde as pictured somewhat fantastically perhaps by Freud in *Totem and Taboo*, with the brothers banding together against the father who has tried to keep all the females to himself.[14]

The Oedipal rivalry is not, however, merely a matter of the Van Helsing group, in which, as Richardson says, "Van Helsing represents the good father figure,"[15] pitted against the Big Daddy, Dracula. Rather, from the novel's beginning, a marked rivalry among the men is evident. This rivalry is defended against by the constant, almost obsessive, assertion of the value of friendship and *agape* among members of the Van Helsing group. Specifically, the defense of overcompensation is employed, most often by Van Helsing in his assertions of esteem for Dr. Seward and his friends. The others, too, repeat expressions of mutual affection *ad* nauseum: they clearly protest too much. Perhaps this is most obviously symbolized, and unintentionally exposed, by the blood transfusions from Arthur, Seward, Quincey Morris, and Van Helsing to Lucy Westenra. The great friendship among rivals for Lucy's hand lacks credibility and is especially strained when Van Helsing makes it clear that the transfusions (merely the reverse of the vampire's blood-letting) are in their nature sexual; others have recognized, too, that Van Helsing's warning to Seward not to tell Arthur that anyone else has given Lucy blood, indicates the sexual nature of the operation.[16] Furthermore, Arthur himself feels that, as a result of having given Lucy his blood, they are in effect married. Thus, the friendships of the novel mask a deep-seated rivalry and hostility.

Dracula does then appear to enact the Oedipal rivalry among sons and between the son and the father for the affections of the mother. The fantasy of parricide and its acting out is obviously satisfying. According to Holland, such a threatening wish-fulfillment can be rewarding when properly defended against or associated with other pleasurable fantasies. Among the other fantasies are those of life after death, the triumph of "good over evil," mere man over super-human forces, and the rational West over the mysterious East.[17] Most likely not frightening and certainly intellectualized, these simplistic abstractions provide a diversion from more threatening material and assure the fantast that God's in his heaven: all's right with the world. On the surface, this is the moral of the end of the novel: Dracula is safely reduced to ashes, Mina is cleansed, the "boys" are triumphant. Were this all the theme of interest the novel presented, however, it would be neither so popular with Victorians and their successors nor worthy of scholarly concern.

Up to now my discussion has been taken from the point of view of reader identification with those who are doing battle against the evil in this world, against Count Dracula. On the surface of it, this is where one's sympathies lie in reading the novel and it is this level of analysis which has been explored by previous critics. However, what is far more significant in the interrelation of fantasy and defense is the duplication of characters and structure which betrays an identification with Dracula and a fantasy of matricide underlying the more obvious parricidal wishes.

As observed, the split between the sexual vampire family and the asexual Van Helsing group is not at all clear-cut: Jonathan, Van Helsing, Seward and Holmwood are all overwhelmingly attracted to the vampires, to sexuality. Fearing this, they employ two defenses, projection[18] and denial: it is not we who want the vampires, it is they who want us (to eat us, to seduce us, to kill us). Despite the projections, we should recall that almost all the on-stage killing is done by the "good guys": that of Lucy, the vampire women, and Dracula. The projection of the wish to kill onto the vampires wears thinnest perhaps when Dr. Seward, contemplating the condition of Lucy, asserts that "had she then to be killed I could have done it with savage delight" (236). Even earlier, when Dr. Seward is rejected by Lucy, he longs for a cause with which to distract himself from the pain of rejection: "Oh, Lucy, Lucy, I cannot be angry with you.... If I only could have as strong a cause as my poor mad friend there [significantly, he refers to Renfield]—a good, unselfish cause to make me work—that would be indeed happiness" (84). Seward's wish is immediately fulfilled by Lucy's vampirism and the subsequent need to destroy her. Obviously, the acting out of such murderous impulses is threatening: in addition to the defenses mentioned above, the use of religion not only to exorcise the evil but to justify the murders is striking. In other words, Christianity is on our side, we *must* be right. In this connection, it is helpful to mention Wasson's observation[19] of the significance of the name "Lord Godalming" (the point is repeated). Additional justification is provided by the murdered themselves: the peace into which they subside is to be read as a thank you note. Correlated with the religious defense is one described by Freud in *Totem and Taboo* in which the violator of the taboo can avert disaster by Lady MacBeth-like compulsive rituals and renunciations.[20] The repeated use of the Host, the complicated ritual of the slaying of the vampires, and the ostensible, though not necessarily conscious, renunciation of sexuality are the penance paid by those in *Dracula* who violate the taboos against incest and the murder of parents.

Since we now see that Dracula acts out the repressed fantasies of the others, since those others wish to do what he can do, we have no difficulty in recognizing an identification with the aggressor on the part of characters and reader alike. It is important, then, to see what it is that Dracula is after.

The novel tells of two major episodes, the seduction of Lucy and of Mina, to which the experience of Harker at Castle Dracula provides a preface, a hero, one whose narrative encloses the others and with whom, therefore, one might readily identify. This, however, is a defense against the central identification of the novel with Dracula and his attacks on the women. It is relevant in this context to observe how spontaneous and ultimately trivial Dracula's interest in Harker is. When Harker arrives at Castle Dracula, his host makes a lunge for him, but only after Harker has cut his finger and is bleeding. Dracula manages to control himself and we hear no more about his interest in Harker's blood until the scene with the vampire women when he says, "This man belongs to me!" (49) and, again a little later, "have patience. Tonight is mine. To-morrow night is yours!" (61) After this we hear no more of Dracula's interest in Jonathan; indeed, when Dracula arrives in England, he never again goes after Jonathan. For his part, Jonathan appears far more concerned about the vampire women than about Dracula—they are more horrible and fascinating to him. Indeed, Harker is relieved to be saved from the women by Dracula. Moreover, the novel focusses on the Lucy and Mina episodes from which, at first, the Jonathan episodes may seem disconnected; actually, they are not, but we can only see why after we understand what is going on in the rest of the novel.

In accepting the notion of identification with the aggressor in *Dracula*, as I believe we must, what we accept is an understanding of the reader's identification with the aggressor's victimization of women. Dracula's desire is for the destruction of Lucy and Mina and what this means is obvious when we recall that his attacks on these two closest of friends seem incredibly coincidental on the narraitve level. Only on a deeper level is there no coincidence at all: the level on which one recognizes that Lucy and Mina are essentially the same figure: the mother. Dracula is, in fact, the same story told twice with different outcomes. In the former, the mother is more desirable, more sexual, more threatening and must be destroyed. And the physical descriptions of Lucy reflect this greater ambivalence: early in the story, when Lucy is not yet completely vampirized, Dr. Seward describes her hair "in its usual sunny ripples;; (180); later, when the men watch her return to her tomb, Lucy is described as "a dark-haired woman" (235). The conventional fair/dark split, symbolic of respective moral casts, seems to be unconscious here, reflecting the ambivalence aroused by the sexualized female. Not only is Lucy the more sexualized figure, she is the more rejecting figure, rejecting two of the three "sons" in the novel. This section of the book ends with her destruction, not by Dracula but by the man whom she was to marry. The novel could not end here, though; the story had to be told again to assuage the anxiety occasioned by matricide. This time, the mother is much less sexually threatening and is ultimately saved. Moreover, Mina is never described physically and is the opposite of rejecting: all the men become her sons, symbolized by the naming of her actual son after them all. What remains constant is the attempt to destroy the mother. What changes is the way the fantasies are managed. To speak of the novel in terms of the child's ambivalence toward the mother is not just to speak psychoanalytically. We need only recall that Luch, as "bloofer lady," as well as the other vampire women, prey on children. In the case of Lucy, the children are as attracted to her as threatened by her.

I have already described the evidence that the Van Helsing men themselves desire to do away with Lucy. Perhaps the story needed to be retold because the desire was too close to the surface to be satisfying; certainly, the reader would not be satisifed had the novel ended with Arthur's murder of Lucy. What is perhaps not so clear is that the desire to destroy Mina is equally strong. Let us look first at the defenses against this desire. I have already mentioned the great professions of affection for Mina made by most of the male characters. Mina indeed acts and is treated as both the saint and the mother (ironically, this is particularly clear when she comforts Arthur for the loss of Lucy). She is all good, all pure, all true. When, however, she is seduced away from the straight and narrow by Dracula, she is "unclean," tainted and stained with a mark on her forehead immediately occasioned by Van Helsing's touching her forehead with the Host. Van Helsing's hostility toward Mina is further revealed when he cruelly reminds her of her "intercourse" with Dracula: "'Do you forget,' he said, with actually a smile, 'that last night he banqueted heavily and will sleep late?'" (328) This hostility is so obvious that the other men are shocked. Nevertheless, the "sons," moreover, and the reader as well, identify with Dracula's attack on Mina; indeed, the men cause it, as indicated by the events which transpire when all the characters are at Seward's hopsital-asylum. The members of the brotherhood go out at night to seek out Dracula's lairs, and they leave Mina undefended at the hospital. They claim that this insures her safety; in fact, it insures the reverse. Furthermore, this is the real purpose in leaving Mina out of the plans and in the hospital. They have clear indications in Renfield's warnings of what is to happen to her and they all, especially her husband, observe that she is not well and seems to be getting weaker. That they could rationalize these signs away while looking for and finding them everywhere else further indicates that they are avoiding seeing what they want to ignore; in other words, they want Dracula to get her. This is not to deny that they also want to save Mina; it is simply to claim that the ambivalence toward the mother is fully realized in the novel.

We can now return to that ambivalence and, I believe, with the understanding of the significance of the mother figure, comprehend the precise perspective of the novel. Several critics have correctly emphasized the regression to both orality and anality[21] in *Dracula*. Certainly, the sexuality is perceived in oral terms. The primal scene already discussed makes abundantly clear that intercourse is perceived in terms of nursing. As C. F. Bentley sees it:

> Stoker is describing a symbolic act of enforced fellation, where blood is again a substitute for semen, and where a chaste female suffers a violation that is essentially sexual. Of particular interest in the ... passage is the striking image of "a child forcing a kitten's nose into a saucer of milk to compel it to drink," suggesting an element of regressive infantilism in the vampire superstition.[22]

The scene referred to is, in several senses, the climax of the novel; it is the most explicit view of the act of vampirism and is, therefore, all the more significant as an expression of the nature of sexual intercourse as the novel depicts it. In it, the woman is doing the sucking. Bierman comments that "The reader by this point in the novel has become used to Dracula doing the sucking, but not to Dracula being sucked and specifically at the breast."[23] While it is true that the reader may most often think of Dracula as the active partner, the fact is that the scenes of vampire sexuality are described from the male perspective, with the females as the active assailants.[24] Only the acts of phallic aggression, the killings, involve the males in active roles. *Dracula*, then, dramatizes the child's view of intercourse insofar as it is seen as a wounding and a killing. But the primary preoccupation, as attested to by the primal scene, is with the role of the female in the act. Thus, it is not surprising that the central anxiety of the novel is the fear of the devouring woman and, in documenting this, we will find that all the pieces of the novel fall into place, most especially the Jonathan Harker prologue.

As mentioned, Harker's desire and primary anxiety is not with Dracula but with the female vampires. In his initial and aborted seduction by them, he describes his ambivalence. Interestingly, Harker seeks out this episode by violating the Count's (father's) injuction to remain in his room; "let me warn you with all seriousness, that should you leave these rooms you will not by any chance go to sleep in any other part of the castle" (42). This, of course, is what Harker promptly does. When Dracula breaks in and discovers Harker with the vampire women, he acts like both a jealous husband and an irate father: "His eyes were positively blazing. The red light in them was lurid ... 'How dare you touch him, any of you?'" (48-49). Jonathan's role as child here is reinforced by the fact that, when Dracula takes him away from the women, he gives them a child as substitute. But most interesting is Jonathan's perspective as he awaits, in a state of erotic arousal, the embraces of the vampire women, especially the fair one: "The other was fair as fair can be, with great wavy masses of golden hair and eyes like pale sapphires. I seemed somehow to know her face and to know it in connection with some dreamy fear, but I could not recollect at the moment how or where" (47). As far as we know, Jonathan never recollects, but we should be able to understand that the face is that of the mother (almost archetypally presented), she whom he desires yet fears, the temptress-seductress, Medusa. Moreover, this golden girl reappears in the early description of Lucy.

At the end of the following chapter, Jonathan exclaims, "I am alone in the castle with those awful women. Faugh! Mina is a woman, and there is nought in common." Clearly, however, there is. Mina at the breast of Count Dracula is identical to the vampire women whose desire is to draw out of the male the fluid necessary for life. That this is viewed as an act of castration is clear from Jonathan's conclusion: "At least God's mercy is better than that of these monsters, and the precipice is steep and high. At its foot a man may sleep—, *as a man*. Good-bye, all! Mina!" (4; emphasis mine).

The threatening Oedipal fantasy, the regression to a primary oral obsession, the attraction and destruction of the vampires of *Dracula* are, then, interrelated and interdependent. What they spell out is a fusion of the memory of nursing at the mother's breast with a primal scene fantasy which results in the conviction that the sexually desirable woman will annihilate if she is not first destroyed. The fantasy of incest and matricide evokes the mythic image of the *vagina dentata* evident in so many folk tales[25] in which the mouth and the vagina are identified with one another by the primitive mind and pose the threat of castration to all men until the teeth are extracted by the hero. The conclusion of *Dracula*, the "salvation" of Mina, is equivalent to such an "extraction": Mina will not remain the *vagina dentata* to threaten them all.

Central to the structure and unconscious theme of *Dracula* is, then, primarily the desire to destroy the threatening mother, she who threatens by being desirable. Otto Rank best explains why it is Dracula whom the novel seems to portray as the threat when he says, in a study which is pertinent to ours:

> through the displacement of anxiety on to the father, the renunciation of the mother, necessary for the sake of life is assured. For this feared father prevents the return to the mother and thereby the releasing of the much more painful primary anxiety, which is related to the mother's genitals as the place of birth and later transferred to objects taking the place of the genitals [such as the mouth].[26]

Finally, the novel has it both ways: Dracula is destroyed[27] and Van Helsing saved; Lucy is destroyed and Mina saved. The novel ends on a rather ironic note, given our understanding here, as Harker concludes with a quote from the good father, Van Helsing:

> "We want no proofs; we ask none to believe us! This boy will some day know what a brave and gallant woman his mother is. Already he knows her sweetness and loving care; later on he will understand how some men so loved her, that they did dare so much for her sake" (416).

NOTES

1. Royce MacGillwray, "*Dracula*: Bram Stoker's Spoiled Masterpiece," *Queen's Quarterly*, LXXIX, 518.

2. See Norman N. Holland, *The Dynamics of Literary Response* (New York: W. W. Norton & Co., 1975).

3. Maurice Richardson, "The Psychoanalysis of Ghost Stories," *Twentieth Century*, CLXVI (December 1959), 427.

4. *Victorian Newsletter*, XLII.

5. Bram Stoker, *Dracula* (New York: Dell, 1974), 103-104. All subsequent references will be to this edition and will appear parenthetically.

6. While it is not my concern in this paper to deal biographically with *Dracula*, the Harry Ludlam biography (a book which is admittedly anti-psychological in orientation despite its provocative title, *A Biography of Dracula: The Life Story of Bram Stoker*) includes some suggestive comments about Bram Stoker's relationship with his mother. Ludlam remarks an ambivalence toward women on the part of Charlotte Stoker who, on the one hand, decried the situation of poor Irish girls in the workhouse which was "the very hot-bed of vice'" and advocated respectability through emigration for the girls and, on the other, "declared often that she 'did not care tuppence' for her daughters." Too, Charlotte told her son Irish folk tales of banshee horrors and a true story of "the horrors she had suffered as a child in Sligo during the great cholera outbreak that claimed many thousands of victims in Ireland alone, and which provoked the most dreadful cruelties" (New York: The Fireside Press, 1962, p. 14). I cannot help but wonder how old Stoker was when his mother discussed these matters with him. Certainly, they made a vivid impression, for later, Charlotte wrote her story down and Bram based his own "The Invisible Giant" on his mother's tale of the cholera epidemic in Sligo.

7. Richardson, p. 419.

8. C. F. Bentley, "The Monster in the Bedroom: Sexual Symbolism in Bram Stoker's *Dracula*," *Literature and Psychology*, XXII, 1 (1972), 29.

9. Joseph S. Bierman, "*Dracula:* Prolonged Childhood Illness and the Oral Triad," *American Image*, XXIX, 194.

10. Bebtketm o, 27,

11. See Tsvetan Todorov, *The Fantastic*, trans, Richard Howard (Cleveland: Case Western Reserve, 1973), pp. 136-39.

12. Richardson, p. 427.

13. MacGillwray, p. 522.

14. Richardson, p. 428. The Oedipal fantasy of the destruction of the father is reinforced by a number of additional, and actually gratuitous, paternal deaths in the novel. See also MacGillwray, p. 523.

15. Richardson, p. 428.

16. See, for instance, Richardson, p. 427.

17. Richard Wasson, "The Politics of *Dracula*," *j English Literature in Translation*, IX, pp. 24-27.

18. Freud, *Totem and Taboo*, trans. James Strachey in *The Standard Edition of the Complete Psychological Works of Sigmund Freud*, Vol. XIII (1913-1914) (London: Hogarth press, 1962), 60-63.

19. Wasson, p. 26.

20. Freud, pp. 37ff.

21. Bentley, pp. 29-30; MacGillwray, p. 522.

22. Bentley, p. 30.

23. Bierman, p. 194. Bierman's analysis is concerned to demonstrate that "*Dracula* mirrors Stoker's early childhood....," and is a highly speculative but fascinating study. The emphasis is on Stoker's rivalry with his brothers but it provides, albeit indirectly, further evidence of hostility toward the rejecting mother.

24. Ludlam cites one of the actors in the original stage production of *Dracula* as indicating that the adaptation was so successful that "Disturbances in the circle or stalls as people felt faint and had to be taken out were not uncommon—and they were perfectly genuine, not a publicity stunt. Strangely enough, they were generally men'" (Ludlam, l. 165).

25. See, for instance, Wolfgang Lederer, M.D., *The Fear of Women* (New York: Harcourt Brace Jovanovich, Inc., 1968), especially the chapter entitled, "A Snapping of Teeth."

26. Otto Rank, *The Trauma of Birth* (New York: Harper & Row, 1973), p. 73.

27. When discussing this paper with a class, two of my students argued that Dracula is not, in fact, destroyed at the novel's conclusion. They maintained that his last look is one of triumph and that his heart is not staked but pierced by a mere bowie knife. Their suggestion that, at least, the men do not follow the elaborate procedures to insure the destruction of Dracula that they religiously observe with regard to that of the women, is certainly of value here, whether one agrees that Dracula still stalks the land. My thanks to Lucinda Donnelly and Barbara Kotacka for these observations.

CAROL A. SENF

Dracula: *The Unseen Face in the Mirror*

> The fault, dear Brutus, is not in our stars,
> But in ourselves, that we are underlings.
>
> *Julius Caesar*, I, ii, 134–35

Published in 1896, *Dracula* is an immensely popular novel which has never been out of print, has been translated into at least a dozen languages, and has been the subject of more films than any other novel. Only recently, however, have students of literature begun to take it seriously, partially because of the burgeoning interest in popular culture and partially because *Dracula* is a work which raises a number of troubling questions about ourselves and our society.[1] Despite this growing interest in Bram Stoker's best-known novel, the majority of literary critics read *Dracula* as a popular myth about the opposition of Good and Evil without bothering to address more specifically literary matters such as style, characterization, and method of narration. This article, on the other hand, focuses on Stoker's narrative technique in general and specifically on his choice of unreliable narrators. As a result, my reading of *Dracula* is a departure from most standard interpretations in that it revolves, not around the conquest of Evil by Good, but on the similarities between the two.

More familiar with the numerous film interpretations than with Stoker's novel, most modern readers are likely to be surprised by *Dracula* and

From *The Journal of Narrative Technique* 9, no. 3 Fall (1979): 160-170.

its intensely topical themes; and both the setting and the method of narration which Stoker chose contribute to this sense of immediacy. Instead of taking place in a remote Transylvanian castle or a timeless and dreamlike "anywhere," most of the action occurs in nineteenth-century London. Furthermore, Stoker de-emphasizes the novel's mythic qualities by telling the story through a series of journal extracts, personal letters, and newspaper clippings—the very written record of everyday life. The narrative technique resembles a vast jigsaw puzzle of isolated and frequently trivial facts; and it is only when the novel is more than half over that the central characters piece these fragments together and, having concluded the Dracula is a threat to themselves and their society, band together to destroy him.

On the surface, the novel appears to be a mythic re-enactment of the opposition between Good and Evil because the narrators attribute their pursuit and ultimate defeat of Dracula to a high moral purpose. However, although his method of narration doesn't enable him to comment directly on his characters' failures in judgment or lack of self-knowledge, Stoker provides several clues to their unreliability and encourages the reader to see the frequent discrepancies between their professed beliefs and their actions. The first clue is an anonymous preface (unfortunately omitted in many modern editions) which gives the reader a distinct warning:

> How these papers have been placed in sequence will be made manifest in the reading of them. All needless matters have been eliminated, so that a history almost at variance with the possibilities of later-day belief may stand forth as simple fact. There is throughout no statement of past things wherein memory may err, for all the records chosen are exactly contemporary, *given from the standpoints and within the range of knowledge of those who made them.*[2]

Writers of Victorian popular fiction frequently rely on the convention of the anonymous editor to introduce their tales and to provide additional comments throughout the text; and Stoker uses this convention to stress the subjective nature of the story which his narrators relate. The narrators themselves occasionally question the validity of their perceptions, but Stoker provides numerous additional clues to their unreliability. For example, at the conclusion, Jonathan Harker questions their interpretation of the events:

> We were stuck with the fact, that in all the mass of material of which the record is composed, there is hardly one authentic document; nothing but a mass of typewriting, except the later

> notebooks of Mina and Seward and myself, and Van Helsing's memorandum. We could hardly ask any one, even did we wish to, to accept these as proofs of so wild a story.[3]

The conclusion reinforces the subjective nature of their tale and casts doubts on everything that had preceded; however, because Stoker does not use an obvious framing device like Conrad in *Heart of Darkness* or James in *The Turn of the Screw* or employ an intrusive editor as Haggard does in *She* and because all the narrators come to similar conclusions about the nature of their opponent, the reader is likely to forget that these documents are subjective records, interpretations which are "given within the range of knowledge of those who made them."

While Stoker's choice of narrative technique does not permit him to comment directly on his characters, he suggests that they are particularly ill-equipped to judge the extraordinary events with which they are faced. The three central narrators are perfectly ordinary nineteenth-century Englishmen: the young lawyer Jonathan Harker, his wife Mina, and a youthful psychiatrist Dr. John Seward. Other characters who sometimes function as narrators include Dr. Van Helsing, Seward's former teacher; Quincy Morris, an American adventurer; Arthur Holmwood, a young English nobleman; and Lucy Westenra, Holmwood's fiancée. With the exception of Dr. Van Helsing, all the central characters are youthful and inexperienced—two dimensional characters whose only distinguishing characteristics are their names and their professions; and by maintaining a constancy of style throughout and emphasizing the beliefs which they hold in common, Stoker further diminishes any individualizing traits.[4] The narrators appear to speak with one voice; and Stoker suggests that their opinions are perfectly acceptable so long as they remain within their limited fields of expertise. The problem, however, is that these perfectly ordinary people are confronted with the extraordinary character of Dracula.

Although Stoker did model Dracula on the historical Vlad V of Wallachia and the East European superstition of the vampire,[5] he adds a number of humanizing touches to make Dracula appear noble and vulnerable as well as demonic and threatening; and it becomes difficult to determine whether he is a hideous bloodsucker whose touch breeds death or a lonely and silent figure who is hunted and persecuted.[6] The difficulty in interpreting Dracula's character is compounded by the narrative technique, for the reader quickly recognizes that Dracula is *never* seen objectively and never permitted to speak for himself while his actions are recorded by people who have determined to destroy him and who, moreover, repeatedly question the sanity of their quest.

The question of sanity, which is so important in *Dracula*, provides another clue to the narrators' unreliability. More than half the novel takes place in or near Dr. Seward's London mental institution; and several of the characters are shown to be emotionally unstable: Renfield, one of Dr. Seward's patients, is an incarcerated madman who believes that he can achieve immortality by drinking the blood of insects and other small creatures; Jonathan Harker suffers a nervous breakdown after he escapes from Dracula's castle; and Lucy Westenra exhibits signs of schizophrenia, being a model of sweetness and conformity while she is awake but becoming sexually aggressive and demanding during her sleepwalking periods. More introspective than most of the other narrators, Dr. Seward occasionally refers to the questionable sanity of their mission, his diary entries mentioning his fears that they will all wake up in straitjackets. Furthermore, his entries on Renfield's condition indicate that he recognizes the narrow margin which separates sanity from insanity: "It is wonderful, however, what intellectual recuperative power lunatics have, for within a few minutes he stood up quite calmly and looked about him" (p. 133).

However, even if the reader chooses to ignore the question of the narrators' sanity, it is important to understand their reasons for wishing to destroy Dracula. They accuse him of murdering the crew of the *Demeter*,[7] of killing Lucy Westenra and transforming her into a vampire, and of trying to do the same thing to Mina Harker. However, the log found on the dead body of the *Demeter*'s captain, which makes only a few ambiguous allusions to a fiend or monster, is hysterical and inconclusive. Recording this "evidence," Mina's journal asserts that the verdict of the inquest was openended: "There is no evidence to adduce; and whether or not the man [the ship's captain] committed the murders there is now none to say" (p. 100). Lucy's death might just as easily be attributed to the blood transfusions (still a dangerous procedure at the time Stoker wrote *Dracula*) to which Dr. Van Helsing subjects her; and Mina acknowledges her complicity in the affair with Dracula by admitting that she did not want to prevent his advances. Finally, even if Dracula is responsible for all the Evil of which he is accused, he is tried, convicted, and sentenced by men (including two lawyers) who give him no opportunity to explain his actions and who repeatedly violate the laws which they profess to be defending: they avoid an inquest of Lucy's death, break into her tomb and desecrate her body, break into Dracula's houses, frequently resort to bribery and coercion to avoid legal involvement, and openly admit that they are responsible for the deaths of five alleged vampires. While it can be argued that *Dracula* is a fantasy and therefore not subject to the laws of verisimilitude, Stoker uses the flimsiness of such "evidence" to focus on the contrast between the narrators' rigorous moral arguments and their all-too-pragmatic methods.

In fact, Stoker reveals that what condemns Dracula are the English characters' subjective responses to his character and to the way of life which he represents. The reader is introduced to Dracula by Jonathan Harker's journal. His first realization that Dracula is different from himself occurs when he looks into the mirror and discovers that Dracula casts no reflection:

> This time there could be no error, for the man was close to me, and I could see him over my shoulder. But there was no reflection of him in the mirror! The whole room behind me was displayed; but there was no sign of a man in it, except myself. This was startling, and, coming on the top of so many strange things, was beginning to increase that vague sense of uneasiness which I always have when the Count is near.
>
> (p. 34)

The fact that vampires cast no reflection is part of the iconography of the vampire in East European folklore, but Stoker translates the superstitious belief that creatures without souls have no reflection into a metaphor by which he can illustrate his characters' lack of moral vision. Harker's inability to "see" Dracula is a manifestation of moral blindness which reveals his insensitivity to others and (as will become evident later) his inability to perceive certain traits within himself.[8]

Even before Harker begins to suspect that Dracula is a being totally unlike himself, Stoker reveals that he is troubled by everything that Dracula represents. While journeying from London to Transylvania, Harker muses on the quaint customs which he encounters; and he notes in his journal that he must question his host about them. Stoker uses Harker's perplexity to establish his character as a very parochial Englishman whose apparent curiosity is not a desire for understanding, but a need to have his preconceptions confirmed. However, instead of finding someone like himself at the end of his journey, a person who can provide a rational explanation for these examples of non-English behavior, Harker discovers a ruined castle, itself a memento of bygone ages, and a man who, reminding him that Transylvania is not England, prides himself on being an integral part of his nation's heroic past:

> ... the Szekleys—and the Dracula as their heart's blood, their brains and their swords—can boast a record that mushroom growths like the Hapsburgs and the Romanoffs can never reach. The warlike days are over. Blood is too precious a thing in these days of dishonourable peace; and the glories of the great races are as a tale that is told.
>
> (p. 39)

To Harker, Dracula initially appears to be an anachronism—an embodiment of the feudal past—rather than an innately evil being; and his journal entries at the beginning merely reproduce Dracula's pride and rugged individualism:

> Here I am noble; I am *boyar;* the common people know me, and I am master. But a stranger in a strange land, he is no one; men know him not—and to know not is to care not for.... I have been so long master that I would be master still—or at least that none other should be master of me.
>
> (p. 28)

It is only when Harker realizes that he is assisting to take this anachronism to England that he becomes frightened.

Harker's later response indicates that he fears a kind of reverse imperialism, the threat of the primitive trying to colonize the civilized world, while the reader sees in his response a profound resemblance between Harker and Dracula:

> This was the being I was helping to transfer to London, where perhaps for centuries to come he might ... satiate his lust for blood, and create a new and ever-widening circle of semi-demons to batten on the helpless. The very thought drove me mad. A terrible desire came upon me to rid the world of such a monster. There was no lethal weapon at hand, but I seized a shovel which the workmen had been using to fill the cases, and lifting it high, struck, with the edge downward, at the hateful face.
>
> (pp. 62–63)

This scene reinforces Harker's earlier inability to see Dracula in the mirror. Taken out of context, it would be difficult to distinguish the man from the monster. Behavior generally attributed to the vampire—the habit of attacking a sleeping victim, violence, and irrational behavior—is revealed to be the behavior of the civilized Englishman also. The sole difference is that Stoker's narrative technique does not permit the reader to enter Dracula's thoughts as he stands over his victims. The reversal of roles here is important because it establishes the subjective nature of the narrators' beliefs, suggests their lack of self-knowledge, and serves to focus on the similarities between the narrators and their opponent. Later in the novel, Mina Harker provides the following analysis of Dracula which ironically also describes the single-mindedness of his pursuers:

> The Count is a criminal and of criminal type.... and *qua* criminal he is of imperfectly formed mind. Thus, in a difficulty he has to seek resource in habit.... Then, as he is criminal he is selfish; and as his intellect is small and his action is based on selfishness, he confines himself to one purpose.
>
> (p. 378)

Both Mina and Jonathan can justify their pursuit of Dracula by labeling him a murderer; and Mina adds intellectual frailty to his alleged sins. However, the narrators show themselves to be equally bound by habit and equally incapable of evaluating situations which are beyond their limited spheres of expertise. In fact, Stoker implies that the only difference between Dracula and his opponents is the narrators' ability to state individual desire in terms of what they believe is a common good. For example, the above scene shows that Harker can justify his violent attack on Dracula because he pictures himself as the protector of helpless millions; and the narrators insist on the duty to defend the innocents.

The necessity of protecting the innocent is called into question, however, when Dr. Van Helsing informs the other characters about the vampire's nature. While most of his discussion concerns the vampire's susceptibility to garlic, silver bullets, and religious artifacts, Van Helsing also admits that the vampire cannot enter a dwelling unless he is first invited by one of the inhabitants. In other words, a vampire cannot influence a human being without that person's consent. Dracula's behavior confirms that he is an internal, not an external, threat. Although perfectly capable of using superior strength when he must defend himself, he usually employs seduction, relying on the others' desires to emulate his freedom from external constraints: Renfield's desire for immortality, Lucy's wish to escape the repressive existence of an upper-class woman, and the desires of all the characters to overcome the restraints placed on them by their religion and their law. As the spokesman for civilization, Van Helsing appears to understand that the others might be tempted by their desires to become like Dracula and he warns them against the temptation:

> But to fail here, is not mere life or death. It is that we become as him; that we henceforward become foul things of the night like him—without heart or conscience, preying on the bodies and the souls of those we love best.
>
> (p. 265)

Becoming like Dracula, they too would be laws unto themselves—primitive [and] irrational—with nothing to justify their actions except the force of their desires. No longer would they need to rationalize their "preying on the bodies and souls of their loved ones" by concealing their lust for power under the rubric of religion, their love of violence under the names of imperialism and progress, their sexual desires within an elaborate courtship ritual.

The narrators attribute their hatred of Dracula to a variety of causes. Harker's journal introduces a being whose way of life is antithetical to theirs—a warlord, a representative of the feudal past and the leader of a primitive cult who he fears will attempt to establish a vampire colony in England. Mina Harker views him as a criminal and as the murderer of her best friend; and Van Helsing sees him as a moral threat, a kind of Anti-Christ. Yet, in spite of the narrators' moral and political language, Stoker reveals that Dracula is primarily a sexual threat, a missionary of desire whose only true kingdom will be the human body. Although he flaunts his independence of social restraints and proclaims himself a master over all he sees, Dracula adheres more closely to English law than his opponents in every area except his sexual behavior. (In fact, Dracula admits to Harker that he invited him to Transylvania so he could learn the subtle nuances of English law and business.) Neither a thief, rapist, nor an overtly political threat, Dracula is dangerous because he expresses his contempt for authority in the most individualistic of ways—through his sexuality. In fact, his thirst for blood and the manner in which he satisfies this thirst can be interpreted as sexual desire which fails to observe any of society's attempts to control it—prohibitions against polygamy, promiscuity, and homosexuality.[9] Furthermore, Stoker suggests that it is generally through sexuality that the vampire gains control over human beings. Van Helsing recognizes this temptation when he prevents Arthur from kissing Lucy right before her death; and even the staid and morally upright Harker momentarily succombs to the sensuality of the three vampire-women in Dracula's castle:

> I felt in my heart a wicked, burning desire that they would kiss me with those red lips. It is not good to note this down, lest some day it should meet Mina's eyes and cause her pain; but it is the truth.
>
> (p. 47)

For one brief moment, Harker does appear to recognize the truth about sexual desire; it is totally irrational and has nothing to do with monogamy, love, or even respect for the beloved. It is Dracula, however, who clearly articulates the characters' most intense fears of sexuality: "Your girls that you all love are mine already; and through them you and others shall yet be mine—my creatures, to do my bidding and to be my jackals when I want to feed" (p. 340). Implicit in Dracula's warning is the similarity between vampire and opponents. Despite rare moments of comprehension, however, the narrators generally choose to ignore this similarity; and their lack of self-knowledge permits them to hunt down and kill not only Dracula and the three women in his castle, but their friend Lucy Westenra as well.

The scene in which Arthur drives the stake through Lucy's body while the other men watch thoughtfully is filled with a violent sexuality which again connects vampire and opponents:

> But Arthur never faltered. He looked like a figure of Thor as his untrembling arm rose and fell, driving deeper and deeper the mercybearing stake, whilst the blood from the pierced heart welled and spurted up around it. His face was set, and high duty seemed to shine through it; the sight of it gave us courage so that our voices seemed to ring through the vault.... There in the coffin lay no longer the foul Thing that we had dreaded and grown to hate that the work of her destruction was yielded as a privilege to the one best entitled to it, but Lucy as we had seen her in life, with her face of unequalled sweetness and purity.
>
> (p. 241)

Despite Seward's elevated moral language, the scene resembles nothing so much as the combined group rape and murder of an unconscious woman; and this kind of violent attack on a helpless victim is precisely the kind of behavior which condemns Dracula in the narrators' eyes. Moreover, Lucy is not the only woman to be subjected to this violence. At the conclusion, in a scene which is only slightly less explicit, Dr. Van Helsing destroys the three women in Dracula's castle. Again Dr. Van Helsing admits that he is fascinated by the beautiful visages of the "wanton Un-Dead" but he never acknowledges that his violent attack is simply a role reversal or that he becomes the vampire as he stands over their unconscious bodies.

By the conclusion of the novel, all the characters who have been accused of expressing individual desire have been appropriately punished: Dracula, Lucy Westenra, and the three vampire-women have been killed; and even Mina Harker is ostracized for her momentary indiscretion. All that remains after the primitive, the passionate, and the individualistic qualities that were associated with the vampire have been destroyed is a small group of wealthy men who return after a period of one year to the site of their victory over the vampire. The surviving characters remain unchanged by the events in their lives and never come to the realization that their commitment to social values merely masks their violence and their sexuality; and the only significant difference in their condition is the birth of the Harkers' son who is appropriately named for all the men who had participated in the conquest of Dracula. Individual sexual desire has apparently been so absolutely effaced that the narrators see this child as the result of their social union rather than the product of a sexual union between one man and one woman.

The narrators insist that they are agents of God and are able to ignore their similarity to the vampire because their commitment to social values such as monogamy, proper English behavior, and the will of the majority enables them to conceal their violence and their sexual desires from each other and even from themselves. Stoker, however, reveals that these characteristics are merely masked by social convention. Instead of being eliminated, violence and sexuality emerge in particularly perverted forms.

Recently uncovered evidence suggests that Bram Stoker may have had very personal reasons for his preoccupation with repression and sexuality. In his biography of his great-uncle, Daniel Farson explains that, while the cause of Stoker's death is usually given as exhaustion, Stoker actually died of tertiary syphillis, exhaustion being one of the final stages of that disease. Farson also adds that Stoker's problematic relationship with his wife may have been responsible:

> When his wife's frigidity drove him to other women, probably prostitutes among them, Bram's writing showed signs of guilt and sexual frustration.... He probably caught syphilis around the turn of the century, possibly as early as the year of Dracula, 1896. (It usually takes ten to fifteen years before it kills.) By 1897 it seems that he had been celibate for more than twenty years, as far as Florence [his wife] was concerned.[10]

Poignantly aware from his own experience that the face of the vampire is the hidden side of the human character, Stoker creates unreliable narrators to tell a tale, not of the overcoming of Evil by Good, but of the similarities between the two. *Dracula* reveals the unseen face in the mirror; and Stoker's message is similar to the passage from *Julius Caesar* which prefaces this article and might be paraphrased in the following manner: "The fault, dear reader, is not in our external enemies, but in ourselves."

Notes

1. Recent full-length studies of *Dracula* include the following books: Radu Florescu and Raymond T. McNally, *In Search of Dracula* (New York:

New York Graphic Society, 1972); Gabriel Ronay, *The Truth About Dracula* (New York: Stein and Day, 1972); and Leonard Wolf, *A Dream of Dracula: In Search of the Living Dead* (Boston: Little, Brown and Company, 1972).

2. Leonard Wolf, *The Annotated Dracula* (New York: Clarkson N. Potter, Inc., 1975), my italics.

3. Bram Stoker, *Dracula* (1896; rpt. New York: Dell Publishing Co., 1971), p. 416. All future references will be to this edition and will be included within the text.

4. Stephanie Demetrakopoulos addresses another facet of this similarity by showing that male and female sexual roles are frequently reversed in *Dracula*. Her article, "Feminism, Sex Role Exchanges, and Other Subliminal Fantasies in Bram Stoker's *Dracula*," is included in *Frontiers: A Journal of Women Studies*, 2 (1977), pp. 104–113.

5. Stoker could have learned of Vlad from a number of sources. Ronay adds in a footnote that "The Millenary of Honfoglalas, the Hungarian invasion of their present-day territory, was being celebrated with great pomp and circumstance in 1896—the year when Stoker was writing *Dracula*" (p. 56). Another possible source is cited by G. Nandris, "A Philological Analysis of Dracula and Rumanian Placenames and Masculine Personal Names in –a/ea," *Slavonic and East European Review*, 37 (1959), p. 371:

> The Rumanian historian I. Bogdan, who published a monograph in 1896 on the prince of Wallachia, Vlad V, nicknamed Tsepesh (The Impaler), and who edited in it two German and four Russian versions of the Dracula legend....

6. Royce MacGillivray explains how Stoker altered the Dracula story:

> In real life Dracula was known for his horrifying cruelty, but Stoker, who wanted a monster that his readers could both shudder at and identify with, omits all mention of the dark side of his reputation and emphasizes his greatness as a warrior chieftain.

"*Dracula*, Bram Stoker's Spoiled Masterpiece," *Queen's Quarterly*, 79 (1972), p. 520.

7. It is significant that Dracula—who is portrayed as a sexual threat—comes to England on a ship named for the Greek goddess of fertility. Furthermore, he returns to his homeland on the *Czarina Catherine*; and Stoker probably expected his readers to know the stories of Catherine's legendary sexual appetite.

8. Wolf comments on this characteristic in the preface to *The Annotated Dracula*:

> Here, then, is the figure that Bram Stoker created—a figure who confronts us with primordial mysteries: death, blood, and love, and how they are bound together. Finally, Stoker's achievement is this: he makes us understand in our own experience why the vampire is said to be invisible in the mirror. He is there, but we fail to recognize him since our own faces get in the way.

9. A number of critics have commented on the pervasive sexuality in *Dracula*. C. F. Bentley, "The Monster in the Bedroom," *Literature and Psychology*, 22 (1972), p. 28:

> What is rejected or repressed on a conscious level appears in a covert and perverted form through the novel, the apparatus of the vampire superstition described in almost obsessional detail in *Dracula* providing the means for a symbolic presentation of human sexual relationships.

Maurice Richardson, "The Psychoanalysis of Ghost Stories," *The Twentieth Century*, 166 (1959), p. 429 describes Dracula as "a vast polymorph perverse bisexual oral-anal-genital sadomasochistic timeless orgy." In *A Dream of Dracula*, Wolf refers to the sexuality of Dracula:

> His kiss permits all unions: men and women; men and men; women and women; fathers and daughters; mothers and sons. Moreover, his is an easy love that evades the usual failures of the flesh. It is the triumph of passivity, unembarrassing, sensuous, throbbing, violent, and cruel.
>
> (p. 303)

Joseph S. Bierman, "Dracula: Prolonged Childhood Illness and the Oral Triad," *American Imago*, 29 (1972), pp. 186–98. Bierman studies Stoker's life and concludes that much of Dracula can be attributed to Stoker's repressed death wishes toward his brothers and toward his employer Henry Irving.

10. Daniel Farson, *The Man Who Wrote Dracula: A Biography of Bram Stoker* (London: Michael Joseph, 1975), p. 234.

GEOFFREY WALL

'Different From Writing': Dracula *In 1897*

> For the aristocracy had asserted the specificity of its body; but it was in the form of *blood*, in terms of ancestral antiquity and prestigious alliances ... The 'blood' of the bourgeoisie was its sex. And this is not just a play on words; many of the themes proper to the caste behaviour of the nobility re-emerge in the nineteenth century bourgeoisie, but in the guise of biological, medical or eugenic notions; the concern for genealogy turned into a preoccupation with heredity.[1]

Published in 1897, the year designated by Lenin as the zenith of imperialism, Bram Stoker's *Dracula* repeats the themes of an ideological crisis, the crisis of the bourgeois family. But read symptomatically, against the grain of its manifest argument for sexual repression, this text allows us to recover not only the content of that crisis, but the forms of its representation in discourses on the family, sexuality, race and empire. *Dracula* repeats this imaginary biology of the 1890s, all those 'scientific' phantasies which took wing in the ideological twilight of an economy which was 'becoming parasitic rather than competitive ... living off the remains of world monopoly.'[2]

Dracula is, persistently, an anxious text. Innocently, unironically, it contemplates its materials and methods, fascinated by the evident

From *Literature and History* 10, no. 1 (Spring 1984): 15-23. © 1984 by Thames Polytechnic.

contradiction between the archaic stuff of its narrative and the contemporary techniques which allow that narrative to emerge. It is a folklore whose improvisations and immediacies have been eroded and reified by being passed through all the most modern means of communication: 'We were struck with the fact that, in all the mass of material of which the record is composed, there is hardly one authentic document; nothing but a mass of typewriting' (332).[3] This final type-written archive includes transcriptions of diverse other kinds of text: a journal written in shorthand, a psychiatric case-history recorded phonographically, telegrames, a polyglot dictionary, title-deeds, a railway timetable, a ship's log translated from the Russian, a newspaper article, the inscription on a tombstone, phonetic renderings of dialect speech, and 'a workman's dogeared notebook which had hieroglyphical entries in thick half-obliterated pencil.' (231) All these materials have been scrupulously compiled so that 'a history almost at variance with the possibilities of latter-day belief may stand forth as simple fact' (Preface). On the one hand, we are left with the dust into which Dracula himself crumbles, on the other 'nothing but a mass of typewriting': on the one hand the spectral desire which invades the bedrooms of the imperial metropolis, on the other hand, its banally material residues, that 'mass of typewriting', empty nets of language which try to capture the history of that desire.

That general anxiety is elaborated as a psychological theme: it afflicts each individual narrator in the activity of their writing. *Dracula*, taking over the multiple subjectivities of the epistolary novel, gives a psychopathological twist to this theme of writing. The writers recognise in their writing a compulsive, obsessional effort to transcribe the uncanny, to establish indications of reality. 'I must,' confides Jonathan Harker to himself, 'keep writing at every chance, for I dare not stop to think. All, big and little, must go down; perhaps at the end the little things may teach us most.' (257) Or, 'I am anxious, and it soothes me to express myself here; it is like whispering to oneself and listening at the same time. And there is also something about the shorthand symbols which makes it different from writing.' (74)

The narrative movement of *Dracula* is towards a social synthesis of these private writings, towards a knowledge which can only be constituted as the relation between diverging phantasies. For there are two distinct moments in the process of the narrative. In the first moment, a self duplication, 'like whispering to oneself and listening at the same time', a self-displacement effected by[4] 'something in the shorthand symbols', a passage from the terrible fluidity of phantasy to the soothing fixity of text. In the second moment, the valorising circulation of what is written, the gift of that text: most conspicuously, the supplementary ritual at the marriage of

Jonathan Harker, when he appoints his new wife as the keeper of his memories, the repository of the journal he kept during his visit to Dracula's castle—'He had his hand over the notebook, and he said to me very solemnly:—"the secret is here and I do not want to know it. I want to take up my life here with our marriage ... Here is the book. Take it and keep it, read it if you will but never let me know ..." I took the book ... and wrapped it up in white paper, and tied it with a little bit of pale blue ribbon which was round my neck, and sealed it over the knot with sealing wax and for my seal I used my wedding-ring.' (104)

It is the wife, Mina, with her 'man's brain' and her 'woman's heart', who is the agent of this process of the circulation of the text. She is the rewriter, the transcriber, the secretary who arranges all the documents in chronological order and composes the case (legal and medical) of Dracula. She acquires an enormous structural importance as the-woman-who-writes. But she also serves to articulate the contradictions posed by the feminism of the 1890s. Before her marriage she has been a school-teacher, but now she will dedicate her cultural skills to the service of the masculine realm of socially productive thought. 'When we are married,' she confides to her friend, 'I shall be able to be useful to Jonathan, and if I can stenograph well enough I can take down what he wants to say in this way and write it out for him on the typewriter.' (57) Mina represents a certain historical transition. She is dimly aware of the contemporary debates on women and marriage, but resolutely traditional in her conception of the duties of a wife and the virtues of subordination. References to the 'New Woman' significantly precede Dracula's first attack on her friend Lucy: 'I believe we should have shocked the New Woman with our appetites.' (90) The appetites in question are innocent, their object is merely an afternoon tea. But they recall Lucy's protest at the prospect of monogamous marriage: 'Why can't they let a girl marry three men, or as many as want her ...? But this is heresy and I must not say it.' (62) Mina, seeing her friend asleep, briefly imagines herself as a man, as her suitor: 'If Mr Holmwood fell in love with her seeing her only in the drawing room, I wonder what he would say if he saw her now?' (91) But this phantasy is then safely projected onto the New Women, rejected as a self-evidently unnatural masculine identification: '... the New Women writers will some day start an idea that men and women should be allowed to see each other asleep before proposing or accepting. But I suppose the New Woman won't condescend in future to accept; she will do the proposing herself. And a nice job she will make of it too!' (91) As we shall see later, Lucy as a vampire, as an openly desiring woman, is offered as an awful example of what will happen if female sexuality is allowed to escape from its lawful subordination within the conjugal family. Mina's writing, in the same gesture of confinement, will be used only to repeat the words of others: 'I shall do what I see lady journalists do: interviewing and writing descriptions and trying to remember conversations. I am told that, with a little practice, one can remember all that goes on or that one hears said during a day.' (57)

But Mina's discursive position is not so simple as either she or others would have it. Her masculine qualities have to be suppressed if masculine discourses are to keep their sovreignty. If we examine the various articulations of gender and discourse in *Dracula*, there emerges a typology which is intriguingly close to that in Breuer and Freud's *Studies in Hysteria* (1895). Indeed, it is Van Helsing, the 'brain-scientist', the hypnotist, the reader of Charcot, who proposes the rule that' ... good women tell all their lives, and by day and by hour and by minute, such things that angels can read; and we men who wish to know have in us something of angel's eyes.' (167) The slide in this sentence, from voice to text to image, from woman's voice to man's eye (though the gaze is ideally ungendered, that of an angel), exemplifies a regression imposed by the men upon the women. The more resolute women can, however, escape this process. Lucy's 'crime', for instance, is to have resisted the masculine-medical gaze of one of her suitors. She writes to Mina, 'I can fancy what a wonderful power he must have over his patients. He has a curious habit of looking one straight in the face, as if trying to read one's thoughts. He tries this on very much with me, but I flatter myself that he has got a very tough nut to crack. I know that from my glass. Do you ever try to read your own face? *I do* ...' (58) Mina, subject to Dracula's power, and warning the men that she will try to deceive them, can be positioned as a 'good woman' by the 'angel eyes' of her husband: 'God saw the look that she turned on me as she spoke, and if there be indeed a Recording Angel that look is noted to her everlasting honour.' (228)

Good women tell all their lives ... first axiom of patriarchal ideology, motto of psychoanalysis. But *Dracula* reaches beyond this simple prescription in its investigation of masculine and feminine. There are so many other patterns of discourse and gender which deviate. Women, for example, will talk to other women behind the backs of men. The early exchange of letters between Mina and Lucy is under the sign of phantasy and the pleasure principle: '... we can talk together freely and build our castles in the air.' (57) It is shaped to a specifically feminine idiom of the erotic and the confidential: '... we have told all our secrets to each other since we were *children* ... I wish I were with you dear, sitting by the fire, undressing, as we used to sit; and I would try to tell you what I feel. I do not know how I am writing this even to you. I am afraid to stop or I should tear up the letter ...' (59) This feminine discourse does not produce knowledge until it has been relayed, submitted to the masculine, deciphered by it. Otherwise it remains enigmatic, shadowy, uncanny. Lucy, for example, on the night of her death, is in bed with her mother when Dracula breaks into the bedroom, heralded by 'the head of a great gaunt grey wolf in the aperture of the broken windowpane'. (134) When the pre-Oedipal domain of mother and daughter is invaded by the phallus the mother dies from the shock, returning, briefly metamorphosed, a modern Philomel: '... the sound of the nightingale seemed like the voice of my dead mother returned to comfort me.' (135)

But this division within discourse, whereby the feminine must be readdressed, completed put into circulation, this division is repeated on the other side. The masculine must relapse and regress, must find again the Mother in order to find its lost feelings. Lucy's mourning lover, Lord Godalming, the very type of aristocratic manhood, 'breaks down' to a woman, to Lucy's friend Mina. She observes. '... there is something in a woman's nature that makes a man free to break down before her and express his feelings on the tender or emotional side without feeling it derogatory to his manhood ... We women have something of the mother in us ...' (204-5) The masculine pattern of intimacy involves 'yarns by the campfire' (64), but also an asexual physical contact: 'that time,' as Van Helsing puts it. 'you suck from my wound so swiftly the poison of the gangrene.' (110) Any display of intense feeling between men is diagnosed as hysterical, as feminine: '... then he cried till he laughed again: and cried and laughed together just as a woman does. I tried to be stern with him, just as one is with a woman under the circumstances ...' (158) This is contrasted with the behaviour of the exemplary Texan who 'bore himself through it like a moral Viking,' (158) Empires, evidently, are founded on a certain masculinity: 'If America can go on breeding men like that, she will be a power in the world indeed,' (158)

Mina, the woman who writes, with her man's brain and her woman's heart, is deliberately excluded, at a crucial moment, from the counsels of the five men who are allied against Dracula: '... now that her work is done, and that it is due to her energy and brains and foresight that the whole story is put together in such a way that every point tells, she may well feel that her part is finished, and that she can henceforth leave the rest to us.' (220) The men have formed themselves into a 'sort of board or committee' (210) for the 'serious work' (212) of destroying that sexuality, aristocratic and perverse, which has insinuated itself into the bourgeois family, fastening adulterously upon its women. 'The girls that you all love,' taunts Dracula, 'are mine already; and through them you and others shall yet be mine ...'. (271) But it is precisely by excluding Mina from the man's work of science that the men condemn her to the enclosed world of phantasy and desire. Left alone, while they are out hunting Dracula, she becomes his victim at the moment when she is resolving to become, precisely, the good woman who tells all her life:

'I still keep my journal as usual. Then if he [her husband] has feared of my trust I shall show it to him, with every thought of my heart put down for his dear eyes to read,' (228) This section of the text enacts, as it were, a fable of repression, a repression that follows the line of sexual difference and the social relations that are constructed upon it. That which is excluded, the woman and her desire, returns, embodied in the secret language of the hysterical symptom, or in the theatricality of the perversion. Mina, like the hysterics treated by Breuer and Freud in the 1880s, 'forms conclusions of her own ... but she will not or she cannot give them utterance ... in some mysterious way Mrs Harker's tongue is tied'. (284) And, like Anna O., Mina proposes the form of her treatment, hypnosis, the talking cure. This secret language released from the hysterical body is both speech and writing: 'The answer came dreamily, but with intention. I have heard her using the same tone when reading her short-hand notes.' (275)

The desire which is transcribed in the conjugal journal, or confided, between women, undressing by the fireside, regulated, ordered and put to work within the conjugal family, deciphered under hypnosis, codified under the masculine and the feminine, this desire is never to be arrested or fixed by its conscious representations. There is, in *Dracula*, that 'other scene', that theatre of the Imaginary where is enacted, corporeally, all that has been banished from the conversations in the drawing room, from the 'small world of happiness'.[5] These erotic *tableaux*, scenes of sexual discovery, follow the codes of a specific theatricality which is not that of Freud's classical Athens, but that of the Victorian theatre, the theatre in which Bram Stoker himself worked for thirty years as secretary to Henry Irving. It was a theatre of spectacle, of melodrama, of clear moral symbolism, a lavish ethical-sentimental picture-book; it was a theatre, in Stoker's own definition, 'whose mechanism of exploiting thoughts is by means of the human body'.[5] The bodies in question, those of Stoker and Irving, spectator and actor, both underwent a profound, reciprocal, erotic crisis in their first encounter. Irving was reciting a poem to a student audience in a Dublin hotel drawing room after dinner. Stoker recalls, in his memoir of Irving, that at the end of the recitation, 'after a few seconds of stony silence, I burst out into something like a violent fit of hysterics ... so profound was the sense of his dominance ... I was as men go a strong man, physically immensely strong ... I was no hysterical subject ... no weak individual yielding to a superior emotional force ... my capacity for receptive emotion was something akin in forcefulness to his power of creating it'. The obvious psychobiographical relation between Irving and Dracula, between Stoker and Harker, is—it seems to me—of less interest than that *theatricalisation of the sexual which informs* the text. The 'scientific, sceptical, matter-of-fact nineteenth century' (212) equips its world-historical representatives, three Englishmen, a Texan and a Dutchman, its present, its future and its past, equips them with phonograph, typewriter and railway timetable in the struggle to defend woman, family and empire against the archaic remnant of a feudal aristocracy. They enter that 'other scene' to find themselves at a performance in Henry Irving's *Lyceum*.

Mina, for example, looking for the sleepwalking Lucy on the cliffs of Whitby, relishes the excellence of the lighting:

> There was a bright full moon, with heavy black driving clouds, which threw the whole scene into a fleeting diorama of light and shade as they sailed across ... as the edge of a narrow band of light ... moved across, the church and the churchyard gradually became visible ... there on our favourite seat, the silver light of the moon struck a half-reclining figure, snowy white. The coming of the cloud was too quick for me to see much, for shadow shut down on light almost immediately ... something dark stood behind the seat where the white figure shone, and bent over it ... something raised a head, and from where I was I could see a white face and gleaming red eyes. (92)

Or, more intimately, more elaborately, the scene disclosed when the men break into Mina's bedroom:

> The moonlight was so bright that through the thick yellow blind the room was light enough to see. On the bed beside the window lay the form of Jonathan Harker, his face flushed and breathing heavily as though in a stupor. Kneeling on the near edge of the bed facing outwards was the white clad figure of his wife. By her side stood a tall, thin man clad in black ... With his left hand he held both Mrs Harker's hands, keeping them away with her arms at full tension; his right hand gripped her by the back of the neck, forcing her face down on his bosom. Her white nightdress was smeared with blood, and a thin stream trickled down the man's bare breast which was shown by his torn-open dress. The attitude of the two had a terrible resemblance to a child forcing a kitten's nose into a saucer of milk to compel it to drink. (249)

What, we might ask, is being enacted in this scene? What anxious phantasy has been given body on this brightly-lit marriage bed? To answer such a question, we need to look at the forms of the family, the social relations which *Dracula* proposes. Dracula himself offers the pleasures of perversion in place of the repressions of hysteria. He is the predatory libertine who will conquer the world by means of an Unholy Family of which he is the incestuous father. He propogates by a sterile metamorphosis, fastening upon the already living, bestowing his grotesque immortality, an eternity of sadistic pleasures emancipated from the imperatives of biology. Dracula's theft of blood defiles the patrimony, disrupts the ordered exchange of women, property and names, dissolves the serene continuity of the imperial Anglo-Saxon race. His object of attack is London itself, the metropolis from which capital sets sail on its world voyages; there, in Jonathan Harker's words, 'for centuries to come he might, amongst its teeming millions, satiate his lust for blood, and create a new and ever-widening circle of semi-demons to batten on the helpless.' (54) A Transylvanian Empire to supplant the British. Dracula, it is important to add, is a richly detailed historical type, the representative of the archaic neo-feudal social formations of Eastern Europe which had survived well into the 'scientific, sceptical, matter-of-fact nineteenth century'. 'Here,' he boasts to Harker, 'I am noble; I am *boyar*: the common people know me and I am master'. (23) In the psychic geography of the continent, this Transylvania is Europe's unconscious:

> There are no maps of this country as yet to compare with our own Ordnance Survey ... one of the wildest and least-known portions of Europe. (23)
>
> ... every known superstition in the world is gathered into the horseshoe of the Carpathians, as if it were the centre of some sort of imaginative whirlpool. (4)
>
> there are deep caverns and fissures that reach none know whither (211)
>
> ... every speck of dust that whirls in the wind a devouring monster in embryo. (311)

Horseshoe, whirlpool, cavern, fissure, every speck of dust, a monster in embryo: as well as the historical-political threat of a counter-empire, Dracula carries a biological phantasy, a masculine nightmare of femininity, of the female body, out of control, ingesting and spawning indiscriminately, violating the territories of the body, the home and the state. It is Lucy, on the eve of her marriage, whose heretically polygamous wish—'Why can't they let a girl marry three men?' (62)—initiates this process, this dissolution of the body politic, which ends only with the birth, on the last page, of Mina's son, the son whose 'bundle of names links all our little band of men together'. (332) Between these two moments, reproduction and circulation of every kind is under threat. All secrecies, all privacies, all territories and rules for contact between bodies are unravelling. Much masculine ingenuity is devoted to the creation of sealed and impregnable spaces, where what is in stays in, where what is out stays out. Bedrooms with charmed windows, asylums with locked doors, coffins with lids screwed down, graves properly inhabited and accurately inscribed, diaries tied in blue ribbon: all in vain. Windows are broken, locks are picked, lunatics escape, coffins open, tombstones tell lies and graves are empty, women walk in their sleep and talk under hypnosis, men have wickedly voluptuous dreams and hysterical attacks, blood is sucked from the neck and transfused from the veins in the arm. 'And so,' laments Van Helsing, 'the circle goes on ever-widening.' (193) The centre of this circle ever-widening is, explicitly, female sexuality. Lucy, in her vampire incarnation, exemplifies that 'sweetness turned to adamantine, heartless cruelty, purity to voluptuous wantonness' (189)

> ... the eyes seemed to throw out sparks of hell-fire, her brows were wrinkled as though the folds of flesh were the coils of Medusa's snakes, and the lovely blood-stained mouth grew to an open square. (190)

Recalling Freud's interpretation of the Medusa,[6] it comes as no surprise that Lucy's punishment-salvation is to be effected by means of a monstruous phallus:

> a round wooden stake some two and a half or three inches thick and about three feet long ... one end hardened in the fire and sharpened to a fine point. (193)

to be wielded by her cheated lover. 'Brave lad!' says Van Helsing, paternally. 'A moment's courage and it is done.' (194) This ritual penetration is enacted on the day after the cancelled wedding:

> He struck with all his might. The Thing in the coffin writhed; and a hideous blood-curdling screech came from the opened red lips. The body shook and quivered and twisted in wild contortions; the sharp white teeth clamped together until the lips were cut and the mouth was smeared with crimson foam. But Arthur never faltered. He looked like a figure of Thor as his

> untrembling arm rose and fell, driving deeper and deeper the mercy-bearing stake, whilst the blood from the pierced heart welled and spurted up round it. (194)

To conclude, a fragment of masculine conversation:

> Then we had supper upstairs in our shirtsleeves (at the moment I am writing in a somewhat more advanced négligé), and then came a lengthy medical conversation on moral insanity and nervous diseases and strange case-histories—your friend Bertha Pappenheim also cropped up—and then we became rather personal and very intimate and he told me a number of things about his wife and children and asked me to repeat what he had said only 'after you are married to Martha'. And then I opened up and said: This same Martha ... is in reality a sweet Cordelia, and we are already on terms of the closest intimacy and can say anything to each other. Whereupon he said he too always calls his wife by that name because she is incapable of displaying affection to others, even including her own father.[7]

Two doctors talking, professionally, speculatively, with all the intimacy and informality of being in shirt-sleeves after supper. Their conversation is that of colleagues, but also that of not-quite-equals, senior and junior, the married and the merely engaged. But professional secrets lead to family secrets, to the danger that these secrets may continue to circulate beyond the closed circle of the medical conversation. They may, through the networks of love and friendship, reach the ears of the patient in question.

The two doctors are Freud and Joseph Breuer, co-authors of the *Studies on Hysteria* (1895), an investigation of femininity and the family written from within the same ideological moment as *Dracula*. This account of their conversation is part of one of the many letters that Freud wrote to Martha Bernays during the four years of their engagement. Martha's friend Bertha Pappenheim, the subject of the 'strange case-history', will be known to posterity as Anna O., the first case of hysteria to be made intelligible. Read alongside that case-history, Freud's letter to Martha exhibits, in its protestations of intimacy and its actual reticence, that same division, those same articulations of gender and discourse that we have found in *Dracula*. We know that Freud and Breuer had discussed the details of Anna O.—Bertha Pappenheim—repeatedly;[8] that Breuer, about this time, had confided despairingly to Freud that Anna-Bertha was 'quite unhinged', wishing that 'she would die and so be released from her suffering';[9] that Breuer had 'fled the house in a cold sweet'[10] when faced with Anna-Bertha's phantom pregnancy at his hands.

None of this emerges in the letter to Martha. Instead, in place of the 'unhinged' Bertha, we meet the figure of 'sweet Cordelia', potent fiction of feminine virtue, one who commands herself to 'love, and be silent'. This Cordelia is summoned to fill the place of those three real women, Bertha Pappenheim, Frau Breuer, Martha Bernays: 'incapable of displaying affection to others', a punctual conjugal desire, cleansed of anxieties, jealousies, hysteria.

Notes

1. M. Foucault, *Histoire de la sexualité: la volonté de savoir* (Paris, 1976) pp.164-5. my translation.
2. E.J. Hobsbawm, *Industry and Empire* (London, 1968) p.192.
3. Page reference to *Dracula* incorporated into the text refer to L. Woolf (ed.), *The Annotated Dracula* (London, 1976).
4. E.L. Freud (ed.), *Letters of Sigmund Freud 1873-1939* (London, 1970) p.45.
5. B. Stoker, 'The Censorship of Fiction' in *The Nineteenth Century* (London, Sept. 1908) p.481.
6. S. Freud, *The Complete Psychological Works* Vol. 18, pp.273-4.
7. *Letters of Sigmund Freud*, p.56.
8. E. Jones, *The Life and Work of Sigmund Freud* (ed. Trilling & Marcus) London, 1964 p.204.
9. *Ibid.* p.204.
10. *Ibid.* p.203.

CHRISTOPHER CRAFT

"Kiss Me with Those Red Lips": Gender and Inversion in Bram Stoker's Dracula

When Joseph Sheridan Le Fanu observed in *Carmilla* (1872) that "the vampire is prone to be fascinated with an engrossing vehemence resembling the passion of love" and that vampiric pleasure is heightened "by the gradual approaches of an artful courtship," he identified clearly the analogy between monstrosity and sexual desire that would prove, under a subsequent Freudian stimulus, paradigmatic for future readings of vampirism.[1] Modern critical accounts of *Dracula*, for instance, almost universally agree that vampirism both expresses and distorts an originally sexual energy. That distortion, the representation of desire under the defensive mask of monstrosity, betrays the fundamental psychological ambivalence identified by Franco Moretti when he writes that "vampirism is an excellent example of the identity of desire and fear."[2] This interfusion of sexual desire and the fear that the moment of erotic fulfillment may occasion the erasure of the conventional and integral self informs both the central action in *Dracula* and the surcharged emotion of the characters about to be kissed by "those red lips."[3] So powerful an ambivalence, generating both errant erotic impulses and compensatory anxieties, demands a strict, indeed an almost schematic formal management of narrative material. In *Dracula* Stoker borrows from Mary Shelley's *Frankenstein* and Robert Louis Stevenson's *Dr. Jekyll and Mr. Hyde* a narrative strategy characterized by a predictable, if variable, triple rhythm. Each of

---

From *Representations* 8 (Fall 1984): 107-133.

these texts first invites or admits a monster, then entertains and is entertained by monstrosity for some extended duration, until in its closing pages it expels or repudiates the monster and all the disruption that he/she/it brings.[4]

Obviously enough, the first element in this triple rhythm corresponds formally to the text's beginning or generative moment, to its need to produce the monster, while the third element corresponds to the text's terminal moment, to its need both to destroy the monster it has previously admitted and to end the narrative that houses the monster. Interposed between these antithetical gestures of admission and expulsion is the gothic novel's prolonged middle,[5] during which the text affords its ambivalence a degree of play intended to produce a pleasurable, indeed a thrilling anxiety. Within its extended middle, the gothic novel entertains its resident demon—is, indeed, entertained by it—and the monster, now ascendent in its strength, seems for a time potent enough to invert the "natural" order and overwhelm the comforting closure of the text. That threat, of course, is contained and finally nullified by the narrative requirement that the monster be repudiated and the world of normal relations restored; thus, the gesture of expulsion, compensating for the original irruption of the monstrous, brings the play of monstrosity to its predictable close. This narrative rhythm, whose tripartite cycle of admission-entertainment-expulsion enacts sequentially an essentially simultaneous psychological equivocation, provides aesthetic management of the fundamental ambivalence that motivates these texts and our reading of them.

While such isomorphism of narrative method obviously implies affinities and similarities among these different texts, it does not argue identity of meaning. However similar *Frankenstein*, *Dr. Jekyll and Mr. Hyde*, and *Dracula* may be, differences nevertheless obtain, and these differences bear the impress of authorial, historical, and institutional pressures. This essay therefore offers not a reading of monstrosity in general, but rather an account of Bram Stoker's particular articulation of the vampire metaphor in *Dracula*, a book whose fundamental anxiety, an equivocation about the relationship between desire and gender, repeats, with a monstrous difference, a pivotal anxiety of late Victorian culture. Jonathan Harker, whose diary opens the novel, provides *Dracula*'s most precise articulation of this anxiety. About to be kissed by the "weird sisters" (64), the incestuous vampiric daughters who share Castle Dracula with the Count, a supine Harker thrills to a double passion:

> All three had brilliant white teeth, that shone like pearls against the ruby of their voluptuous lips. There was something about them that made me uneasy, *some longing and at the same time some*

> *deadly fear*. I felt in my heart a wicked, burning desire that they would kiss me with those red lips. (51; emphasis added)

Immobilized by the competing imperatives of "wicked desire" and "deadly fear," Harker awaits an erotic fulfillment that entails both the dissolution of the boundaries of the self and the thorough subversion of conventional Victorian gender codes, which constrained the mobility of sexual desire and varieties of genital behavior by according to the more active male the right and responsibility of vigorous appetite, while requiring the more passive female to "suffer and be still." John Ruskin, concisely formulating Victorian conventions of sexual difference, provides us with a useful synopsis: "The man's power is active, progressive, defensive. He is eminently the doer, the creator, the discoverer, the defender. His intellect is for speculation and invention; his energy for adventure, for war, and for conquest. ..." Woman, predictably enough, bears a different burden: "She must be enduringly, incorruptibly, good; instinctively, infallibly wise—wise, not for self-development, but for self-renunciation ... wise, not with the narrowness of insolent and loveless pride, but with the passionate gentleness of an infinitely variable, because infinitely applicable, modesty of service—the true changefulness of woman."[6] Stoker, whose vampiric women exercise a far more dangerous "changefulness" than Ruskin imagines, anxiously inverts this conventional pattern, as virile Jonathan Harker enjoys a "feminine" passivity and awaits a delicious penetration from a woman whose demonism is figured as the power to penetrate. A swooning desire for an overwhelming penetration and an intense aversion to the demonic potency empowered to gratify that desire compose the fundamental motivating action and emotion in *Dracula*.

This ambivalence, always excited by the imminence of the vampiric kiss, finds its most sensational representation in the image of the Vampire Mouth, the central and recurring image of the novel: "There was a deliberate voluptuousness which was both thrilling and repulsive ... I could see in the moonlight the moisture shining on the red tongue as it lapped the white sharp teeth" (52). That is Harker describing one of the three vampire women at Castle Dracula. Here is Dr. Seward's description of the Count: "His eyes flamed red with devilish passion; the great nostrils of the white aquiline nose opened wide and quivered at the edges; and the white sharp teeth, behind the full lips of the blood-dripping mouth, champed together like those of a wild beast" (336). As the primary site of erotic experience in *Dracula*, this mouth equivocates, giving the lie to the easy separation of the masculine and the feminine. Luring at first with an inviting orifice, a promise of red softness, but delivering instead a piercing bone, the vampire mouth fuses and confuses what Dracula's civilized nemesis, Van Helsing and his Crew of Light,[7] works so hard to separate—the gender-based categories of the penetrating and the receptive, or, to use Van Helsing's language, the complementary categories of "brave men" and "good women." With its soft flesh barred by hard bone, its red crossed by white, this mouth compels opposites and contrasts into a frightening unity, and it asks some disturbing questions. Are we male or are we female? Do we have penetrators or orifices? And if both, what does that mean? And what about our bodily fluids, the red and the white? What are the relations between blood and semen, milk and blood? Furthermore, this mouth, bespeaking the subversion of the stable and lucid distinctions of gender, is the mouth of all vampires, male and female.

Yet we must remember that the vampire mouth is first of all Dracula's mouth, and that all subsequent versions of it (in *Dracula* all vampires other than the Count are female)[8] merely repeat as diminished simulacra the desire of the Great Original, that "father or furtherer of a new order of beings" (360). Dracula himself, calling his children "my jackals to do my bidding when I want to feed," identifies the systematic creation of female surrogates who enact his will and desire (365). This should remind us that the novel's opening anxiety, its first articulation of the vampiric threat, derives from Dracula's hovering interest in Jonathan Harker; the sexual threat that this novel first evokes, manipulates, sustains, but never finally represents is that Dracula will seduce, penetrate, drain another male. The suspense and power of *Dracula*'s opening section, of that phase of the narrative which we have called the invitation to monstrosity, proceeds precisely from this unfulfilled sexual ambition. Dracula's desire to fuse with a male, most explicitly evoked when Harker cuts himself shaving, subtly and dangerously suffuses this text. Always postponed and never directly enacted, this desire finds evasive fulfillment in an important series of heterosexual displacements.

Dracula's ungratified desire to vamp Harker is fulfilled instead by his three vampiric daughters, whose anatomical femininity permits, because it masks, the silently interdicted homoerotic embrace between Harker and the Count. Here, in a displacement typical both of this text and the gender-anxious culture from which it arose, an implicitly homoerotic desire achieves representation as a monstrous heterosexuality, as a demonic inversion of normal gender relations. Dracula's daughters offer Harker a feminine form but a masculine penetration:

> Lower and lower went her head as the lips went below the range of my mouth and chin and seemed to fasten on my throat.... I could feel the soft, shivering touch of the lips on the supersensitive skin of my throat, and the hard dents of the two

> sharp teeth, just touching and pausing there. I closed my eyes in a langorous ecstasy and waited—waited with a beating heart. (52)

This moment, constituting the text's most direct and explicit representation of a male's desire to be penetrated, is governed by a double deflection: first, the agent of penetration is nominally and anatomically (from the mouth down, anyway) female; and second, this dangerous moment, fusing the maximum of desire and the maximum of anxiety, is poised precisely at the brink of penetration. Here the "two sharp teeth," just "touching" and "pausing" there, stop short of the transgression which would unsex Harker and toward which this text constantly aspires and then retreats: the actual penetration of the male.

This moment is interrupted, this penetration denied. Harker's pause at the end of the paragraph ("waited—waited with a beating heart"), which seems to anticipate an imminent piercing, in fact anticipates not the completion but the interruption of the scene of penetration. Dracula himself breaks into the room, drives the women away from Harker, and admonishes them: "How dare you touch him, any of you? How dare you cast eyes on him when I had forbidden it? Back, I tell you all! This man belongs to me" (53). Dracula's intercession here has two obvious effects: by interrupting the scene of penetration, it suspends and disperses throughout the text the desire maximized at the brink of penetration, and it repeats the threat of a more direct libidinous embrace between Dracula and Harker. Dracula's taunt, "This man belongs to me," is suggestive enough, but at no point subsequent to this moment does Dracula kiss Harker, preferring instead to pump him for his knowledge of English law, custom, and language. Dracula, soon departing for England, leaves Harker to the weird sisters, whose final penetration of him, implied but never represented, occurs in the dark interspace to which Harker's journal gives no access.

Hereafter *Dracula* will never represent so directly a male's desire to be penetrated; once in England Dracula, observing a decorous heterosexuality, vamps only women, in particular Lucy Westenra and Mina Harker. The novel, nonetheless, does not dismiss homoerotic desire and threat; rather it simply continues to diffuse and displace it. Late in the text, the Count himself announces a deflected homoeroticism when he admonishes the Crew of Light thus: "My revenge is just begun! I spread it over the centuries, and time is on my side. Your girls that you all love are mine already; and *through them you and others shall yet be mine ...*" (365; italics added). Here Dracula specifies the process of substitution by which "the girls that you all love" mediate and displace a more direct communion among males. Van Helsing, who provides for Lucy transfusions designed to counteract the dangerous influence of the Count, confirms Dracula's declaration of surrogation; he knows that once the transfusions begin, Dracula drains from Lucy's veins not her blood, but rather blood transferred from the veins of the Crew of Light: "even we four who gave our strength to Lucy it also is all to him [*sic*]" (244). Here, emphatically, is another instance of the heterosexual displacement of a desire mobile enough to elude the boundaries of gender. Everywhere in this text such desire seeks a strangely deflected heterosexual distribution; only through women may men touch.

The representation of sexuality in *Dracula*, then, registers a powerful ambivalence in its identification of desire and fear. The text releases a sexuality so mobile and polymorphic that Dracula may be best represented as bat or wolf or floating dust; yet this effort to elude the restrictions upon desire encoded in traditional conceptions of gender then constrains that desire through a series of heterosexual displacements. Desire's excursive mobility is always filtered in *Dracula* through the mask of a monstrous or demonic heterosexuality. Indeed, Dracula's mission in England is the creation of a race of monstrous women, feminine demons equipped with masculine devices. This monstrous heterosexuality is apotropaic for two reasons: first, because it masks and deflects the anxiety consequent to a more direct representation of same sex eroticism; and second, because in imagining a sexually aggressive woman as a demonic penetrator, as a usurper of a prerogative belonging "naturally" to the other gender, it justifies, as we shall see later, a violent expulsion of this deformed femininity.

In its particular formulation of erotic ambivalence, in its contrary need both to liberate and constrain a desire indifferent to the prescriptions of gender by figuring such desire as monstrous heterosexuality, *Dracula* may seem at first idiosyncratic, anomalous, merely neurotic. This is not the case. *Dracula* presents a characteristic, if hyperbolic, instance of Victorian anxiety over the potential fluidity of gender roles,[9] and this text's defensiveness toward the mobile sexuality it nonetheless wants to evoke parallels remarkably other late Victorian accounts of same sex eroticism, of desire in which the "sexual instincts" were said to be, in the words of John Addington Symonds, "improperly correlated to [the] sexual organs."[10] During the last decades of the nineteenth century and the first of the twentieth, English writers produced their first sustained discourse about the variability of sexual desire, with a special emphasis upon male homoerotic love, which had already received indirect and evasive endorsement from Tennyson in "In Memoriam" and from Whitman in the "Calamus" poems. The preferred taxonomic label under which these writers categorized and examined such sexual desire was not, as we might anticipate, "homosexuality" but rather "sexual inversion," a classificatory term involving a complex negotiation between socially encoded gender norms and a sexual mobility that would seem at first unconstrained by those norms. Central polemical texts contributing to this discourse include Symonds's *A Problem in Greek Ethics* (1883), and his *A Problem in Modern Ethics* (1891); Havelock Ellis's *Sexual Inversion*, originally written in collaboration with Symonds, published and suppressed in England in 1897, and later to be included as volume 2 of Ellis's *Studies in the Psychology of Sex* (1901); and Edward Carpenter's *Homogenic Love* (1894) and his *The Intermediate Sex* (1908). Admittedly polemical and apologetic, these texts argued, with considerable circumspection, for the cultural acceptance of desire and behavior hitherto categorized as sin, explained under the imprecise religious term "sodomy,"[11] and repudiated as "the crime *inter Christianos non nominandum*."[12] Such texts, urbanely arguing an extremist position, represent a culture's first attempt to admit the inadmissible, to give the unnamable a local habitation and a name, and as Michel Foucalt has argued, to put sex into discourse.[13]

"Those who read these lines will hardly doubt what passion it is that I am hinting at," wrote Symonds in the introduction to *A Problem in Modern Ethics*, a book whose subtitle—*An Inquiry into the Phenomenon of Sexual Inversion, Addressed Especially to Medical Psychologists and Jurists*—provides the OED *Supplement* with its earliest citation (1896) for "inversion" in the sexual sense. Symonds's coy gesture, his hint half-guessed, has the force of a necessary circumlocution. Symonds, Ellis, and Carpenter struggled to devise, and then to revise, a descriptive language untarnished by the anal implications, by suggestions of that "circle of extensive corruption,"[14] that so terrified and fascinated late Victorian culture. Symonds "can hardly find a name that will not seem to soil" his text "because the accomplished languages of Europe in the nineteenth century provide no term for this persistant feature of human psychology without importing some implication of disgust, disgrace, vituperation." This need to supple a new term, to invent an adequate taxonomic language, produced more obscurity than clarity. A terminological muddle ensued, the new names of the unnameable were legion: "homosexuality," "sexual inversion," "intermediate sex," "homogenic love," and "uranism" all coexisted and completed for terminological priority. Until the second or third decade of this century, when the word "homosexuality," probably because of its medical heritage, took the terminological crown, "sexual inversion"—as word, metaphor, taxonomic category—provided the basic tool with which late Victorians investigated, and constituted, their problematic desire. Symonds, more responsible than any other writer for the establishment of "inversion" as Victorian England's preferred term for same sex eroticism, considered it a "convenient phrase" "which does not prejudice the matter under consideration." Going further, he naively claimed that "inversion" provided a "neutral nomenclature" with which "the investigator has good reason to be satisfied."[15]

Symonds's claim of terminological neutrality ignores the way in which conventional beliefs and assumptions about gender inhabit both the label "inversion" and the metaphor behind it. The exact history of the word remains obscure (the *OED Supplement* defines sexual inversion tautologically as "the inversion of the sex instincts" and provides two perfunctory citations) but it seems to have been employed first in English in an anonymous medical review of 1871; Symonds later adopted it to translate the account of homoerotic desire offered by Karl Ulrichs, an "inverted" Hanoverian legal official who wrote in the 1860s in Germany "a series of polemical, analytical, theoretical, and apologetic pamphlets" endorsing same sex eroticism.[16] As Ellis explains it, Ulrichs "regarded uranism, or homosexual love, as a congenital abnormality by which a female soul had become united with a male body—*anima muliebris in corpore virili inclusa*."[17] The explanation for this improper correlation of anatomy and desire is, according to Symonds's synopsis of Ulrichs in *Modern Ethics*, "to be found in physiology, in that obscure department of natural science which deals with the evolution of sex."[18] Nature's attempt to differentiate "the indeterminate ground-stuff" of the foetus—to produce, that is, not merely the "male and female organs of procreation" but also the "corresponding male and female appetites"—falls short of complete success: "Nature fails to complete her work regularly and in every instance. Having succeeded in differentiating a male with full-formed sexual organs from the undecided foetus, she does not always effect the proper differentiation of that portion of the physical being in which resides the sexual appetite. There remains a female soul in a male body." Since it holds nature responsible for the "imperfection in the process of development," this explanation of homoerotic desire has obvious polemical utility; in relieving the individual of moral responsibility for his or her anomalous development, it argues first for the decriminalization and then for the medicalization of inversion. According to this account, same sex eroticism, although statistically deviant or abnormal, cannot then be called unnatural. Inverts or urnings or homosexuals are therefore "abnormal, but natural, beings"; they constitute the class of "the naturally abnormal." Symonds, writing to Carpenter, makes his point succinctly: "The first thing is to force people to see that the passions in question have their justification in nature."[19]

As an extended psychosexual analogy to the more palpable reality of physical hermaphroditism, Ulrichs's explanation of homoerotic desire provided the English polemicists with the basic components for their metaphor of inversion, which never relinquished the idea of a misalignment between inside and outside, between desire and the body, between the hidden truth of sex and the false sign of anatomical gender. ("Inversion," derived from the Latin verb *vertere*, "to turn," means literally to turn in, and the *OED* cites the following meaning from pathology: "to turn outside in or inside out.") This argument's intrinsic doubleness—its insistence of the simultaneous inscription within the individual of two genders, one anatomical and one not, one visible and one not—represents an accommodation between contrary impulses of liberation and constraint, as conventional gender norms are subtilized and manipulated but never fully escaped. What this account of same sex eroticism cannot imagine is that sexual attraction between members of the same gender may be a reasonable and natural articulation of a desire whose excursiveness is simply indifferent to the distinctions of gender, that desire may not be gendered intrinsically as the body is, and that desire seeks its objects according to a complicated set of conventions that are culturally and institutionally determined. So radical a reconstitution of notions of desire would probably have been intolerable even to an advanced reading public because it would threaten the moral priority of the heterosexual norm, as the following sentence from Ellis suggests: "It must also be pointed out that the argument for acquired or suggested inversion logically involves the assertion that normal sexuality is also acquired or suggested."[20] Unable or unwilling to deconstruct the heterosexual norm, English accounts of sexual inversion instead repeat it; desire remains, despite appearances, essentially and irrevocably heterosexual. A male's desire for another male, for instance, is from the beginning assumed to be a feminine desire referable not to the gender of the body (*corpore virili*) but rather to another invisible sexual self composed of the opposite gender (*anima muliebris*). Desire, according to this explanation, is always already constituted under the regime of gender—to want a male cannot not be a feminine desire, and vice versa—and the body, having become an unreliable signifier, ceases to represent adequately the invisible truth of desire, which itself never deviates from respectable heterosexuality. Thus the confusion that threatens conventional definitions of gender when confronted by same sex eroticism becomes merely illusory. The body, quite simply, is mistaken.

Significantly, this displaced repetition of heterosexual gender norms contains within it the undeveloped germ of a radical redefinition of Victorian conventions of feminine desire. The interposition of a feminine soul between erotically associated males inevitably entails a certain feminization of desire, since the very site and source of desire for males is assumed to be feminine (*anima muliebris*). Implicit in this argument is the submerged acknowledgment of the sexually independent woman, whose erotic empowerment refutes the conventional assumption of feminine passivity.

Nonetheless, this nascent redefinition of notions of feminine desire remained largely unfulfilled. Symonds and Ellis did not escape their culture's phallocentrism, and their texts predictably reflect this bias. Symonds, whose sexual and aesthetic interests pivoted around the "pure & noble faculty of understanding & expressing manly perfection."[21] seems to have been largely unconcerned with feminine sexuality; his seventy-page *A Problem in Greek Ethics*, for instance, offers only a two-page "parenthetical investigation" of lesbianism. Ellis, like Freud, certainly acknowledged sexual desire in women, but nevertheless accorded to masculine heterosexual desire an ontological and practical priority: "The female responds to the stimulation of the male at the right moment just as the tree responds to the stimulation of the warmest days in spring."[22] (Neither did English law want to recognize the sexually self-motivated woman. The Labouchère Amendment to the Criminal Law Amendment Act of 1885, the statute under which Oscar Wilde was convicted of "gross indecency," simply ignored the possibility of erotic behavior between women.) In all of this we may see an anxious defense against recognition of an independent and active feminine sexuality. A submerged fear of the feminization of desire precluded these polemicists from fully developing their own argumentative assumption of an already sexualized feminine soul.

Sexual inversion, then, understands homoerotic desire as misplaced heterosexuality and configures its understanding of such desire according to what George Chauncey has called "the heterosexual paradigm," an analytical model requiring that all love repeat the dyadic structure (masculine/feminine, husband/wife, active/passive) embodied in the heterosexual norm.[23] Desire between anatomical males requires the interposition of an invisible femininity, just as desire between anatomical females requires the mediation of a hidden masculinity. This insistent ideology of heterosexual mediation and its corollary anxiety about independent feminine sexuality return us to *Dracula*, where all desire, however, mobile, is fixed within a heterosexual mask, where a mobile and hungering woman is represented as a monstrous usurper of masculine function, and where, as we shall see in detail, all erotic contacts between males, whether directly libidinal or thoroughly sublimated, are fulfilled through a mediating female, through the surrogation of the other, "correct," gender. Sexual inversion and Stoker's account of vampirism, then, are symmetrical metaphors sharing a fundamental ambivalence. Both discourses, aroused by a desire that wants to elude or flaunt the conventional prescriptions of gender, constrain that desire by constituting it according to the heterosexual paradigm that leaves conventional gender codes intact. The difference between the two discourses lies in the particular articulation of that paradigm. Sexual inversion, especially as argued by Symonds and Ellis, represents an urbane and civilized accommodation of the contrary impulses of liberation and constraint. Stoker's vampirism, altogether more hysterical and hyperbolic, imagines mobile desire as monstrosity and then devises a violent correction of that desire; in *Dracula* the vampiric abrogation of gender codes inspires a defensive reinscription of the stabilizing distinctions of gender. The site of that ambivalent interplay of desire and its correction, of mobility and fixity, is the text's prolonged middle, to which we now turn.

ENGENDERING GENDER

Our strong game will be to play our masculine against her feminine.
—Stoker, The Lair of the White Worm

The portion of the gothic novel that I have called the prolonged middle, during which the text allows the monster a certain dangerous play, corresponds in *Dracula* to the duration beginning with the Count's arrival in England and ending with his flight back home; this extended middle constitutes the novel's prolonged moment of equivocation, as it entertains, elaborates, and explores the very anxieties it must later expel in the formulaic resolution of the plot. The action within this section of *Dracula* consists, simply enough, in an extended battle between two evidently masculine forces, one identifiably good and the other identifiably evil, for the allegiance of a woman (two women actually—Lucy Westenra and Mina Harker nee Murray).[24] This competition between alternative potencies has the apparent simplicity of a black and white opposition. Dracula ravages and impoverishes these women, Van Helsing's Crew of Light restores and "saves" them. As Dracula conducts his serial assaults upon Lucy, Van Helsing, in a pretty counterpoint of penetration, responds with a series of defensive transfusions; the blood that Dracula takes out Van Helsing then puts back. Dracula, isolated and disdainful of community, works alone; Van Helsing enters this little English community, immediately assumes authority, and then works through surrogates to cement communal bonds. As critics have noted, this pattern of opposition distills readily into a competition between antithetical fathers. "The vampire Count, centuries old," Maurice Richardson wrote twenty-five years ago, "is a father figure of huge potency" who competes with Van Helsing, "the good father figure."[25] The theme of alternate paternities is, in short, simple, evident, unavoidable.

This oscillation between vampiric transgression and medical correction exercises the text's ambivalence toward those fundamental dualisms—life and death, spirit and flesh, male and female—which have served traditionally to constrain and delimit the excursions of desire. As doctor, lawyer, and sometimes priest ("The Host. I brought it from Amsterdam. I have an indulgence."), Van Helsing stands as the protector of the patriarchal institutions he so emphatically represents and as the guarantor of the traditional dualisms his religion and profession promote and authorize.[26] His largest purpose is to reinscribe the dualities that Dracula would muddle and confuse. Dualities require demarcations, inexorable and ineradicable lines of separation, but Dracula, as a border being who abrogates demarcations, makes such distinctions impossible. He is *nosferatu*, neither dead nor alive but somehow both, mobile frequenter of the grave and boudoir, easeful communicant of exclusive realms, and as such as he toys with the separation of the living and the dead, a distinction critical to physician, lawyer, and priest alike. His mobility and metaphoric power deride the distinction between spirit and flesh, another of Van Helsing's sanctified dualisms. Potent enough to ignore death's terminus, Dracula has a spirit's freedom and mobility, but that mobility is chained to the most mechanical of appetites: he and his children rise and fall for a drink and for nothing else, for nothing else matters. This conor inter-fusion of spirit and appetite, of eternity and sequence, produces a madness of activity and a mania of unceasing desire. Dracula lives an eternity of sexual repetition, a lurid wedding of desire and satisfaction that parodies both.

But the traditional dualism most vigorously defended by Van Helsing and most subtly subverted by Dracula is, of course, sexual: the division of being into gender, either male or female. Indeed, as we have seen, the vampiric kiss excites a sexuality so mobile, so insistent, that it threatens to overwhelm the distinctions of gender, and the exuberant energy with which Van Helsing and the Crew of Light counter Dracula's influence represents the text's anxious defense against the very desire it also seeks to liberate. In counterposing Dracula and Van Helsing, Stoker's text simultaneously threatens and protects the line of demarcation that insures the intelligible division of being into gender. This ambivalent need to invite the vampiric kiss and then to repudiate it defines exactly the dynamic of the battle that constitutes the prolonged middle of this text. The field of this battle, of this equivocal competition for the right to define the possible relations between desire and gender, is the infinitely penetrable body of a somnolent woman. This interposition of a woman between Dracula and Van Helsing should not surprise us; in England, as in Castle Dracula, a violent wrestle between males is mediated through a feminine form.

The Crew of Light's conscious conception of women is, predictably enough, idealized—the stuff of dreams. Van Helsing's concise description of Mina may serve as a representative example: "She is one of God's women fashioned by His own hand to show us men and other women that there is a heaven we can enter, and that its light can be here on earth" (226). The impossible idealism of this conception of women deflects attention from the complex and complicitous interaction within this sentence of gender, authority, and representation. Here Van Helsing's exegesis of God's natural text reifies Mina into a stable sign or symbol ("one of God's women") performing a fixed and comfortable function within a masculine sign system. Having received from Van Helsing's exegesis her divine impress, Mina signifies both a masculine artistic intention ("fashioned by His own hand") and a definite didactic purpose ("to show us men and other women" how to enter heaven), each of which constitutes an enormous constraint upon the significative possibilities of the sign or symbol that Mina here becomes. Van Helsing's reading of Mina, like a dozen other instances in which his interpretation of the sacred determines and delimits the range of activity permitted to women, encodes woman with a "natural" meaning composed according to the textual imperatives of anxious males. Precisely this complicity between masculine anxiety, divine textual authority, and a fixed conception of femininity—which may seem benign enough in the passage above—will soon be used to justify the destruction of Lucy Westenra, who, having been successfully vamped by Dracula, requires a corrective penetration. To Arthur's anxious importunity "Tell me what I am to do." Van Helsing answers: "Take this stake in your left hand, ready to place the point over the heart, and the hammer in your right. Then when we begin our prayer for the dead—I shall read him; I have here the book, and the others shall follow—strike in God's name ..." (259). Here four males (Van Helsing, Seward, Holmwood, and Quincey Morris) communally read a masculine text (Van Helsing's mangled English even permits Stoker the unidiomatic pronominalization of the genderless text: "I shall read him").[27] in order to justify the fatal correction of Lucy's dangerous wandering, her insolent disregard for the sexual and semiotic constraint encoded in Van Helsing's exegesis of "God's women."

The process by which women are construed as signs determined by the interpretive imperatives of authorizing males had been brilliantly identified some fifty years before the publication of *Dracula* by John Stuart Mill in *The Subjection of Women*. "What is now called the nature of women," Mill writes, "is an extremely artificial thing—the result of forced repression in some directions, unnatural stimulation in others."[28] Mill's sentence, deftly identifying "the nature of women" as an "artificial" construct formed (and deformed) by "repression" and "unnatural stimulation," quietly unties the lacings that bind something called "woman" to something else called "nature." Mill further suggests that a correct reading of gender becomes almost impossible, since the natural difference between male and female is subject to cultural interpretation: " ... I deny that anyone knows, or can know, the nature of the two sexes, as long as they have only been seen in their present relation to one another." Mill's agnosticism regarding "the nature of the sexes" suggests the societal and institutional quality of all definitions of the natural, definitions which ultimately conspire to produce "the imaginary and conventional character of women."[29] This last phrase, like the whole of Mill's essay, understands and criticizes the authoritarian nexus that arises when a deflected or transformed desire ("imaginary"), empowered by a gender-biased societal agreement ("conventional"), imposes itself upon a person in order to create a "character." "Character" of course functions in at least three senses: who and what one "is," the role one plays in society's supervening script, and the sign or letter that is intelligible only within the constraints of a larger sign system. Van Helsing's exegesis of "God's women" creates just such an imaginary and conventional character. Mina's body/character may indeed be feminine, but the signification it bears is written and interpreted solely by males. As Susan Hardy Aiken has written, such a symbolic system takes "for granted the role of women as passive objects or signs to be manipulated in the grammar of privileged male interchanges."[30]

Yet exactly the passivity of this object and the ease of this manipulation are at question in *Dracula*. Dracula, after all, kisses these women out of their passivity and so endangers the stability of Van Helsing's symbolic system. Both the prescriptive intention of Van Helsing's exegesis and the emphatic methodology (hypodermic needle, stake, surgeon's blade) he employs to insure the durability of his interpretation of gender suggest the potential unreliability of Mina as sign, an instability that provokes an anxiety we may call fear of the mediatrix. If, as Van Helsing admits, God's women provide the essential mediation ("the light can be here on earth") between the divine but distant patriarch and his earthly sons, then God's intention may be distorted by its potentially changeable vehicle. If woman-as-signifier wanders, then Van Helsing's whole cosmology, with its founding dualisms and supporting texts, collapses. In short, Van Helsing's interpretation of Mina, because endangered by the proleptic fear that his mediatrix might destabilize and wander, necessarily imposes an *a priori* constraint upon the significative possibilities of the sign "Mina." Such an authorial gesture, intended to forestall the semiotic wandering that Dracula inspires, indirectly acknowledges woman's dangerous potential. Late in the text, while Dracula is vamping Mina, Van Helsing will admit, very uneasily, that "Madam Mina, our poor, dear Madam Mina is changing" (384). The potential for such a change demonstrates what Nina Auerbach has called this woman's "mysterious amalgam of imprisonment and power."[31]

Dracula's authorizing kiss, like that of a demonic Prince Charming, triggers the release of this latent power and excites in these women a sexuality so mobile, so aggressive, that it thoroughly disrupts Van Helsing's compartmental conception of gender. Kissed into a sudden sexuality,[32] Lucy grows "voluptuous" (a word used to describe her only during the vampiric process), her lips redden, and she kisses with a new interest. This sexualization of Lucy, metamorphosing woman's "sweetness" to "adamantine, heartless cruelty, and [her] purity to voluptuous wantonness" (252), terrifies her suitors because it entails a reversal or inversion of sexual identity; Lucy, now toothed like the Count, usurps the function of penetration that Van Helsing's moralized taxonomy of gender reserves for males. *Dracula*, in thus figuring the sexualization of woman as deformation, parallels exactly some of the more extreme medical uses of the idea of inversion. Late Victorian accounts of lesbianism, for instance, superscribed conventional gender norms upon sexual relationships to which those norms were anatomically irrelevant. Again the heterosexual norm proved paradigmatic. The female "husband" in such a relationship was understood to be dominant, appetitive, masculine, and "congenitally inverted"; the female "wife" was understood to be quiescent, passive, only "latently" homosexual, and, as Havelock Ellis argued, unmotivated by genital desire.[33] Extreme deployment of the heterosexual paradigm approached the ridiculous, as George Chauncey explains:

> The early medical case histories of lesbians thus predictably paid enormous attention to their menstrual flow and the size of their sexual organs. Several doctors emphasized that their lesbian patients stopped menstruating at an early age, if they began at all, or had unusually difficult and irregular periods. They also inspected the woman's sexual organs, often claiming that inverts had unusually large clitorises, which they said the inverts used in sexual intercourse as a man would his penis.[34]

This rather pathetic hunt for the penis-in-absentia denotes a double anxiety: first, that the penis shall not be erased, and if it is erased, that it shall be reinscribed in a perverse simulacrum; and second, that all desire repeat, even under the duress of deformity, the heterosexual norm that the metaphor of inversion always assumes. Medical professionals had in fact no need to pursue this fantasized amazon of the clitoris, this "unnatural" penetrator, so vigorously, since Stoker, whose imagination was at least deft enough to displace that dangerous simulacrum to an isomorphic orifice, had by the 1890s already invented her. His sexualized women are men too.

Stoker emphasizes the monstrosity implicit in such abrogation of gender codes by inverting a favorite Victorian maternal function. His New Lady Vampires feed at first only on small children, working their way up, one assumes, a demonic pleasure thermometer until they may feed at last on full-blooded males. Lucy's dietary indiscretions evoke the deepest disgust from the Crew of Light:

> With a careless motion, she flung to the ground, callous as a devil, the child that up to now she had clutched strenuously to her breast, growling over it as a dog growls over a bone. The child gave a sharp cry, and lay there moaning. There was a cold-bloodedness in the act which wrung a groan from Arthur; when she advanced to him with outstretched arms and a wanton smile, he fell back and hid his face in his hands.
>
> She still advanced, however, and with a langorous, voluptuous grace, said:
>
> "Come to me Arthur. Leave those others and come to me. My arms are hungry for you. Come, and we can rest together. Come, my husband, come!" (253–254)

Stoker here gives us a *tableau mordant* of gender inversion: the child Lucy clutches "strenuously to her breast" is not being fed, but is being fed upon. Furthermore, by requiring that the child be discarded that the husband may be embraced, Stoker provides a little emblem of this novel's anxious protestation that appetite in a woman ("My arms are hungry for you") is a diabolic ("callous as a devil") inversion of natural order, and of the novel's fantastic but futile hope that maternity and sexuality be divorced.

The aggressive mobility with which Lucy flaunts the encasements of gender norms generates in the Crew of Light a terrific defensive activity, as these men race to reinscribe, with a series of pointed instruments, the line of demarcation which enables the definition of gender. To save Lucy from the mobilization of desire, Van Helsing and the Crew of Light counteract Dracula's subversive series of penetrations with a more conventional series of their own, that sequence of transfusions intended to provide Lucy with the "brave man's blood" which "is the best thing on earth when a woman is in trouble" (180). There are in fact four transfusions, which begin with Arthur, who as Lucy's accepted suitor has the right of first infusion, and include Lucy's other two suitors (Dr. Seward, Quincey Morris) and Van Helsing himself. One of the established observations of *Dracula* criticism is that these therapeutic penetrations represent displaced marital (and martial) penetrations; indeed, the text is emphatic about this substitution of medical for sexual penetration. After the first transfusion, Arthur feels as if he and Lucy "had been really married and that she was his wife in the sight of God"

(209); and Van Helsing, after his donation, calls himself a "bigamist" and Lucy "this so sweet maid ... a polyandrist" (211–212). These transfusions, in short, are sexual (blood substitutes for semen here)[35] and constitute, in Nina Auerbach's superb phrase, "the most convincing epithalamiums in the novel."[36]

These transfusions represent the text's first anxious reassertion of the conventionally masculine prerogative of penetration; as Van Helsing tells Arthur before the first transfusion. "You are a man and it is a man we want" (148). Countering the dangerous mobility excited by Dracula's kiss. Van Helsing's penetrations restore to Lucy both the stillness appropriate to his sense of her gender and "the regular breathing of healthy sleep," a necessary correction of the loud "stertorous" breathing, the animal snorting, that the Count inspires. This repetitive contest (penetration, withdrawal; penetration, infusion), itself an image of *Dracula*'s ambivalent need to evoke and then to repudiate the fluid pleasures of vampiric appetite, continues to be waged upon Lucy's infinitely penetrable body until Van Helsing exhausts his store of "brave men," whose generous gifts of blood, however efficacious, fail finally to save Lucy from the mobilization of desire.

But even the loss of this much blood does not finally enervate a masculine energy as indefatigable as the Crew of Light's, especially when it stands in the service of a tradition of "good women whose lives and whose truths may make good lesson [*sic*] for the children that are to be" (222). In the name of those good women and future children (very much the same children whose throats Lucy is now penetrating), Van Helsing will repeat, with an added emphasis, his assertion that penetration is a masculine prerogative. His logic of corrective penetration demands an escalation, as the failure of the hypodermic needle necessitates the stake. A woman is better still than mobile, better dead than sexual:

> Arthur took the stake and the hammer, and when once his mind was set on action his hands never trembled nor even quivered. Van Helsing opened his missal and began to read, and Quincey and I followed as well as we could. Arthur placed the point over the heart, and as I looked I could see its dint in the white flesh. Then he struck with all his might.
>
> The Thing in the coffin writhed; and a hideous, blood-curdling screech came from the opened red lips. The body shook and quivered and twisted in wild contortions; the sharp white teeth champed together till the lips were cut and the mouth was smeared with a crimson foam. But Arthur never faltered. He looked like the figure of Thor as his untrembling arm rose and fell, driving deeper and deeper the mercy-bearing stake, whilst

> the blood from the pierced heart welled and spurted up around it. His face was set, and high duty seemed to shine through it; the sight of it gave us courage, so that our voices seemed to ring through the little vault.
>
> And then the writhing and quivering of the body became less, and the teeth ceased to champ, and the face to quiver. Finally it lay still. The terrible task was over. (258–259)

Here is the novel's real—and the woman's only—climax, its most violent and misogynistic moment, displaced roughly to the middle of the book, so that the sexual threat may be repeated but its ultimate success denied: Dracula will not win Mina, second in his series of English seductions. The murderous phallicism of this passage clearly punishes Lucy for her transgression of Van Helsing's gender code, as she finally receives a penetration adequate to insure her future quiescence. Violence against the sexual woman here is intense, sensually imagined, ferocious in its detail. Note, for instance, the terrible dimple, the "dint in the white flesh," that recalls Jonathan Harker's swoon at Castle Dracula ("I could feel ... the hard dents of the two sharp teeth, just touching and pausing there") and anticipates the technicolor consummation of the next paragraph. That paragraph, masking murder as "high duty," completes Van Helsing's penetrative therapy by "driving deeper and deeper the mercy-bearing stake." One might question a mercy this destructive, this fatal, but Van Helsing's actions, always sanctified by the patriarchal textual tradition signified by "his missal," manage to "restore Lucy to us as a holy and not an unholy memory" (258). This enthusiastic correction of Lucy's monstrosity provides the Crew of Light with a double reassurance: it effectively exorcises the threat of a mobile and hungering feminine sexuality, and it counters the homoeroticism latent in the vampiric threat by reinscribing (upon Lucy's chest) the line dividing the male who penetrates and the woman who receives. By disciplining Lucy and restoring each gender to its "proper" function. Van Helsing's pacification program compensates for the threat of gender indefinition implicit in the vampiric kiss.

The vigor and enormity of this penetration (Arthur driving the "round wooden stake," which is "some two and a half or three inches thick and about three feet long," resembles "the figure of Thor") do not bespeak merely Stoker's personal or idiosyncratic anxiety but suggest as well a whole culture's uncertainty about the fluidity of gender roles. Consider, for instance, the following passage from Ellis's contemporaneous *Studies in the Psychology of Sex*. Ellis, writing on "The Mechanism of Detumescence" (i.e., ejaculation), employs a figure that Stoker would have recognized as his own:

> Detumescence is normally linked to tumescence. Tumescence is the piling on of the fuel; detumescence is the leaping out of the devouring flame whence is lighted the torch of life to be handed on from generation to generation. The whole process is double yet single; it is exactly analogous to that by which a pile is driven into the earth by the raising and the letting go of a heavy weight which falls on the head of the pile. In tumescence the organism is slowly wound up and force accumulated; in the act of detumescence the accumulated force is let go and by its liberation the sperm-bearing instrument is driven home.[37]

Both Stoker and Ellis need to imagine so homely an occurrence as penile penetration as an event of mythic, or at least seismographic, proportions. Ellis's pile driver, representing the powerful "sperm-bearing instrument," may dwarf even Stoker's already outsized member, but both serve a similar function: they channel and finally "liberate" a tremendous "accumulated force" that itself represents a transor supra-natural intention. Ellis, employing a Darwinian principle of interpretation to explain that intention, reads woman's body (much as we have seen Van Helsing do) as a natural sign—or, perhaps better, as a sign of nature's overriding reproductive intention:

> There can be little doubt that, as one or two writers have already suggested, the hymen owes its development to the fact that its influence is on the side of effective fertilization. It is an obstacle to the impregnation of the young female by immature, aged, or feeble males. *The hymen is thus an anatomical expression of that admiration of force which marks the female in her choice of a mate.* So regarded, it is an interesting example of the intimate matter in which sexual selection is really based on natural selection.[38] (italics added)

Here, as evolutionary teleology supplants divine etiology and as Darwin's texts assume the primacy Van Helsing would reserve for God's, natural selection, not God's original intention, becomes the interpretive principle governing nature's text. As a sign or "anatomical expression" within that text, the hymen signifies a woman's presumably natural "admiration of force" and her invitation to "the sperm-bearing instrument." Woman's body, structurally hostile to "immature, aged, or feeble males," simply begs for "effective fertilization." Lucy's body, too, reassures the Crew of Light with an anatomical expression of her admiration of force. Once fatally staked, Lucy is restored to "the so sweet that was." Dr. Seward describes the change:

> There in the coffin lay no longer the foul Thing that we had so dreaded and grown to hate that the work of her destruction was yielded to the one best entitled to it, but Lucy as we had seen her in her life, with her face of unequalled sweetness and purity.... One and all we felt that the holy calm that lay like sunshine over the wasted face and form was only an earthly token and symbol of the calm that was to reign for ever. (259)

This post-penetrative peace[39] denotes not merely the final immobilization of Lucy's body, but also the corresponding stabilization of the dangerous signifier whose wandering had so threatened Van Helsing's gender code. Here a masculine interpretive community ("One and all we felt") reasserts the semiotic fixity that allows Lucy to function as the "earthly token and symbol" of eternal beatitude, of the heaven we can enter. We may say that this last penetration is doubly efficacious: in a single stroke both the sexual and the textual needs of the Crew of Light find a sufficient satisfaction.

Despite its placement in the middle of the text, this scene, which successfully pacifies Lucy and demonstrates so emphatically the efficacy of the technology Van Helsing employs to correct vampirism, corresponds formally to the scene of expulsion, which usually signals the end of the gothic narrative. Here, of course, this scene signals not the end of the story but the continuation of it, since Dracula will now repeat his assault on another woman. Such displacement of the scene of expulsion requires explanation. Obviously this displacement subserves the text's anxiety about the direct representation of croticism between males: Stoker simply could not represent so explicitly a violent phallic interchange between the Crew of Light and Dracula. In a by now familiar heterosexual mediation, Lucy receives the phallic correction that Dracula deserves. Indeed, the actual expulsion of the Count at novel's end is a disappointing anticlimax. Two rather perfunctory knife strokes suffice to dispatch him, as *Dracula* simply forgets the elaborate ritual of correction that vampirism previously required. And the displacement of this scene performs at least two other functions: first, by establishing early the ultimate efficacy of Van Helsing's corrective technology, it reassures everyone—Stoker, his characters, the reader—that vampirism may indeed be vanquished, that its sexual threat, however powerful and intriguing, may be expelled; and second, in doing so, in establishing this reassurance, it permits the text to prolong and repeat its flirtation with vampirism, its ambivalent petition of that sexual threat. In short, the displacement of the scene of expulsion provides a heterosexual locale for Van Helsing's demonstration of compensatory phallicism, while it also extends the duration of the text's ambivalent play.

This extension of the text's flirtation with monstrosity, during which Mina is threatened by but not finally seduced into vampirism, includes the novel's only explicit scene of vampiric seduction. Important enough to be twice presented, first by Seward as spectator and then by Mina as participant, the scene occurs in the Harker bedroom, where Dracula seduces Mina while "on the bed lay Jonathan Harker, his face flushed and breathing heavily as if in a stupor." The Crew of Light bursts into the room; the voice is Dr. Seward's:

> With his left hand he held both Mrs. Harker's hands, keeping them away with her arms at full tension: his right hand gripped her by the back of the neck, forcing her face down on his bosom. Her white nightdress was smeared with blood, and a thin stream trickled down the man's bare breast, which was shown by his torn-open dress. The attitude of the two had a terrible resemblance to a child forcing a kitten's nose into a saucer of milk to compel it to drink. (336)

In this initiation scene Dracula compels Mina into the pleasure of vampiric appetite and introduces her to a world where gender distinctions collapse, where male and female bodily fluids intermingle terribly. For Mina's drinking is double here, both a "symbolic act of enforced fellation"[40] and a lurid nursing. That this is a scene of enforced fellation is made even clearer by Mina's own description of the scene a few pages later; she adds the graphic detail of the "spurt":

> With that he pulled open his shirt, and with his long sharp nails opened a vein in his breast. When the blood began to spurt out, he took my hands in one of his, holding them tight, and with the other seized my neck and pressed my mouth to the wound, so that I must either suffocate or swallow some of the—Oh, my God, my God! What have I done? (343)

That "Oh, my God, my God!" is deftly placed: Mina's verbal ejaculation supplants the Count's liquid one, leaving the fluid unnamed and encouraging us to voice the substitution that the text implies—this blood is semen too. But this scene of fellation is thoroughly displaced. We are at the Count's breast, encouraged once again to substitute white for red, as blood becomes milk: "the attitude of the two had a terrible resemblance to a child forcing a kitten's nose into a saucer of milk." Such fluidity of substitution and displacement entails a confusion of Dracula's sexual identity, or an interfusion of masculine and feminine functions, as Dracula here becomes a lurid mother offering not a breast but an open and bleeding wound. But if the Count's sexuality is double, then the open wound may be yet another displacement (the reader of *Dracula* must be as mobile as the Count himself). We are back in the genital region, this time a woman's, and we have the suggestion of a bleeding vagina. The image of red and voluptuous lips, with their slow trickle of blood, has, of course, always harbored this potential.

We may read this scene, in which anatomical displacements and the confluence of blood, milk, and semen forcefully erase the demarcation separating the masculine and the feminine, as *Dracula*'s most explicit representation of the anxieties excited by the vampiric kiss. Here *Dracula* defines most clearly vampirism's threat of gender indefinition. Significantly, this scene is postponed until late in the text. Indeed, this is Dracula's last great moment, his final demonstration of dangerous potency; after this, he will vamp no one. The novel, having presented most explicitly its deepest anxiety, its fear of gender dissolution, now moves mechanically to repudiate that fear. After a hundred rather tedious pages of pursuit and flight, *Dracula* perfunctorily expels the Count. The world of "natural" gender relations is happily restored, or at least seems to be.

A Final Dissolution

If my last sentence ends with an equivocation, it is because *Dracula* does so as well; the reader should leave this novel with a troubled sense of the difference between the forces of darkness and the forces of light. Of course the plot of *Dracula*, by granting ultimate victory to Van Helsing and a dusty death to the Count, emphatically ratifies the simplistic opposition of competing conceptions of force and desire, but even a brief reflection upon the details of the war of penetrations complicates this comforting schema. A perverse mirroring occurs, as puncture for puncture the Doctor equals the Count. Van Helsing's doubled penetrations, first the morphine injection that immobilizes the woman and then the infusion of masculine fluid, repeat Dracula's spatially doubled penetrations of Lucy's neck. And that morphine injection, which subdues the woman and improves her receptivity, curiously imitates the Count's strange hypnotic power; both men prefer to immobilize a woman before risking a penetration.[41] Moreover, each penetration announces through its displacement this same sense of danger. Dracula enters at the neck, Van Helsing at the limb; each evades available orifices and refuses to submit to the dangers of vaginal contact. The shared displacement is telling: to make your own holes is an ultimate arrogance, an assertion of penetrative prowess that nonetheless acknowledges, in the flight of its evasion, the threatening power imagined to inhabit woman's available openings. Woman's body readily accommodates masculine fear and desire, whether directly libidinal or culturally refined. We may say that Van Helsing and his tradition have polished teeth into hypodermic needles, a cultural refinement that masks violation as healing. Van Helsing himself, calling his medical instruments "the ghastly paraphernalia of our beneficial trade," employs an adjectival oxymoron (ghastly/beneficial) that itself glosses the troubled relationship between paternalism and violence (146). The medical profession licenses the power to penetrate, devises a delicate instrumentation, and defines canons of procedure, while the religious tradition, with its insistent idealization of women, encodes a restriction on the mobility of desire (who penetrates whom) and then licenses a tremendous punishment for the violation of the code.

But it is all penetrative energy, whether re-fanged or refined, and it is all libidinal; the two strategies of penetration are but different articulations of the same primitive force. *Dracula* certainly problematizes, if it does not quite erase, the line of separation signifying a meaningful difference between Van Helsing and the Count. In other words, the text itself, in its imagistic identification of Dracula and the Crew of Light, in its ambivalent propensity to subvert its own fundamental differences, sympathizes with and finally domesticates vampiric desire; the uncanny, as Freud brilliantly observed, always comes home. Such textual irony, composed of simultaneous but contrary impulses to establish and subvert the fundamental differences between violence and culture, between desire and its sublimations, recalls Freud's late speculations on the troubled relationship between the id and the superego (or ego ideal). In the two brief passages below, taken from his late work *The Ego and the Id*, Freud complicates the differentiation between the id and its unexpected effluent, the superego:

> There are two paths by which the contents of the id can penetrate into the ego. The one is direct, the other leads by way of the ego ideal.

And:

> From the point of view of instinctual control, of morality, it may be said of the id that it is totally non-moral, of the ego that it strives to be moral, and of the super-ego that it can be supermoral and then become as cruel as only the id can be.[42]

It is so easy to remember the id as a rising energy and the superego as a suppressive one, that we forget Freud's subtler argument. These passages, eschewing as too facile the simple opposition of the id and superego, suggest instead that the id and the superego are variant articulations of the same primitive energy. We are already familiar with the "two paths by which the contents of the id penetrate the ego." "The one is direct," as Dracula's penetrations are direct and unembarrassed, and the other, leading "by way of the ego ideal," recalls Van Helsing's way of repression and sublimation. In providing an indirect path for the "contents of the id" and in being "as cruel as only the id can be," the superego may be said to be, in the words of Leo Bersani, "the id which has become its own mirror."[43] This mutual reflectivity of the id and superego, of course, constitutes one of vampirism's most disturbing features, as Jonathan Harker, standing before his shaving glass, learns early in the novel: "This time there could be no error, for the man was close to me, and I could see him over my shoulder. But there was no reflection of him in the mirror! The whole room behind me was displayed; but there was no sign of a man in it, except myself" (37). The meaning of this little visual allegory should be clear enough: Dracula need cast no reflection because his presence, already established in Harker's image, would be simply redundant; the monster, indeed, is no one "except myself." A dangerous sameness waits behind difference: tooth, stake, and hypodermic needle, it would seem, all share a point.

This blending or interfusion of fundamental differences would seem, in one respect at least, to contradict the progress of my argument. We have, after all, established that the Crew of Light's penetrative strategy, subserving Van Helsing's ideology of gender and his heterosexual account of desire, counters just such interfusions with emphatic inscriptions of sexual difference. Nonetheless, this penetrative strategy, despite its purposive heterosexuality, quietly erases its own fundamental differences, its own explicit assumptions of gender and desire. It would seem at first that desire for connection among males is both expressed in and constrained by a traditional articulation of such fraternal affection, as represented in this text's blaring theme of heroic or chivalric male bonding. The obvious male bonding in *Dracula* is precipitated by action—a good fight, a proud ethic, a great victory. Dedicated to a falsely exalted conception of woman, men combine fraternally to fulfill the collective "high duty" that motivates their "great quest" (261). Van Helsing, always the ungrammatical exegete, provides the apt analogy: "Thus we are ministers of God's own wish.... He have allowed us to redeem one soul already, and we go out as the old knights of the Cross to redeem more" (381). Van Helsing's chivalric analogy establishes this fraternity within an impeccable lineage signifying both moral rectitude and adherence to the limitation upon desire that this tradition encodes and enforces.

Yet beneath this screen or mask of authorized fraternity a more libidinal bonding occurs as male fluids find a protected pooling place in the body of a woman. We return, for a last time, to those serial transfusions which, while they pretend to serve and protect "good women," actually enable the otherwise inconceivable interfusion of the blood that is semen too. Here displacement (a woman's body) and sublimation (these are medical penetrations) permit the unpermitted, just as in gang rape men share their semen in a location displaced sufficiently to divert the anxiety excited by a more direct union. Repeating its subversive suggestion that the refined moral conceptions of Van Helsing's Crew of Light express obliquely an excursive libidinal energy, an energy much like the Count's, *Dracula* again employs an apparently rigorous heterosexuality to represent anxious desire for a less conventional communion. The parallel here to Dracula's taunt ("Your girls that you all love are mine already; and through them you ... shall be mine") is inescapable; in each case Lucy, the woman in the middle, connects libidinous males. Here, as in the Victorian metaphor of sexual inversion, an interposed difference—an image of manipulable femininity—mediates and deflects an otherwise unacceptable appetite for sameness. Men touching women touch each other, and desire discovers itself to be more fluid than the Crew of Light would consciously allow.

Indeed, so insistent is this text to establish this pattern of heterosexual mediation that it repeats the pattern on its final page. Jonathan Harker, writing in a postscript that compensates clearly for his assumption at Castle Dracula of a "feminine" passivity, announces the text's last efficacious penetration:

> Seven years ago we all went through the flames: and the happiness of some of us since then is, we think, well worth the pain we endured. It is an added joy to Mina and to me that our boy's birthday is the same day as that on which Quincey Morris died. His mother holds, I know, the secret belief that some of our brave friend's spirit has passed into him. His bundle of names links all our little band of men together; but we call him Quincey. (449)

As offspring of Jonathan and Mina Harker, Little Quincey, whose introduction so late in the narrative insures his emblematic function, seemingly represents the restoration of "natural" order and especially the rectification of conventional gender roles. His official genesis is, obviously enough, heterosexual, but Stoker's prose quietly suggests an alternative paternity: "His bundle of names links all our little band of men together."

This is the fantasy child of those sexualized transfusions, son of an illicit and nearly invisible homosexual union. This suggestion, reinforced by the preceding pun of "spirit," constitutes this text's last and subtlest articulation of its "secret belief" that "a brave man's blood" may metamorphose into "our brave friend's spirit." But the real curiosity here is the novel's last-minute displacement, its substitution of Mina, who ultimately refused sexualization by Dracula, for Lucy, who was sexualized, vigorously penetrated, and consequently destroyed. We may say that Little Quincey was luridly conceived in the veins of Lucy Westenra and then deftly relocated to the purer body of Mina Harker. Here, in the last of its many displacements, *Dracula* insists, first, that successful filiation implies the expulsion of all "monstrous" desire in women and, second, that all desire, however mobile and omnivorous it may secretly be, must subject itself to the heterosexual configuration that alone defined the Victorian sense of the normal. In this regard, Stoker's fable, however hyperbolic its anxieties, represents his age. As we have seen, even polemicists of same sex eroticism like Symonds and Ellis could not imagine such desire without repeating within their metaphor of sexual inversion the basic structure of the heterosexual paradigm. Victorian culture's anxiety about desire's potential indifference to the prescriptions of gender produces everywhere a predictable repetition and a predictable displacement: the heterosexual norm repeats itself in a mediating image of femininity—the Count's vampiric daughters, Ulrichs's and Symonds's *anima muliebris*, Lucy Westenra's penetrable body—that displaces a more direct communion among males. Desire, despite its propensity to wander, stays home and retains an essentially heterosexual and familial definition. The result in *Dracula* is a child whose conception is curiously immaculate, yet disturbingly lurid: child of his fathers' violations. Little Quincey, fulfilling Van Helsing's prophecy of "the children that are to be," may be the text's emblem of a restored natural order, but his paternity has its unofficial aspect too. He is the unacknowledged son of the Crew of Light's displaced homoerotic union, and his name, linking the "little band of men together," quietly remembers that secret genesis.

NOTES

1. Joseph Sheridan Le Fanu, *Carmilla*, in *The Best Ghost Stories of J. S. Le Fanu* (New York, 1964), p. 337; this novella of lesbian vampirism, which appeared first in Le Fanu's *In A Glass Darkly* (1872), predates *Dracula* by twenty-five years.

2. Franco Moretti, *Signs Taken for Wonders* (Thetford, 1983), p. 100.

3. Bram Stoker, *Dracula* (New York, 1979), p. 51. All further references to *Dracula* appear within the essay in parentheses.

4. The paradigmatic instance of this triple rhythm is Mary Shelley's *Frankenstein*, a text that creates—bit by bit, and stitch by stitch—its resident demon, then equips that demon with a powerful Miltonic voice with which to petition both its creator and the novel's readers, and finally drives its monster to polar isolation and suicide. Stevenson's *Dr. Jekyll and Mr. Hyde* repeats the pattern: Henry Jekyll's chemical invitation to Hyde corresponds to the gesture of admission; the serial alternation of contrary personalities constitutes the ambivalent play of the prolonged middle; and Jekyll's suicide, which expels both the monster and himself, corresponds to the gesture of expulsion.

5. Readers of Tzvetan Todorov's *The Fantastic* (Ithaca, 1975) will recognize that my argument about the gothic text's extended middle derives in part from his idea that the essential condition of fantastic fiction is a duration characterized by readerly suspension of certainty.

6. John Ruskin, *Sesame and Lilies* (New York, 1974), pp. 59–60.

7. This group of crusaders includes Van Helsing himself. Dr. John Seward, Arthur Holmwood. Quincey Morris, and later Jonathan Harker; the title Crew of Light is mine, but I have taken my cue from Stoker: Lucy, *lux*, light.

8. Renfield, whose "zoophagy" precedes Dracula's arrival in England and who is never vamped by Dracula, is no exception to this rule.

9. The complication of gender roles in *Dracula* has of course been recognized in the criticism. See, for instance, Stephanie Demetrakopoulos, "Feminism, Sex Role Exchanges, and Other Subliminal Fantasies in Bram Stoker's *Dracula*," *Frontiers*, 2 (1977), pp. 104–113. Demetrakopoulos writes: "These two figures I have traced so far—the male as passive rape victim and also as violator-brutalizer—reflect the polarized sex roles and the excessive needs this polarizing engendered in Victorian culture. Goldfarb recounts the brothels that catered to masochists, sadists, and homosexuals. The latter aspect of sexuality obviously did not interest Stoker...." I agree with the first sentence here and, as this essay should make clear, emphatically disagree with the last.

10. John Addington Symonds, *A Problem in Modern Ethics* (London, 1906), p. 74.

11. The semantic imprecision of the word "sodomy" is best explained by John Boswell, *Christianity, Social Tolerance, and Homosexuality* (Chicago, 1980), pp. 91–116. "Sodomy," notes Boswell, "has connoted in various times and various places everything from ordinary heterosexual intercourse in an atypical position to oral sexual contact with animals" (93).

12. This is the traditional Christian circumlocution by which sodomy was both named and unnamed, both specified in speech and specified as unspeakable. It is the phrase, according to Jeffrey Weeks, "with which Sir Robert Peel forbore to mention sodomy in Parliament," quoted in Weeks, *Coming Out* (London, 1977), p. 14.

13. Michel Foucault, *The History of Sexuality* (New York, 1980). My argument agrees with Foucault's assertion that "the techniques of power exercised over sex have not obeyed a principle of rigorous selection, but rather one of dissemination and implantation of polymorphous sexualities" (12). Presumably members of the same gender have been copulating together for uncounted centuries, but the invert and homosexual were not invented until the ninteenth century.

14. I cite this phrase, spoken by Mr. Justice Wills to Oscar Wilde immediately after the latter's conviction under the Labouchère Amendment to the Criminal Law Amendment Act of 1885, as an oblique reference to the orifice that so threatened the homophobic Victorian imagination; that Wilde was never accused of anal intercourse (only oral copulation and mutual masturbation were charged against him) seems to me to confirm, rather than to undermine this interpretation of the phrase. Wills's entire sentence reads: "And that you, Wilde, have been the centre of a circle of extensive corruption of the most hideous kind among young men, it is equally impossible to doubt"; quoted in H. Montgomery Hyde, *The Trials of Oscar Wilde* (New York, 1962), p. 272. The Labouchère Amendment, sometimes called the blackmailer's charter, punished "any act of gross indecency" between males, whether in public or private, with two years' imprisonment and hard labor. Symonds, Ellis, and Carpenter argued strenuously for the repeal of this law.

15. Symonds, *A Problem in Modern Ethics*, p. 3.

16. Ibid., p. 84. To my knowledge, the earliest English instance of "inversion" in this specific sense is the phrase "Inverted Sexual Proclivity" from *The Journal of Mental Science* (October, 1871), where it is used anonymously to translate Carl Westphal's neologism *die conträre Sexualempfindung*, the term that would dominate German discourse on same gender eroticism. I have not yet been able to date precisely Symonds's first use of "inversion."

17. Havelock Ellis, *Sexual Inversion*, volume 2 of *Studies in the Psychology of Sex* (Philadelphia, 1906), p. 1.

18. This and the two subsequent quotations are from Symonds's *Modern Ethics*, pp. 86, 90, and 85 respectively.

19. Symonds's letter to Carpenter, December 29, 1893, in *The Letters of John Addington Symonds*, volume 3, eds. H. M. Shueller and R. L. Peters (Detroit, 1969), p. 799; also quoted in Weeks, p. 54.

20. Ellis, *Sexual Inversion*, p. 182.

21. Symonds in *Letters*, volume 2, p. 169.

22. Ellis, quoted in Weeks, p. 92.

23. George Chauncey, Jr., "From Sexual Inversion to Homosexuality: Medicine and the Changing Conceptualization of Female Deviance," *Salamagundi*, 58–59 (1982), pp. 114–146.

24. This bifurcation of woman is one of the text's most evident features, as critics of *Dracula* have been quick to notice. See Phyllis Roth, "Suddenly Sexual Women in Bram Stoker's *Dracula*," *Literature and Psychology*, 27 (1977), p. 117, and her full-length study *Bram Stoker* (Boston, 1982). Roth, in an argument that emphasizes the pre-Oedipal element in *Dracula*, makes a similar point: "... one recognizes that Lucy and Mina are essentially the same figure: the Mother. Dracula is, in fact, the same story told twice with different outcomes." Perhaps the most extensive thematic analysis of this split in Stoker's representation of women is Carol A. Senf's "*Dracula:* Stoker's Response to the New Woman," *Victorian Studies*, 26 (1982), pp. 33–39, which sees this split as Stoker's "ambivalent reaction to a topical phenomenon—the New Woman."

25. Maurice Richardson, "The Psychoanalysis of Ghost Stories," *The Twentieth Century*, 166 (1959), p. 427–428.

26. On this point see Demetrakopoulos, p. 104.

27. In this instance at least Van Helsing has an excuse for his ungrammatical usage; in Dutch, Van Helsing's native tongue, the noun *bijbel* (Bible) is masculine.

28. John Stuart Mill, *The Subjection of Women* in *Essays on Sex Equality*, ed. Alice Rossi (Chicago, 1970), p. 148.

29. Ibid., p. 187.

30. Susan Hardy Aiken, "Scripture and Poetic Discourse in *The Subjection of Women*," *PMLA*, 98 (1983), p. 354.

31. Nina Auerbach, *Woman and the Demon*, (Cambridge, 1982), p. 11.

32. Roth, "Suddenly Sexual Women," p. 116.

33. An adequate analysis of the ideological and political implications of the terminological shift from "inversion" to "homosexuality" is simply beyond the scope of this essay, and the problem is further complicated by a certain imprecision or fluidity in the employment by these writers of an already unstable terminology. Ellis used the word "homosexuality" under protest and Carpenter, citing the evident bastardy of any term compounded of one Greek and one Latin root, preferred the word "homogenic." However, a provisional if oversimplified discrimination between "inversion" and "homosexuality" may be useful: "true" sexual inversion, Ellis argued, consists in "sexual instinct turned by *inborn constitutional abnormality* toward

persons of the same sex" (*Sexual Inversion*, p. 1; italics added), whereas homosexuality may refer to same sex eroticism generated by spurious, circumstantial (*faute de mieux*), or intentionally perverse causality. The pivotal issue here is will or choice: the "true" invert, whose "abnormality" is biologically determined and therefore "natural," does not choose his/her desire but is instead chosen by it; the latent or spurious homosexual, on the other hand, does indeed choose a sexual object of the same gender. Such a taxonomic distinction (or, perhaps better, confusion) represents a polemical and political compromise that allows, potentially at least, for the medicalization of congenital inversion and the criminalization of willful homosexuality. I repeat the caution that my description here entails a necessary oversimplification of a terminological muddle. For a more complete and particular analysis see Chauncey, pp. 114–146; for the applicability of such a taxonomy to lesbian relationships see Ellis, *Sexual Inversion*, pp. 131–141.

34. Chauncey, p. 132.

35. The symbolic interchangeability of blood and semen in vampirism was identified as early as 1931 by Ernest Jones in *On The Nightmare* (London, 1931), p. 119: "in the unconscious mind blood is commonly an equivalent for semen...."

36. Auerbach, p. 22.

37. Havelock Ellis, *Erotic Symbolism*, volume 5 of *Studies in the Psychology of Sex* (Philadelphia, 1906), p. 142.

38. Ibid., 140.

39. Roth correctly reads Lucy's countenance at this moment as "a thank you note" for the corrective penetration; "Suddenly Sexual Women," p. 116.

40. C. F. Bentley, "The Monster in the Bedroom: Sexual Symbolism in Bram Stoker's *Dracula*," *Literature and Psychology*, 22 (1972), p. 30.

41. Stoker's configuration of hypnotism and anaesthesia is not idiosyncratic. Ellis, for instance, writing at exactly this time, conjoins hypnosis and anaesthesia as almost identical phenomena and subsumes them under a single taxonomic category: "We may use the term 'hypnotic phenomena' as a convenient expression to include not merely the condition of artificially-produced sleep, or hypnotism in the narrow sense of the term, but all those groups of psychic phenomena which are characterized by a decreased control of the higher nervous centres, and increased activity of the lower centres." The quality that determines membership in this "convenient" taxonomy is, to put matters baldly, ap elvis pumped up by the "increased activity of the lower centres." Ellis, in an earlier footnote, explains the antithetical relationship between the "higher" and "lower" centers: The persons best adapted to propagate the race are those with the large pelves,

and as the pelvis is the seat of the great centres of sexual emotion the development of the pelvis and its nervous and vascular supply involves the greater heightening of the sexual emotions. At the same time the greater activity of the cerebral centres enables them to subordinate and utilise to their own ends the increasingly active sexual emotions, so that reproduction is checked and the balance to some extent restored." The pelvic superiority of women, necessitated by an evolutionary imperative (better babies with bigger heads require broader pelves), implies a corresponding danger—an engorged and hypersensitive sexuality that must be actively "checked" by the "activity of the cerebral centres" so that "balance" may be "to some extent restored." Hypnotism and anaesthesia threaten exactly this delicate balance, and especially so in women because "the lower centres in women are more rebellious to control than those of men, and more readily brought into action." Anaesthesiology, it would seem, is not without its attendant dangers: "Thus chloroform, ether, nitrous oxide, cocaine, and possibly other anaesthetics, possess the property of exciting the sexual emotions. Women are especially liable to these erotic hallucinations during anaesthesia, and it has sometimes been almost impossible to convince them that their subjective sensations have had no objective cause. Those who have to administer anaesthetics are well aware of the risks they may thus incur." Ellis's besieged physician, like Stoker's master monster and his monster master, stands here as a male whose empowerment anxiously reflects a prior endangerment. What if this woman's lower centers should take the opportunity—to use another of Ellis's phrases—"of indulging in an orgy"? Dracula's kiss, Van Helsing's needle and stake, and Ellis's "higher centres" all seek to modify, constrain, and control the articulation of feminine desire (But, it might be counter-argued, Dracula comes precisely to excite such an orgy, not to constrain one. Yes, but with an important qualification: Dracula's kiss, because it authorizes only repetitions of itself, clearly articulates the destiny of feminine desire; Lucy will only do what Dracula has done before.) Havelock Ellis, *Man and Woman* (New York, 1904), pp. 299, 73, 316, and 313 respectively. I have used the fourth edition; the first edition appeared in England in 1895.

42. Sigmund Freud, *The Ego and the Id* (New York, 1960), pp. 44–45.

43. Leo Bersani, *Baudelaire and Freud* (Berkeley, 1977), p. 92.

JOHN ALLEN STEVENSON

A Vampire in the Mirror: The Sexuality of Dracula

Near the end of *Dracula*, as the band of vampire hunters is tracking the count to his Carpathian lair, Mina Harker implores her husband to kill her if her partial transformation into a vampire should become complete. Her demand for this "euthanasia" (the phrase is Dr. Seward's [340]) is itself extraordinary, but equally interesting is the way she defines her position and the duty of the men around her: "Think, dear, that there have been times when brave men have killed their wives and womenkind, to keep them from falling into the hands of the enemy.... It is men's duty towards those whom they love, in such times of sore trial!" (336). Why is this "duty" incumbent on "brave men"? Why are "wives and womenkind" a treasure better destroyed than lost to the "enemy"? In the context of Bram Stoker's novel, it is evident that the mercy implied by such euthanasia is not salvation from the loathsome embraces of a lewd foreigner. It is too late for that. Mina, after all, has already been the object of Dracula's attention. The problem is one of loyalty: the danger is not that she will be captured but that she will go willingly. She makes this clear: "this time, if it ever come, may come quickly ... and ... you must lose no time in using your opportunity. At such a time, I myself might be—nay! if the time ever comes, *shall be*—leagued with your enemy against you" (337). Kill me, she says, before I can betray you.

That *Dracula* concerns competition between men for women can hardly be questioned—passages like these can be multiplied almost

From *PMLA* 103, no. 2 (March 1988): 139-149.

indefinitely. But what is the nature of that competition? Certainly, a number of readers have agreed on one interpretation. As they would have it, the horror we feel in contemplating Dracula is that his actions, when stripped of displacement and disguise, are fundamentally incestuous and that Stoker's novel is finally a rather transparent version of the "primal horde" theory Freud advanced—only about fifteen years after publication of the novel—in *Totem and Taboo*.[1] According to this interpretation (as one adherent has it, "almost a donnée of *Dracula* criticism" [Twitchell, *Living Dead* 135]), the count, undeniably long in the tooth, attempts to hoard all the available women, leaving the younger generation, his "sons," no recourse but to rise up and kill the wicked "father," thus freeing the women for themselves. The novel does concern how one old man ("centuries-old," he tells us) struggles with four young men (and another old, but good, man, Dr. Van Helsing) for the bodies and souls of two young women. But to call that strife intrafamilial (Twitchell, *Dreadful Pleasures* 139) or to say that all the characters, including Dracula, are linked "as members of one family" (Richardson 428) seems to be more of a tribute to the authority psychoanalysis enjoys among literary critics than it is an illuminating description of Stoker's narrative.

I would like to rethink the way sexual competition works in *Dracula* from the perspective of that frequent antagonist of psychoanalysis, anthropology. Nowhere is the gulf between these universalizing disciplines greater, perhaps, than it is on the subject that obsesses them both, incest.[2] A good deal of recent anthropological work argues that, as one prominent scholar puts it, "human beings [do] not *want* to commit incest all that much" (Fox, *Red Lamp* 7). My intention in this essay is to apply this anti-incestuous model of human desire to *Dracula* in the place of the more customary Freudian model. As Mina's remarks above indicate, the novel insistently—indeed, obsessively—defines the vampire not as a monstrous father but as a foreigner, as someone who threatens and terrifies precisely because he is an outsider. In other words, it may be fruitful to reconsider Stoker's compelling and frequently retold story in terms of inter*racial* sexual competition rather than as intrafamilial strife. Dracula's pursuit of Lucy and Mina is motivated, not by the incestuous greed at the heart of Freud's scenario, but by an omnivorous appetite for difference, for novelty. His crime is not the hoarding of incest but a sexual theft, a sin we can term excessive exogamy. Although the old count has women of his own, he is exclusively interested in the women who belong to someone else. This reconsideration can yield a fresh appreciation of the appeal of Stoker's story and can suggest ways in which the novel embodies a quite powerful imagining of the nature of cultural and racial difference.

Before explaining how *Dracula* represents this kind of exogamous threat, I want to review briefly some basic anthropological ideas about marriage customs, particularly as they relate to the incest taboo.[3] While not, as was once imagined, an absolute universal of human behavior, the taboo is very common, and various benefits—genetic diversity, family peace, social stability, the existence of society itself—have been ascribed to it. More relevant to *Dracula* than the origin of the taboo, however, is the so-called rule of exogamy that is one result. Sex and marriage, of course, are not the same thing, but since sex is typically a part of the marital relation, the taboo's injunction against sex within the family means that people must "marry out." Anthropology has devoted considerable energy to discovering the remarkable and often arbitrary rules humanity has established to govern just which women are "inside" the family and hence forbidden and which are "outside" and therefore available. But the word *exogamy* is also somewhat misleading, because most cultures place significant limitations on how far out a mate may be sought. As Robin Fox says, "Of course, [exogamy] had to have some boundaries.... Groups speaking the same language and being alike in other ways might well exchange wives among themselves—but the connubium stopped at the boundaries of the language, territory, or colour, or whatever marked 'us' off from 'them'" (*Kinship* 78). The exchange of women that is the essence of exogamy has its limits. If most cultures have forbidden marriage within the family, they have also wanted to maintain the integrity of the group. *Group* is, admittedly, a vague term, an inherently cultural construct encompassing all manner of classifications: tribe, caste, class, race, religion, nation, and so on. But its vagueness does not diminish the importance of the distinction Fox speaks of, that boundary between "us" and "them," however artificially that line might be drawn. And according to these lights, marriage, or even a sexual relation, that crosses that boundary ceases to be a social act that simultaneously denies incest and affirms the group and becomes instead a threat, what I earlier called excessive exogamy. This was the problem worrying the Deuteronomist when he cautioned the Jews that intermarriage would "turn away thy sons ... that they may serve other gods" (7.3), and this was the kind of exogamy the great pioneer of the anthropology of marriage, Edward Westermarck, was thinking about when he coined the memorable phrase "social adultery" (2:51). Here, then, is the real horror of Dracula, for he is the ultimate social adulterer, whose purpose is nothing if it is not to turn good Englishwomen like Lucy and Mina away from their own kind and customs. Mina's fear, we recall, is that she "*shall be* ... leagued with your enemy against you."

What sort of enemy, foreigner, stranger is Count Dracula? I have claimed that interracial sexual competition is fundamental to the energies that motivate this novel, but in what way are vampires another "race"? As a rigorous scientific concept, race enjoys little credence today, despite the many attempts—particularly as part of the nineteenth-century zeal for classification—to elevate it to a science involving physical criteria like jaws, cheekbones, cranial capacities, and so on. It is, however, a convenient metaphor to describe the undeniable human tendency to separate "us" from "them." An idea like race helps us grapple with human otherness—the fact that we do not all look alike or believe alike or act alike. Dracula is, above all, strange to those he encounters—strange in his habits, strange in his appearance, strange in his physiology. At one point, Van Helsing calls him "the other" (297), and the competition for women in the novel reflects a conflict between groups that define themselves as foreign to each other. My use of the term *interracial*, then, is a way to speak of what happens when any two groups set themselves at odds on the basis of what they see as differences in their fundamental identity, be that "racial," ethnic, tribal, religious, national, or whatever.[4]

The problem of interracial competition would have probably had an especial resonance in 1897, the year *Dracula* appeared. For several decades, Great Britain had been engaged in an unprecedented program of colonial expansion: four and one quarter million square miles were added to the empire in the last thirty years of the century alone (Seaman 332). British imperialism, of course, was not new, nor was suspicion of foreigners a novelty in a country where, as one eighteenth-century wit put it, "Before they learn there is a God to be worshipped, they learn there are Frenchmen to be detested" (qtd. in Porter 21). Yet the late nineteenth century saw the rise of that great vulgarization of evolution (and powerful racist rationalization), social Darwinism, and heard Disraeli say, "All is race; there is no other truth" (qtd. in Faber 59). *Dracula*'s insistence on the terror and necessity of racial struggle in an imperialist context (the count, after all, has invaded England and plans to take it over) must reflect that historical frame. My emphasis in this essay, however, is on Stoker's novel as a representation of fears that are more universal than a specific focus on the Victorian background would allow. Westermarck's comment about exogamy as social adultery is indeed contemporary with *Dracula* (his *History of Human Marriage* was first published in 1891), but the anthropologist was expressing nothing not on the mind of the Deuteronomist millennia before. And the difficulty facing the men who fight the vampire is not unlike that expressed by Roderigo to Brabantio, in lines first spoken at a much earlier time in British imperial history: Desdemona, he says, has made "a gross revolt, / Tying her duty, beauty, wit, and fortunes / In an extravagant and wheeling stranger ..." (1.1.131–33). Let us look more specifically, then, at this stranger, Count Dracula.

First, appearances. Dracula is described repeatedly, always in the same way, with the same peculiar features emphasized. Take Mina's first sight of him:

> I knew him at once from the description of the others. The waxen face; the high aquiline nose, on which the light fell in a thin, white line; the parted red lips, with the sharp white teeth showing between; and the red eyes that I had seemed to see in the sunset on the windows of St. Mary's Church at Whitby. I knew, too, the red scar on his forehead where Jonathan had struck him.
> (292–93)

Dracula is remarkable locking for his nose, for the color of his lips and eyes and skin, for the shape of his teeth, for the mark on his forehead; elsewhere, we learn also that he has a strange smell (257). Color, in fact, which is commonly used in attempts at racial classification, is a key element in Stoker's creation of Dracula's foreignness. Here, and throughout the novel, the emphasis is on redness and whiteness. In a brief description, each color is mentioned three times (I count "waxen" as white), and the combination of the two colors is one of the count's most distinguishing racial features. That it is racial, and not personal, becomes clear when we note how Stoker consistently uses a combination of red and white to indicate either incipient or completed vampirism. The women Harker encounters at Castle Dracula, while one is blond and two are dark, are all primarily red and white ("All three had brilliant white teeth that shone like pearls against the ruby of their voluptuous lips" [46]). More significant, Lucy and Mina take on this coloration as Dracula works his will on them. There is first of all the reiterated image of red blood on a white night-gown (103, 288), a signature that Dracula leaves behind after one of his visits (and a traditional emblem of defloration). Even more striking is the scar left when Van Helsing, in a futile attempt at inoculation, presses the host into Mina's forehead to protect Mina against renewed attack. Harker calls it the "red scar on my poor darling's white forehead" (321). The scar, a concentration of red and white that closely resembles the mark on Dracula's own forehead (cf. esp. 312), thus becomes a kind of caste mark, a sign of membership in a homogeneous group—and a group that is foreign to the men to whom Mina supposedly belongs.

The scar shared by Dracula and Mina, one of the richest details in the novel, has a significance even beyond its function as a caste mark. After all, the wounds are not self-inflicted but given by members of the group of vampire hunters (Dracula's by Harker, Mina's by Van Helsing), so that they represent an attempt by the nonvampires to "mark off" the vampires—much as God puts a mark on Cain, the original type of an alien breed. But the caste mark is also a kind of venereal scar, not only because it results from the count's seduction of Mina but also because the echo of Hamlet's accusation against Gertrude is far too strong to be accidental: "Such an act / That blurs the grace and blush of modesty, / Calls virtue hypocrite, takes off the rose / From the fair forehead of an innocent love, / And sets a blister there ..." (3.4.41–45).[5] The scar is thus a sign of defilement (seeing it, Mina cries out, "Unclean! Unclean!" [302]), of sexual possession by the outsider. Finally, it is curious to think of a scar on Dracula at all. He is remarkably protean, able to change his form (he leaves the shipwreck at Whitby as a dog) or even involve himself in rising mist. Why should he allow this disfigurement to remain? John Freccero, discussing the scar Dante describes on the purgatorial form of Manfred, insists that a mark like this on a supernatural being must be seen, not as literal and physical, but as a text, as something meant especially to be *read*. In that sense, the scars on the vampires serve a dense semiotic function, marking Dracula and Mina (potentially, anyway) as simultaneously untouchable, defiled, and damned—above all, different.

Red and white are, of course, the colors we associate with the typically "English" complexion, and I want to emphasize that vampire coloration is something different; at the same time, however, the coincidence of coloration is meaningful. On the one hand, a "rosy" English complexion is created by the perception of red *through* white—blood coursing beneath pale skin. The vampire inverts this order. He or she displays red *on* white, as with the scars or the effect of ruby lips against waxen skin. The result is rather like a mortician's makeup—a parody of what we expect and, as with a corpse, an effect that finally signals difference and not similarity. That is, the vampire has no rosy glow but presents what looks like dead flesh stained with blood (or drained flesh indicating the food it requires)—a grotesque inversion of good health. On the other hand, the vampire and his English competitors may have more in common than they wish to acknowledge. As we explore vampire sexuality, we will encounter a series of traits that initially assert themselves as foreign or strange but that are revealed as inversions (as in the coloration example), parodies, exaggerations, or even literalizations. Thus, the perception of otherness can be an accurate response to difference and, at the same time, an act that conceals or represses deeper connections.

The allies against the count are not described in comparable detail, and their descriptions tend to be moral rather than physical. Three of their qualities recur almost formulaically—*good*, *brave*, and *strong*. "Oh, thank God for good, brave men!" says Mina, and Van Helsing insists later, "You men are brave and strong" (316, 332). *Good* is also often attached to the women in their unvamped condition: "there are good women left still to make life happy" (190). The distinction between the moral excellence of the insiders and the physical peculiarity of the foreigner underlines the outsider's inherent danger. As Mina puts it, "[T]he world seems full of good men—even if there *are* monsters in it" (230). The familiar is the image of the good, while foreignness merges with monstrosity.

But looks are only one way to construct our images of the foreign, and, as we might expect, Dracula's habits are as bizarre as his appearance. The introductory section of the novel—Harker's diary account of his journey to Transylvania and of his stay at Castle Dracula—gradually reveals Dracula's distinctive customs, moving from the merely odd to the unequivocally horrifying. So, we learn early that Dracula lacks servants, that he is nocturnal, that he likes to eat alone, and that he despises mirrors, and only later do we watch him crawl down walls head first, feed small children to his women, and sleep in his coffin. All Dracula's peculiarities, however, reflect fundamental differences in the most basic human activities that signal group identity. Dracula is strange to Harker—and to us—because of what food he eats and how he obtains and prepares it, because of where and when he sleeps, because of his burial customs. To Harker as to so many, what is foreign is monstrous, even if it is only a matter of table manners.

In the structure of group identity, the regulation of sexuality has an especially privileged place, and *Dracula* is most fundamentally concerned with both distinguishing the differences between the way vampire "monsters" and "good, brave men" reproduce and identifying the threat those differences pose to Van Helsing and the other men. Our introduction to Dracula in the novel's first six chapters—what Christopher Craft calls the "admission" to monstrosity (108)—establishes the count's foreignness; after that, the novel primarily shows us Dracula's attempts to reproduce and the struggle of the band of young men under Van Helsing to stop him. The tale horrifies because the vampire's manner of reproduction appears radically different and because it requires the women who already belong to these men.

Although the vampire reproduces differently, the ironic thing about vampire sexuality is that, for all its overt peculiarity, it is in many ways very like human sexuality, but human sexuality in which the psychological or metaphoric becomes physical or literal. It initially looks strange but quite often presents a distorted image of human tendencies and behavior. What is frightening about Dracula, then, is that his sexuality is simultaneously different and a parodic mirror. This seeming paradox probably reflects the full complexity of the way one group responds to the sexual customs of another.

We note first the remarkable economy at the heart of the vampire's survival instinct. Like human beings, Dracula has the need for self-preservation, which asserts itself in the drive to preserve both the life of the individual and the life of the species. The difference, of course, is that the vampire can satisfy the two needs simultaneously—the same action, vamping, answers the need for nourishment and procreation. But that equation of eating and sexual intercourse literalized by the vampire is a connection we all make metaphorically and one that, as Lévi-Strauss is fond of pointing out, a number of primitive tribes acknowledge by making the same verb do service for both actions (*Raw and Cooked* 269, *Savage Mind* 105). Dracula says he needs new women so that he can "feed" (312), but we know that is not all he means.

While the physiology of vampire sexuality literalizes a connection between sex and eating that, for human beings, operates metaphorically, the expression of that sexuality grotesquely exaggerates the typical human pattern of incest avoidance and exogamy. The vampire's "marriage" laws are first suggested when Harker is almost seduced by the three vampire women he encounters at Castle Dracula. Critical opinion about these women differs considerably, betraying how badly vampire sexuality has been misunderstood. The problem arises in part because the text does not explicitly define the women's relation to Dracula—who are they? Both Craft and Maurice Richardson call them Dracula's "daughters" (110, 427); Carol Frye terms them "wives" (21); Leonard Wolf the count's "beautiful brides" (249); and C. F. Bentley says that "they are either Dracula's daughters or his sisters" but insists that an "incestuous" relation existed between them in the past (29). The difficulty here is a false either/or: these women must either be kin or be wives. What these readers ignore is the possibility that Dracula's relation to these women has, quite simply, changed, that they have occupied both roles—not simultaneously, as in incest, but sequentially, because of the way vampire reproduction works.

A speech Dracula makes to Mina late in the novel clarifies his relation to the women at the castle: "And you, their best beloved one, are now to me, flesh of my flesh; blood of my blood; kin of my kin; my bountiful wine-press for a while; and shall be later on my companion and helper" (293). According to the count's description, he and Mina are like husband and wife (he uses the "flesh of my flesh" from Genesis and the marriage ceremony), but through the very fact of their union, they are also becoming "kin." Thus, because of the vampire's incest taboo, she can be his "wine-press" only for a "while," and in time, when her transformation from "good" Englishwoman to vampire is complete, she will become a daughterly "companion and helper." The vampire women at the castle have undergone a similar change. When one of them reproaches Dracula with the accusation, "You yourself never loved; you never love!" he can answer, "Yes, I too can love; you yourselves can tell it from the past. Is it not so?" (47).

Dracula's relation to his women changes in this way because of another economy in vampire sexuality. Not only do vampires combine feeding with reproduction, they collapse the distinction between sexual partners and offspring. "Wives," that is, become daughters in an extraordinarily condensed procedure in which penetration, intercourse, conception, gestation, and parturition represent, not discrete stages, but one undifferentiated action.[6] Dracula re-creates in his own image the being that he is simultaneously ravishing. But the transformation, once complete, is irreversible—Dracula makes it clear that once Mina becomes his daughter, his "companion and helper," she can never again be his "wine-press."[7] We confront here one large inadequacy of the *Totem and Taboo* reading. In the primal horde, as female offspring mature, they fall under the sexual sway of their fathers—daughters become wives. In *Dracula*, this role transformation is reversed and is accompanied, moreover, by a powerful incest taboo that seems to preclude Dracula's further sexual interest in his onetime partners. In fact, unlike the greedy patriarch of the horde, Dracula encourages his women to seek other men. He tells the female vampires at his castle that, when Harker's usefulness to him is over, they can have their way with the Englishman: "Well, now I promise you that when I am done with him you shall kiss him at your will" (47).

The inevitable question arises for vampires as well as for human beings: why is there an incest taboo? The answer, however, is not that incest avoidance has been ingrained in the vampire's conscience, if such a thing should exist; instead, vampires appear incapable of committing this particular crime, since they face a physical barrier to incest, not just a psychological one—another dramatic instance of vampire literalization. Such a barrier is an example of the many physical changes that mark the transformation into a vampire, as we learn on the day that Lucy dies to her old identity as Englishwoman and is reborn as one of Dracula's own kind. (Vampire victims, it seems, always die in childbirth.) Van Helsing and Seward examine her neck and discover, to their horror, that the punctures in her throat "had absolutely disappeared" (167). Dracula could not commit incest even if he wanted to; he has no orifice to penetrate.

With the exaggeration of human tendencies characteristic of vampire sexuality, the vampire's incest taboo creates its own iron rule of exogamy. Just as there is a physical obstacle to vampire incest, so the vampire's need to marry out is not a matter of custom or of a long-term evolutionary benefit but an immediate and urgent biological necessity. Westermarck approvingly quotes another nineteenth-century anthropologist, who speaks of "mankind's instinctive hankering after foreign women" (2: 165). For Dracula, though, the need for "foreign women" is no mere hankering. Rather, because his sexual partner is also his food, the vampire must marry out or die.[8] A world without foreign women would represent not only sterility but famine.

The vampire as a sexual being is thus strangely familiar—he avoids incest and he seeks sexual partners outside his family. But that sexuality is also a parody of human sexuality, a literalization that makes him seem very odd: he *cannot* commit incest, he *must* marry out. And that necessity, in turn, creates his primary danger. Since all vampires are kin, they cannot simultaneously seek likeness (i.e., marry within the confines of the group) and avoid incest, as human beings do. Dracula thus cannot respect group or racial boundaries with regard to women; his particular physiology demands instead that he take "foreign women" away from the men they already belong to, a theft that continues his own kind. Moreover, his physically insistent need to steal threatens the existence of the group on which he preys. As he tells Van Helsing and his allies, "Your girls that you all love are mine already; and through them you and others shall yet be mine" (312). Dracula is thus doubly frightening—he is the foreigner whose very strangeness renders him monstrous, and, more dangerous, he is an imperialist whose invasion seeks a specifically sexual conquest; he is a man who will take other men's women away and make them his own.[9]

And Dracula will make "foreign women" his own in a radical way. He does not simply kidnap or alter cultural allegiances; his sexual union with women like Lucy and Mina physically deracinates them and re-creates them as members of his own kind.[10] This point will be clearer if we look at Stoker's manipulation of the novel's central image, that of blood. Blood means many things in *Dracula*; it is food, it is semen, it is a rather ghastly parody of the Eucharist, the blood of Christ that guarantees life eternal. But its meaning also depends on the way humanity has made blood a crucial metaphor for what it thinks of as racial identity. Blood is the essence that somehow determines all those other features—physical and cultural—that distinguish one race from another. And this connection of blood and race explains most fully that fascinating sequence when each of the good, brave men in turn gives Lucy a transfusion. Ostensibly, they are replacing what the count has removed, so that she will not perish from loss of blood. But Dracula's action is not feeding, nor is it only a combination of feeding and copulation. The men are desperate to transfuse their blood into Lucy because they understand that sexual intercourse with a vampire deracinates. Dracula's threat is not miscegenation, the mixing of blood; instead, he gives his partners a new racial identity. And he can do this because the source of their original identity, their blood, has been taken away. In only one more of the remarkable literalizations that give this novel mythic power, the answer to the kind of genocide that the vampire threatens is to reinfuse Lucy with the "right" blood, "young and strong ... and so pure" (131), as Van Helsing says.

Such deracination is one effect of the economy we observed above, that of the vampire's sexual partners becoming his offspring. But what I have been calling the racial element needs emphasis here; not only do wives become daughters but brides who were originally foreign to Dracula become pure vampires. This is what the Deuteronomist understood: the problem with mixed marriages is that they produce new loyalties, not confused ones. As Mina says, "I ... *shall be* ... leagued with your enemy against you." And why? Because, with her own blood removed, she will be like Dracula, and it is that loss of women's loyalty that the good, brave men cannot abide. As Van Helsing explains it to Mina: "He have infect you in such a wise, that ... in time, death ... shall make you like to him. This must not be! We have sworn together that it must not. Thus are we ministers of God's own wish: that the world ... will not be given over to monsters ..." (325). The desperation these men feel about the threat from Dracula is suggested, perhaps, by the multiple transfusions they give Lucy. Van Helsing recognizes that these transfusions are sexual and that they imply a kind of promiscuity in Lucy; as he puts it in his distinctively incompetent English: "Ho, ho! then this so sweet maid is a polyandrist, and me, with my poor wife dead to me, but alive by Church's law, though no wits, all gone—even I, who am faithful husband to this now-no-wife, am bigamist" (182). Lucy's promiscuity—her "polyandry," as the propriety of the Dutchman would have it—is forgivable, because finally her loyalty to her own kind is more vital than her absolute chastity. Clearly, it is more important that the group maintain its hold over her than that any one man has exclusive rights. In the face of such anxiety, too, there is always the option we began with, euthanasia, the killing by brave men of their women, to keep them from falling into the hands of the enemy.

In the light of all this, it is very hard to see as "incestuous" the competition for women that constitutes the primary action of the novel. *Dracula* does touch on primal fears and urges, but they are not the horror or allure of incest. Stoker's perdurable myth reflects the ancient fear that "they" will take away "our" women, and Dracula is at his most horrifying not when he drinks blood or travels in the form of a bat but when he, a man of palpable foreignness, can say, "Your girls that you all love are mine." An old black ram, he says, is tupping your white ewe. Richardson is right to find the count a figure of "huge potency" (427), but Dracula's power is not that of the father, as Richardson suggests, but that of the "extravagant stranger," or, in Van Helsing's words, "the other." But such power raises a new set of questions. The men are anxious about losing their women, but what of the women themselves? How do they respond to Dracula's frightful glamour? What is this novel's attitude toward women?

Stoker's description of the first women we see in *Dracula*, the vampire women at the castle, strongly emphasizes their overt sexuality. The word *voluptuous* is repeated—they have "voluptuous lips" and a "deliberate voluptuousness" in their approach to Harker (46). And he, in turn, is quickly aroused by their seductive appeal, as he feels "a wicked, burning desire that they would kiss me with those red lips" (46). They project themselves as sexualized beings and have power to inspire a sexual response in others. The pattern is exactly repeated when Lucy's transformation into a vampire is complete. Shortly after Van Helsing and Seward note the disappearance of the wounds in her neck, the young doctor reports that she speaks in a "soft, voluptuous voice, such as I had never heard from her lips" (167); and when the whole band confronts the undead Lucy outside her tomb, "we recognised the features of Lucy Westenra. Lucy Westenra, but yet how changed. The sweetness was turned to ... cruelty, and the purity to voluptuous wantonness" (217). Within the next three paragraphs, we hear that she has a "voluptuous smile" and a "wanton smile" and that she speaks with "a languorous, voluptuous grace." As is typical when Stoker discusses the characteristics of a group, his vocabulary shrinks, and he resorts to formulas—*good*, *brave*, and, for vampire females, *voluptuous*. And when the posse of racial purity hammers the stake through Lucy's heart, that merciful penetration which undoes the undead, the transformation is a return to her former state of desexualization: the "foul Thing" with its "voluptuous mouth" and its "carnal and unspiritual appearance" disappears, replaced with "Lucy as we had seen her in her life, with her face of unequalled sweetness and purity" (220–22).

There are several ways to interpret the novel's attitude toward the sexuality these female vampires project. The first—developed by a number of critics—is that Stoker is expressing what have usually been regarded as typical Victorian attitudes about female sexuality. According to these readers, the violence against women in *Dracula*, most vividly rendered in the staking of Lucy, reflects a hostility toward female sexuality felt by the culture at large. Women should not be "wanton" or "voluptuous"; they should be "pure" and "spiritual." So, Phyllis Roth contends that "much of the novel's great appeal derives from its hostility to female sexuality" ("Suddenly Sexual" 113), Judith Weissman insists that *Dracula* "is an extreme version of the stereotypically Victorian attitudes toward sexual roles" (392), and Gail Griffin argues that, among other things, Dracula represents "a subliminal voice in our heros, whispering that, at heart, these girls ... are potential vampires, that their angels are, in fact, whores" (463). Very recently, Bram Dijkstra has renewed the charge, calling the book a "central document in the late nineteenth-century war on woman" (341).[11]

Undoubtedly, *Dracula* exhibits hostility toward female sexuality. Women who are "pure" are not only good, they are recognizable as members of the group—after the staking, Lucy again looks like "we had seen her in her life." By contrast, "voluptuous" women are monsters, loathsome creatures fit only for destruction. What interests me, however, is not the possibility that *Dracula* is yet another misogynist text but the way in which the novel incorporates its portrayal of women into its consideration of foreignness. A careful look at the women in *Dracula* reveals that the primary fear is a fear of the foreign and that women become terrifying insofar as they are associated with the kind of strangeness vampires represent. Lucy and those women at Castle Dracula are, as Van Helsing puts it, "like him," members of that "new order of beings" that the count wishes to "father" (308). Two issues are important in this regard. First, there is the bisexuality of female vampires (and males, too), a consideration that complicates any attempt to generalize about the place of gender in this novel. Second, the women here do not transform themselves. The count is the indispensable catalyst for their alteration into sexual beings, a catalytic role that exposes again *Dracula*'s deep anxieties about excessive exogamy. I would like to look briefly at both these issues before concluding.

A famous psychoanalytic comment on vampirism occurs in Ernest Jones's *On the Nightmare*:

> The explanation of these fantasies is surely not hard. A nightly visit from a beautiful or frightful being, who first exhausts the sleeper with passionate embraces and then withdraws from him a vital fluid; all this can point only to a natural and common process, namely to nocturnal emissions.... In the unconscious mind blood is commonly an equivalent for semen.
>
> (119)

Dracula does indeed make blood and semen interchangeable fluids,[12] and this equivalence may offer another clue why the combination of red and white is the vampire's distinct coloration. But the striking omission from Jones's rather condescending comment is that, in Stoker's novel, the "vital fluid" is being withdrawn from women, that the nightly visitor is a man. Vampirism may have something to do with nocturnal emissions, but surely it is important that in *Dracula* women have all the wet dreams. Clearly, in the vampire world traditional sexual roles are terribly confused. Dracula penetrates, but he receives the "vital fluid"; after Lucy becomes a vampire, she acts as a "penetrator" (and becomes sexually aggressive), but she now receives fluid from those she attacks. Nowhere is this confusion greater than at the moment the brave band interrupts Dracula's attack on Mina:

> With ... his right hand [he] gripped her by the back of the neck, forcing her face down on his bosom. Her white nightdress was smeared with blood, and a thin stream trickled down the man's bare breast which was shown by his torn-open dress. The attitude of the two had a terrible resemblance to a child forcing a kitten's nose into a saucer of milk to compel it to drink.
>
> (288)

As many have remarked, there is a powerful image of fellatio here (and there is also an exchange of fluids—a point not made clear in the description of Dracula's attack on Lucy); but in this scene Dracula, in a breathtaking transformation, is a mother as well, engaged in an act that has a "terrible resemblance" to breast-feeding. What is going on? Fellatio? Lactation? It seems that the vampire is sexually capable of everything.

Like Tiresias, the vampire has looked at sex from both sides, and that fact is significant for several reasons. First, it makes it difficult to say, simply, that the novel is hostile to female sexuality, when the nature of the "female" has itself been made problematic; it is more accurate to say that the primary fear is of vampire sexuality, a phenomenon in which "our" gender roles interpenetrate in a complicated way. Female vampires are not angels turned into whores but human women who have become something very strange, beings in whom traditional distinctions between male and female have been lost and traditional roles confusingly mixed. Moreover, we encounter again here the central paradox of *Dracula*'s representation of the foreign. For the bisexuality of the vampire is not only monstrously strange, it is also a very human impulse—an impulse that, once more, the vampire has made astonishingly literal. As we have seen throughout this essay, the sexuality of vampires—here their bisexuality—is both strange and familiar, both an overt peculiarity to be seen and dreaded and a reflection to be repressed.

If female vampires are powerfully bisexual, they are also creatures who have been profoundly changed. The pure and spiritual become voluptuous, the passive become aggressive, and so on. As Van Helsing says, "Madame Mina, our poor dear Madame Mina, is changing" (328). The novel makes it clear that these changes do not come from within—Dracula brings them about as part of that complex process of deracinative reproduction discussed above. In other words, the erotic energy of the female vampires is somehow the count's creation. And that, in turn, suggests another way in which he is terrifying to the band of good, brave men. What if the problem is not that women like Lucy and Mina have become sexual but that their sexuality has been released in the wrong way, by a foreigner, a foreigner who has achieved what the men fear they may be unable to accomplish?[13] That is, the anxiety of Van Helsing and his band may be partly a fear of aggressive or demanding women, but it may also be a fear of superior sexual potency in the competition. The boy next door may be no match for an extravagant stranger.

The fear of excessive exogamy, so much a part of the terror that Dracula inspires, is thus both a racial and a sexual problem. As I suggested earlier, Dracula is a sexual imperialist, one who longs to be "the father or furtherer of a new order of beings" (308). And he can beget this race only on the bodies of other men's women, imperiling the racial integrity of the West. The fear he inspires, however, is also personal, for his is not merely an imperialism that takes women, it is especially an imperialism of seduction—if he initially approaches these women through violence, in the end they are converts, "leagued with your enemy against you." Dracula threatens to destroy both the "good" men's race and their masculinity, to destroy them as a group and emasculate them as individuals. No wonder they are so desperate to stop him.

Dracula emerges, then, as a remarkable meditation on foreignness, in at least two ways. The surface of the tale is a memorable myth of interracial sexual competition, a struggle between men who wish to retain their control over women defined as members of their group and a powerful and attractive foreigner, who wishes to make the women his own. This battle, finally, is between two kinds of desire. The desire of the good, brave men is a force that must be called conservative, for it is an urge to protect possessions, to insist on the integrity of racial boundaries, to maintain unmixed the blood of their group. Hence, we see their xenophobic insistence that "the world"—meaning their world and their women—"not be given over to monsters." Dracula's desire is the antithesis of such conservatism: what the count has once possessed is useless to him in his continuing struggle for survival. His constantly renewed desire for difference may be "monstrous" in terms of the marriage practices of most cultures, but it is hardly the monstrosity of incest. The threat Dracula represents is not the desire of the father to hoard his own women; it is an urgent need to take, to violate boundaries, a desire that must incorporate foreign blood for the very survival of his kind. For the vampire, the blood he needs, both for sex and for food, always belongs to somebody else.

Dracula thus uncovers for us the kind of mind that sees excessive exogamy as a particularly terrifying threat. Such thinking is common in human experience: we tend to divide ourselves into groups and to fret about sexual contact across group lines. At the same time, such fears must have been acute in late nineteenth-century Britain, plump with imperial gain, but given perhaps to the bad dream that *Dracula* embodies: what if "they" should try to colonize *us*?[14] *Dracula* is interesting, however, as something more than a representation of the xenophobic mind, in either its Victorian or its aboriginal avatar—fascinating as that representation is. For xenophobia requires, first of all, a concept of what is foreign, and the remarkable thing about Stoker's novel is the way it is able to undermine that very conception of the "foreign" on which so much of its narrative energy depends. That is, *Dracula* both exemplifies what Hannah Arendt terms "race-thinking" (158) and calls such thinking radically into question. Again and again Stoker depicts vampire sexuality as a curiously doubled phenomenon—always overtly bizarre, but also somehow familiar.[15] Such a paradox possibly is inherent in the enterprise by which foreignness, that ancient need to separate "us" from "them," is constructed in the human imagination. As *Dracula* represents that process, it is a simultaneous movement, in which differences are perceived and reified, while likenesses are repressed and denied. The refusal of some recognition may thus always be a part of the perception of foreignness—even (or maybe especially) the extreme foreignness of monstrosity.

Vampires, we all know, cast no reflection. Virtually the first frightening oddity that Harker notices at Castle Dracula is that "there was no reflection of [the count] in the mirror" (34). In the light of this discussion, that missing image presents a striking metaphor. The vampire, "the other," "the monster"—everything that Dracula represents, and represents so powerfully—depends on our refusal to see the ways in which he is also a mirror. After all, it is Harker who can see nothing in the glass. When we say that the vampire is absent from the mirror, perhaps what we are saying is that we are afraid to see a reflection—however uneasy and strange—of ourselves.

Notes

1. The first critic to insist on a parallel between *Dracula* and *Totem and Taboo* was Maurice Richardson. In his wake have come James Twitchell's *The Living Dead* (134–35), *Dreadful Pleasures* (99–104, 137), and *Forbidden Partners* (69–70), and Phyllis Roth's "Suddenly Sexual Women" (115) and *Bram Stoker* (114). Richard Astle also brings up the theory but notes that there are two "fathers" in Stoker's novel, Dracula and Van Helsing, a "wish-fulfillment" situation that enables the "sons" simultaneously to kill and obey the father (98–99).

2. For a valuable discussion of the differences between anthropology and psychoanalysis, see W. Arens (40–43 esp.). In *The Red Lamp of Incest*,

Robin Fox attempts to reconcile recent anthropological and biological work on incest with *Totem and Taboo*. The result has been controversial, and in any event I am not sure Freud would recognize his theories in their rehabilitated form. The approach I use in this essay does not imply that I believe anthropology to be "right," psychoanalysis "wrong." I do want to substitute one model of human behavior for another (and models are what I believe both approaches are) and see what happens.

3. The discussion that follows is much indebted to Arens and to the two volumes by Fox, all three of which provide good summaries of the vast anthropological literature on these subjects. Also, while I am aware that Lévi-Strauss's theories have been much debated in the anthropological community and that they are not, perhaps, entirely original, I must acknowledge that I could not have arrived at the ideas developed in this essay without his powerfully expressed notion of the interrelation between an incest taboo and the exchange of women among allied men.

The existence of an incest taboo does not contradict the idea that humans have an instinctive aversion to committing incest. See Arens 14.

4. Pierre Van den Berghe provides a useful summary of the history and current status of attempts at racial classifications (ch. 1). A dictionary (*American Heritage*) definition of *race* suggests the range of essentially metaphoric meanings attached to the word. Those definitions include "a distinct group [defined by] genetically transmitted physical characteristics"; "a group united" on the basis of history, geography, or nationality; and "a genealogical line." As a "race," vampires partake of all these meanings.

5. Stoker would have known *Hamlet* intimately, having been associated for many years with the actor Henry Irving and having long served as manager of the Lyceum Theatre in London. In fact, a review Stoker wrote of Irving's performance as Hamlet first brought the two together, and Stoker's management of the Lyceum began with a ninety-eight-night run of *Hamlet*. See Daniel Farson 17, 56.

There is a further biographical consideration here if it is true, as Farson argues, that Stoker died of syphilis. Farson claims that in view of the typical progression of the disease Stoker might have caught the infection at about the time he wrote *Dracula* (233–35).

6. For this reason, there is no such thing as birth control for vampires, except coitus interruptus, whose efficacy seems uncertain. The good men certainly interrupt Dracula's last attack on Mina, but her salvation from rebirth as a vampire seems more a function of Dracula's death than the result of the interruption. The impossibility of separating sexuality from reproduction in *Dracula* inverts the pattern in the other great nineteenth-century monster novel, *Frankenstein*, which insists on that separation. In a

sense, these novels anticipate the contemporary debate between Catholic conservatives and technological interventionists on the issue of reproduction. *Dracula*, with its crucifixes, its use of the host as a kind of disinfectant, and especially its literalization of certain Catholic preoccupations about sex, emerges as an oddly Catholic novel, with vampires representing a fantasy of sexual orthodoxy. Neither of the biographies I consulted had anything to say on the subject of the novelist's religion, but Stoker was Irish.

7. Again, there is a deliciously gossipy biographical sidelight here. According to Farson, who is Stoker's great-nephew, family gossip maintains that Stoker's wife ceased to have sexual relations with her husband after the birth of their one child in 1879 (214). Of course, it is impossible to know how far to trust such evidence, but the parallel is worth noting.

8. Here we see an exaggerated and literalized version of the sociobiological argument that outbreeding is genetically useful for humanity. See Arens 22.

9. It is Dracula's status as an invader that sets him apart from other supernatural beings. Most of the terror ghosts create is bound up with the belief that dead people haunt the places they knew in life: houses are normally haunted by former residents, or at least by someone who had a significant relation to the place. Dracula, however, must leave his old home to do his dreadful work. This supernatural imperialism suggests again that the fear Dracula creates is linked to his strangeness, to his remote origins. In a sense, Dracula is a demonic version of Abraham, who also must leave his old home and go to another place to begin his new race.

10. A powerful expression of this mentality dominates John Ford's great western *The Searchers* (1956). At one point, John Wayne and an army doctor are looking over a group of women, all of them very blond, recently rescued from long captivity (the chief who has been holding them is named, interestingly, "Scar"). The women are behaving strangely, and the doctor remarks, "It's hard to believe they're white." Wayne's reply tersely reveals his character's belief in sexual deracination: "They're not white—anymore. They're Comanche."

11. There is, however, another school of thought that finds at least glimmers of real sympathy for women in *Dracula*. Nina Auerbach sees in Lucy and Mina a "self-transforming power surging beneath apparent victimization," observing that "we are struck by the kinds of power that [Stoker] grant[s]" to his women (34, 17). Stephanie Demetrakapoulous insists that the novel expresses hidden desires in Victorian culture, particularly women's desire to be sexually alive, and Alan Johnson says that the count "symbolizes" these women's "inner rebelliousness," which the novel portrays as "justified" (21). Carol Senf suggests that Stoker's

"treatment of women ... does not stem from his hatred of women in general but ... from his ambivalent reaction to a topical phenomenon—the New Woman" (34).

12. It seems inevitable that, at some point soon, the phenomenon of AIDS and the vampire myth will converge. In fact, we may already be seeing a "vampirization" of high-risk groups for the disease. One heterosexual was quoted in the *New York Times Magazine* as saying, "[Avoiding sex with members of high-risk groups] is, in a way, a tyranny, a part of the inexorable return to conservatism. It's so antithetical to intermingling.... People are saying you should sleep only with your own kind" (Davis 35).

13. Some important recent historical work suggests that the standard view of Victorian attitudes toward female sexuality is seriously flawed. Both Peter Gay and Carl Degler argue that there was no monolithic suppression or denial of women's erotic potential in the era and that a notorious figure like Dr. William Acton (who thought "normal" women had no sexual feelings) should not be viewed as a spokesperson for the age.

14. Jerome Buckley's comment is interesting in this regard: "All through the nineties there lay behind the cult of empire a half-hushed uneasiness, a sense of social decline. a foreboding of death ..." (228).

15. Such doubleness calls to mind Freud's analysis of the "uncanny," in which the *heimlich* and the *unheimlich* converge. For Freud, however, the "uncanny is that class of the frightening which leads back to what is known of old and long familiar" ("'Uncanny'" 220). My understanding of Dracula here depends on the poles of the strange and familiar remaining simultaneously present. Freud's "leads back to" suggests the priority Freud assigns to the family romance even in the realm of the literature of fright. In insisting on concealed points of similarity between vampires and human beings, I have not been led "back to" an incestuous reading of the novel. Rather, I mean to show how foreignness is perhaps an inevitably compromised perception.

Works Cited

Arendt, Hannah. *The Origins of Totalitarianism*. Cleveland: Meridian, 1958.

Arens, W. *The Original Sin: Incest and Its Meaning*. New York: Oxford UP, 1986.

Astle, Richard. "Dracula as Totemic Monster: Lacan, Freud, Oedipus, and History." *Sub-stance* 25 (1980): 98–105.

Auerbach, Nina. *Woman and the Demon: The Life of Victorian Myth*. Cambridge: Harvard UP, 1982.

Bentley, C. F. "The Monster in the Bedroom: Sexual Symbolism in Bram Stoker's *Dracula*." *Literature and Psychology* 22 (1972): 27–32.

Buckley, Jerome. *The Victorian Temper: A Study in Literary Culture*. New York: Vintage, 1964.

Craft, Christopher. "'Kiss Me with Those Red Lips': Gender and Inversion in Bram Stoker's *Dracula*." *Representations* 8 (1984): 107–33.

Davis, Peter. "Exploring the Kingdom of AIDS." *New York Times Magazine* 31 May 1987: 32–35.

Degler, Carl. "What Ought to Be and What Was: Women's Sexuality in the Nineteenth Century." *American Historical Review* 79 (1974): 1467–90.

Demetrakapoulous, Stephanie. "Feminism, Sex-Role Exchanges, and Other Subliminal Fantasies in Bram Stoker's *Dracula*." *Frontiers* 2 (1977): 104–13.

Dijkstra, Bram. *Idols of Perversity: Fantasies of Evil in Fin-de-Siècle Culture*. New York: Oxford UP, 1986.

Faber, Richard. *The Vision and the Need: Late Victorian Imperialist Aims*. London: Faber, 1966.

Farson, Daniel. *The Man Who Wrote* Dracula: *A Biography of Bram Stoker*. London: Joseph, 1975.

Ford, John, dir. *The Searchers*. Warner Brothers, 1956.

Fox, Robin. *Kinship and Marriage: An Anthropological Perspective*. Harmondsworth: Penguin, 1967.

———. *The Red Lamp of Incest*. New York: Dutton, 1980.

Freccero, John. "Manfred's Wounds and the Poetics of the *Purgatorio*." *Centre and Labyrinth: Essays in Honour of Northrop Frye*. Ed. Eleanor Cook et al. Toronto: U of Toronto P, 1983. 69–82.

Freud, Sigmund. *Totem and Taboo. The Standard Edition of the Complete Psychological Works of Sigmund Freud*. Ed. James Strachey. Vol. 13. London: Hogarth, 1955. 1–162. 24 vols. 1953–74.

———. "The 'Uncanny.'" *The Standard Edition of the Complete Psychological Works of Sigmund Freud*. Ed. James Strachey. Vol. 17. London: Hogarth, 1955. 218–52. 24 vols. 1953–74.

Frye, Carol L. "Fictional Conventions and Sexuality in *Dracula*." *Victorian Newsletter* 42 (1972): 20–22.

Gay, Peter. *Education of the Senses*. New York: Oxford UP, 1984.

Griffin, Gail. "'Your Girls That You All Love Are Mine': Dracula and the Victorian Male Sexual Imagination." *International Journal of Women's Studies* 3 (1980): 454–65.

Johnson, Alan P. "'Dual Life': The Status of Women in Stoker's *Dracula*." *Sexuality and Victorian Literature*. Ed. Don Richard Cox. Knoxville: U of Tennessee P, 1984. 20–39.

Jones, Ernest. *On the Nightmare*. New York: Liveright, 1951.

Lévi-Strauss, Claude. *The Elementary Structures of Kinship*. Boston: Beacon, 1969.

———. *The Raw and the Cooked*. New York: Harper, 1975.

———. *The Savage Mind*. Chicago: U of Chicago P, 1966.

Porter, Roy. *English Society in the Eighteenth Century*. Harmondsworth: Penguin, 1982.

Richardson, Maurice. "The Psychoanalysis of Ghost Stories." *Twentieth Century* 166 (1959): 419–31.

Roth, Phyllis. *Bram Stoker*. Boston: Twayne, 1982.

———. "Suddenly Sexual Women in Bram Stoker's *Dracula*." *Literature and Psychology* 27 (1977): 113–21.

Seaman, Lewis Charles Bernard. *Victorian England: Aspects of English and Imperial History, 1837–1901*. London: Methuen, 1973.

Senf, Carol A. "*Dracula*: Stoker's Response to the New Woman." *Victorian Studies* 26 (1982): 33–49.

Stoker, Bram. 1897. *Dracula*. New York: Signet, 1965.

Twitchell, James. *Dreadful Pleasures: An Anatomy of Modern Horror*. New York: Oxford UP, 1985.

———. *Forbidden Partners: The Incest Taboo in Modern Culture*. New York: Columbia UP, 1986.

———. *The Living Dead: A Study of the Vampire in Romantic Literature*. Durham: Duke UP, 1981.

Van den Berghe, Pierre. *Race and Racism: A Comparative Perspective*. New York: Wiley, 1967.

Weissman, Judith. "Women and Vampires: *Dracula* as Victorian Novel." *Midwest Quarterly* 18 (1977): 392–405.

Westermarck, Edward. *The History of Human Marriage*. 3 vols. New York: Allerton, 1922.

Wolf, Leonard. *The Annotated* Dracula. New York: Potter, 1975.

DANIEL PICK

'Terrors of the night': Dracula *and 'degeneration' in the late nineteenth century*

'It is nineteenth century up-to-date with a vengeance.' (*Dracula*, p. 36)[1]

This essay seeks to address *Dracula* historically and to suggest some of its crucial discursive contexts. Bram Stoker's text was published in 1897, the very year after the term 'psychoanalysis' is said to have been coined.[2] Nevertheless, *Dracula* inhabits, like many other late nineteenth-century fictions, a world of representation which now seems insistently and tantalisingly pre-Freudian.[3] The adjacent dates—signalling for Stoker as for Freud a critical, albeit relatively late, 'career launch' into fame—mask the enduring separation between their languages on fantasy and demons, as between their respective interpretations of dreams. They were not at all, as one commentator has recently claimed, 'telling the same story'.[4]

Part of the novel's task was to represent, externalise and kill off a distinct constellation of contemporary fears. Corruption and degeneration, the reader discovers, are identifiable, foreign and superable; but the text also recognises a certain sense of failure—an element of horror is always left over, uncontained by the terms of the story as by the intrepid party who stalked the Count: an English aristocrat, a brave American hunter, two doctors, a lawyer and his devoted, dutiful (but endangered) wife. The vampire is allowed no direct voice or expression, but nor is any other figure given full

From *Critical Quarterly* 30, no. 4 (Winter 1988): 71-87.

narrative mastery. The novel refuses to provide a synthesis, proceeding instead through a series of separate diaries, reports and letters. It seeks to deal with a number of contemporary social debates, but reaches in the face of them a kind of paralysis, as though the narrative never came to represent the danger it hints. There are points where the description seems frozen at the threshold between Victorian evolutionism and psychoanalysis:

> ... I saw around us a ring of wolves, with white teeth and lolling red tongues, with long, sinewy limbs and shaggy hair. They were a hundred times more terrible in the grim silence which held them than even when they howled. For myself, I felt a sort of paralysis of fear. It is only when a man feels himself face to face with such horrors that he can understand their true import. (p. 13)

Although Professor Van Helsing is famed for his 'absolutely open mind' (p. 112), the novel chronically reverts to closed, cautionary tale, warning of the perils of a wandering consciousness or body, the potentially fatal risks of entering mysterious new places and knowledges: Trance/Trans/Transylvania. But the narrative is itself prone to carelessness, wandering off the point or hinting too much. As Montague Summers observed in his early study of the vampire (1928): 'If we review *Dracula* from a purely literary point of approach it must be acknowledged that there is much careless writing....'[5] The text is careless in some respects but painstaking in its insistence on the inadequacy of nineteenth-century materialism and determinism. *Dracula* thirsts to cross the threshold into a new conception of subjectivity and science, say psychoanalytic, towards which, simultaneously, it seems to be remarkably resistant. We are shown how the doctors in the novel kept coming up against an impasse, rejecting any organic explanation of Lucy Westenra's illness, but reluctant to follow through to any alternative explanation: '... but as there must be a cause somewhere, I have come to the conclusion that it must be something mental' (p. 111); 'I have made careful examination but there is no functional cause' (p. 114).

Stoker and Freud could have known nothing of one another at the time of *Dracula*. Even in 1913 Freud made no mention of this horror story when he discussed vampires in *Totem and Taboo*.[6] By then the tale was something of a *cause célèbre*—nine English editions had already appeared as well as a considerable subsidiary literature.[7] But perhaps Freud's omission is unsurprising. The context of his brief observations on the vampire was strictly anthropological, nothing to do with the popular novel.

Although Freud said nothing about *Dracula*, he did discuss a book published the year after, Rudolf Kleinpaul's *Die Lebendigen und die Toten in Volksglauben, Religion und Sage* (1898), which had included a useful account of the vampire myth. Indeed according to this authority, as recounted by Freud, once upon a time '*all* of the dead were vampires, all of them had a grudge against the living and sought to injure them and rob them of their lives' (p. 59). In the course of history, so the argument continued, the perceived malignity of the dead diminished and narrowed, frequently restricted to those with a particular right to feel resentment, for instance, murdered people, or 'brides who had died with their desires unsatisfied' (*ibid*). Kleinpaul described various tribes in which the dead were cast as murderously threatening creatures. They lusted to bring the living within their fold: 'The living did not feel safe from the attacks of the dead till there was a sheet of water between them. That is why men liked to bury the dead on islands or on the farther side of rivers; and that, in turn, is the origin of such phrases as 'Here and in the Beyond' (*ibid*).

In reading the various recent studies on tribal taboos around death, Freud had been struck by the frequency with which the dead were imbued with evil designs and a will to 'infect' the living. 'We know that the dead are powerful rulers; but we may perhaps be surprised when we learn that they are treated as enemies. The taboo upon the dead is—if I may revert to the simile of infection—especially virulent among most primitive peoples (p. 51). In many tribes, for instance in Polynesia, Melanesia and Africa, those who had had a close relationship or intimate dealings with the dead were seen to have been themselves morally touched and contaminated by death. They became anathema for the community. Thus there were villages in the Philippine Islands where:

> a widow may not leave her hut for seven or eight days after the death; and even then she may only go out at an hour when she is not likely to meet anybody, for whoever looks upon her dies a sudden death. To prevent this fatal catastrophe, the widow knocks with a wooden peg on the trees as she goes along, thus warning people of her dangerous proximity; and the very trees on which she knocks soon die. (p. 53)

Evidence from Frazer and others was given to show that widowers too were subject to restrictions of contact with other members of the community; restrictions which were in fact barriers to *temptation*. The taboos operated to prevent the fulfilment of the bereaved's desire to find a substitute partner: 'Substitutive satisfactions of such a kind run counter to the sense of mourning and they would inevitably kindle the ghost's wrath' (p. 54). The wrathful dead themselves were often unnameable: indeed anything which might evoke and hence invoke the dead had to be prevented, '[f]or they [e.g. the Tuaregs of the Sahara] make no disguise of the fact that they are *afraid* of the presence or of the return of the dead person's ghost; and they perform a great number of ceremonies to keep him at a distance or drive him off' (p. 57).

Freud linked such myths and taboos to the guilt, remorse, pain and hate experienced by the bereaved, remarking that these folk tales and taboos had to be reversed. In fact the tale inverted the relation of subject and predicate: it was not the demons that produced guilt, but the other way round. Demons and spirits, Freud argued, were 'only projections of man's own emotional impulses' (p. 92). He noted the unconscious desire to protect the 'innocence' of the mourner, to project the evil wishes on to the dead, as though thereby, despite the impossibility, to free the living of ambivalence. Ghosts, vampires, demons, spirits functioned at once to punish and exonerate the living, threatening and reprieving at the same moment. The trouble with the dead, it seemed, was that they would not stay dead and buried, least of all in the memories of the living. Like blood-sucking vampires, they haunted the memory of the bereaved and drained them of their vitality.

Freud's own concern here was at the juncture of psychoanalysis and anthropology, not social history. The aim, after all, was not specifically the analysis of recent culture, but the pursuit of the 'primitive' as royal road to the understanding of the origin of more widely shared terrors, totems and projections. In *Totem and Taboo* there is no exploration of the significance of the *renewed* late nineteenth-century interest in the uncanny, the immaterial, the supernatural and the beyond; yet that interest was to be found repeatedly and variedly in fiction, anthropology, psychology and criminology, as well as at the Society for Psychical Research of which Freud became a corresponding member.[8] The Society was founded in 1882 with a commitment to the 'open-minded' investigation of the occult, ghosts, haunted houses, possession and trances. It connected with a much wider European intellectual reappraisal of positivism and naturalism which crystallised in the 1890s. Van Helsing would no doubt have been an ideal member; after all he constantly doubted his senses and questioned his rationalist assumptions, always striving to see beyond 'our scientific, sceptical matter-of-fact nineteenth century' (*Dracula*, p. 238).

To try to read *Dracula* historically, rather than anthropologically or trans-historically, involves, initially, a certain capacity of resistance on the part of the reader. For it is tempting to 'fall prey' to the mythological, folkloristic connotations of the vampire story and declare the novel merely a new twist to an old tale, the reiteration of antique taboos on death. The cinema often contributes to this collapse of history, by eliding the differences between *Dracula* and *Frankenstein*, placing them together in much the same castle, the same period, as if there were one undifferentiated 'gothic' nineteenth century, homogenous from beginning to end. To say that Stoker's best-seller was very much a Victorian, or indeed more specifically a late nineteenth-century text may even appear perverse. It was, after all, only the latest in a long history of literary representations of the vampire which itself ran back into a vast range of myths. In 1819 Polidori's *The Vampyre* had appeared (under the name of Byron) and made just this point; the 'superstition', we are told, was very general in the East and had spread into Europe through Hungary, Poland, Austria and Lorraine.[9] Or as a subsequent account put it: 'Assyria knew the vampire long ago and he lurked amid the primaeval forests of Mexico before Cortes came.'[10]

Any specific representation of the vampire, it could then be argued, fades into a longer history which in turn dissolves into timeless myth. Some things, we are reminded in *Dracula*, are historically recalcitrant, unamenable to 'modern' transformation: '... the old centuries had, and have powers of their own which mere "modernity" cannot kill' (p. 36). Perhaps one could seek in Proppian fashion to pare away the idiosyncracies of Stoker's tale in order to locate across the centuries the basic shared form of vampire narratives, the essential morphological elements into which, apparently, any tale might be decomposed.[11] Thus a recent study of the vampire from the nineteenth century through to contemporary cinema has insisted that despite the 'unique achievement' of each classic of the genre, '[a] close extended look ... will allow us to see the shape and the particular significance of the entire series ...'.[12] What is offered in that particular approach to the vampire is certainly a useful compendium of examples, but *Dracula* as such is largely displaced from the later nineteenth century; there is indeed only the briefest consideration of any of the wider historical questions and debates at the time of its writing.

Dracula, however, has many contemporary references and resonances not even to be found in one of its most immediate 'sources', Le Fanu's *Carmilla* (1872).[13] Above all, whilst Le Fanu's tale had been securely located in Styria, Stoker's novel brings Dracula to London, articulating a vision of the bio-medical degeneration of the race in general and the metropolitan population in particular. Although versions of such a theory had found expression in specialist journals and treatises since the 1850s, it had only become a major issue of social debate and political speculation in the 1880s and 1890s.[14] The network of *Dracula's* images and terrors can be read in the context of a multitude of other contemporary representations: from government inquiries to popular pamphlets, statistical surveys, laboratory experiments, political programmes and philosophical investigations. The ambiguities of representation in the novel were in part bound up with contradictions in that wider discourse of degeneration throughout the period: the process of pathological decay, it seemed, was at once precisely contained (there were certain identifiable degenerate categories of being who eventually became sterile) and ubiquitous, affecting whole populations. The reassuring function of the novel—displacing perceived social and political dangers on to the horror story of a foreign Count finally staked through the heart—was undermined by the simultaneous suggestion of an invisible and remorseless morbid accumulation within, distorting the name and the body of the West (Lucy Westenra), transmitting unknown poisons from blood to blood.

The novel, excruciatingly, says nothing of the sexual fantasies and fears it articulates so graphically as vampire attack and blood pollution. The text resists the 'temptation' of spelling out any notion of sexuality, for which, indeed, it lacks any developed terms of description: resistance, frustration, failure of insight are crucial 'themes' in Stoker's story, and it is as if the narrative itself takes a certain delight in resistance, deafness to the very words on the page, despite its own admonition: '[Van Helsing to Seward] You do not let your eyes see nor your ears hear ...' (p. 191). Harker proposes to his future wife a union of ignorance: 'Are you willing, Wilhelmina, to share my ignorance? Here is the book. Take it and keep it, read it if you will, but never let me know ...' (p. 104). Yet denial provides no defence against Dracula. To be asleep or merely careless is to risk the vampire's bite and the fall into hypnotic fascination.

Orthodox medicine itself is shown to be in much the state of a sleepwalker, semi-consciously stumbling along well-worn routes, unable to cross conceptual frontiers and understand the condition of its patients: Dr Seward [of his patient Renfield] '... I do not follow his thought'; 'I wish I could get some clue to the cause'; 'I wish I could fathom his mind' (pp. 107, 116). Renfield constantly escapes the doctor's grasp: he slips all too easily out of his cell and of any existing psychiatric schema. Seward never does get to the 'heart' of the 'mystery', never succeeds in becoming 'master of the facts of his hallucination' (p. 60), persisting too single-mindedly in his materialist research on the brain. Only very slowly does he come to sense that his patient's condition is bound up with Dracula and some wider contemporary perversion of the evolutionary 'struggle for survival' which has blurred the question of 'fitness' and 'unfitness': 'My homicidal maniac is of a peculiar kind. I shall have to invent a new classification for him, and call him a zoophagous (life-eating) maniac; what he desires is to absorb as many lives as he can, and has laid himself out to achieve it in a cumulative way' (pp. 70–1). Seward's 'obtuse' reluctance to make any unconventional diagnosis about Lucy Westernra finally exasperates even his mentor, Van Helsing: 'Do you mean to tell me, friend John, that you have no suspicion as to what poor Lucy died of; not after all the hints given, not only by events, but by me?' (p. 191).

The subjects of hysteria and hypnotism, which for a long time in the nineteenth century had been pushed out to the fringes and beyond of orthodoxy and respectability, had lately been returned to the medical centre-stage, at least in Paris, and could no longer be dismissed as mere occult practice or superstition by the modern doctor: '[Van Helsing] I suppose now that you do not believe in corporeal transference. No? Nor in materialisation. No? Nor in astral bodies. No? Nor in the reading of thought. No? Nor in hypnotism?—' '[Seward] Yes' I said. 'Charcot has proved that pretty well' (p. 191).

But the medical audience 'lured' from abroad by Charcot's famous Tuesday demonstrations at the Salpêtrière was frequently appalled to learn of the presence of another theatre of hysteria where quacks, charlatans and music-hall actors entertained large crowds. The individual could, supposedly, be seduced or induced to commit terrible crimes. Crowds and mobs could be whipped up into anarchic frenzies by the hypnotic potential of 'morbid, excitable leaders'.[15] This is the period indeed that sees the reappearance of great hypnotists: Charcot *and* Donato, stage-name of a former Belgian naval officer, D'Hont, who causes sensation and scandal as he tours the European theatres, provoking furious debate on the very legality of the public sepctacle of magnetism and hypnotism.[16] The 'hypnotic menace' becomes a matter of forensic investigation and grave public concern—famous cases and trials underscore the possibility of subliminal manipulation, of innocent women induced to commit hideous crimes, even 'murder under hypnosis'[17] —at the same time that it is a terrain of new artistic and medical exploration towards the unconscious.

Of how much Stoker, a man of the theatre who was later to express a particular interest in the question of imposture (and Donato was unmasked on stage for his tricks),[18] knew of this directly we cannot be sure, but echoes of the criminal trials, public performances and dubious private consultations will have reached him. Certainly Dracula too is cast as a form of hypnotist on the stage of Europe, part fake, part genius: '[Harker] I felt myself struggling to awake some call of my instincts ... I was becoming hypnotised' (p. 44). '[Mina Murray] I was bewildered, and strangely enough, I did not want to hinder him' (p. 287). The novel sets up a contest of hypnotic powers: the good scientist and the evil vampire compete for the loyalty of the wavering hysterical women, for whom there is always only one step from 'horrid flirt' (p. 58) to the 'nightmare' of a demonic possessed sexuality: 'She seemed like a nightmare of Lucy as she lay there; the pointed teeth, the bloodstained voluptuous mouth—which it made one shudder to see—the whole carnal and unspiritual appearance, seeming like a devilish mockery of Lucy's sweet purity' (p. 214).

Everyone, it appears in the novel, is obliged to doubt not only their own descent but their own health and mental order or else to fall into mere self-delusion. Thus Mina Murray is forced to 'suppose I was hysterical ...' (p. 184). Lord Godalming 'grew quite hysterical' (p. 230); even Van Helsing, the seemingly secure centre of reason and wisdom—'one of the most advanced scientists of the day', 'both in theory and in practice' (p. 112)—enigmatically collapses at one point into a 'disturbed' and disturbing condition. Seward records how in the face of Lucy's death, Van Hesling became hysterical: '... he gave way to a regular fit of hysterics ... He laughed till he cried and I had to draw the blinds lest anyone should see us and misjudge ...' (p. 174). Strange perturbations are repeatedly described, and not simply in relation to the external figure of Dracula, casting doubt on whether anyone can be, as Lucy Westenra considers Seward, 'absolutely imperturbable' (p. 55). Indeed, thwarted in love, the doctor is forced to rely on drugs to put him to sleep (p. 101). It is increasingly unclear what could constitute a protection from illness and vice in the novel; whether for instance 'good breeding' means anything; for who could be better bred than Count Dracula himself? Amidst the 'whirlpool of races' (p. 28) which made up European history, the Count was descended from a noble line of 'survivors': 'for in our veins flows the blood of many brave races who fought as the lion fights, for lordship' (p. 28).

The novel is in one sense committed to the contradistinction of vice and virtue, purity and corruption, human and vampire; but it tacitly questions the possibility of such sharp separations, in this like so many medical-psychiatrists of the period convinced that no complete dividing line lay between sanity and insanity but rather a vast and shadowy borderland: '[Van Helsing] For it is not the least of its terrors that this evil thing is rooted deep in all good ...' (p. 241). Darwin too, it should be remembered, had already dealt his 'blow' to 'human narcissism' (as Freud was later to view it) by warning that there was no absolute evolutionary separation from the world of the animals, no escape from the stigma of that descent. Behind even the most imperiously 'contemptuous' human smile, one usually caught the glint of a set of once ferocious teeth:

> He who rejects with scorn the belief that his own canines, and their occasional great development in other men, are due to our

> early progenitors having been provided with these formidable weapons, will probably reveal by sneering the line of his descent. For though he no longer intends, nor has the power, to use these teeth as weapons, he will unconsciously retract his 'snarling muscles' ... —so as to expose them ready for action, like a dog prepared to fight.[19]

Stoker's text was paralysed at a threshold of uncertainty, at the turning point between a psychiatric positivism (which the novel derided) and the glimpsed possibility of a new exploration of the unconscious. The rejection of conventional science in the novel was conceived to involve not so much a leap into the future as a return to an earlier knowledge: Van Helsing stoically accepts and manipulates folklore, amalgamating it with the latest evidence from the laboratory and the clinic. He is repeatedly forced to point out the power of the irrational and the inexplicable, the fact that there were more wonders in heaven and earth than were dreamt of in nineteenth-century naturalist philosophy. Nevertheless he finally explains to the other protagonists that the fearful enigma of the vampire has to be approached not through a popular physiognomy but through the insights of a craniometry currently being developed in modern criminal anthropology:

> The criminal always works at one crime—that is the true criminal who seems predestinate to crime, and who will of none other. This criminal has not full man-brain. He is clever and cunning and resourceful; but he be not of manstature as to brain. He be of child-brain in much. Now this criminal of ours is predesinate to crime also; he too have child-brain ... The Count is a criminal and of criminal type. Nordau and Lombroso would so classify him, and *qua* criminal he is of imperfectly formed mind. (pp. 341–2)

Stoker's novel refers to Max Nordau and Cesare Lombroso, to a whole realm of investigation into degeneration and atavism, which itself wavered between a taxonomy of visible stigmata and the horror of invisible maladies, between the desired image of a specific, identifiable criminal type (marked out by ancestry) and the wider representation of a society in crisis, threatened by waves of degenerate blood and moral contagion.[20] Like Lombroso and the earlier important French theorist of degeneration, Bénédict-Augustin Morel,[21] Jonathan Harker journeys from specific images of deformity (goitre in particular: 'Here and there we passed Cszeks [*sic*] and Slovaks, all in picturesque attire, but I noticed that goitre was painfully prevalent' (p. 7), towards the citadel of full-blown degeneracy. From early work on cretinism and goitre, a medico-psychiatric theory had emerged in which the degenerate was cast as a kind of social vampire who corrupted the nation and desired, in Lombroso's words, 'not only to extinguish life in the victim, but to mutilate the corpse, tear its flesh and drink its blood'.[22]

The possible identification of the delinquent and the degenerate through physiognomy were part of the problematic of many late nineteenth-century novels as of criminal anthropology itself in the period. The idea that different categories of delinquent possessed specific traits and that a new science might chart precisely the features of the 'born criminal' aroused vast interest and enthusiasm, but also growing criticism and ridicule. By the 1890s, the cruder versions of Lombrosian and other degenerationist schema (the simian eyebrows, handle-shaped ears and so on) were being challenged and even satirised by dissenting experts in medical lecture courses and at international congresses of criminal anthropology.[23] New biological determinist arguments emerged, concentrating not on the face of the criminal, but on the supposedly obscure anomalies of the blood, internal organs, nervous system and brain.

Dracula is full of aspiring physiognomists, seeking to probe demeanours, features and expressions: '[Harker] Doctor, you don't know what it is to doubt everything, even yourself. No you don't; you couldn't with eyebrows like yours.' '[Van Helsing] seemed pleased, and laughed as he said: "So! You are a physiognomist"' (p. 188). Lucy points out to Mina how Seward 'tries to read your thoughts', and then asks '[d]o you ever try to read your own face? *I do*, and I can tell you it is not a bad study ...' (p. 55). Good and evil are sometimes written in the features, sometimes erased by them. Distance and perspective alter the nature of what is seen. Thus the 'women looked pretty, except when you got near them ...' (p. 3). Physiognomy is seen to be an enigmatic and potentially counter-productive study; the face is at once a camouflage and a symptom. Dracula after all can change his form at will, and even when in human shape his appearance seems to mislead. Thus the Count's hands, for instance look initially to be 'rather white and fine', but on closer inspection, 'they were rather coarse—broad with squat fingers ... [and] hairs in the centre of the palm' (p. 18). 'The marked physiognomy' of his face is described in meticulous detail:

> ... high bridge of the thin nose and peculiarly arched nostrils; with lofty domed forehead, and hair growing scantily round the temples, but profusely elsewhere. His eyebrows were very massive, almost meeting over the nose, and with bushy hair that seemed to curl in its own profusion. The mouth, so far as I could see it under the heavy moustache, was fixed and rather cruel-

> looking, with peculiarly sharp white teeth; these protruded over the lips, whose remarkable ruddiness showed astonishing vitality in a man of his years. For the rest, his ears were pale and at the tops extremely pointed; the chin was broad and strong, and the cheeks firm though thin. The general effect was one of extraordinary pallor. (pp. 17–18)

Dracula picked up a wider debate on the physiognomy of the 'born criminal' and the nature of the recidivist (a figure who had increasingly dominated European debate on law and order in the last quarter of the century);[24] it might even be said to be *parasitic*, like its own villain, feeding off a social moral panic about the reproduction of degeneration, the poisoning of good bodies and races by bad blood, the vitiation of healthy procreation. The novel provided a metaphor for current political and sexual political discourses on morality and society, representing the price of selfish pursuits and criminal depravity. The family and the nation, it seemed to many, were beleagured by syphilitics, alcoholics, cretins, the insane, the feeble-minded, prostitutes and a perceived 'alien invasion' of Jews from the East who, in the view of many alarmists, were feeding off and 'poisoning' the blood of the Londoner.[25] Significantly, it was an unscrupulous Jew who aided and abetted Dracula's flight from his hunters: 'We found Hildescheim in his office, a Hebrew of rather the Adelphi type, with a nose like a sheep, and a fez. His arguments were pointed with specie—we doing the punctuation—and with a little bargaining he told us what he knew' (p. 349).

The parasite might be called a key-word of the period; it cropped up at decisive moments in a multitude of social and political discussions. In 'The science of the future: a forecast', in *Civilization: Its Cause and Cure* (1889), for instance, Edward Carpenter had argued that primitive tribes might be more barbarous than the civilised but they were healthier and biologically stronger. Their society was 'not divided into classes which prey upon each other; nor is it consumed by parasites. There is more true social unity'.[26] Or take the American Eugene Talbot's *Degeneracy. Its Signs, Causes and Results* (1898) which summed up advances in current European criminological research with the view that the essence of crime was to be found in 'parasitology':

> The essential factor of crime is its parasitic nature. Parasites, in a general way, may be divided into those which live on their host, without any tendency to injure his well-being (like the dermodex in the skin follicules); those which live more or less at his expense, but do not tend to destroy him; and finally those which are

> destructive of the well-being of man and lack proper recognition of individual rights which constitute the essential foundation of society.[27]

The image of the parasite and the blood-sucker informed late nineteenth-century eugenics and the biological theory of degeneration. The parasite argued Edwin Ray Lankester, famous zoologist and curator at the British Museum, in his important 'revisionist' work, *Degeneration, a Chapter in Darwinism* (1880) demonstrated the possibility of a successful evolutionary adaptation to the environment which constituted nevertheless degeneration, the return from the heterogeneous to the homogeneous, the complex to the simple.[28] Darwin it seemed to many had been too optimistic, had suggested, despite his relative caution in extrapolating from the biological to the political, that evolution and progress were tied together. He had thought too little about who and what might best survive in an arguably noxious and degenerate environment—late nineteenth-century London, for instance.[29]

Dracula descended on that London, thus descending in a sense into the much wider social debate of the 1880s and 1890s about the morbidity and degeneracy of the average inhabitant of the metropolis. The city dweller, it seemed, had become a monstrous physical travesty. One of the vexed questions of the debate in degenerationist medical psychiatry was whether such stunted creatures tended eventually towards sterility and self-extinction or, on the contrary, towards a dreadful fecundity, which defied death, spawning offspring to infinity; like the undead in *Dracula* who 'cannot die, but must go on age after age adding new victims and multiplying the evils of the world' (p. 214). As the evil Count gloats, the bad blood he disseminates will spread ever further, constantly finding new carriers: 'My revenge is just begun! I spread it over centuries, and time is on my side' (p. 306). Early in the novel, Dracula amazes Harker by his perfect command of the English language and his familiarity with the layout of London. The Count explains that he had mastered this knowledge because he longed to 'go through the crowded streets of your mighty London, to be in the midst of the whirl and rush of humanity, to share its life, its change, its death ...' (p. 20). As he warns his guest/prisoner, 'you dwellers of the city cannot enter into the feelings of the hunter' (p. 18). When Harker finally realises what 'sharing' London's life and death actually means, he is utterly appalled by the vision of a future vampire-ridden city; '... perhaps for centuries to come, he might amongst its teeming millions, satiate his lust for blood, and create a new and ever widening circle of semi-demons to batten on the helpless' (p. 51).

The theory of degeneration seemed to raise difficult moral questions about the relation between the victim and the agent. The degenerates had inherited an affliction, which they then risked visiting upon the next generation. The potential carriers had a duty to protect themselves (for the good of society) from a process of morbidity which, like Dracula, had many forms and disguises. As a French expert, Dr Legrain, was to put it in 1889: 'Le dégénéré apparaît alors comme une vaste synthèse, un conglomérat d'états morbides différents, au milieu desquels il est obligé de se frayer une voie, en conservant très difficilement son équilibre. Ses délires sont multiples, polymorphes, protéiformes'.[30]

Stoker's story continually hinted at a whole set of questions about 'polymorphous perversity', fantasy, desire and will, which could only be characterised very obliquely as the 'strange and uncanny' (p. 14) or the 'living ring of terror' (p. 13). Incarcerated in the castle, Harker declares: '... I am either being deceived, like a baby, by my own fears, or else I am in desperate straits ...' (p. 27). But Harker in fact is shown to succumb to sexual fantasies without being bitten; it is seemingly his own thoughts which place him in desperate danger. Whilst kept prisoner, he wanders beyond the bounds of his permitted space, unable to heed Dracula's warning: 'Let me advise you, my dear young friend—nay, let me warn you with all seriousness, that should you leave these rooms you will not by any chance go to sleep in any other part of the castle. It is old, and has many memories, and there are bad dreams for those who sleep unwisely' (p. 33).

It is with good reason that the novel's characters fear sleep: '[Lucy] I tried to go to sleep, but could not. Then there came to me the old fear of sleep, and I determined to keep awake' (p. 142). When Harker falls asleep in the wrong room, he awake 'uneasily' to find three young women before him, a prisoner to his own 'wicked, burning desire' (p. 37), captivated by a 'thrilling' and 'repulsive' scene:

> I was afraid to raise my eyelids, but looked out and saw perfectly under the lashes. The fair girl went on her knees and bent over me, fairly gloating. There was a deliberate voluptuousness which was both thrilling and repulsive, and as she arched her neck she actually licked her lips like an animal, till I could see in the moonlight the moisture shining on the scarlet lips and on the red tongue as it lapped the white sharp teeth. Lower and lower went her head as the lips went below the range of my mouth and chin and seemed about to fasten on my throat ... I could feel the soft, shivering touch of the lips on the super-sensitive skin of my throat, and the hard dents of two sharp teeth, just touching and pausing there. I closed my eyes in a langourous ecstasy and waited—waited with beating heart. (p. 38)

At this decisive moment, the Count reappears with a fury beyond 'the demons of the pit ...' (p. 38), to reclaim the young man as his own: 'This man belongs to me!': '[y]es I too can love ...' (p. 39). Dracula protected Harker from himself. As the young lawyer had earlier admitted, 'of all the foul things that lurk in this hateful place the Count is the least dreadful to me ...' (p. 36).

Stoker's novel, for all its 'mythological' and folkloristic insistence, must be read in relation to a whole set of late nineteenth- and early twentieth-century concerns, images and problems. The novel in part explored and was in part imprisoned by its own situation: that powerful felt moment of interim ('this dreadful thrall of night and gloom and fear', p. 45), on the verge of the new century, in a kind of corridor between different forms of knowledge and understanding. The novel at once sensationalised the horrors of degeneration and charted reassuringly the process of their confinement and containment. The terrors and the contradictions were never quite banished, despite the deeply consoling, conservative representation of cheerful beer-swilling, cap-doffing London labourers, Jonathan Harker's dramatic upward social mobility (he rises 'from clerk to master in a few years', p. 158), and Mina Harker's restoration as subservient, faithful wife and mother.

By 1905, something had changed in Stoker's work; the vision of paralysis had shifted, as though he could now represent the nineteenth century as a long period of dark superstition which had given way to twentieth-century clarity and enlightenment. Perhaps the new tone owed something to certain recent events. In the immediately preceding years the theory of the degeneration of the Londoner in particular and the race in general had been used to explain the reverses of the Boer War, but had been subjected to serious cross-examination and some devastating criticism in the much publicised inter-departmental government report of 1904.[31] The wilder claims of the existence of a huge, stunted degenerate urban population had been discounted: the process of 'deterioration', the inquiry concluded, was confined to certain slum areas. Moreover something, it seemed, was being done about alien immigration—the Royal Commission had been completed in 1903 and a new Act was passed in 1905.[32]

Where *Dracula* had turned on the vision of degeneration and corruption, Stoker's new novel, entitled *The Man* (1905),[33] was a kind of 'positive eugenic' homily, the saga of the struggle to get good stock together, in order to achieve female beauty, pride and self-reliance (p. 3) and male strength, intelligence, bravery and determination (p. 4). Although petrified in an interminable, hackneyed romance, the text uttered prosaically and routinely the words 'sex' and 'sexuality', for as we are reminded, 'sex is sex all through. It is not, like whiskers or a wedding-ring, a garnishment of maturity' (p. 19). The very perception of sex and childhood had changed, it was suggested, from an ill-informed past where the infant was treated by adults as a kind of neuter object without feelings—'the baby was "it" to a man' (p. 18)—and, one might add, the representation of fear, desire and subjectivity had shifted in Stoker's own writing from the earlier novel where the vampire had constituted an ambiguous, threatening third person: 'I saw It—Him'; 'He—It!' (*Dracula*, p. 85); 'It—like a man' (p. 84).

The coincidence of timing was again striking: 1905 was the year of Freud's *Three Essays on the Theory of Sexuality*.[34] Stoker no doubt knew little or nothing of this, but he too charted masculinity, feminity and their discontents, through the destiny of the daughter of Stephen Norman, who has been brought up as a 'tom boy' and indeed christened Stephen herself, at the instigation of her dying mother ('let her be indeed our son! Call her by the name we both love!', p. 16), in order to console the father for his bitter disappointment at the gender of his child.

In *The Man* women are still shown to be constantly in danger not only from 'a certain [male] resentment' (p. 20) but also from themselves. Stephen's very physiognomy, we are told, suggests the prospect of 'some trouble which might shadow her whole after life' (p. 3); moreover her description is strangely reminiscent of the female vampires in the earlier text; she too has a trace of Eastern blood and a seductive mouth 'the voluptuous curves of the full, crimson lips' (p. 3), albeit no sharp, deadly teeth. The total effect is declared to be 'admirable', emblematic of a fine lineage: 'In her the various elements of her race seemed to have cropped out' (p. 3). She has a 'wide, fine forehead', 'black eyes', 'raven eyebrows', 'acquiline nose', a face which 'marked the high descent from Saxon through Norman'. The dangers are all internal, there are no monsters: the only 'wolf' in the story is not 'the wicked wolf that for half a day had paralysed London' (*Dracula*, p. 140), but in fact her saviour: Harold An Wolf. The crisis stems from Stephen's wilfulness and forwardness: she comes close to disaster in usurping the male role and proposing marriage to a worthless man only to be rejected and humiliated.

A hint of the new story had certainly been there in *Dracula* when Mina Murray speaks scathingly of the 'New Woman' writers who 'will some day start an idea that men and women should be allowed to see each other asleep before proposing or accepting' and even speculates that 'the New Woman won't condescend in future to accept; she will do the proposing herself' (p. 89), but in *The Man*, a certain style of indirectness and displacement has gone, as though the author is insisting that the veil of the vampire can now be seen through, leaving in place of the Count's castle and its surrounding wolves, only the occasional necessary sexual euphemism where total frankness still remained out of the question. We are presented with knock-about adventure, patriotism, long descriptions of the true qualities of fine men and women amongst the superior races, and various 'matter of fact' comments on the distance still to be traversed to dispel all remaining sexual mystery: 'Perhaps some day, when Science has grappled successfully with the unseen, the mysteries of sex will be open to men ...' (p. 103). Through hundreds of pages, the protagonists battle with those enduring mysteries of sexuality, caught up in a drama of profound misunderstanding, a personal 'trial' culminating in shipwreck and temporary blindness. Before their final union, the hero and the heroine are to be overwhelmed by emotional frustration, remorse and the most painful confusions of identity.

Thus in 1905 *Dracula* was banished and replaced with a melodrama of psychological suffering, neurosis, cruelty and redemption, full of 'longings and outpourings of heart and soul and mind' (p. 104). Of course, vampires have returned in innumerable guises in cinema, theatre and writing since then. But at that moment for Stoker, there were no psychotic, 'undead' blood-sucking creatures needed. For the lovely, impetuous Stephen and the lovesick Harold there were only long and lonely private mental torments—'the tortures and terrors of the night' (p. 104).

Notes

1. Bram Stoker, *Dracula, A Tale* [1897]. The World's Classics (Oxford: Oxford University Press, 1983).

2. See Peter Gay, *Freud, A Life for our Time* (London, J.M. Dent & Sons), p. 103.

3. For a related discussion on this point which has already appeared in *Critical Quarterly*, see Stephen Heath, 'Psychopathia sexualis: Stevenson's strange case', XXVIII (spring–summer 1986), pp. 93–108.

4. Gregory A. Waller, *The Living and the Undead. From Stoker's Dracula to Romero's Dawn of the Dead* (Urbana and Chicago: University of Illinois Press, 1986), p. 66.

5. Montague Summers, *The Vampire: His Kith and Kin* (London: Kegan Paul, 1928), p. 334.

6. Sigmund Freud, *Totem and Taboo* [1913], *The Standard Edition of the Complete Psychological Works of Sigmund Freud* (London: Hogarth, 1955), 24 vols., vol. XIII. Note that Ernest Jones followed Freud in his disregard of *Dracula*. There is no mention of Stoker's novel in Jones's chapter on 'The Vampire' in *On the Nightmare* (London: Hogarth, 1931).

7. The ninth edition was published in London in 1912; c.f. Summers, *op. cit.*, ch. 5, pp. 271–340, 'The Vampire in Literature'.

8. See the list of members, *Proceedings of the Society for Psychical Research*, XXV (1911).

9. 'The vampyre: a tale by Lord Byron', *The New Monthly Magazine and Universal Register*, II (January–June 1819), pp. 195–206, p. 195.

10. Summers, *op. cit.*, p. ix.

11. See V. Propp, *Morphology of the Folktale* [1928] (Austin and London: University of Texas Press, 1968, p. 96.

12. Waller, *op. cit.*, p. 6.

13. J. Sheridan Le Fanu, *Carmilla, In a Glass Darkly* (London: R. Bentley & Son, 1872), 3 vols., vol. III.

14. See Gareth Stedman Jones, *Outcast London: A Study in the Relationship Between Classes* [1971] (Harmondsworth: Penguin, 1984).

15. See for instance Gustave Le Bon, *The Crowd. A Study of the Popular Mind*, trans. from the French (London: T. F. Unwin, 1896). For a general survey, see Robert A. Nye, *The Origins of Crowd Psychology. Gustave Le Bon and the Crisis of Mass Democracy in the Third Republic*, (London and Beverley Hills: Sage, 1975); and Susanna Barrows, *Distorting Mirrors. Visions of the Crowd in Late Nineteenth-Century France* (New Haven and London: Yale University Press, 1981).

16. See for instance Clara Gallini, *La sonnambula meravigliosa. Magnetismo e ipnotismo nell'ottocento italiano* (Milan: Feltrinelli, 1983).

17. See Ruth Harris, 'Murder under hypnosis in the case of Gabrielle Bompard: psychiatry in the courtroom in belle époque Paris', in *The Anatomy of Madness. Essays in the History of Psychiatry*, ed. W. Bynum, R. Porter and M. Shepherd (London: Tavistock, 1985), vol. II, ch. 10.

18. Bram Stoker, *Famous Imposters* (London: Sidgwick & Jackson, 1910).

19. Charles Darwin, *The Descent of Man and Selection in Relation to Sex* (London: John Murray, 1871), 2 vols., vol. I, p. 127.

20. See for instance Cesare Lombroso, *L'uomo delinquente* (Milan: Hoepli, 1876); Max Nordau, *Degeneration* [1892], translated from the 2nd German edition (London: W. Heinemann, 1895); for various general discussions, cf. Sander Gilman and J. Chamberlin eds., *Degeneration. The Dark Side of Progress* (New York: Columbia University Press, 1985). With regard to Lombroso, I have tried to analyse this contradiction or at least double connotation further, in an essay in *History Workshop Journal*, Issue 21 (spring 1986), pp. 60–86.

21. See Bénédict-Augustin Morel, *Traité des dégénérescences physiques, intellectuelles et morales de l'espèce humaine* (Paris: J. B. Baillière, 1857).

22. Cesare Lombroso, *Criminal Man According to the Classification of Cesare Lombroso Briefly Summarised by his Daughter, Gina Lombroso Ferrero* (New York and London: G. P. Putnam, 1911), p. xv.

23. See the heated exchanges on the work of Lombroso at the first, second and third congresses of criminal anthropology; *Actes du Premier*

Congrès International d'anthropologie criminelle, Turin, 1886; *Actes du Deuxième Congrès ...*, Paris 1889; *Actes du Troisième Congrès ...*, Brussels, 1893; note the highly critical appendix on 'degeneration', Benjamin Ball, *Leçons sur les Maladies Mentales*, 2nd ed. (Paris: Asselin & Houzeau, 1890).

24. See Robert Nye, *Crime, Madness and Politics in Modern France. The Medical Concept of National Decline* (Princeton: Princeton University Press, 1984); and L. Radzinowicz and R. Hood, 'Incapacitating the habitual criminal, the English experience', *Michigan Law Review*, LXXVIII (1980), pp. 1305–89.

25. See for example the testimony of Arnold White to the *Royal Commission on Alien Immigration. Minutes of Royal Commission on Alien Immigration* [vol. II of the report] (1903), pp. 15–16; cf. David Feldman, 'The importance of being English: social policy, patriotism and politics in response to Jewish immigration, 1885–1906', in *Between Neighbourhood and Nation: Essays in the History of London*, ed. Feldman and Stedman Jones (London: Routledge, in press).

26. Edward Carpenter, *Civilization: its Cause and Cure and Other Essays* (London: Swan Sonnenschein, 1889), pp. 8–9.

27. Eugene S. Talbot, *Degeneracy: its Causes, Signs and Results* (London: Walter Scott, 1898), p. 318; cf. Francis Galton's observation that there was an absolute 'contrariety of ideals between the beasts that prey and those they prey upon, between those of the animals that have to work hard for their food and the sedentary parasites that cling to their bodies and suck their blood' *Essays in Eugenics* (London: The Eugenics Education Society, 1909), p. 36.

28. Edwin Ray Lankester, *Degeneration. A Chapter in Darwinism* (London: Macmillan, 1880).

29. Cf. 'Degeneration amongst Londoners', *The Lancet*, I (February 1885), p. 265.

30. M. Legrain, *Hérédité et alcoolisme. Étude psychologique et clinique sur les dégénérés buveurs et les familles d'ivrognes* (Paris: O. Doin, 1889), p. 6.

31. *The Report of the Inter-Departmental Committee on Physical Deterioration* (1904), *Reports from Commissioners, Inspectors and Other Series*, vol. XXXII.

32. *Report of the Royal Commission on Alien Immigration* (1903); *Aliens Act* (1905).

33. Bram Stoker, *The Man* (London: W. Heinemann, 1905).

34. Sigmund Freud, *Three Essays on the Theory of Sexuality* [1905], *The Standard Edition of the Complete Psychological Works of Sigmund Freud* (London: Hogarth, 1953), 24 vols., vol. VII.

KATHLEEN L. SPENCER

Purity and Danger: Dracula, *the Urban Gothic, and the Late Victorian Degeneracy Crisis*

> I believe that ideas about separating, purifying, demarcating and punishing transgressions have as their main function to impose system on an inherently untidy experience. It is only by exaggerating the difference between within and without, above and below, male and female, with and against, that a semblance of order is created.
>
> —Mary Douglas, *Purity and Danger*[1]

> The construction of categories defining what is appropriate sexual behavior ("normal"/"abnormal"), or what constitutes the essential gender being ("male"/"female"); or where we are placed along a continuum of sexual possibilities ("heterosexual," "homosexual," "paedophile," "transvestite" or whatever); this endeavor is no neutral, scientific discovery of what was already there. Social institutions which embody these definitions (religion, the law, medicine, the educational system, psychiatry, social welfare, even architecture) are constitutive of the sexual lives of individuals. *Struggles around sexuality are, therefore, struggles over meanings*—over what is appropriate or not appropriate—meanings which call on the resources of the body and the flux of desire, but are not dictated by them.
>
> —Jeffrey Weeks, *Sexuality and its Discontents* (emphasis added)[2]

From *ELH* 59 (1992): 197-225.

Interpreting *Dracula*'s sexual substrata has become something of a cottage industry of late, so much so that one more reading of the text's unconscious may seem a bit pointless. Yet there is something curious going on here: despite certain disagreements as to what kind of sexuality is present in the novel, almost all readings presume a given sexuality that is repressed and displaced throughout the text, which it is the critical task to uncover and articulate. In other words, despite local disagreements, all of these readings approach the text from a fairly orthodox version of depth psychology.[3] While this focus has certainly been productive, there are other questions about the text that cannot be answered by focusing on the unconscious sexuality of the author, or a character, or even, as in Freudian/Marxist readings, on the class system.

What I propose is a different kind of historical reading of *Dracula* to supplement the previous approaches; my concern is less with Stoker's position as a representative late-Victorian man that with the novel as a representative late-Victorian *text*. For *Dracula* is not an isolated phenomenon, but is part of a literary/cultural discourse comprised not only of other tales about vampires, but of other fantastic novels and stories that also focus on sexual dynamics, whether covertly or overtly.[4] Whatever it is that *Dracula* is saying about sex, then, it is saying not in isolation but as part of a dialogue.

The first step in this broader historical explication of Stoker's novel is to identify its literary context: the "romance revival" of the 1880s and 1890s—more explicitly, that species of romance called "the fantastic." Having located the text generically, we can then clarify its cultural context—the late-Victorian world of imperialism and degeneracy theories, purity crusades and the New Woman, materialist medicine and its opponents (continental psychology on the one hand, Spiritualism and assorted occultisms on the other). To illuminate this social context I will read the novel against models of cultures in crisis drawn from René Girard and anthropologist Mary Douglas. Finally I will consider the relationship between *Dracula*'s genre, its historical context, and its popularity, to see what light this analysis can shed on a larger question—why the fantastic as a genre should have flourished so dramatically in this period of cultural transformation.

I: THE FANTASTIC

Like "romance" itself, "the fantastic" is a much-disputed term. While some theorists use "fantasy" and "the fantastic" interchangeably, others see them as referring to two quite different kinds of stories, and still others see the fantastic not as a genre at all but as an element that can appear in many kinds of tales (as the term "gothic" can be applied either to a specific fictional configuration common at the end of the eighteenth century, or to a literary mode which can appear in works of any period).

The most famous definition of the term "fantastic" is Tzvetan Todorov's, but what seems to me the most functional, precise explanation of the fantastic is that proposed by the Polish semiotician Andrzej Zgorzelski. For Zgorzelski, the fantastic as a genre is signaled by "the breaching of the internal laws which are initially assumed in the text to govern the fictional world." The opening of the text indicates that the fictive world is based on a "mimetic world model," a model that is violently breached by the entrance of the fantastic element and changed into a different world, one in which the fantastic element does not violate the laws of reality. A fantastic text, then, builds its fictional world as "*a textual confrontation of two models of reality*."[5]

Two elements are essential for the characteristic *frisson* of the fantastic: first, the impossible event must genuinely be happening (not a dream, a hallucination, a mistake, or a deliberate trick); and second, the tone of the narrative emphasizes initial disbelief, and (usually) horror. The characters react with fear and revulsion at encountering what is not only unexpected, but *unnatural* according to the laws of the world they inhabit, and readers usually respond with the same feelings, not only because we identify with the characters, but because the world the characters initially inhabit is our own world. Further, the narrative voice insistently emphasizes violation and transgression, the logical contradiction between the impossibility of the occurrence and its actuality. For example, when Dracula appears in Picadilly at high noon, the characters react initially with disbelief and a kind of horrified vertigo at discovering that the monstrous is real and walking the streets of their ordinary modern city.

Defined in this way, the fantastic as a genre is relatively modern. The low mimetic (to use Northrop Frye's familiar term) must be a well-established fictional convention before we can conventionalize its violation, a condition that does not obtain till the mid-eighteenth century. Before the convention of realism became the norm—in the medieval quest narrative or Renaissance romance, for example—the intrusion of the supernatural or monstrous did not create an experience of the fantastic for either the characters or the readers. A questing knight may be seriously dismayed to discover a dragon or a magician in his path, but the mere existence of the supernatural does not force him to rethink reality, because it does not violate the laws of nature. For Prince Hamlet, seeing his father's ghost is certainly alarming; but it is the ghost's message, not its presence, which so distresses him. The serious question for Hamlet is not whether the ghost is real but whether it is "honest"—genuinely his father's spirit or a demon sent to tempt him to regicide.

Modern readers of these texts need not believe in the actual existence of dragons or ghosts to recognize that the text treats these occurrences as natural. The conventions of fictional realism do not apply, any more than they apply to modern fantasy or science fiction, whose readers learn to respond without astonishment to the presence of wizards or of faster-than-light space vessels. But a wizard or faster-than-light ship introduced into a text whose opening pages signal a contemporary realistic setting would produce reactions from the characters, the narrator, and the readers that would signal the presence of the fantastic.

In light of this requirement, I would argue that the Gothic tales of the late eighteenth century are the first fantastic fictions, Horace Walpole and Anne Radcliffe among the first writers to experiment with the emotional possibilities (for both characters and readers) of violating the laws of nature. Since such violations are radically new, the earliest writers tend to soften the effects a bit. In the first place, Gothic fictions are traditionally distanced somewhat from the world of their audience, set back in time and "away" in space—preferably in Spain or Italy during the Inquisition—making the stories more plausible (to an English audience) by the superstitiousness of their settings, and at the same time lessening the intensity of the fear, for the readers if not the characters. As another softening device, some of the early Gothic writers, notably Radcliffe, tidy away the fantastic by giving us rational explanations for the apparent supernatural events—though not till the end of the novel, so we have plenty of time to experience the fantastic *frisson* first. However, this tidying strategy was soon abandoned. While second-generation Gothic writers like Monk Lewis and Charles Maturin still set their novels in Inquisition Europe, they apparently felt less need to reassure their readers at the end that the ordinary rational laws of reality governed the world inside the text as well as outside.

But the fantastic that develops at the end of the nineteenth century (exclusive of the ghost story, a popular but traditional form) is identifiably different from the Gothic of one hundred years before. First and most important, the new authors insist on the modernity of the setting—not on the distance between the world of the text and the world of the reader, but on their *identity*. A modern setting means, most profoundly, an urban setting, as by the end of the nineteenth century well over half the population of the British Isles lived in cities. To be modern also means that science is the metaphor that rules human interactions with the universe, so the new fantastic adopts the discourse of empiricism even to describe and manipulate supernatural phenomena.

These characteristics of the modern fantastic, as distinct from the earlier variety, suggest we need a new term to refer to it; and I would argue that "Urban Gothic" is particuiarly appropriate for the new type, acknowledging the eighteenth-century ancestry while identifying the major modifications that have been made to adapt the fantastic to the needs of a new era.

The change from Gothic to Urban Gothic allows writers to call on the powers of what Henry James, in a review of the sensation novels of Mary Elizabeth Braddon, called "those most mysterious of mysteries, the mysteries which are at our own doors." As James observed, the innovation of bringing the terror next door gave an entirely new direction to horror literature. The new strategy

> was fatal to the authority of Mrs. Radcliffe and her everlasting castle in the Apennines. What are the Apennines to us, or we to the Apennines? Instead of the terrors of "Udolpho", we were treated to the terrors of the cheerful country house and the busy London lodgings. And there is no doubt that these were infinitely more terrible.

In 1865, James was moderately scornful of the supernatural as a fictional device, remarking in this same review that "a good ghost-story, to be half as terrible as a good murder-story, must be connected at a hundred points with the common objects of life."[6] But twenty-five years later he himself found uses for the supernatural by following his own advice and connecting it "at a hundred points to the common objects of life"—and so did his "fellow" (if we can so call them) romancers. In short, James, along with many of his contemporaries, explored the Urban Gothic.

II: THE ROMANCE REVIVAL

But the Urban Gothic was only part, if a crucial part, of a larger literary movement of the last two decades of the century: the romance revival. "Romance" is another of those protean literary terms whose meaning varies with the frame of reference, but in the context of the 1880s, the term has a fairly stable meaning. The "romance revival" began as a reaction against the "high realism" of the 1870s, which was, in its turn, a reaction against the "sensation novels" of the 1860s. The theorists of high realism rejected the sensation novel's emphasis on plot, arguing that it demanded less of readers than novels that required them to interpret the subtleties of human motives. In addition, it was believed, too strong an emphasis on plot would interfere with the "naturalness" of characters.

By the 1880s, these novels of "character analysis" themselves came under attack. First, being limited to and by "gross" reality, the novels (their critics argued) were dull and trivial. Second, these novelists had chosen to adopt the "heartless" methods of science ("vivisection" is a common metaphor), treating their characters with no sympathy or decorum, dissecting them in public. Then, when "high realism" transposes into naturalism, new grounds for rejection appear. For one thing, naturalist novels persistently tried to introduce moral, middle-class readers to the kinds of persons—prostitutes, criminals, beggars, and other "undeserving" or unappealing poor people—whom they had no desire to meet. For another, realism, especially when pushed to the extremes of naturalist determinism, allowed no room for the higher workings of Providence, no room for the reward of the virtuous and the punishment of the guilty. Finally, since naturalism was identified in the minds of English readers with Zola, James, and Howells, it became for some readers and critics a patriotic duty to resist "foreign influences," and to call for a healthy *English* fiction.[7]

The result was a resurgence of interest in bold, high-stakes adventure, larger-(and simpler)-than-life characters, exotic locales and incidents, idealistic quests, world-class criminals, disguises and escapes, rescues and disasters. Anthony Hope Hawkins, author (as Anthony Hope) of one of the best-known romances of the period, *The Prisoner of Zenda* (1893), exclaimed that in romance,

> Emotion must be taken at high pitch. It must be strong, simple, confident; otherwise it lacks the quality needed for romance. ... romance becomes an expression of some of the deepest instincts of humanity.
>
> It has no monopoly of this expression, but it is its privilege to render it in a singularly clear, distinct, and pure form; it can give to love an ideal object, to ambition a boundless field, to courage a high occasion; and these great emotions, revelling in their freedom, exhibit themselves in their glory. Thus in its most worthy forms, in the hands of its masters, it can not only delight men, but can touch them to the very heart. It shows them what they would be if they could, if time and fate and circumstances did not bind, what in a sense they all are, and what their acts would show them to be if an opportunity offered. So they dream and are happier, and at least none the worse for their dreams.[8]

Robert Louis Stevenson, Rudyard Kipling, H. Rider Haggard, Arthur Conan Doyle, and (in his early works) H. G. Wells are the best-known figures of this new movement, along with Arthur Machen, Algernon Blackwood, and Andrew Lang, several of whom also wrote manifestos for the critical journals in favor of romance.[9] In addition to these relatively familiar names, a whole army of romancers, once popular but now practically unread and in many cases entirely forgotten, produced large quantities of this fiction to supply the new markets.[10]

But if the revived romance of the 1880s takes its declared form from an ancient tradition, the new romancers (like the authors of the Urban Gothic) draw on contemporary interests for their characters, settings, and themes: the exotic reaches of the empire—Africa, Egypt, India, Australia—as well as such regions as China, the South Pacific, and South and Central America; dead civilizations of the ancient past (Egyptian, Peruvian, Celtic, Neanderthal), their tales enlivened by information culled from the newest archaeological reports; lost races inside volcanoes, at the bottom of the sea, in the polar regions, on other planets, in the future; the thrilling possibilities of modern technology (electrically-induced immortality or eternal youth; brain transplants; memory recordings; time travel); or the beliefs and rituals of that other revival of the 1880s, the occult revival (Spiritualism, Theosophy, the Society for Psychical Research, and the magicians of the Order of the Golden Dawn).[11]

III: PURITY AND DANGER

Thus not only the Urban Gothic but the romance revival as a whole transforms a traditional literary genre by an infusion of modern perspectives. But the Urban Gothic and the romance share another crucial characteristic beyond their common reliance on contemporary adventure and exoticism: a concern for purity, for the reduction of ambiguity and the preservation of boundaries. Both attempt to reduce anxiety by stabilizing certain key distinctions, which seemed, in the last decades of the nineteenth century, to be eroding: between male and female, natural and unnatural, civilized and degenerate, human and nonhuman. At issue, finally, underneath all these distinctions, is the ground of individual identity, the ultimate distinction between self and other.

Where once a complex web of traditional roles and relationships grounded individual identity, in the new capitalist world of the cash-nexus, Anthony Giddens observes, the bulwarks of identity were reduced essentially to two: the arena of intimate relationships (that is, the family, personal and highly sexualized), and the arena of "mass ritual," of sporting events and political ceremonies, especially the fervent impersonal group identity we call nationalism. "In such conditions of social life," writes Giddens, "the ontological security of the individual in day-to-day life is more fragile than in societies dominated by tradition and the meshings of kinship across space and time."[12]

Instead of being broadly supported by a web of interlocking kinship links, work groups, ceremonial societies, traditions, routines, and even the continuities of place and seasonal cycle, identity for the ordinary middle-class Briton now hung delicately on two slender threads at the extreme margins of scale, the intimate and the national. So it is hardly surprising that many people grew anxious to preserve the clarity and purity of the distinctions that supported this system.

However, even at this time of their heightened significance, these very distinctions came under attack. Darwinian evolutionary theory blurred the boundaries between human and animal in not one but two ways: by the famous argument that humans and apes had a common ancester, but also by the implied hierarchy at the end of *The Descent of Man* which leads from the ape-like ancestor through primitive peoples to civilized Europeans. The imputed inferiority of the lower races, as George Stocking points out, "although still in the first instance cultural, was now in most cases at least implicitly organic as well."[13] Thus the boundary between human and ape became a matter of scientific doctrine, but (as Wells's *The Island of Dr. Moreau* pointed out) an ambiguous one: what was actually a philosophic and political debate was concealed under the language of science. Yet since "scientific" language could not hope to stabilize a fundamentally unscientific boundary, the issue continued unresolved.

Nor was this boundary a matter of abstract speculation for civilized Europeans; for if humans could evolve, it was thought they could also *de*volve or degenerate, both as nations and as individuals. At what point in a downward slide did a human being cross over the line into animality? Lombroso addressed this question with his new "science" of criminal anthropology, which purported to demonstrate through elaborate measurements and charts of facial angles that habitual criminals were throwbacks to primitive ancestors, with more of the ape than the human about them. Fear of such national "degeneracy" was further highlighted for Britons by the Boer War of 1899–1902, first by the series of unprecedented defeats handed the greatest army in the world by a handful of Dutch farmers, and second by the recruiting campaign that discovered the physical inadequacies of the men from London's East-End slums, who were alarmingly undersized, frail, and sickly.[14] Such concerns underlay the tremendous public anxiety at the end of the century about the condition of the British Empire and the warnings that, like its Roman predecessor, it could fall, and for what were popularly perceived as the same reasons—moral decadence leading to racial degeneration.

Another crucial distinction under attack was that between male and female. By all the superficial criteria of appearance, behavior, and legal status, Victorian men and women must have seemed almost like two different, though symbiotically related, species. It has been argued that never in western society have gender roles been more rigid or more distinct (at least in the middle classes) than in the late nineteenth century. Victorian science, especially Victorian medicine, lent the weight of its prestige to the position that the physical distinctions between women and men were absolute, and absolutely determinate. In their very nature and essence, said the doctors, women were unlike men; and this difference explained their limitations—physical, moral, and intellectual—and justified their legal and social disabilities.[15]

It was woman's special nature that fitted her for the task she had been assigned by Victorian society. In her guises of maiden, wife, and above all mother, Woman (with a capital) had been appointed the guardian of moral virtue; the home, Woman's realm, became both a refuge from the hard necessities of the utilitarian business world and the temple of a new religion that served to supplement or substitute for the weakening Christian orthodoxy—the religion of romantic love as the source of salvation, and of the family as a haven for all the human warmth, grace and affection that had been banished from the father's daily life in the world. Woman, as the Angel in the House, was to save Man from his own baser instincts and lead him toward heaven.

Jenni Calder's study of the Victorian home further clarifies the significance of this domestic religion. While Victorians genuinely desired to make the world a better place, Calder argues, the social problems facing them were so massive and so intractable that they usually had to settle for making the home, as the only part of the world responsive to their actions, a better place instead. Thus "the angel in the house was at the root of multitudes of Victorian assumptions and ideas, and Victorian rationalizations and ideals."[16]

But this position did not go unchallenged. Throughout the century, women argued for reforms of marriage and divorce laws, and in particular for the right of married women to own property in their own names. The kind of resistance they faced is revealed most potently in the comments of Lord St. Leonards, who argued against the passage of the Married Women's Property Bill of 1857 on the grounds that it would "place the whole marriage law ... on a different footing and give a wife all the distinct rights of citizenship," an argument that indicates that for this distinguished jurist and former Lord Chancellor the categories of "wife" and "citizen" were mutually exclusive.[17] A few men joined the fray on the distaff side, most notably John Stuart Mill, who argued against such logic in *The Subjection of Women* in 1869 and even tried to get women the vote, on the grounds that only if they could vote for their representatives would Parliament take their needs seriously; but considerable discussion produced little substantive action.

The debate grew even more heated in the last few decades of the century when the New Woman arrived on the scene, wanting higher education, striving to enter the learned professions, and ever more frequently working outside the home for money (that is, middle-class women began to do so, for of course lower-class women had long been so employed). And some of the most radical New Women even argued that they were entitled to the same freedom of sexual expression as men. In short, more and more women insisted on leaving the house of which they had been appointed angel, the house that, if a refuge for men, became for many middle-class wives and daughters a more or less pleasant prison. But in the eyes of most Victorian men, for women to deny their traditional role was to deny their womanhood, to challenge the distinctions between women and men upon which the family—and therefore society—depended.

Nor was the New Woman the only source of threat to gender categories. Homosexuality was brought into the consciousness of a horrified public, first by the Cleveland Street scandal in 1889, which revealed a homosexual brothel catering to the upper classes (including the Prince of Wales's closest friend and, by rumor, the Prince's eldest son as well).[18] More dramatic still was the infamous Wilde trial in 1895, which made "homosexuality" both as an ontological state and as a chosen lifestyle available to ordinary middle-class imaginations for the first time.[19] To late Victorians, if the New Woman's desire to achieve higher status by "becoming" a man was at least understandable, though outrageous, what could be said about men who deliberately refused to be men? Such depravity challenged not just the distinction between male and female but that between natural and unnatural as well.[20]

The debates about sex and sex roles in the nineteenth century, argues Ludmilla Jordanova, "hinged precisely on the ways in which sexual boundaries might become blurred. It is as if the social order depended on clarity with respect to certain distinctions whose symbolic meanings spread far beyond their explicit context."[21] In this perception she is quite right: anthropologists tell us that social order depends precisely on the clarity of such distinctions. But anthropologists can tell us more: they can help us see the dynamics at work in late Victorian England in a larger social context—the context of a culture in crisis.

Mary Douglas's work on pollution fears and witchcraft societies is surprisingly appropriate here.[22] All cultures that explain evil as a product of witchcraft—from certain African tribes to Salem Village in the seventeenth century—share certain characteristics, she notes. Most importantly, there is strong pressure on group members to conform, but the classification system of the society is somehow ineffective in structuring reality: it is too narrow and rigid to deal with the variety of actual experience, or it is inconsistent, or has gaps, or is in competition with another system of classification that weakens the effectiveness of both.

In such a society, the universe is dualistic: what is inside is good, what is outside is bad. The group boundary is therefore both a source of magical danger and the main definer of rights: you are either a member or a stranger. Evil is a foreign danger introduced by foreign agents in disguise, but abetted by deviant members of the group who must be identified and expelled for allowing the outside evil to infiltrate. Since not only the society itself but the entire cosmos is endangered by the vile, irrational behavior of these human agents of evil, a witchcraft society is preoccupied with rituals of cleansing, the expulsion of spies or witches, and the redrawing of boundaries to mark the pure (inside) and the evil (outside).

Though the late Victorians did not explicitly attribute evil to witches, they manifested the same fears of pollution from outsiders, the same suspicion of deviants as traitors, and the same exaggerated estimation of what was at stake—in short, the same social dynamics as more traditional witchcraft societies. The pressures on middle-class Victorians to conform were intense (and too well known to need documentation), while the model to which they were required to conform was losing its clarity. The old consensus on the central distinctions of their society—on which distinctions were indeed central, and on how those distinctions were to be defined and maintained—was breaking down. In the last twenty years of the century, an intense debate developed between those who sought to shore up the old crumbling distinctions and those demanding change—nontraditional women, homosexuals, socialists, some artists and intellectuals, a few scientists, working-class men who had acquired some education. One side strove to widen or redefine cultural boundaries, to let some of the "outside" in, while the other fought desperately to maintain the "purity" of the inside by expelling as traitors those who breached the boundaries.

Douglas mentions one other key factor in a witchcraft society that the Victorians also shared: the leadership of the group is precarious or under dispute, and the roles within the group ambiguous or undefined. Because no one person or faction has sufficient authority to stabilize the situation, the struggle for leadership prompts what we might call "purity competitions": who is most vigilant at ferreting out enemies, especially those disguised enemies lurking within the society itself? In other words, the struggle for power and stability under these social conditions leads inevitably to scapegoat rituals.[23]

The struggle for leadership of a divided and confused people also characterized late Victorian society. For the Victorians, neither traditionalist nor "rebel" forces could take complete command: the traditionalists had the numbers and most of the worldly power, but the rebels tended to be educated and articulate, many were influential, and all had ready access to a public forum in the wide-open periodical market of the 1880s and '90s. As a result, they could make their voices heard in disproportion to their numbers and official positions. The battle produced numerous cries of "seize the witch!"—directed both at groups (Jews, Germans, Slavs, Orientals, birth control advocates, promiscuous women, decadent French authors [especially Zola], homosexuals) and at individuals—most spectacularly, though by no means solely, Oscar Wilde.

And here is where we reconnect the social and the literary. The romance, I would argue, and in particular the Urban Gothic, not only in its characteristic subject matter but more importantly in its very form, is the perfect literary reflection of the cultural crisis Britain experienced between 1880 and 1914. In such an atmosphere, the modern fantastic became a potent vehicle for social drama—potent because the images of the fantastic are always drawn from our dreams and nightmares. The fantastic as a genre is based on violations of reality, which means it is fundamentally concerned with *defining* reality; and the nature of reality is exactly the question at issue in late-nineteenth-century England. Finally, since at the end of a fantastic tale the violating element is characteristically expelled and the mimetic world, the status quo, is reestablished, the fantastic proved ideal for symbolically reaffirming the traditional model of reality.

As Northrop Frye told us long ago, the romance is traditionally a *psychomachia*, a struggle between the forces of good and evil in which evil is defeated, and the modern romance (as Hope's quotation suggests, with its emphasis on clarity and purity and "great emotions in their glory") retains this pattern. The Urban Gothic extends the tradition in a peculiarly modern way by defining the enemy as not only evil but *unnatural*: she/he/it has no right to exist at all. In the very form of both the romance and the Urban Gothic, then, we find repeated the contemporary drive to purify the inside and expel the foreign pollution: at the heart of both lies the scapegoat ritual.

And this finally brings us to *Dracula*, a classic example of the conservative fantastic: in the end Dracula is killed, the alien element expelled and the ordinary world restored. But what exactly is being expelled? In particular, how would Stoker's original audience have read this novel? In the cultural context of 1897, what threat did Dracula represent that needed so desperately and at such cost to be driven out? How was the culture being instructed to protect itself, and from what?

Another way to put the question is this: who is the scapegoat in *Dracula*, and to what end is that scapegoat sacrificed?

IV: RITUAL VICTIMS IN *DRACULA*

As René Girard tells us in *Violence and the Sacred*, what all sacrificial victims have in common is that they must recognizably belong to the community, but must at the same time be somehow marginal, incapable of fully participating in the social bond—slaves, criminals, the mad, the deformed. They are enough of the community to substitute for it, but between them and the community "a crucial social link is missing, so they can be exposed to violence without fear of reprisal. Their death does not automatically entail an act of vengeance." As a result, sacrificing them will end communal violence rather than prolonging it.[24]

In *Dracula*, I argue, Lucy Westenra fills the category and the social function of the surrogate victim who is sacrificed to restore a lost order. On the surface, it would seem that Lucy belongs to the class Victorians would find *least* sacrificeable rather than most—a young, beautiful, virtuous girl—and that, in any case, she is a victim not of her own community but of a monstrous outsider. However, we are given numerous indications that Lucy, for all her sweetness, purity, and beauty, is a marginal figure. In the first place, her social connections are alarmingly tenuous: her father is dead, and she has no brothers or other family to protect her except her mother, who is herself very weak both psychologically and physically (and in fact predeceases her daughter). There is no one to protect Lucy from attack, or to revenge her death at the hands of her own community.

More crucially, Lucy's character is "flawed" in a way that makes her fatally vulnerable to the vampire. She is a woman whose sexuality is under very imperfect control. She is loved devotedly by three different young men, which in itself is not a fault, but her reaction to this situation reveals a problem. When she writes to Mina about her suitors, she can't help gloating about "THREE proposals in one day."[25] Worse, although she says she is greatly in love with Arthur, she also feels very badly about turning down those two splendid fellows, John Seward and Quincey Morris, and bursts out, "Why can't they let a girl marry three men, or as many as want her, and save all this trouble?" Immediately afterward she admits that "this is heresy, and I must not say it" (59); but even so, we sense that she means what she says: she really would like to marry all of them.

And, according to the novel's own semiotics, she gets her wish. At her funeral Arthur declares that, because he has given Lucy his blood, he feels that she is his true wife in the sight of God. Under the circumstances, his friends naturally refrain from telling him about the transfusions Lucy had received from her other two lovers and Dr. Van Helsing; but later, alone with Seward, Van Helsing bursts out in uncontrollable laughter thinking of it. True, as Seward observes, the thought is very comforting for Arthur. But if

Arthur is right in his belief, Van Helsing points out, what about the other three donors? "Then this so sweet maid is a polyandrist" (176).

Nor is this desire to marry all three of her suitors the only sign of Lucy's suspect character. She is a sleepwalker, a habit traditionally associated with sexual looseness. She is therefore doubly vulnerable to Dracula's approach; in the symbol-system of the novel, she has signaled her sexual receptivity. It cannot be an accident that on the night of the storm, when Dracula's ship lands, Lucy indulges again in sleepwalking, leaving the house dressed only in her nightgown. Considering the armor-like characteristics of the ordinary Victorian woman's daytime clothing—the heavily-boned corsets, the immense weight of petticoats, the endless layers of cloth—Lucy in her nightdress might as well be naked. Worse yet, she goes to the old cemetery, alone, and to the grave of a suicide (the only spot of unsanctified ground in the churchyard). The traditional equation of sexuality and death could hardly be clearer, nor her invitation of Dracula more explicit.

What makes Lucy's sexuality threatening to the community—sufficiently threatening that she becomes an appropriate surrogate victim—is that she will not limit herself to one man. While she does officially choose one of her three suitors, her choice is insufficiently absolute to control the competition among the three for her possession. Stoker downplays the competition by making the men such good friends and such decent, self-controlled characters that the threat of disorder is concealed, but nonetheless that competition remains as a source of potential violence.

But in order to function as a surrogate victim who can purge the community of its universal violence, something further is required: Lucy has to take on the aspect of the monstrous. In one light, Lucy functions as the monstrous double of Mina, the virtuous wife; seen another way, she functions as her own monstrous double, for there are two aspects to her personality whose separation becomes increasingly marked throughout her transformation into a vampire. She is both the image of purity, sweetness, and beauty—the traditional blond angel in the house—and the creature of sexual appetites, the sleep-walker who accedes to violent penetration by the vampire. Her saving grace, according to Van Helsing, is that she yielded to Dracula only during a trance—that is, when her conscious personality was not in command—so her unconscious personality alone has become vampiric.[26] During her last hours, she manifests both sides of her personality in alternation, sometimes the sweet pure Lucy they all love, and sometimes the wanton, voluptuous creature with cruel mouth and hard eyes. When she is awake and thus "herself," she clutches the garlic flowers to her; but in her sleep, she thrusts away that protection, embracing her monstrous fate. Since she dies in her sleep, her future as one of the Un-Dead is inescapable.

As a vampire she is even more beautiful than in life, but no longer the Lucy they had known. "The sweetness was turned to adamantine, heartless cruelty, and the purity to voluptuous wantonness.... Lucy's eyes [have become] unclean and full of hell-fire, instead of the pure, gentle orbs we knew"; they blaze with "unholy light" and she is as "callous as a devil" (211). Again and again, Seward uses the words "wanton" and "voluptuous" to describe Un-Dead Lucy's smile, her tones "diabolically sweet"—until she is thwarted, at which point she becomes overtly monstrous, her eyes throwing out "sparks of hellfire," the brows "wrinkled as though the folds of the flesh were the coils of Medusa's snakes" (212). These same images are repeated when the four men, Dr. Van Helsing and Lucy's three suitors, return the next day to free Lucy's soul, to save her by killing her. "She seemed like a nightmare of Lucy as she lay there; the pointed teeth, the bloodstained, voluptuous mouth—which it made one shudder to see—the whole carnal and unspirited appearance, seeming like a devilish mockery of Lucy's sweet purity" (214).

But the rite of sacrifice, an act of terrible violence, restores both Lucy and the community she had threatened. As Stoker describes it, the final killing of Lucy is quite clearly both a religious act and a communal one. The setting is a solitary tomb lit only by candles. Arthur drives the stake through Lucy's heart, as the one with the best right to so violate her offending body and release the innocent soul, and he is supported in his work by the priestly figure of Dr. Van Helsing and by his two closest friends, Lucy's other lovers, who read the prayer for the dead as he strikes home.

> The thing in the coffin writhed; and a hideous, bloodcurdling screech came from the opened red lips. The body shook and quivered and twisted in wild contortions; the sharp white teeth champed together till the lips were cut, and the mouth was smeared with a crimson foam. But Arthur never faltered. He looked like a figure of Thor as his untrembling arm rose and fell, driving deeper and deeper the mercy-bearing stake, whilst the blood from the pierced heart welled and spurted up around it. His face was set, and high duty seemed to shine through it; the sight of it gave us courage so that our voices seemed to ring through the little vault....
>
> There, in the coffin lay no longer the foul Thing that we had so dreaded and grown to hate that the work of her destruction was yielded as a privilege to the one best entitled to it, but Lucy as we had seen her in life, with her face of unequalled sweetness and purity. (216)[27]

In death Lucy becomes again the angel she had been in life; she also becomes a bond between her three rivals, where in life she could only have been a source of division. Despite their personal grief, it is for them an ideal solution to the problem she represented. In sacrificing Lucy, the four men purge not only their fear of female sexuality generally, of which she is the monstrous expression, but also—and more importantly—their fear of their own sexuality and their capacity for sexually-prompted violence against each other.

The scene in the tomb exemplifies a key element of the sacrificial rite, "the atmosphere of terror and hallucination that accompanies the primordial religious experience."[28] The violent hysteria, the decisive act of violence perceived as religious experience, the succeeding calm and the atmosphere of holy mystery covering the participants, all function to fuse the men into a closed and harmonious community. Although Lucy is no longer available to any of the men as a bulwark of his personal identity, her death serves to reinforce their common bond, their dedication to each other and to a sense of shared interest, thus bolstering that other pole of Victorian identity that Giddens defines as nationalism.

But Lucy is not the only scapegoat in the novel. Count Dracula himself is also sacrificed for the common good. Like all sacrificial victims, he must be both connected and marginal. His links to the community are literally *blood* ties—the blood of Jonathan, Lucy, and Mina. Further, he resembles his enemies in several important ways: he is (or was once) human, he is European, he is extremely intelligent and has a most powerful will. But his roots are in *Eastern* Europe—Slavic, Catholic, peasant, and superstitious where England is Anglo-Saxon, Protestant, industrial, and rationalist. Further, unlike Arthur, the bourgeois aristocrat, Dracula belongs to a much older, more feudal sort of aristocracy, one that was was going out of favor in England.[29] In fact, the most unmistakable sign of his allegiance to that older pattern may be his sexuality, which partakes of the ancient *droit du seigneur*. "Your girls that you all love are mine already," he gloats (306), taunting his opponents; and throughout the novel he lets his appetites run rampant, voracious and (as Freud says of the child's sexuality) polymorphously perverse—a most appropriate phrase, since the narrative repeatedly emphasizes Dracula's "child brain" (335), as opposed to the adult brains of his enemies. Even Mina has, we are told, a *man's* brain to go with her woman's heart (234).

But we know that civilized adult men control their appetites; his failure to do so marks the crucial distinction between Dracula and his opponents: he is *degenerate*, "a criminal and of criminal type" according to the theories of Lombroso and Nordau, which means he has an "imperfectly formed mind"

(342).[30] Consequently he can only work on one project at a time, and in emergencies must fall back on habit—which is why, closely pursued, he can do nothing but flee to his castle, while his opponents are able to innovate strategies for his defeat. As criminal and degenerate, Dracula is by definition selfish, evil, solitary; despite his pride in his descent from Attila and in his people's valiant struggles against the Turk, as a vampire he has no true "national" identity, no "community" to belong to. Even the three vampire women at the castle who could conceivably function as a family for him, if not a nation, do not appear to do so. By contrast the "band of brothers" is selfless, good, and unified into a community both by their shared sacrifice of Lucy and their shared devotion to Mina. It is, as Van Helsing tells them, one of their great advantages over Dracula—the "power of combination," along with the "sources of science" and "devotion in a cause" (238).

However, despite all these differences, the truth gradually emerges: the Count represents precisely those dark secret drives that the men most fear in themselves, which are most destructive to both poles of identity—the intimate self of the family man, threatened by unrestrained sexual appetites, and the communal self of the nation, undermined by violent internal competition more than by external invasion. Representing a real aspect of his enemies, but one that they consciously wish to reject, Dracula has both the necessary connections to the community and the necessary separation from it to fulfill the scapegoat's purgative function.

And like Lucy's sacrifice, the scene of Dracula's death contains all the elements of the primordial religious experience. The atmosphere is terrifying and hallucinatory: the two parties desperately racing the sun, each fighting for life—Dracula to reach his castle, the band of heroes to catch the vampire before sunset restores his deadly power; the Count's glaring eyes and "horrible vindictive look" as he lies helpless in his coffin, and his triumphant expression as he sees the sun setting and anticipates his revenge. Like the earlier sacrifice, this act is communal: two of the young men together pry off the lid of the coffin with their knives and strike simultaneously, one slashing the Count's throat, the other plunging a knife into his heart—all described in words that intensify the terror of the moment ("sweep," "flash," "shriek," "shear," "plunge" [377]).

"It was like a miracle," cries Mina in relief; but, as the Count's body crumbles into dust before their eyes, she adds, "Even in that moment of final dissolution, there was in the face a look of peace, such as I never could have imagined might have rested there" (377). As at the moment of Lucy's death, the sacrificial victim is pictured as at peace, almost grateful to die for the greater good of the community. And indeed, there may be a reason for both Lucy's and Dracula's curious passivity at the moment of death. Mary Douglas remarks in *Purity and Danger* that "if a person has no place in the social system and is therefore a marginal being, all precaution against danger must come from others. He cannot help his abnormal situation." But to say that he cannot help his situation is to suggest that he would *like* to help it, that he does not want to be a danger to others.

However we read this reaction, the atmosphere of the scene changes dramatically at the moment of the vampire's death: Castle Dracula is suddenly seen standing out against the sunset sky as we have never seen it before, every stone blazing in the light. The violence and horror is succeeded by holy awe and peace, which is capped when Quincey Morris sees Mina's forehead now clear of its shameful scar, and vows with his last breath that this outcome is worth dying for. It is the ultimate confirmation that the community has been saved.

But it has been a near thing, and the cost high: Lucy is lost to them (though her soul was saved), Quincey is dead, and both Jonathan and Mina suffer severely before Dracula is defeated. Stoker's novel, then, reveals two complementary perspectives on its subject. If Lucy and Dracula demonstrate the terrifying powers of degeneracy, so threatening that they must at all costs be expelled from the community and from life itself, Jonathan's and Mina's experiences exemplify the difficulties and the rewards of resistance.

According to Victorian sexology, in Dracula's castle Jonathan is a man at risk: he is engaged to Mina, but they are not yet married, so that his sexual fantasies are inflamed but not yet lawfully satisfied. Further, he is far from home and isolated from other living human beings. For the Victorians, solitude greatly increased sexual danger: the solitude of privacy allowed one to indulge in masturbation, while the different solitude of anonymity left one free to indulge in the kinds of sexual experiences one would, as member of a family, have been ashamed to admit desiring.[31] Jonathan is both alone and anonymous. Confronted with the three mysterious and beautiful women in the moonlit room, he admits, "I felt in my heart a wicked, burning desire that they would kiss me with those red lips" (37). The scene that follows, when he very nearly (and disastrously) gets his wish, is recorded with incandescent detail:

> The girl went on her knees and bent over me, simply gloating. There was a deliberate voluptuousness which was both thrilling and repulsive, and as she arched her neck she actually licked her lips like an animal, till I could see in the moonlight the moisture shining on the scarlet lips and on the red tongue as it lapped the white sharp teeth. Lower and lower went her head as the lips went below the range of my mouth and seemed to fasten on my

> throat.... I could feel the soft, shivering touch of the lips on the super-sensitive skin of my throat, and the hard dents of two sharp teeth, just touching and pausing there. I closed my eyes in languorous ecstasy and waited—waited with beating heart. (38)

The erotic charge of the scene is quite remarkable, as is Jonathan's fascinated passivity in surrendering to his sexual fantasies, even while admitting the wickedness of what he desires. What we see and he does not, at this moment, is that he is risking not the "little death" of orgasm, but the real thing. Ironically, Jonathan is saved from the women not by his own virtue, but by Count Dracula's opportune arrival. However, he is rescued from the evils of feminine sexuality only to be plunged into the horrors of homosexual passions. "How dare you cast eyes on him when I had forbidden it?" Dracula furiously asks his handmaids. "This man belongs to me!" The women answer, with a laugh of "ribald coquetry," "You yourself never loved; you never love!" The Count looks at Jonathan's face "attentively," and says in a soft whisper, "Yes, I too can love" (39). As Dracula approaches him, Jonathan conveniently sinks into unconsciousness—into the same state in which Lucy had yielded to the vampire's blandishments. If we had had any doubts about the equation of violence and sex in the novel, this scene would dispel them: Dracula's own language conflates erotic desire and feeding; the mouth both kisses and consumes, the same organ gratifying two distinct hungers.

The encounter seems to "cure" Jonathan of his sexual desires (desires he will later pay for in the brain fever which sends him to his wedding an invalid). The text attributes his reaction to the fact that he now understands who, or rather, *what* the fatally beautiful creatures are, and thus sees them with horror rather than his earlier guilty fascination. "I am alone in the castle with those awful women. Faugh! Mina is a woman, and there is nought in common. They are devils of the Pit!" (53). His beloved, he insists, though a woman, has nothing in common with these creatures. He means, of course, that she does not have their evil capabilities—but neither, we notice, does she have their voluptuousness. He never records any erotic reaction to Mina at all, let alone one of this feverish intensity. In fact, since their marriage begins with her nursing him through his illness, Mina's relationship to her husband always seems more maternal than wifely. But in late-Victorian theory, that is as it should be. Marriage is designed to tame the sexual impulses of husbands; and as for wives, as Krafft-Ebing remarks, "Woman, if physically and mentally normal, and properly educated, has but little sensual desire. If it were otherwise, marriage and family life would be empty words."[32]

Victorian sexual theory also helps us to understand the difference between Lucy and Mina, to explain why Mina takes longer to succumb to the vampire count, and why she is able to resist more effectively than her friend. In the first place, while Lucy satisfies her own unconscious desires in yielding to Dracula, Mina's vulnerability results as much from the failures of others as her own weakness. It is no action of Mina's that allows the count access to her bedroom, but Renfield's betrayal in giving his master the necessary permission to enter the house. Further, her husband and her friends, who should be protecting her, instead become so obsessed with the fight against Dracula—a fight from which they deliberately, and with the best motives, exclude her—that they leave her too much alone. Solitude is a danger to her as it was to Jonathan; and while Mina has presumably had little personal experience of sexual desire, she has, we must remember, read Jonathan's journal in the process of transcribing it. That means she has read his description of his adventure with the three female vampires. Her own husband, then, in another sort of betrayal, has exposed Mina to his sexual fantasies.

Thus isolated and exposed, Mina's experience of marital sex, such as it has been, gives her no protection against the count's powers of sexual fascination. When she recognizes him in her bedroom, she is appalled but paralyzed, unable to respond or cry out as he bares her throat to refresh himself. Such paralysis is bad enough, but worse, to her bewilderment she discovers that, "strangely enough, I did not want to hinder him. I suppose it is a part of the horrible curse that such is [*sic*], when his touch is on his victim" (287). Dracula has drained not only her blood, but also her will to resist. He is, in sexual terms, more seducer than rapist. For a modern reader, this might lessen the crime, but for Victorians seduction would have been infinitely worse. In Victorian theory, it is sexual desire rather than sexual activity that is the true source of danger; and as Mina herself makes clear, she experiences desire under Dracula's attentions.

This explains why Mina's forehead is scarred by the Host, why she herself suffers such (to us disproportionate) agonies of guilt and self-revulsion. But once she is no longer isolated, once she is included in the community of her husband and their friends, she is able to resist desire, to exert her will against Dracula to help defeat him. Thus when he dies, the shameful scar disappears from her forehead. With help, Mina has conquered temptation and the dangers of degeneracy. It is this effort of will, the effort to conquer her own sexual imagination, that makes her worthy of the sacrifices of the others—that makes her worthy, in the end, of salvation.

What, then, has been achieved? By the end of the novel Lucy is dead, Quincey Morris is dead, Mina and Jonathan have both come close to death—or worse, to the death-in-life of the degeneracy which vampirism represents; but they have, after all, repented and are now stronger than ever. Dracula has been killed, and England and the world preserved. The fantastic element has been expelled, and we return to the safe, ordinary reality of the opening.

In fact, the novel ends quite abruptly, barely a full page after Dracula's death. In a brief note we are told that Mina and Jonathan have a son, that Seward and Gadalming are happily married (Lucy's role filled by other women), and that Van Helsing is now incorporated into the extended family. We also learn that the story we have just been told is, despite its elaborate detail and fundamentally documentary nature, unsupported by any original documents—nothing exists but Mina's typescript, which is hardly proof of the remarkable narrative we have just read. Thus we, the fictive audience, are left to accept or reject based purely on the internal evidence, and—since the danger is safely past—need not react at all if we choose.[33]

VI: *DRACULA* AND THE URBAN GOTHIC

But if comparatively little has happened in the world of the fictive audience, in the world of the actual audience Stoker's novel has accomplished a good deal. With Dracula's death, the "natural" superiority of Englishmen over the "lesser" races has been once again convincingly portrayed. More importantly, a number of profoundly disruptive elements have been symbolically expelled from society and the crumbling boundaries between certain key categories reaffirmed: between life and death, civilization and degeneracy, human and non-human, desire and loathing—all of which boundaries Dracula had blurred or violated. The even more fundamental boundary between self and other, which Dracula's ability to override his victims' willpower so terrifyingly challenges, is seen once again triumphant in Mina's recovered purity and self-control.

In *Sexuality and Its Discontents*, Jeffrey Weeks connects the development of sociology with the simultaneous development of sexology. As these two new disciplines struggled to define the "laws" of behavior in their respective realms, he argues, a powerful interdependency sprang up between them. At the same time as sexuality was being constituted as a key area of social relations, where it helped to define personal identity, sex as what Freud would soon call a "drive" came to be perceived as "a force outside, and set against society," as "part of the eternal battle of individual and society."[34] Thus sex is paradoxically seen as both social and anti-social; it helps to define individual identity while at the same time threatening the collective. No wonder, then, that sex is such an explosive issue for the late Victorians, for whom these two poles of identity had become so crucial and so fragile. (It may also help to explain why sex is still an explosive issue for us, their grandchildren, a hundred years later—apparently so different from them, but living in a society which, like theirs, balances precariously on the same two poles.)

The sex/society formulation, Weeks continues, "evokes and replays all the other great distinctions which attempt to explain the boundaries of animality and humanity"—like nature/culture, freedom/regulation—the "two rival absolutes."[35] As we have already seen, these are some of the central categories at play in *Dracula*. The outcome of the novel suggests Stoker was arguing that the solution to the late Victorian crisis lay in privileging society over sex, that in order to preserve the nation it was necessary to sacrifice some degree of personal freedom. That would explain the novel's insistent pattern of the many against the one, the community against the scapegoat; it might also help explain the novel's popularity at a time of imperialist fervor concealing deep anxieties about the future of the empire.

And it is the generic conventions of the fantastic that have made this resolution possible, by creating an imaginative way simultaneously to affirm and deny the reality of chosen cultural elements. The fantastic allows writers and readers to take those aspects of their own culture that are most emotionally charged, most disruptive, and identify them as monstrous—that is, as violations not just of human law but of the very nature of reality—so that society can be symbolically purged of its pollution.

However, *Dracula* is not merely fantastic; it is an example of the Urban Gothic, that modern version of the fantastic marked by its dependence on empiricism and the discourse of science. The difference can be seen most clearly by comparing *Dracula* to its immediate predecessor and reputed inspiration, Sheridan Le Fanu's *Carmilla* (1871). Le Fanu's story of a female (and lesbian) vampire is, in fact, quite powerful and subtle, but the tale is set in a remote country house in eighteenth-century Transylvania, whereas Stoker goes out of his way repeatedly to emphasize the modernity of his setting. For example (more or less at random): Van Helsing observes, "A year ago which of us would have received [i.e., believed] such a possibility, in the midst of our scientific, sceptical, matter-of-fact nineteenth century?" (266); or again, in "this enlightened age, when men believe not even what they see, the doubting of wise men would be [Dracula's] greatest strength" (321). In addition to such references, which could easily be multiplied, the band of heroes relies readily and matter-of-factly on modern technology like blood transfusions, typewriters, telegraphs, and Dr. Seward's "phonograph diary" (219).

But these are mere decorations on the surface of the text. More important, the approach of the characters to their tasks in each tale shows the same contrast. Carmilla is tracked to her lair and killed by reference to the past—her own history, and the traditional religious knowledge of the community, while Dracula is identified and defeated by painstaking investigation of his present actions. Dr. Van Helsing's knowledge of vampire lore eventually becomes essential, but it is of no use until Dracula can be conclusively identified as a vampire. Thus the most crucial event in *Dracula* occurs when Mina types up all the documents of the case (Jonathan's diary, Seward's records, her own correspondence with Lucy, newspaper clippings, even telegrams) and assembles them in chronological order—the order in which we read them. Only with chronology does narrative emerge; only then does a collection of data turn into a hypothesis. And, as in science, hypothesis is a necessary prelude to action. In other words, while *Carmilla* resembles a traditional ghost story, *Dracula* is constructed like that other form which comes into its own in the 1890s, the detective story.[36]

The implications of this difference are crucial. The ghost story, like the eighteenth-century Gothic to which it is closely related, usually finds its methods in the shared knowledge of the community, whether this means traditional religious approaches to the supernatural or the ancient remedies of the folk. In either case, the necessary knowledge is both implicit and communal. In the modern world, and therefore in the Urban Gothic, there is no implicit knowledge: everything must be tested and proved. A method for dealing with the supernatural must be created, drawing on the most powerful and prestigious tools at their disposal: the methods of science, shaped by a secular world view—paradoxically, the very world view that was initially overthrown by the fantastic intrusion.[37]

How are we to read this paradox, so central to the Urban Gothic? Is the primary effect to invalidate the supernatural, seeing it as an alien intruder in the modern world? Is it, on the contrary, to affirm the reality of the supernatural in the very act of expelling it? Or is it to demonstrate the efficacy of the scientific method in addressing any kind of crisis? I would argue instead that the central appeal of fantastic literature is that, like the violent scapegoat rituals it mimics, it allows its writers and readers simultaneously to acknowledge and deny those aspects of themselves and their world that they find most troubling—to see them both as part of the community and as available for sacrifice.

Douglas observes that one of the sources of ritual pollution is "the interplay of form and formlessness. Pollution dangers strike when form has been attacked."[38] Dracula is a perfect example of the "formless" attacking form (he is, after all, a shape-changer); but at the same time, our cultural experience of the novel suggests that, in creating his vampire count, Stoker has given to formlessness itself a form of continuing potency.

NOTES

Some of the research for this essay was done during an NEH Summer Seminar for College Teachers on "British Literature and Culture 1840–1900" given at Brown University in 1989. I am grateful to the NEH, to the seminar's directors, Profs. Roger Henkle (English) and L. Perry Curtis (History), and to my colleagues in the seminar for their advice and support.

1. Mary Douglas, *Purity and Danger: An Analysis of Concepts of Pollution and Taboo* (New York: Praeger, 1966), 4.

2. Jeffrey Weeks, *Sexuality and Its Discontents: Meanings, Myths, and Modern Sexualities* (London: Routledge and Kegan Paul, 1985), 178.

3. The most common positions are that *Dracula* is either about male sexuality threatening passive female innocence, or about the need to control rampant female sexuality. But it has also been argued that the novel is about covert homoerotic desire displaced onto women, and even that all the sex in the book is sadomasochistic. For a convenient collection of the best recent criticism of *Dracula*, see Margaret L. Carter, *The Vampire and the Critics* (Ann Arbor: UMI Research Press, 1988). For some non-psychological readings of the novel, see Nina Auerbach, *Woman and the Demon: The Life of a Victorian Myth* (Cambridge: Harvard Univ. Press, 1982), and Elaine Showalter, *Sexual Anarchy: Gender and Culture at the Fin de Siècle* (New York: Viking Penguin, 1990).

4. For example: Rosa Campbell Praed, *Affinities: A Romance of Today* (1885); Rider Haggard, *She* (1887); Arthur Conan Doyle, *The Parasite* (1894); Richard Marsh, *The Beetle* (1897); Somerset Maugham, *The Magician* (1907); Algernon Blackwood, "The Camp of the Dog" in *John Silence, Physician Extraordinaire* (1908); Sax Rohmer, *The Brood of the Witch-Queen* (1918); Jessie Kerruish, *The Undying Monster* (1922).

5. Tzvetan Todorov, *The Fantastic: A Structural Approach to a Literary Genre*, trans. Richard Howard (Ithaca: Cornell Univ. Press, 1975); Andrzej Zgorzelski, "Is Science Fiction a Genre of Fantastic Literature?" *Science-Fiction Studies* 6 (1979): 289 (emphasis in original). Todorov defines the fantastic in relation to two other genres, the "uncanny" and the "marvellous." In a realistic world—that is, a textual world modeled on the world we inhabit—an event occurs that appears to violate the laws of this world. The character who experiences this seemingly abnormal event (and, more importantly, the reader of the text) must choose between two explanations: either the event is a product of illusion, or imagination, or deliberate deception—in which case the familiar laws remain intact (and the text is an example of the uncanny); or else the event has genuinely occurred,

is a part of reality, in which case the laws must be modified to allow for the existence of, say, ghosts or the Devil. In that case, the text belongs to the category of the marvellous. If, on the other hand, it is impossible for character or reader to decide whether or not the event is genuine, the text is, by Todorov's definition, fantastic. "The fantastic is that *hesitation* experienced by a person who knows only the laws of nature, confronting an *apparently supernatural* event" (25; emphasis added). The problem with Todorov's definition is that most texts do actually commit themselves about the event; thus very few texts that we normally think of as fantastic end up qualifying as such by Todorov's definition. For a more extended discussion of Zgorzelski's definition and its implications, see Kathleen L. Spencer, "Naturalizing the Fantastic: Narrative Technique in the Novels of Charles Williams," *Extrapolation* 28 (1987): 62–74.

6. Henry James, "Miss Braddon," *The Nation*, 9 Nov. 1865, 593–94; reprinted in *Notes and Reviews* (Cambridge: Dunster House, 1921), 110. Jane Austen makes a similar point in *Northanger Abbey*, contrasting the imaginary horrors in th. Gothic novels her heroine is so fond of reading with the more mundane but very real cruelties she finds practiced in her own modern, ordinary England.

7. For a fuller discussion of this material, see George Kenneth Graham, *English Criticism of the Novel 1865–1900* (Oxford: Clarendon, 1965), 51–109. For a more traditional (that is, judgmental) treatment of the romance-realism debate see Lionel Stevenson, *The English Novel: A Panorama* (Boston: Houghton Mifflin, 1960) and John Halperin, "The Theory of the Novel: A Critical Introduction" in *The Theory of the Novel: New Essays*, ed. John Halperin (London, New York: Oxford Univ. Press, 1974), 3–22. For the patriotic argument for rejecting naturalism, see William C. Frierson, "The English Controversy Over Realism in Fiction 1885–1895," *PMLA* 43 (1928): 533–50.

8. Cited in Sir Charles Mallett, *Anthony Hope and His Books* (London: Hutchinson, 1935), 114.

9. See, for example: R. L. Stevenson, "A Gossip on Romance," *Longman's Magazine* 1 (November 1882): 69–79; Stevenson, "A Humble Remonstrance," *Longman's Magazine* 5 (December 1884): 139–47; H. Rider Haggard, "About Fiction," *Contemporary Review* 51 (February 1887): 172–80; Andrew Lang, "Realism and Romance," *Contemporary Review* 52 (1887): 683–93; George Saintsbury, "The Present State of the Novel.I," *Fortnightly Review*, n.s., 48 (September 1887): 410–17; "The Present State of the Novel.II," *Fortnightly Review*, n.s., 49 (January 1888): 112–23; and Hall Caine, "The New Watchwords of Fiction," *Contemporary Review* 57 (April 1890): 479–88.

10. For example, Marie Corelli, George Griffith, Guy Boothby, William Le Queux, Sax Rohmer.

11. For a fuller discussion of the late Victorian fascination with the far reaches of empire, see Patrick Brantlinger, *Rule of Darkness: British Literature and Imperialism, 1839–1914* (Ithaca: Cornell Univ. Press, 1988). Though the futuristic plot settings of some of these novels may make them sound very much like science fiction, they do not as a rule qualify as such by any reasonably rigorous criteria, not even the novels set on other planets. Their generic affiliations are rather with the imaginary voyage and the utopia, which are quite different traditions. For a survey of these texts and an alternate view of their genre, see Darko Suvin, *Victorian Science Fiction in the UK: The Discourses of Knowledge and Power* (Boston: G. K. Hall, 1983). For a brief description of the occult revival, see Kathleen L. Spencer, "The Urban Gothic In British Fantastic Fiction 1880–1930" (Ph.D. diss., University of California, Los Angeles, 1987), 34–98. For more detail, see John J. Cerullo, *The Secularization of the Soul: Psychical Research in Modern Britain* (Philadelphia: Institute for the Study of Human Issues, 1982); Frank Miller Turner, *Between Science and Religion* (New Haven: Yale Univ. Press, 1974); Alan Gauld, *The Founders of Psychical Research* (New York: Schocken Books, 1968); and Ellic Howe, *Magicians of the Golden Dawn: A Documentary History of a Magical Order 1887–1923* (London: Routledge and Kegan Paul, 1972).

12. Anthony Giddens, *A Contemporary Critique of Historical Materialism, Vol. I: Power, Property, and the State* (Berkeley: Univ. of California Press, 1981), 194.

13. George W. Stocking, Jr., *Race, Culture, and Evolution: Essays in the History of Anthropology* (London: Collier-Macmillan, 1968), 121.

14. For a discussion of the East End and degeneracy, see Gareth Steadman Jones, *Outcast London: A Study in the Relationships Between Classes in Victorian Society* (Oxford: Clarendon, 1971), 149.

15. For discussions of this point, see (for example) Mary Poovey, *Uneven Developments: The Ideological Work of Gender in Mid-Victorian England* (Chicago: Univ. of Chicago Press, 1988), and Elaine Showalter, *The Female Malady: Women, Madness, and English Culture 1830–1980*, 2nd ed. (New York: Penguin, 1987). While the female role as constituted in theory was quite rigid, in practice both working-class and aristocratic women experienced some relaxation of its rigors, especially in economic and (therefore?) in sexual activities: aristocrats, because of the traditional privileges of their class and the sense that their lives are not bound by the same rules as everyone else; and working-class women, because they were needed in the paid work force by both their families and their employers.

16. Jenni Calder, *The Victorian and Edwardian Home* (London: Batsford, 1977), 132.

17. 3 Hansard, CXLV, 800. Quoted by Lee Holcombe, "Victorian Wives and Property: Reform of the Married Women's Property Law, 1857–1882" in *A Widening Sphere: Changing Roles of Victorian Women*, ed. Martha Vicinus (Bloomington: Indiana Univ. Press, 1977), 12. Holcombe's article as a whole (3–28) is an illuminating and scholarly discussion of the struggle of Victorian wives to reform property laws.

18. For detailed discussions of the Cleveland Street brothel, see H. Montgomery Hyde, *The Cleveland Street Scandal* (New York: Coward, McCann, and Geoghagan, 1976), and Colin Simpson et al., *The Cleveland Street Affair* (Boston: Little, Brown, 1976).

19. For a discussion of the way the Wilde trial helped turn "homosexual" from an adjective describing certain kinds of behaviors into a noun indicating a kind of person and the significance of this change for the subsequent history of homosexuality, see Jeffrey Weeks, *Sex, Politics, and Society: The Regulation of Sexuality Since 1800* (London: Longman, 1981). To give one small example of the trial's effect on the general cultural atmosphere (beyond the terror it struck in the hearts of homosexuals): in the late 1880s and early '90s, there had been an explosion of novels treating sympathetically such previously untouchable subjects as female sexuality, free love, and fallen women. Thomas Hardy's *Tess of the D'Urbervilles* (1891), for example, was received not without controversy, certainly, but with a good bit of support for Hardy's sympathetic treatment of Tess. But *Jude the Obscure*, published in 1896 after Wilde's public disgrace, was greeted with such a firestorm of disapproval that Hardy swore off writing fiction forever (for this argument, see Eric Trudgill, *Madonnas and Magdalenes: The Origins and Development of Victorian Sexual Attitudes*, [London: Heinemann, 1976]). *Dracula*, published in 1897, reached the public at the height of this antisexual hysteria; it should not surprise us to find reflections of this mood in such a popular text—meaning both one that was addressed to a less sophisticated audience and one that was very widely read at the time.

20. In this same decade, the "unnaturalness" of homosexuality was also being challenged by Havelock Ellis, along with several prominent apologists like Edward Carpenter and John Addington Symonds who in the 1890s published books arguing that homosexuals were not "failed" or "unnatural" men or women but were instead members of a third or "intermediate" sex (Ellis, who was married to a lesbian, was the first to write sympathetically about lesbianism). In the early editions of *Psychopathia Sexualis*, Richard von Krafft-Ebing argued that all homosexual behavior was degenerate, but after the turn of the century he softens this judgment, concluding that *some* homosexuals indeed seemed to be "born" not "made,"—in his words, "congenital." See, for example, the lengthy discussion of "Homosexual Feeling as an Abnormal Congenital Manifestation" (356–90). He explores

the available explanations of "sexual inversion" from the traditional "vice" to the more "scientific" cause, excessive and/or early masturbation, and finally concludes that in some cases an explanation based on physiological factors—something in the structure of the brain, something therefore not subject to the will of the "invert"—rather than the old medico-moral explanation of "willful indulgence in depravity," is the only logical conclusion. He does not altogether abandon degeneracy as an explanation even in these cases, arguing that "In fact, in all cases of sexual inversion, a taint *of a hereditary character* may be established"; but he admits that "What causes produce this factor of taint and its activity is a question which cannot be well answered by science in its present stage" (370; emphasis added). By allowing for the possibility of inherited tendencies to degeneracy, Krafft-Ebing simultaneously takes back and lets stand his uneasy conclusion that some homosexuals do not seem to be morally responsible for their sexual orientation. (Richard von Krafft-Ebing, *Psychopathia Sexualis: A Medico-Forensic Study*, Latin trans. Harry E. Wedeck [New York: G. P. Putnam's Sons, 1965]. This edition, with an introduction by Ernest Van Den Haag, is described as "The first unexpurgated edition, with the Latin texts translated into English for the first time" by Dr. Wedeck, but does not specify who translated the German parts of the text. I suspect this edition is based on the translation of the 12th German edition by F. J. Rebman published in 1934 by the Physicians and Surgeons Book Company, but cannot verify my suspicion at this time.)

21. Ludmilla Jordanova, "Natural Facts: An Historical Perspective on Science and Reality" in *Nature, Culture, and Gender*, ed. Carol MacCormack and Marilyn Strathern (Cambridge: Cambridge Univ. Press, 1980), 44.

22. The following discussion is drawn primarily from Mary Douglas's *Natural Symbols: Explorations in Cosmology* (New York: Random House, 1972).

23. For other examples of modern "witchcraft" societies, consider Nazi Germany and McCarthy-era America. Indeed, the current struggle between social liberals and religious fundamentalists over issues like abortion and pornography manifests many of the same dynamics.

24. René Girard, *Violence and the Sacred*, trans. Patrick Gregory (Baltimore: Johns Hopkins Univ. Press, 1977), 13. Interestingly enough, despite the fact that in many cultures women are not afforded full status, they are seldom chosen as surrogate victims. Girard speculates that because a married woman retains ties with her parents' social group as well as her husband's, to sacrifice her would be to run the risk of one group or the other interpreting the sacrifice as "an act of murder committing it to a reciprocal act of revenge," and so not ending the communal violence, but increasing it (13).

25. Bram Stoker, *Dracula* (Oxford: Oxford Univ. Press, 1983), 59. All further citations will be to this text. Showalter in *Sexual Anarchy* (note 3),

which I did not see until after this essay was submitted, makes the same essential point about Lucy.

26. Simon Williams, analyzing Charles Nodier's play, *Vampire* (1820), part of the response to Polidori's *The Vampyre* (1819), finds a very similar pattern. "Sexual desire is exhibited as supernatural possession that causes the heroine to wander deliriously in caverns and shady places in search of her demon lover. But once she returns to consciousness, she is totally unaware of the dark forces that have briefly taken over her body" ("Theatre and Degeneration: Subversion and Sexuality," in *Degeneration: The Dark Side of Progress*, ed. J. Edward Chamberlin and Sander L. Gilman [New York: Columbia Univ. Press, 1985], 246). The terms "conscious" and "unconscious" may seem anachronistic, but the English had casually accepted the idea of an unconscious mind by the latter part of the nineteenth century; the idea is expounded in a number of different places in the last two decades. It was not the concept of the unconscious that made Freud so shocking, but his notion of what kinds of material the unconscious contained. As Nina Auerbach (note 3) points out, Stoker might well have known of Freud by the time he wrote *Dracula*, since F. W. Myers had presented a lecture to the Society for Psychical Research on Freud and Breuer's work with hysterics in 1893; and in the novel itself Dr. Seward mentions Charcot, Freud's teacher (22–23).

27. Most critics discuss this scene as symbolic of sexual intercourse and orgasm, even going so far in one case as to liken it to the "painful deflowering of a virgin, which Lucy still is" (C. F. Bentley, "The Monster in the Bedroom: Sexual Symbolism in Bram Stoker's *Dracula*," *Literature and Psychology* 22 [1972]: 31). While I recognize the elements of the scene that make it possible to draw the parallel, what most strikes me in the description (and, I suspect, most women readers) is the violence—which is, because of the religious overtones of the scene, weirdly impersonal. Indeed, it is rather alarming to me to think that this scene can be read so easily, and apparently without qualms or qualifiers, as an image of sexual intercourse. What does such a reading suggest about our culture's confusion of sex and violence?

28. Girard (note 24), 161.

29. This popular disapproval of the aristocracy became particularly apparent after the publication of Sir Francis Galton's *Hereditary Genius* in 1869, which attacked both inherited wealth and the titled nobility.

30. For a detailed discussion of Dracula as Lombroso's "criminal man," see Ernest Fontana, "Lombroso's Criminal Man and Stoker's *Dracula*," in Carter (note 3), 159–66. For a more thorough examination of the place of degeneracy theory in late Victorian thinking, see Chamberlin and Gilman (note 26).

31. Douglas (note 1), 97. Richard Sennett and Michael Foucault, "Sexuality and Solitude," in *Humanities in Review* 1, ed. Sennett et al. (New York: Cambridge Univ. Press, 1982), 4.

32. Krafft-Ebing (note 20), 42. Not all Victorian doctors agreed with this, but it does seem to have been a majority opinion, expressed categorically, publically, and often. Poovey in *Uneven Developments* (note 15) offers the clearest explanation of the thinking behind what now seems a ludicrous position. Victorian doctors knew so little about female physiology, she observes, that the only model they had for sexual response was the familiar male tumescence/ejaculation sequence. Failing to find this sequence in women, they concluded that women normally did not experience orgasm. Of course, this does not explain Krafft-Ebing's value judgment about the incompatibility of female sexual desire with marriage and family life; that, after all, is a matter of culture, not science. Nonetheless, Poovey's observation does give us a welcome alternative to the reductive explanation of "sexism" as to how otherwise intelligent men could arrive at such absurd conclusions.

33. This detail is characteristic of fantastic texts, that finally we are left with just the testament itself, and no "external" proofs.

34. Weeks (note 2), 81.

35. Weeks, 97.

36. Rather than pointing to *Carmilla*, I think that Stoker's most important literary source is Polidori's *The Vampyre* (1819), or more likely (since Stoker was a theatrical man) one of its many dramatic redactions. Polidori's text creates a modern fantastic effect, deriving its potency from the device of bringing his nobleman/vampire into the city of London—seventy-five years before Stoker does the same thing.

37. One way to distinguish between the traditional ghost story and the Urban Gothic is that the ghost story, although genuinely fantastic, is much closer in tone to the original Gothic. In addition, ghosts generally have quite a limited repertory of objects, motives, and behaviors: to get revenge, to make restitution, to finish an important task left incomplete at death, to warn the living (generally family members or descendants), or to reenact endlessly the crucial event of their lives (as in Yeats' "Purgatory"). In the Urban Gothic, the supernatural powers have a much broader scope for action.

38. Douglas (note 1), 104.

JENNIFER WICKE

Vampiric Typewriting: Dracula *and its Media*

In the Introduction to the *Grundrisse* Marx asks, thinking about the relation of Greek art to the present day: "What chance has Vulcan against Roberts & Co., Jupiter against the lightning-rod and Hermes against the Credit-Mobilier? All mythology overcomes and dominates and shapes the forces of nature ... it therefore vanishes with the advent of real mastery over them. What becomes of Fama alongside Printing House Square?"[1] The incongruity—and mastery—of *Dracula* lies in its willingness to set the mythological, Gothic, medieval mystery of Count Dracula squarely in the midst of Printing House Square. The *Grundrisse* is Marx's complex meditation on the intertwined fates of production, consumption and distribution, prefaced by these worries about the place of the aesthetic in the modern socioeconomic landscape. Within its novelistic form, *Dracula* too could be said to pose and to enact the occultation of those three processes, by its privileging of consumption, which subsumes the other two. This engorgement is staged by the collision of ancient mythologies with contemporary modes of production.

Miss Mina Murray writes to Miss Lucy Westenra about her current preoccupations: "I have been working very hard lately, because I want to keep up with Jonathan's studies, and I have been practicing shorthand very assiduously. When we are married I shall be able to be very useful to

From *ELH* 59 (1992): 467-493.

Jonathan, and if I can stenograph well enough I can take down what he wants to say in this way and write it out for him on the typewriter, which I am also practicing very hard. He and I sometimes write letters in shorthand, and he is keeping a stenographic journal of his travels abroad."[2] While such girlish pursuits, if slavishly dutiful, scarcely seem ominous, it is Mina's very prowess with the typewriter that brings down Dracula on unsuspecting British necks, even including her very own. In what follows I want to propose that as radically different as the sexy act of vamping and such prosaic labor on the typewriter appear, there are underlying ties between them that can ultimately make sense of the oxymoron of vampiric typewriting. The argument will turn attention to the technologies that underpin vampirism, making for the dizzy contradictions of this book, and permitting it to be read as the first great *modern* novel in British literature. In doing so, I will be concentrating on the shabby, dusty corners of *Dracula*, inspecting its pockets for lint rather than examining its more delicious excesses, and putting pressure on the aspects of *Dracula* that have received less attention because they, like practicing shorthand, don't immediately seem as pleasurable. *Dracula* cannot help but be a heady cocktail, even under inauspiciously stringent critical circumstances, and part of what I hope to show in so pursuing its media are its connections to the everyday life of typewriters, neon, advertisement and neoimperialism we are still living today. To drain *Dracula* of some of its obvious terrors may help to highlight the more banal terrors of modern life.

Franco Moretti bifurcates his stimulating analysis of *Dracula*: one strand follows a Marxist allegorical path, examining the abstract fears aroused by the specter of monopoly capital rising up in Britain's free trade society, and centering on Count Dracula as the metaphoric instantiation of monopoly capital gone wild in its eerie global perambulations; his second appraisal locates Dracula's terror, rather unsurprisingly, in the realm of eros, and advances the notion that the root fear vampirism expresses is the child's ambivalent relation to its mother, and the psychosexual repressions that ambivalence exacts. Both vectors are vigorously and excellently argued, but my concern here is with Moretti's ultimate acknowledgment that these are discrete analyses: "I do not propose here to reconstruct the many missing links that might connect socio-economic structures and sexual-psychological structures in a single conceptual chain. Nor can I say whether this undertaking ... is really possible. I would merely like to explain the two reasons that—in this specific case—persuaded me to use such different methodologies ... Marxism and psychoanalysis thus converge in defining the function of this literature: to take up within itself determinate fears in order to present them in a form different from their real one ..."[3] These are two disparate fears, then, with only overdetermination to account for their co-presence. The theoretical split Moretti chooses to elide is just as fraught as he describes it to be; I think it is possible, however, to find a way of addressing this text without accepting such hermetically sealed compartments of analysis. There can be more traffic across these divides; my choice of *Dracula* rests on a desire to investigate the uncoupled chain of materialist and psychosexual readings, because I see *Dracula* lodged at the site of that difficulty, at a crux that marks the modernist divide for both theory and literature. It is necessary to juggle several balls in the air at once, to force a collision between these vocabularies. What causes Moretti's economic and sexual allegories to diverge so thoroughly, in my view, is the paradoxical absence of the category of consumption; what I will work through here is the uneasy status of consumption as it is poised between two seemingly exclusionary vocabularies that nonetheless intersect (often invisibly) precisely there.

In considering *Dracula*, I am turning the text to face forward into the twentieth century, rather than assessing its status as Victorian mythography, since what I want to give is a reading that opens up into a thesis about the modernity we can then read off the wildly voluptuous, and even Medusan, *volte face* thereby revealed. This is not to discount the probing and incisive readings that do annex *Dracula* to its very real Victorian contexts, but rather to shift the agenda in critical terms to the work that the text can do as a liminal modernist artifact, an exemplary text that then lies hauntingly behind the uncanny creations of modernism, at the borders of what is accepted as "high modernism," the high art tradition of its literature.[4] The vampirism this text articulates is crucial to the dynamics of modernity, as well as to giving a name to our current theoretical predicaments. *Dracula* is not a coherent text; it refracts hysterical images of modernity. One could call it a chaotic reaction-formation in advance of modernism, wildly taking on the imprintings of mass culture.

To begin by eliminating all the suspense of my own theoretical trajectory: the social force most analogous to Count Dracula's as depicted in the novel is none other than mass culture, the developing technologies of the media in its many forms, as mass transport, tourism, photography and lithography in image production, and mass-produced narrative. To take seriously the status of mass culture in an incipiently mass cultural artifact is to have a privileged vantage on the dislocations and transformations it occasions, especially because *Dracula* has been so successful in hiding the pervasiveness of the mass cultural within itself, foregrounding instead its exotic otherness.

What has been little remarked about the structure of *Dracula* is precisely how its narrative is ostensibly produced, its means of production. A narrative patchwork made up out of the combined journal entries, letters, professional records and newspaper clippings that the doughty band of vampire hunters had separately written or collected, it is then collated and typed by the industrious Mina, wife of the first vampire target and ultimately a quasi-vampire herself.[5] The multiplicity of narrative viewpoints has been well discussed, but the crucial fact is that all of these narrative pieces eventually comprising the manuscript we are said to have in our hands emanate from radically dissimilar and even state-of-the-art media forms. *Dracula*, draped in all its feudalism and medieval gore, is textually completely au courant. Nineteenth-century diaristic and epistolary effusion is invaded by cutting edge technology, in a transformation of the generic materials of the text into a motley fusion of speech and writing, recording and transcribing, image and typography.

Dr. Seward, for example, the young alienist who operates the private insane asylum so fortuitously located next to Count Dracula's London property, produces his voluminous journal not by writing it, but by recording his own words on gramophone records, which then must be transcribed. Since the gramophone is in 1897 an extremely recently invented device, even Dr. Seward is confused by some of its properties; his worst realization is that in order to find some important gem of recorded insight, he will have to listen to all the records again.[6] Never fear, since the incomparable Madame Mina offers to transcribe all the cylinders to typewritten form after she has listened to them, realizing their value as part of the puzzle of tracking the vampire. "I put the forked metal to my ears and listened," she writes. And later, "that is a wonderful machine, but it is cruelly true ... No one must hear them (his words) spoken ever again! I have copied out the words on my typewriter." Despite the apparent loss of "aura," in Benjamin's sense, ostensibly found in the mechanical reproduction of Seward's diary, what Mina is struck by is the latent emotional power of the recorded voice, whose spectacular emotion the typewriter can strip away. Her transcription of Dr. Seward's wax cylinders occurs mid-way in the text, when the search for Dracula in London is begun in earnest. What that timing implies is that all Dr. Seward's previous entries, and there are many, are recordings, as it were, voicings coded in the most up-to-date inscription, speaking to us from out of the text. There is ample textual confusion swirling about this point, and much inconsistency, since Dr. Seward's diary includes abbreviations and chemical formulas that do not have meaning "orally"; moreover, when the machine is used by others, there is a vampiric exchange involved—a chapter title tells us, "Dr. Seward's Phonograph Diary, spoken by Van Helsing." The burden this mode of production puts on narration is expressed when Dr. Seward reacts to hearing the burial service read over Mina, a prophylactic act in case they have to kill her. "I—I cannot go on—words—and—v-voice—fail m-me!" (352). Such doughty sentimentality cannot mask the fact that Seward's diary constitutes the immaterialization of a voice, a technologized zone of the novel, inserted at a historical point where phonography was not widespread, because still quite expensive, but indicative of things to come. We are not dealing here with pure speech in opposition to writing, but instead with speech already colonized, or vampirized, by mass mediation.

The other materials forming the narrative's typed body are equally mass-culturally produced. Jonathan Harker's journal, which begins the novel and recounts the fateful discovery of Count Dracula as a vampire, only to have the memory of this insupportable revelation wiped out by a bout of brain fever, is "actually" a document in stenographic form, later itself uncoded by Mina's act of typewriting. Stenography is a fortuitous code for Jonathan, since Dracula, who seems to know everything else, does not take shorthand, and doesn't confiscate the journal, an act that would deprive us of the first-hand frisson of narrative in progress. We as readers don't see on the page the little swirls and abbreviations we might expect from a manuscript in shorthand, since that would keep us from reading; it would produce cognitive dissonance for readers to be reminded that the terrifying narrative his diary unfolds is meant to be inscribed in that elliptical, bureaucratized form of writing known as shorthand. What, after all, is the stenographic version of "kiss me with those red lips," Jonathan's hot inner monologue as he lies swooning on the couch surrounded by his version of Dracula's angels? Shorthand may seem to fall innocently outside the sphere of mass cultural media, but in fact it participates in one of the most thoroughgoing transformations of cultural labor of the twentieth-century, the rationalization (in Weber's sense) of the procedures of bureaucracy and business, the feminization of the clerical work force, the standardization of mass business writing. The modern office is very far afield from Transylvania, the doomed castle, and the ghastly doings Jonathan experiences there, but shorthand is utterly material to the ramifications of vampirism. Vampirism springs up, or takes command, at the behest of shorthand. Although the pages we open to start our reading of the book look like any printed pages, there is a crucial sense in which we are inducted into Count Dracula lore by the insinuation of this invisible, or translated, stenography. This submerged writing is the modern, or mass cultural, cryptogram; the linkage of this mode of abbreviated writing with the consumption process is made apparent by our willingness to invest these abbreviations with the fully-fleshed body of typed and printed writing. Shorthand flows through us, as readers, to be transubstantiated as modern, indeterminate, writing.

Jonathan has begun his journey to that foreboding place as a tourist of sorts; the impressions he jots down with most relish initially are the recipes for strange foods he would like Mina to try—the "national dishes," as he calls them: "(*Mem.*, get recipe for Mina)" (1). He first tastes a chicken dish made with red pepper that, insidiously enough, makes him thirsty; even the red peppers are suspicious in a text with such a fixed color scheme of red and white. Count Dracula, of course, has a national dish as well, only it is comprised of the bodies not yet belonging to his nation, and Mina, who was going to get the chance to whip up the national dish of the Carpathians, is to become his food for thought. The local color Jonathan drinks in, as recipes and customs and costumes, has the form of regularized tourism; Dracula's castle becomes an unwonted departure from the Transylvanian Baedeker. This may be the point at which to broach the larger argument that will dog the more local one I am making. I am trying to give a reading of the society of consumption and its refraction in *Dracula*, but that society rests on, is impossible without, the imperial economy. It is overly glib to talk about commodity culture without this insistent awareness; what particularly draws me to *Dracula*, and what makes it a modern text, is the embeddedness there of consumption, gender, and empire. Jonathan's travels are made not to a specific British colonial or imperial possession, but to a place with a dense history of conquest and appropriation. He is funneled into this history by means of the accoutrements of modern travel and leisure; Jonathan, who is on business, is nonetheless a tourist *manqué*. In this instance too, Count Dracula and his extraordinary logic of production are encountered through the lens of mass cultural preoccupations and techniques.

Jonathan bears a gift of sorts for Dracula, a set of Kodak pictures of the British house the latter is interested in purchasing, although Dracula in fact has another motive for having brought the rather drab young law clerk so far from England: he wants to borrow his speech, to learn English perfectly from his captive, Harker Jonathan, as he occasionally slips in addressing him. The presence of the Kodak camera in the midst of such goings on is unexpected and yet far from accidental. Photography joins the list of new cultural techniques or processes juxtaposed with the story of the medieval aristocratic vampire, but the Kodak snapshot camera so many people were wielding at the time is really also a celluloid analog of vampirism in action, the extraction out of an essence in an act of consumption. For a time at the turn of the century, "kodak" meant eye-witness proof; a testimony to the accuracy of Joseph Conrad's portrayal of circumstances in the Belgian Congo was headed "A Kodak on the Congo." The photographic evidence Jonathan brings to Count Dracula is also a talismanic offering, a simulacrum of the communion wafer Professor Van Helsing will put to Mina's forehead with such disastrously scarring results. In the latter case, the alembic contamination of vampire blood produces the "image" of vampirism as a red mark on white skin; photography makes its images in a similarly alchemical, if less liturgical, fashion. Jonathan Harker and Count Dracula come into a relation of exchange with one another through the mediation of the photographic image; more than that, the untoward aspects of vampirism are first signaled by the mention of the Kodak, which precedes the Count's version of vampirism by several pages. Both the history of photography as a domestic practice, as well as photography's connection to ethnography and travel, are summoned up textually by Jonathan's kodaks. Even the subsequent descriptions of what the Count looks like are altered by these initial references to photography, since his frightful looks bear such resemblance to the photographically cataloged "deviants" of Lombroso and others, and his quaint alterity seems to cry out for immortalization by the National Geographic (that is, photographic) touch. It is possible to speculate that if a vampire's image cannot be captured in a mirror, photographs of a vampire might prove equally disappointing. That scary absence from the sphere of the photographable shunts the anxiety back onto vampirism itself: vampirism as a stand-in for the uncanny procedures of modern life.

The consumption of journalism's anonymous textuality marks the book's dialectic with mass culture as well. Large sections of the putatively typewritten manuscript derive from newspaper articles salvaged by the haggard participants in this dark tale—a reader is asked to imagine either that Mina's transcript has redundantly retyped the newsprint, or that the newspaper pieces are literally collated with those typewritten pages, a collage or bricolage of versions of print. Mina, for example, preserves the newspaper accounts of the shipwreck that, it later emerges, has brought Dracula to Britain's shores, there to wreak his havoc on Lucy Westenra, who has already begun to go into an insomniac decline. These extensive mass-mediated narrations are uncannily inserted amongst the other, purportedly "first-hand" reports of Jonathan, Mina, Lucy, Dr. Seward and Professor Van Helsing. Clearly there is a pragmatic narrative reason for this, since otherwise the exposition of such events would be highly suspect—how would Mina on her own have managed to gather the deceased ship captain's log and find out about the mysterious cargo of boxes of earth the tragic ship carried? Beyond textual mechanics, however, lies the more intriguing fact that the anonymously-authored newspaper reports are coextensive with, and equally authoritative as, the other voices of the text. The text's action absolutely depends on the inclusion of mass-produced testimony; it absorbs these extraneous pieces within itself just as Dracula assimilates the life-blood of his victims. Even at the narrative level *Dracula* requires an immersion into mass-cultural discourse; its singular voices, however technologically-assisted, are in themselves not sufficient to exorcise an event which is unfolding at the level of collective consumption.

The transmogrification of the narrative's nominal events into mass cultural shards reaches its height when the posthumous whereabouts of Lucy Westenra, now a vampire in earnest, are revealed to the alert Professor Van Helsing and Dr. Seward by her mass-cultural incarnation as the "bloofer lady" of tabloid fame. Lucy has been preying on the lower-class children of London in her role as un-dead, stalking them after dark in the large London parks where they are left unaccountably alone. Her upper-middle class beauty is so miraculous to these waifs that she has achieved legendary status and a mass-cultural name. Without her tabloidization the men would have no chance to eliminate her with their ritualistic objects that can succeed in exorcising her—neck-laces of garlic, doughy paste made up of communion wafers, stakes driven through the heart. As much as Lucy is taken up into the pantheon of Dracula's girls ("your girls that you love are mine"), she is also become currency within mass culture, where she circulates in the mass blood stream with a delicious thrill as the "bloofer lady." Lucy becomes an object of the mass press simultaneously with her assimilation into the vampiric fold; the two phenomena are intertwined in the logic of this vampirism. Unless and until Lucy is commoditized out over an adoring, and titillated, public by virtue of her exciting vampiric identity, she cannot be said to have consummated that identity in the terms of the text. While her vamping by Count Dracula precedes her "bloofer lady" role and indeed causes it, the un-dead Lucy is similarly vamped by the press, and vamps all those who come under her thrall by just reading about her in the morning newspaper. *Dracula* does not make distinctions among these consuming ontologies.

Other peculiar newspaper moments in the text include the Pall Mall Gazette account of a zookeeper whose wolf has escaped. We as readers are aware that Dracula has taken over its body for a night of rampaging, but the newspaper story is excitedly fixated on the raffish Cockney persona of the zookeeper, and on including his diction in the piece about this strange disappearance. Here as elsewhere the text pauses for a sustained entry into mass cultural territory; in this case there is not even the excuse of plot description, just the need to filter the vampiric through the mesh of a mediated response. Inclusion of the newspaper story also keeps up the pressure on the distinction between speech and writing that so fissures the text, because the point of the article seems as much to be transcribing the loquacious dialect of the zookeeper as adding to anyone's knowledge of the habits of Dracula. The newspaper page serves as a theater for the staging of class differences when its "standard" written English can erupt with the quoted, vigorous orality of lower-class modes of speech. Lucy breaks the charmed circle of class by becoming a twilight apparition of interest to all classes, as they read about her in the newspaper. The zookeeper perhaps occupies so much textual space in *Dracula* because vampirization, or consumption, originally seems to threaten class distinctions.

A final irony in a novel so deranged by the mass voice of journalism is the fact that the band of fearless vampire killers manages to keep any notice of vampirism out of the papers, reserving that for its own "truthful" pages; the mass cultural forms skirt the knowledge of Dracula but never come to be in possession of it—in my argument, because *Dracula* himself is an articulation of, a figuration for, that same mass culture, as a consequence supervening any of its individual media, which are shown to be limited in scope unless taken together. Dracula's individual powers all have their analogue in the field of the mass cultural; he comprises the techniques of consumption.

Consider all the media technologies the novel so incessantly displays and names: the telegraph that figures so largely in the communicative strategies that allow the band to defeat Dracula is an equivalent to the telepathic, telekinetic communication Dracula is able to have with Mina after sealing her into his race with her enforced drinking of his blood. The phonographic records Dr. Seward uses are the reproduction of a voice, of a being, without any body needing to be present, just as Dracula can insinuate himself as a voice into the heads of his followers, or call them from afar. The Kodak camera captures an image and then allows it to be moved elsewhere, freezing a moment of temporality and sending it across space, in a parallel to Dracula's insubstantiality and his vitiation of temporality. Like such images, he continues to circulate even when separated from his source; in other words, his blood can circulate and have its drastic effects even when he is not bodily present. Dracula also vitiates space, of course, and in this shares the very ubiquity of the mass media: advertising's anticipation of its readers into all the corners and matchbooks of their lives, the mass ceremonial of the press, a daily bestseller that has no shelf life and must be consumed immediately. Mass culture is protean, with the same horrific propensity to mutate that also defines Dracula's anarchic power, as he becomes a bat or a white mist at will. Even the subway, the Underground used by Mina and Dr. Seward in the novel, has its fearsome vampiric echoes, since like Dracula the subway uses an underground place for transport across space, a subterranean vault encrypted by modern transportation.

When Madame Mina, "pearl among women," provides the typescript that resolves the incommensurabilities of the assorted documents, phonographic records and so on, she is able to do this because, as she tells Dr. Seward with rightful pride, her typewriter has a function called

"Manifold" that allows it to make multiple copies in threes. This function is positively vampiric, even to the name it has been given, reverberating with the multiplicity of men Dracula is, the manifold guises of the vampire, and the copying procedure which itself produces vampires, each of which is in a sense a replica of all the others. Here we step into the age of mechanical reproduction with a vengeance, since the reproductive process that makes vampires is so closely allied to the mechanical replication of culture. The perverse reversals of human reproduction that vampirism entails, making a crazy salad of gender roles and even of anatomical destiny, have been well discussed, and assuredly impinge on the terrors of *Dracula*. The ties to cultural reproduction and to cultural consumption need to be acknowledged as well, to place the book in its genuine context of modernity. Because Mina operates the manifold function her relation to Dracula is as close as it is later perverse. Typewriting itself partakes of the vampiric, although paradoxically in this text it can serve also as an instrument used to destroy it.[7]

The gender division of labor in consumption strongly pervades the representation of this mass cultural vampire and helps to situate Dracula unmistakably as a figure for consumption. Dracula cannot enter your home and molest you unless invited in; that same invitation is the one extended to the mass cultural, in the sense that it is its seductive invasion of the home that allows the domestic to become the site, the opening puncture wound, for all the techniques of mass culture. Mass culture or consumption can be said to transform culture from within the home, despite the obvious fact that many of its cultural technologies are encountered elsewhere, in the department store, on the billboard, in the nickelodeon parlor, at the newsstand or the telegraph office. The book is obsessed with all these technological and cultural modalities, with the newest of the new cultural phenomena, and yet it is they that shatter the fixed and circumscribed world the novel seems designed to protect through those very means, as the home is opened up to the instabilities of authority and the pleasures that lie outside the family as a unit of social reproduction. The same science, rationality and technologies of social control relied on to defend against the encroachments of Dracula are the source of the vampiric powers of the mass cultural with which Dracula, in my reading, is allied. Homes are the most permeable membrane possible for this transfusion, since by installing the middle-class and even the lower-class woman in economic isolation there by the end of the nineteenth century, a captive audience for the vampiric ministrations of commoditized culture, consumption and so-called "leisure," in the case of upper-class women, is thereby created.[8] Women are the ones who ineluctably let Dracula in.

It may seem that I accept the text's ambivalence about mass cultural transformation in connecting Dracula to it, but what I want to propose is a very different spin on the notion of consumption—the need to see it as, as Pierre Bourdieu calls it, "the production that is consumption." These changes are extraordinary and have powerful political effects; they are also, as I have claimed, premised on a cannibalization of resources from invisible places "elsewhere," in global economic terms. The contradictions of consumption run like fault lines through this text, and correspondingly in our own contemporary theory. It should be underscored, however, that consumption is always a labor—I don't at all mean the work of shopping, but a form of cultural labor, including the producing of meanings.[9] Because *Dracula* focuses on the entry into mass culture, it becomes one of our primary cultural expressions of that swooning relation and thus has needed to be revived incessantly, in films, books, and other cultural forms. The vampiric embrace is now a primary locus for our culture's self-reflexive assessment of its cultural being, since that being is fixed in the embrace of material consumption.

In the madman Renfield, Dr. Seward's star patient as an example of "zoophagy," we have a gloss on the psychic interiorizations of consumption. He is of course finally shown to be a disciple of Dracula, his master, in a theological partnership that runs roughshod over the psychoanalytic diagnoses Dr. Seward has been trying to make. Renfield's underlying sanity seems to inhere in his acceptance of racial and class differences as a matter of blood, his stalwartly hierarchical common sense, and in his staunch support for imperialist projects. He praises the country of the Texan Quincey Morris: "Mr. Morris, you should be proud of your great state. Its reception into the Union was a precedent which may have far-reaching effects hereafter, when the Pole and the Tropics may hold alliance to the Stars and Stripes. The power of Treaty may yet prove a vast engine of enlargement, when the Monroe doctrine takes its true place as a political fable" (257). Renfield actually adheres to an imperialism that has the vastest engine of enlargement in Dracula, but he is also able to admire a rival imperialism of great promise. The imperial nexus is also tied to the mass cultural through Renfield. When Mina Harker asks to meet this bizarre inmate, he agrees to converse with her, and he speaks about his own desire to devour living things as if it were in the remote past: "The doctor here will bear me out that on one occasion I tried to kill him for the purpose of strengthening my vital powers by the assimilation with my own body of his life through the medium of his blood—relying, of course, upon the Scriptural phrase, 'For the blood is the life'" (247). The theological monologue represents vampirism's literalization of Christian practices, so embedded that it will require equivalent literalizations to supercede it. But Renfield goes on to reflect on a new cultural instance:

"Though indeed, the vendor of a certain nostrum has vulgarised the truism to the very point of contempt. Isn't that true, Doctor?" (247) There was a British blood tonic that had adopted this phrase in its advertisements in "real life," but what Renfield objects to is amusingly crazy: advertising's debasement of the religious signification when Dracula, the original blood tonic man, is on his way to give the phrase his own supernally horrific debasement. This denigration of the popularizing and secularizing rhetoric of advertisement serves to underscore the conflation of Dracula with the world of advertisement and mass media made by the text, even where Renfield may make an invidious distinction. Advertisement itself, among many other forms, was a powerful recasting of the religious vocabulary, its translation into the promises of a salvational commodity culture; that language was, in a manner of speaking, lying around loose in a secularizing culture, and advertisement appropriated it for its own uses, as it recirculates all evacuated social languages.[10] This may often look like a vulgarization, when it is additionally a resurrection; the vampire enters into this circulatory economy as well. Count Dracula's more pointedly terrifying manifestation covers over the lurking fears, as well as pleasures, found in the deflating of spiritual rhetoric as it is recirculated as the currency of advertisement. Renfield's erratic "madness," his eating of live animals, is itself almost a pun on the tremors of consumption. He is unvampirized in the literal sense, only vampirized from afar, so at a double remove Renfield hypostatizes the consumer, directed by invisible longings and compelled by ghostly commands to absorb everything in sight. His is one cautionary tale of the "phagous" nature of consumption.

Dracula's own biorhythms are, paradoxically, very much those of everyday life under the altered conditions of the mass cultural; Dracula *must* consume on a daily basis. The outlandishness of Dracula's behavior is simultaneously made quotidian, regularized, indeed, everyday, in the extended sense that word is given by Henri Lefebvre.[11] It can be no accident that the overwhelming trope of this novel is also the word for this new social economy—consumption. Dracula drinks his victims dry, takes all their blood and *consumes* it, rather than ingesting it. Ingesting or digesting these sanguinary meals would imply a rather more stolid, alimentary process than the one we witness. Van Helsing tactlessly reminds Mina that the previous night Dracula "banqueted" on her, but this word too has some of the baroque bravura of consumption.

The vampiric consumption of blood in *Dracula* is simultaneously and complexly a sexual act, as commentators like Nina Auerbach, Christopher Craft and John Stevenson have variously shown, and its process holds both victim and perpetrator in a version of sexual thrall or ecstasy. I want to comment on the sexual thrust of *Dracula*'s dynamic, if you will, but first I want to trace out the implications of seeing these exchanges also in sumptuary terms.[12]

Dracula takes blood, but he also gives something, that intangible but quite ineluctable gift of vampirism, which enters invisibly into victims during their act of expenditure. A model of the consumptive paradigm is enacted in their bloody congress; something is interiorized in the giving over to Dracula. Once the mass cultural makes its appearance it unleashes pleasure, it transforms attention, it mobilizes energies outside the norms of authority. I'm not giving this a utopian cast, simply remarking on the rearrangements of the social and the psychic consumption exacts, nowhere more specifically than in the realm of sexuality. The modern discourse of sexuality is indeed based on consumption, as Foucault's work has demonstrated, and recently Lawrence Birkin's book has annexed sexology to the epistemic shift of consumption.[13] *Dracula* bears this out. The history of mass culture is at least in part the history of regaining and reasserting control over sexuality; in *Dracula*, this battle is still so new that the enemy is us.

The vampire yokes himself to the feminine because the mass cultural creeps in on little female feet, invades the home and turns it inside out, making it a palace of consumption. Dracula consumes but thereby turns his victims into consumers; he sucks their blood and renders them momentarily compliant and passive and then wild, powerful and voluptuous. What the text can't decide, nor can we, is how to determine which of these is likely, and then, which of these is preferable. This may help us to understand why Dracula, unlike, say, Jack the Ripper, feasts exclusively on British middle-class women, when, it would seem, the rest of the population, female and even male, is more readily available for his delectation. Lucy, for example, directs her vampire attentions to children of the lower orders; there is some evidence in the text that female vampires do tend to subsist on children, unless particularly enticing erotic possibilities present themselves. In this way the three vampire ladies of Dracula's castle are thrown little children in sacks, but hunger for Jonathan Harker when he is within their spectral chambers; Lucy hunts the parks, but turns to her fiance Arthur when she hopes to consummate her vampirism with an erotic meal. The connection between mass culture and the feminine has been made since its beginnings, and is arrestingly refigured in *Dracula*, since mass culture is appraised as feminizing, passive, voluptuous, carnal and anti-imperial, in the case of Lucy, and labor-intensive, productive and properly imperial where Mina is involved.

Lucy and Mina have shown themselves to be appetitive even before the attacks Dracula makes on them. The very day of Lucy's vamping by Dracula, who as a secret stowaway on the ship that has wrecked against the coast has just arrived at the seaside town of Whitby where the two are staying, the women go out to share that very British meal of "tea," a meal defined as a beverage. Mina says: "I believe we should have shocked the New Women with our appetites. Men are more tolerant, God bless them." The tea that they devour so sensually, in defiance of the putative austerity of the New Women, is a foreshadowing of their exposure to vampiric lust, but also an index of their placement in the chain of consumption. Another striking detail of the text attests to the propriety and discipline of Mina, yet also hints at unexplored depths of commodity desire. She rescues Lucy, although too late, from her vamping by Dracula as she sits in a zombie state by the sea. Since Lucy has walked out to meet Dracula in a somnambulant trance, she has neglected to put on shoes, so Mina gives hers over to Lucy upon hastening to her side. This leaves Mina with an awkward predicament: if she is seen by any townspeople on the midnight trip back to the relative safety of bourgeois girlhood's boudoir, they will draw inferences from her lack of footgear. Mina hits upon a startling trick, but one in keeping with her plucky pragmatism. She daubs her feet with mud, so that no reflection of white foot or ankle twinkling in the night can alert any sleepy voyeur who might be looking out a window. So Mina makes the trip back with her feet coated in mud; that expedient is a brilliant one, but also presents us subliminally with the image of a Mina thoroughly earth-bound, enmired. The scandal occurs for the reader's eyes alone, so that Mina's earthiness will be underscored even in her hour of intense decorum. The text's surface establishes the two women's purity and asexuality, yet slips in a glimpse of their susceptibility to consumption—a consumption that also demarcates them favorably in opposition to the New Women who eschew marriage and home. You're damned if you do, and damned if you don't consume.

Lucy has given signs that she is not utterly passive prior to her vampirization; she has been proposed to by three men on one day—by Dr. Seward, the gallant Texan Quincey Morris, and by the Honorable Arthur Holmwood, whom she does indeed accept. Yet in her letter to Mina recounting all this she bursts out: "Why can't they let a girl marry three men, or as many as want her, and save all this trouble? But this is heresy, and I must not say it" (62). Lucy gets her wish, in one way: all of these men, with the addition of Professor Van Helsing, will have to give her a blood transfusion, thus becoming her husbands, as Van Helsing piquantly points out: "Ho, ho! Then this so sweet maid is a polyandrist, and me, with my poor wife dead to me, but alive by Church's law, though no wits, all gone—even I, who am faithful husband to this now-nonwife, am bigamist" (187). Lucy is so metaphorized by the text, in contrast to Mina, typist extraordinaire, that the wavering boundary of her sexual appetite has serious consequences. If one considers her name, Luce, light and illumination, emanating out of the West-enra, she is clearly an overdetermined being, more than a woman, a civilizational cause. The sexual torque put on her vamping is indeed amazing, but I would claim that this must be considered beyond the level of the fear of women's sexuality and examined also as a very particular convergence of questions. Lucy stands in for the project of empire; it is her ineffable whiteness that is so valuable an icon to her male protectors—these are men who, as Quincey Morris points out, have served together in exotic places of danger and violence, in some inexplicable blend of Indiana Jones-style ethnographic adventure and military colonial exploits (65). Their devotion to Lucy continues to unite them, and she becomes a kind of allegory of their mutual project in taming the rest of the world. Mina does not have this resonance, since she is resolutely plain and intelligent, and has not been sought over by a trio of explorers; her sole proposal was from Jonathan Harker, and he a home-bound lawyer. Lucy's white westernness becomes totemic in her vamping; the crepuscular universe she inhabits is a twilight of the gods of Western hegemony. An advertisement for Pear's soap of 1887, showing the legend "Pear's Soap is the Best" spelled out in shining white against a glowering dark rock, as astonished natives fall in awe before the handwriting on the wall, also reads, "The Formula of British Conquest," and in glossing its own trope, quotes the words of Phil Robinson, a war correspondent to the London Daily Telegraph, as follows: "Even if our invasion of the Soudan has done nothing else it has at any rate left the Arab something to puzzle his fuzzy head over, for the legend Pear's Soap is the Best, inscribed in white characters on the rock which marks the farthest point of our advance toward Berber, will tax all the wits of the Dervishes of the Desert to translate."[14] Lucy's vampirization comments directly on the dark side of that boast and its certainty, since even the joint ministrations of her band of admirers are ineffective in staving off the return of the imperial repressed. It would be far too reductive to read Dracula as a transposition of the fear of a massive colonial uprising, a revenge taken on the imperial seat by those so dominated, in the person of Count Dracula. To extirpate the imperial context, however, makes even the sexuality of the text denatured, decontextualized, since Lucy's iconic presence has as much to do with extended cultural preoccupations of the discourse of imperialism as it does with the "anxiety" about women's changing roles. These aspects can be made to mesh, without reductive narrowing, through the complex of consumption, a process equally invoked and implicated by imperial discourse and psychosexual representation.

All the more shocking, then, when the living, female impetus for imperial energies succumbs to the lures of consumption. Van Helsing has to convince the other men that their Miss Lucy could indeed be doing such a thing as biting children, and to do that he takes them to a park where they watch her in action. This scene is renowned for its excesses; although Lucy is out for children's blood, she's described as wantonly voluptuous, red-lipped and voluptuous, extremely voluptuous—they've never seen her this way before, flushed with desire and flaunting her sexual charms. She actually offers Arthur a taste of the delights he has missed, since she was snatched away on the eve of the wedding: "Come to me, Arthur. Leave these others and come to me. My arms are hungry for you. Come, and we can rest together" (223). Arthur has to be restrained, of course, and when they prevent Lucy from getting into her tomb by the application of the communion wafer weather-stripping, there is a hilarious pun as she is compared to Medusa, the archetype of destructive female sexuality, giving them a hideous grimace as if, Dr. Seward says, "looks could kill." Medusa's "look" could turn men to stone; here it's really Lucy's *looks*, her voluptuous looks—her appearance, not her *regard*—that are so appalling and must be expunged. It should not seem trivializing to suggest that at least some of the fixation on carmine lips and cheeks is actually cosmetic—that Miss Lucy has been made over cosmetically by the pleasures of these new feminine products, the "paint" beginning to be available, if not worn by the middle-class virgin—in her posthumous state. Her sexuality is indeed excessive per se, but a large measure of its horror is yoked to its consumerist incarnadine as well, as if Lucy had availed herself of the rouge pot and the rice powder in dressing herself to kill. Such widely read "manuals" as Lily Langtry's treatise on the art of cosmetic use seem to have found their way into the lascivious descriptions of Lucy's unwonted sex appeal, and are consequently references to an arena of choice for women, however dimly articulated. Note too that the early Lucy of the text writes to Mina of her absence of interest in fashion, which actually displeases Arthur at that innocent stage! (69) This strange irony reverberates with Lucy's love of fashionable slang.

That these men are on a sex hunt is borne out from the beginning, when Van Helsing tells Dr. Seward that Lucy has become a vampire and then must take the enraged doctor to the cemetery to show him proof. Van Helsing is holding a candle in order to light up the coffin to be able to drill a hole in it; the text says that his "sperm" dropped in "white patches" which congeal on the coffin plate bearing her name. Even if we know that sperm is short for the spermaceti still used in making the candle wax, this is a vivid description of Van Helsing's premature ejaculation onto Lucy, a prelude of things to come. Arthur does the honors when the group of adventurers has agreed that this Un-Dead must be dispatched, even especially because she has the body of a provocative Lucy—a "carnal" appearance, the text says. As the men surround the coffin, Arthur puts the point of the stake to her heart, "and as I [Dr. Seward] looked I could see its dint in the white flesh. Then he struck with all his might. The Thing in the coffin writhed; and a hideous, blood-curdling screech came from the opened red lips. The body shook and quivered and twisted in wild contortions; the sharp white teeth champed together till the lips were cut, and the mouth was smeared with crimson foam. But Arthur never faltered. He looked like a figure of Thor ..." (227). John Stevenson and others rightly view this as the picture of orgasm. It can't be denied that the text is fascinated with this spectacle of sexual violation, and Lucy is undeniably being punished for her sexuality as a vampire; as the imperturbable Van Helsing asks Arthur after this, with postcoital nonchalance, "May I cut off Miss Lucy's head?" The punishment is additionally inflicted for the separation of sexuality from reproduction, or its amalgamation; Lucy only procreates in the sense that vampiric attacks produce more vampires from the liaison. If this were all the text did with the cataclysm of female sexuality it would become yet another symptomatic document of sexual hierarchization. Yet more is entertained here than just the effacement of Lucy as a female character; what I want to urge is that there is a dialectical intertwining of the racial and national on the one hand, and consumption and femaleness on the other, that roughens such tidy analyses. It makes a difference that Lucy is the victim, so to speak, of the group of men who accompanied one another on their colonial voyages and who, as Quincey Morris puts it, "told yarns by the camp-fire in the prairies; and dressed one another's wounds after trying a landing at the Marquesas; and drunk healths on the shore of Titicaca" (65). Their investment in expunging Lucy the vampire is inflected by this mutual history, and by Lucy's emblematic status as Western icon.

The textual investment shifts when Mina is vamped. For one thing, as Van Helsing has already pointed out, Madame Mina "has man-brain," so her relation to the equilibration of consumption and empire alters. Mina is an anomaly in evolutionary terms, and as such is affiliated to Dracula; her brain is not a female one, but instead is white, male and European, according to the brain science not merely of this book but of Western racial science generally until it peters out in the 1930s, to persist in Schockley and the sociobiologies. On that evolutionary scale the female brain, the criminal brain and the so-called savage or primitive brain are on a par; the adult white male brain is the evolutionary summit.[15] By leaping over this divide Mina occupies unclear territory, and one way of reading what happens to her is to assume that she is set up as Dracula's next victim as a means of establishing her femininity. With lavish abandon and extravagant bad faith her so-called protectors leave her alone in the insane asylum to spend the night, and congratulate themselves at every turn on having shielded her from unbearably painful knowledge; this, of the woman who has typed all the previous vampire documents, and is therefore the most fully in the know.

Having been imprinted with vampirism in a uniquely mediated way, by nursing from and fellating Dracula at the same moment, as she is forced to suck his blood from a wound in his breast, Mina becomes his telepathic double. There's a kinky notion of cerebral sex involved in this, to be sure; at the same time, it begins to make perfect sense that Dracula would have this intimate cognitive relationship with Mina. If it is the case that at least part of *Dracula*'s marshaling of fear has to do with assigning a status to the mass cultural, and working through the anxieties it evokes, then the gender slippage that surrounds the characterization of Mina helps account for this. Consumption is psychosexual, yet also socioeconomic. Mina occupies a strange niche between these two, since she is consumed by Dracula, who banquets on her, and also consumes him, but without longing, without desire, and with all her cognitive faculties intact. She could be said to be a perfect replica of the labor of consumption in this regard: she is always doing something with it, always is consciously co-present with the act, unlike Lucy's white zombiedom. The text wants to protect itself from Mina's brain, from her knowledge. After her vamping, the men alternately need to tell her everything, and want to tell her nothing. Oscillating back and forth between these positions, Mina becomes more and more the author of the text; she takes over huge stretches of its narration, she is responsible for giving her vampire-hunting colleagues all information on Dracula's whereabouts, and she is still the one who coordinates and collates the manuscripts, although she has pledged the men to kill her if she becomes too vampiric in the course of time. Her act of collation is by no means strictly secretarial, either; Mina is the one who has the idea of looking back over the assembled manuscripts for clues to Dracula's habits and his future plans. Despite the continual attempts both consciously by the characters and unconsciously by the text itself to view Mina as a medium of transmission, it continually emerges that there is no such thing as passive transmission—invariably, intelligent knowledge is involved, and Mina goes to the heart of things analytically and structurally.

Mina is treated as a medium when Professor Van Helsing hypnotizes her repeatedly to allow her to reveal Dracula's whereabouts; of course we recognize in this a version of the psychoanalytic "cures" beginning to be effected through hypnotism, by Freud and others.[16] The woman is placed in a state where she does not know her own knowledge, she simply relates it as it is drawn from her by a man who knows what to make of it. All the reverberations to Freud's Dora are in place; the mesmeric and hypnotic world of Charcot is an open intertext of the novel. On all these grounds, including the professional activities of Dr. Seward and the psychoanalytic mutterings of Van Helsing as he repudiates surface meanings for deeper trance states and hysterical body signs, psychoanalysis does a duet with *Dracula*. This should point us to Dracula's role in making vivid the split nature of consciousness and the predatory energies of the libidinal unconscious, and yet it should also be an alert that psychoanalysis and the novel *Dracula* are up against the same problematic: describing or figuring a process that is both productive and consumptive, contradictorily placed both psychically and socially. Mina does tell what her shared or double consciousness is up to, as if she were in the enviable and dangerous position of having her unconscious, which she has in a sense swallowed, speak to her with an audible voice, absent the condensations and displacements of lesser mortals. And yet she is not a controllable medium for Van Helsing, nor just a transparent recording device of the id within, Count Dracula. She is productive in her consumptive possession: Mina essentially becomes the detective of the final segment of the story.

The situation has gotten desperate in London; the men have found all but one of the Count's magic boxes and consecrated them, but he only needs one, and he has obviously departed in it from London. As the men fall prostrate in one or another ways, Mina sends them to lie down and vigorously applies herself to deducing the precise route Dracula must take to get himself carried back in his box to the Castle. For the first time an entry reads "Mina's Memorandum" (371). With relentless logic, the keen use of maps, geometrical calculations and brilliant speculation, she provides them all with a plan of attack, deciding which river Dracula will need to use to get home and how he can best be countered. "Once again Madam Mina is our teacher," Van Helsing cries out. "Her eyes have been where ours were blinded" (374). In a text that claims again and again that women need to be shielded from the reality of vampirism, a woman is responsible for seeing the way out. Yet Mina's prescience and logical ability are predicated on her proximity to the mass cultural forms she has mastered: for example, her hobby is memorizing the train schedule, since she is, in her own words, "a train fiend," which allows her to recreate Dracula's line of escape. Additionally, she is a typist with a portfolio. "I feel so grateful to the man who invented the 'Traveller's' typewriter," she testifies in eerie simulation of the traveling count (371). Mina is that hybrid creature, the consumed woman whose consumption is a mode of knowledge, as Georg Simmel predicted. Mina is simply closer to what Dracula is than the men can be. In saying this, I am not privileging Mina as a heroine, or claiming that her deductive actions are some kind of subversion of patriarchal domination. For one thing, in my understanding of texts the characters aren't really people; to valorize Mina as if she had some existence outside the dynamics of the text is, I think, to insert an allegory of our own making. Moreover, there is no neatly definable patriarchy available for subverting; the class and racial lines form a web that denies transgressive primacy to any one figure here, whether or not a female.

When Dracula comes to press his attentions on Mina he criticizes her for having played her brain against his, and he warns her that her male companions should feel grateful to him: "They should have kept their energies for use closer to home. Whilst they played wits against me—against me who commanded nations, and intrigued for them, and fought for them, hundreds of years before they were born—I was countermining them. And you, their best beloved one, are now to me, flesh of my flesh; blood of my blood; kin of my kin; my bountiful winepress for a while; and shall be later on my companion and my helper" (304). It is worth remarking that this extended speech by Dracula is recounted by Mina herself, not available first-hand from the eyewitnesses to the vamping. Here is the paradox of Dracula. While he is perforce racially other, of the alien vampire race, and while he has as a result of his racial otherness what Van Helsing calls a "child-brain" and a criminal brain, making him vulnerable to the tactics of the European adult male brain at its peak, he is also a partner in imperialism. In the "whirlpool of races" he describes to Jonathan at the beginning of the text, it is his race that emerges as the purest European, a noble race that in conquering this eastern territory in fact makes it historically possible to acquire the fruits of empire for the British, Dutch and Texan men who hunt him. One can readily imagine that the imperial situation produced a fear of that unspecified otherness coming for retaliation, but Dracula is not simply that apparition; he is an ally of imperial forces, and in some ways annexes his own project to that of imperial Britain's, as an extension to it or an elaboration of it. This is why he is not content with any vampiric empire that would take shape in archaic ways—even the Oriental despotism Marx speaks of is too *recherché* for the Count. He must come to London to modernize the terms of his conquest, to master the new imperial forms and to learn how to supplement his considerable personal powers by the most contemporary understanding of the metropolis. Dracula has, in short, felt himself to be on the periphery, however powerful he might be there, and by coming to England he has an opportunity to meld vampirism to the modern forces of imperial control.

Benedict Anderson has shown that nations are, in his phrase, "imagined communities," and that the chief means of establishing these relatively fictive national unities has been through language, the "print-languages" made possible by capitalism. As Anderson says: "Nothing served to assemble related vernaculars more than capitalism, which, within the limits imposed by grammars and syntaxes, created mechanically-reproduced print-languages, capable of dissemination through the market."[17] *Dracula* is a veritable whirlpool of language, a farrago of accents and dialects and classed speech; this polyglottal quality is the other determinative feature of the novel's form. As much as it is extruded, so to speak, in and through the modern technologies of production that elsewhere the text so abhors, so also the text relies on pushing at the limits of the common language of English to mark out its national boundary, and controlling the unruliness of speech by technologizing it—typing it—as a print-language of hegemony.

"The captain swore polyglot—very polyglot—polyglot with bloom and blood" (336), comes Dr. Van Helsing's report on the captain who has taken Dracula's box on board his vessel. Of course, the bloom and blood are the sprinklings of the most common British curses, but they also connect to the polyglot nature of national "blood" or language. Both Dr. Van Helsing and Count Dracula speak English with idiosyncratic results, especially in the doctor's voluble case. Dracula had wanted to perfect his English by using Jonathan as a model; he fears being a stranger when he goes to London. "Here I am boyar, I am noble, the common people know me and I am master. But a stranger in a strange land, he is no one; men know him not—and not to know is not to care not for" (21). Why Dracula needs linguistic proof of being master when he has so much physical proof is unclear, and he exhibits no particular longing for people to know him. Remarkably enough, I would suggest that Dracula experiences some of the poignant sense of estrangement of the colonial intellectual, who has utterly mastered the print language, is an adept in all things English, including the ascot, and yet who lacks that touch of spoken familiarity. Rather than seeing Count Dracula as a simple stand-in for the "fear of otherness" an imperial nation might well exhibit, his situation has a subtle specificity. He *does* permit the text to express its confidence in the levels of mastery of English that "prove" the nationality. The text then veers off into the extended monologues of, for example, one Mr. Swales, the one hundred-year-old sailor whose speech is almost impossible to read as English, let alone to imagine being spoken, and the report of the cockney zookeeper that is similarly impenetrable as writing. What unifies them is what must now be called vampiric typewriting, the face of print-language that can extirpate difference even at the margins of comprehensibility, an effacement devoutly to be wished, and brought about by the alchemy of a mass-cultural form.

The nation "has an inner incompatibility with empire," acutely shown in the predicaments that *Dracula* helps to reveal.[18] The empire fans out across the globe, collecting its grab-bag of completely incongruous possessions, while at the same time the maintenance of a national community back in the metropole, as it were, siphons off tremendous amounts of ideological energy. "From the start," Anderson claims, "the nation was conceived in language, not in blood, and [one] could be invited into the imagined community" (133). Such an invitation would rest on linguistic grounds, language being a synecdoche for cultural solidarity. And the only means of producing a language center on a vast enough scale to indeed make a nation lay in and through the techniques of mass cultural dissemination.

Count Dracula is matched on the linguistic plane by Dr. Van Helsing, the Dutch lawyer, doctor and sage who produces the most amazing word salad put on the page. It is not incidental to the polyglot logic of the text that one of its chief characters would fracture English so magnificently; Van Helsing's flights of oratory are foreignness bounded by a rigid adherence to the primacy of English goals in the world. Where his side-kick Dr. Seward will concentrate on minds, Van Helsing's first loyalty is to blood, the purity and strength of which he seems able to determine intuitively. Van Helsing compares Dracula to a tiger: "Your man-eater, as they of India call the tiger who has once tasted blood of the human, care no more for the other prey, but prowl unceasing till he get him" (339). The professor is also knowledgeable about Dracula's motives for becoming a modern vampire. "What does he do? He find out the place of all the world most of promise for him. Then he deliberately set himself down to prepare for the task. He find in patience just how is his strength, and what are his powers. He study new tongues. He learn new social life; new environment of old ways, the politic, the law, the finance, the science, the habit of a new land and a new people who have come to be since he was. His glimpse that he have had, whet his appetite only and enkeen his desire" (339). Dracula's last attack on the vampire group is not represented in his taking over of Mina's soul; before he departs from London, Dracula mounts an attack on language, the language of print culture itself. He finds the manuscript of their trials and burns it to ashes, also throwing in the stray gramophone disk recordings of Dr. Seward's diary he finds until these are reduced to wax. Thankfully, Mina has kept a copy. This fortuitous reclamation of their labors, and also of the text held in the hand of the reader, all too ironically derives from a copy. If copying is the inevitable fate of the mass-produced, here it is also the salvation. The vampire hunters do not need sacral, original, authentic or auratic texts—copies will do, the more reproduced the better. Dracula's pyro-technic outrage implies the desire for a primal relation to texts, and certainly a desire to replace writing with speech, but his little apocalypse in the fireplace cannot succeed in annihilating the reproductive powers of technologized language.

As Van Helsing sees it, Dracula's appetite is not for blood, but for a kind of knowledge and power he has become aware of as the attributes of modern, consumer capitalist culture. His "desire is keen" surely not just to enlarge the vampire dominions, but to transform vampire-dom, to take it to the heart of the metropolis, where it feeds on the forces already set in motion by technological development. "What more may he not do when the greater world of thought is open to him," the professor muses, imagining Dracula's feelings as he lies on the periphery in his moldy Carpathian tomb. This should make it clear that it is not merely the atavism of Dracula that makes his appearance in England so frightful; it is his relative modernity, his attempt to be more British than the British in consolidating his goals. Franco Moretti interestingly hypothesizes Dracula as the figure for the circulation of money in late capitalism; Dracula does have a vivid scene where coins shower out of his clothes. Nonetheless, that symbology may take too literally the meaning of the "economic," since Dracula's economy is so mediated by its relation to consumption and to the forces of empire.

Understandably, *Dracula* concludes haltingly, and can only end by letting the modern, urban world of technology and consumption recede altogether. The final confrontation with the vampire takes place on horseback in the countryside, Dracula's coffin protected by a group of gypsy cart drivers. This low-tech ending allows the religiosity the text nervously relies on to resurface with less apparent anachronism, but the ancient and the modern cannot be made to converge. They each move on separate curves, asymptotically, never coalescing. Mina, the typist, has lost all her office equipment by the end, although she does narrate Dracula's death and records his last look of peace—a far cry from the orgasmic turbulence that passes over Lucy's visage. Mina's vampire mark, the red scar burned into her forehead by its contact with a holy wafer, recedes with the setting sun, and Mina is free to become a mother, to reproduce what she has heretofore only copied.

The novel doesn't forget its complex relation to the techniques of modernity, however; the religious apotheosis is not its last gasp. *Dracula* is an unstable brew, because it is made up out of mass cultural forms, and yet tries to use this loose collection to mount a retrogressive search and destroy mission against itself. Only the Bible seems to be a text with enough authority to confront Count Dracula—a text that seems (although it is not) to be unscathed by the market forces of commodity culture, a written assemblage of the spoken holy word, as composite and palimpsestic as the textual production this novel itself claims. It would appear that Mina's sudden unscarring would be proof of those powers, but the novel has already shown us again and again that these sacred words are not powerful enough, do not address the conditions of modern life, are not sufficiently passed through the crucible of mass culture to answer the problems of foreignness, otherness, and the unstable self. The baptismal font of language in this book has to be the typewriter, and it seems blasphemous to direct attention to the printed nature of the Bible, its role as the first printed book of Western culture, by Gutenberg's hand.

As a final proof of the divisions within the text, divisions that fruitfully and fearfully show us the dislocations in cultural authority that prompt its new world of language, consider the last and then the first words of the text. The group gets together years later, huddling around the boy who is, through Lucy's transfusions and the passage of her blood to Dracula, and hence to Mina, the putative son of all of the men and all the women, the "sexual history" going back to Dracula and his three brides, and "we were struck with the fact that, in all the masses of material of which the record is composed, there is hardly one authentic document: nothing but a mass of typewriting" (400). The only proof of the ravages of Dracula is the existence of the boy, young Quincey, named after the gallant Texan who gave his life for Mina's unvamping, and while he may constitute bodily proof for the friends, his unmarked state would represent the opposite to most people. But the first thing we read as we begin the text is this: "How these papers have been placed in sequence will be made manifest in the reading of them ... there is throughout no statement of past things wherein memory may err, for all the records chosen are exactly contemporary, given from the standpoints and within the range of knowledge of those who made them." Which is it, truth, origin, the authority of knowledge, or a "mass of typewriting"? What makes this text so modern, not to say modernist, is that it knows that it will be consumed—it stages the very act of its own consumption, and problematizes it. The energies of modernity flow out of these same ineluctable wounds, and the undecidable nature of consumption. Most of all, the modernist text follows *Dracula* in acknowledging, however repressedly, the necessary relation of the modern world to its dialectical other, the rest of the globe. In that encounter, which *Dracula* enacts, a modernist writing begins.

The reading of the mass of typewriting is the labor of consumption the text requires of us. This mass is vampiric typewriting, this vampire is mass typewriting, this typewriting is mass vampirism. Under the sign of modernity we are vampires at a banquet of ourselves, we are Dracula and Madame Mina, the one who bites and the one who is bitten, the one who types and the one who is typewritten.

NOTES

1. Karl Marx, *Grundrisse*, trans. Martin Nicolaus (London: Penguin, 1973), 110.

2. All quotes from Dracula refer to Bram Stoker, *Dracula* (1897; reprint, New York: Bantam, 1981). The citation of this perenially and immensely popular work from a mass-cultural paperback source seems appropriate; Mina's remarks are found on page 57.

3. Franco Moretti, "Dialectic of Fear," in *Signs Taken For Wonders* (London: Verso, 1983), 105.

4. Among the best treatments of the Victorian legacy to be discovered, in one form or another, in the book are Nina Auerbach's commentary on the text in her *Woman and the Demon: The Life of Victorian Myth* (Cambridge: Harvard Univ. Press, 1982); John Stevenson's essay "A Vampire in the Mirror: The Sexuality of *Dracula*," *PMLA* 103 (1988): 139–149; and Daniel Pick's essay "'Terrors of the Night': Dracula and 'Degeneration,'" *Critical Quarterly* 30 (Winter 1988): 71–87.

5. David Seed touches on this in his "The Narrative Method of Dracula," *Nineteenth Century Fiction* 40 (June 1985): 61–75.

6. Dr. Seward follows recent medical practice in this, as Leonard Wolf's *The Annotated Dracula* (New York: Ballantine Books, 1975) notes (118).

7. See in this connection of course Walter Benjamin's "The Work of Art in an Age of Mechanical Reproduction," in *Illuminations*, trans. Harry Zohn (New York: Schocken, 1969), 212–251, since despite its Brechtian utopianism, this essay forges the vocabulary for apprehending the mass cultural in modern critical theory.

8. Fine accounts of the relation of women to mass culture can be found in Andreas Hussen's *After the Great Divide: Modernism and Mass Culture* (New York: Columbia Univ. Press, 1987), and in Tania Modleski's essay "Femininity and Mas(s)querade," in *Feminism Without Women: Culture and Criticism in a "Post Feminist" Age* (New York: Routledge, 1991), 23–34.

9. I have argued for the revisionary nature of consumption elsewhere; some of the theorists who provide ballast for the rethinking of the process of consumption include Pierre Bourdieu, especially in his *Distinction: A Social Critique of the Judgment of Taste* (Cambridge: Harvard Univ. Press, 1984), Michel de Certeau's work, especially *The Practice of Everyday Life* (Berkeley, Univ. of California, 1984), and John Fiske's *Understanding Popular Culture* (Boston: Unwin Hyman, 1989).

10. I argue for this in *Advertising Fictions: Literature, Advertising, and Social Reading* (New York: Columbia Univ. Press, 1988); the classic essay is Leo Spitzer's "American Advertising Explained as Popular Art," in *Leo Spitzer: Representative Essays*, ed. Alban K. Forcione, Herbert Lindenberger, and Madeline Sutherland (Stanford: Stanford Univ. Press, 1988), wherein Spitzer shows the relation of the Protestant spirit of capitalism, as it were, to the language of advertising.

11. See Henri Lefebvre, *Everyday Life in the Modern World* (London: Verso, 1971).

12. Auerbach (note 4) allegorizes the sexuality in Dracula as a grappling with the explosion of female power, and its consequent suppression. Christopher Craft's essay "'Kiss Me with those Red Lips': Gender and Inversion in Bram Stoker's *Dracula*," *Representations* 8 (1984): 107–133, makes a persuasive case for the novel's imbrication in the formation of a medicalized and legal discourse of homosexuality in the late nineteenth century. Additional essays speak tellingly to the presence of the sexual in Dracula: see Robin Wood, "Burying the Undead: The Use and Obsolescence of Count Dracula," *Mosaic* 16 (1983): 175–187; John L. Greenway, "Seward's Folly: *Dracula* as a critique of 'Normal Science,'" *Stanford Literature Review* 3 (Fall 1986): 213–230; Marjorie Howes, "The Mediation of the Feminine: Bisexuality, Homoerotic Desire and Self-Expression in Bram Stoker's *Dracula*," *Texas Studies in Language and Literature* 30 (1988): 4–19; and Judith Weissman, "Women and Vampires: *Dracula* as Victorian Novel," *Midwest Quarterly* 18 (1977): 392–405. It is not possible to write about *Dracula* without raising the sexual issue; John A. Stevenson's "A Vampire in the Mirror: The Sexuality of *Dracula*" (note 4) has perhaps the best formulation of the renegade and yet all too familiar sexual practices of Dracula, which he grafts onto a stimulating argument about the implied anthropology of the novel.

13. In *Consuming Desire: Sexual Science and the Emergence of a Culture of Abundance, 1871–1914* (Ithaca: Cornell Univ. Press, 1988) Lawrence Birken suggestively argues that the climate of modern sexual discourse is affiliated with the culture of consumption.

14. See E. J. Hobsbawm, *The Age of Empire 1875–1914* (New York: Pantheon Books, 1987), Illustration Number 21.

15. Stephen Jay Gould's *The Mismeasure of Man* (New York: Norton, 1981) effectively synopsizes these developments. Anne McWhir interestingly approaches the anthropological background in her essay, "Pollution and Redemption in *Dracula*," *Modern Language Studies* 17 (Summer 1987): 31–40.

16. Often mentioned, this link to a nascent psychoanalysis is laid out in John L. Greenway (note 12). Greenway concentrates on the historical forms of science *Dracula* is able to enact.

17. Benedict Anderson, *Imagined Communities: Reflections on the Origin and Spread of Nationalism* (London, Verso, 1983), 47. Eric Hobsbawm adduces further empirical claims for the importance of print culture in Britain's nationalism, particularly, in *The Age of Empire* (note 14), chapter six and following.

18. Anderson (note 17), 89.

LAURA SAGOLLA CROLEY

The Rhetoric of Reform in Stoker's Dracula: *Depravity, Decline, and the Fin-de-Siècle "Residuum"*

In the past decade, critics of Bram Stoker's *Dracula* (1897) have discovered the fruits of historicizing a novel previously read chiefly in psychoanalytic, anthropological, and transhistorical terms.[1] This new attention to the "embeddedness" of Stoker's text has produced a number of persuasive attempts to flesh out what the Count might represent to late Victorian readers: criminality and degeneracy, foreignness, and homosexuality, to name the more noteworthy assertions.[2] While in many ways dissimilar, these readings all recognize *Dracula*'s capacity to shape and to be shaped by the late-Victorian discourses that together constitute national identity—the colonial project, scientific theory, race, and sexuality certainly among them. Moreover, many of these readings share the understanding that the Count transgresses boundaries near and dear to the late Victorian frame of mind, and that the novel, betraying a fear of cultural decline occasioned by these sorts of transgression, struggles throughout to preserve boundaries and restore cultural order.[3]

The reading I offer here seeks to illustrate how Stoker's novel associates crossed boundaries and potential decline, as did many social commentators of the 1890s, with a particular segment of the English population. I will argue that Stoker's Count is associated and allied with the poorest of the poor—not the industrious artisan but the vagrant, not the

From *Criticism* 37, no. 1 (Winter 1995): 85-108. © 1995 by the Wayne State University Press.

respectable working class but its supposedly shiftless, slum-dwelling underclass[4]—and that the threat of Dracula and vampirism stands in for the late-century threat of the lumpenproletariat.[5] If the wandering and slum-dwelling poor, like the vampire, presented a material threat to the sound health and social harmony of England, their moral threat was at least equally important. Stoker and nineties commentators cast vampire and lumpen alike as representing—sometimes even causing—cultural decline effected, above all, by a disregard of middle-class norms, including domesticity, motherhood, and female sexual purity. Read in tandem with works such as William Booth's 1890 *In Darkest England and the Way Out*, Stoker's novel betrays a similar preoccupation with cultural collapse effected by the lumpenproletariat. In order to halt that collapse, both Booth and Stoker prescribe for the lowest classes "the way out" of England—expulsion or, put more politely, emigration.

1

The very poor were never more in the Victorian imagination than in the decade and a half before the publication of Stoker's *Dracula*. When scores of homeless poor "slept-out" in Trafalgar Square and St. James park in the summer of 1887, "the existence of these unfortunates was somewhat rudely forced upon the attention of Society."[6] Overwhelmed by the sheer number of vagrants (there were 300–400 people in Trafalgar Square alone), constables let them stay put, declining to arrest them for their clear violation of vagrancy law.[7] The first half of the 1890s brought a period of recession which caused still more vagrancy: one London casual ward which reported the relief of under 5,000 on January 1, 1884, relieved 8,300 on the same night in 1894 (Rose, 84).

If the plight of the poor became more visible in the nineties, the written account of that plight magnified it considerably. In the year of the Trafalgar Square sleep-outs, the first comprehensive English history of vagrancy, J. Ribton Turner's *A History of Vagrants and Vagrancy and Beggars and Begging*, was published. A few years earlier, in 1883, John Thomas Smith's 1817 *Vagabondiana*, a lavishly-illustrated catalogue of urban beggars, was reprinted. And the beggar's sibling in extreme poverty, the slum-dweller, figured prominently in 1880s newspaper exposes by W. T. Stead and G. R. Sims, as well as in the "realistic" fiction of Arthur Morrison, Israel Zangwill, and George Gissing in the 1890s. The most famous and (arguably) most thorough commentators on homelessness and slumlife in the nineties were the Booth brothers, William and Charles. Along with extensive work on the aged poor, Charles conducted a census of London's East End in the late eighties to ascertain how many "paupers," "homeless," "starving," and "the very poor" (all separate categories) lived there. Charles's brother William had created the Salvation Army in 1878, by his own account moved by the dozens of vagrants sleeping-out near the London Bridge he encountered during a nighttime walk (Rose, 60). His 1890 *In Darkest England and the Way Out*, which will be referred to throughout, outlined an intricate plan for "saving" morally and physically the poorest of the London poor.

It is against the work of the Booths and against earlier accounts of the lower classes that Stoker's *Dracula* should be read. In 1861 Henry Mayhew opens his massive, four-volume *London Labour and the London Poor* with the insistence that there are "socially, morally, and perhaps even physically considered—but two distinct and broadly marked races, viz., the wanderers and the settlers—the vagabond and the citizen—the nomadic and the civilized tribes." More important for present purposes, Mayhew also insists that "each civilized tribe has generally some wandering horde intermingled with, and in a measure preying upon, it."[8] For Mayhew, that "wandering horde" is the London poor; the "civilized tribe" are the middle- and upper-classes, and even the portion of the poor who have permanent homes and respect middle-class mores. Claiming that the nomad "preys" upon the settled, Mayhew sets up an antagonism not unlike that between the industrious middle-class "Crew of Light" (as Christopher Craft calls Harker, Van Helsing, Seward, Godalming,[9] Morris, and sometimes Mina [Craft, 218]) and parasitic Dracula, who is, after all, spatially mobile—a nomad. Mayhew ascribes to "nomad races" in general several of Dracula's traits: a "delight in warfare," "pleasure ... in witnessing the suffering of sentient creatures," "comparative insensibility to pain," "desire for vengeance," and "disregard of female honor" (1:2).

This mid-century notion of poverty as active parasitism did not apply to the industrious working class (factory hands, domestic servants, shop-girls, etc.) but to a group the Victorians would have called, according to Gertrude Himmelfarb, the "residuum"—gypsies, beggars, vagrants, petty criminals, madmen, slum-dwellers, all of whom were most often unemployed and unattached to middle-class norms (356). Middle- and upper-class Victorians took great pains to distinguish the industrious poor from the residuum or, in Marx's terms, the proletariat from the lumpenproletariat. The New Poor Law of 1834 was instituted with an eye to just such a demarcation, and Mayhew's categories of "those who will work" and "those who will not work" lent the demarcation pseudo-scientific weight.[10]

By the time Stoker writes *Dracula*, the rhetoric describing the Victorian residuum or lumpenproletariat has changed little from the forties, when intrepid social explorer Edwin Chadwick first "penetrated" the *terra incognita* of the London rookeries to argue the necessity of sanitary reform. This rhetoric, including the metaphors of disease, animality, and foreignness, figures prominently in descriptions of Stoker's Count. When the Crew of Light invades Carfax Abbey to destroy Dracula's boxes of dirt, Harker's description seems to come straight out of Chadwick's 1842 *Sanitary Report*: "here the place was small and close, and the long disuse had made the air stagnant and foul. There was an earthy smell, as of some dry miasma, which came through the fouler air."[11] The Count seems to inhabit the sort of "low lodging house" visited and colorfully described by journalists and social reformers throughout the century—broken down, empty of furniture, and extremely dusty: "the place was thick with dust. The floor was seemingly inches deep.... The walls were fluffy and heavy with dust, and in the corners were masses of spiders' webs whereon the dust had gathered till they looked like old tattered rags as the weight had torn them partly down" (250). In his 1883 *How the Poor Live*, George Sims notes similar "heaps of dust," "rags, dirt, filth, wretchedness" in the slums he visits.[12] In the Reverend Andrew Mearns's pamphlet of the same year, "The Bitter Cry of Outcast London," the picture is identical: "poverty, rags, and dirt everywhere."[13]

And Carfax Abbey houses a "dry miasma," the medium by which disease was believed for most of the century to spread, and a quintessential element of slum descriptions. Mearns, for instance, notes the "poisonous and malodorous gases" (94) of the London slums. Assuming the shape of a "mist" in his attacks on Lucy (144), Mina (258), and Renfield (278, 280), the Count personifies miasma. Even Renfield, the Count's most loyal follower, is made uncomfortable by this power: "He slid in through the window.... His white face looked out of the mist with His red eyes gleaming, and He went on as though he owned the place, and I was no one. He didn't even smell the same as He went by me. I couldn't hold Him" (280). Like the vampiric miasma, the Count's "rank" breath (18) speaks the language of disease. Just a few years before the publication of *Dracula*, William Booth noted the "foul and fetid breath of our slums" (14), referring in tandem, as did many Victorian social commentators, to the moral and physical contagion of slum-life.

While this language of disease applied to the poor in general, it became heightened in discussions of "nomads" like Dracula, for if physical and moral disease could be somewhat contained in the slums, it became mobile and invasive with the moving body. Vagrants traveled the country carrying "tramp-fever" and, according to Mayhew, a "moral pestilence as terrible and devastating as the physical pest that accompanies it" (quoted in Himmelfarb, 340); they were a "stream of vice and disease," a "tide of iniquity and fever" (3:397).

Vampirism is throughout *Dracula* similarly figured as a disease with palpable physical effects—pallor, loss of appetite, loss of blood, and eventually death (or "un-death")—and moral effects—libidinousness, selfishness, and a rejection of domesticity and motherhood. But because Stoker's readers and critics have so often concentrated on what the disease of vampirism might *represent*, the pairing itself of physical and moral contagion has gone unnoticed. Scrutinizing this particular aspect of vampirism—one that, like so many others, seems "natural" to the generations of Westerners familiar with the vampire myth—reveals yet another link to contemporary representations of the residuum. For it seems that no where else in Stoker's culture were physical and moral deterioration paired and figured as contagious but in descriptions of the lumpenproletariat.

Like the metaphor of disease, the metaphor of animality figures prominently in the pages of both Victorian reform literature and Stoker's novel. Dracula is "panther-like" and "lion-like" with "long and pointed" eye-teeth (305). His homes and dirt-boxes Van Helsing repeatedly refers to as "lairs" (291–92, 303), echoing Booth's (25, 40) and other reformers' descriptions of the slums as "lairs" or "dens" where the poor live like dangerous animals.[14] As Peter Stallybrass and Allon White point out, the claim that the poor live like animals or among animals deteriorates quickly into the claim that the poor *are* animals.[15] And Dracula makes literal this claim in his metamorphosis into various animals—a wolf, a stray dog, a bat, and in the Carfax Abbey scene a pack of rats. Dracula's victims also become animal-like: at Dracula's castle, Jonathan begins to behave "like a rat in a trap" (27); Renfield, a "zoophagous [life-eating] maniac" [70], is compared to a dog (69, 141), a tiger (102), and a "wild beast" (102, 155); and Lucy's teeth grow long and sharp as her disease progresses (153).

Reform literature's rhetoric of colonization and miscegenation also plays a part in the Count's persona. Although Stephen J. Arata has rightly pointed out that Stoker's novel is shot through with anxieties of reverse colonization, with the fear that the dark-skinned other will invade England and compromise its racial purity, Arata fails to see the class implications of Dracula's racial invasion. Social reformers and journalists throughout the century used the language of race to talk about the very poor, from Mayhew's straightforward insistence in 1861 that costermongers "appear to be a distinct race" (1:6) to the controlling metaphor of Booth's 1890 *In Darkest England*, the title an allusion to Sir Henry Morton Stanley's *In Darkest Africa* published in the same year. Dracula's racial otherness may say as much about class, then, as it does about race. When Mayhew uses water metaphors to describe vagrancy—vagrants constitute a "stream of vice and disease" and a "tide of iniquity and fever, continually flowing from town to town"—his "tide" and "stream" are literally inside England. But they also stand in for the

English channel, "continually flowing" and bringing the foreigner with it. This is the same tide Dracula rides to England and must, in the end, be made to ride home. This is the same water in which William Booth imagines his "submerged tenth"—not the working class but "paupers," the "homeless," the "starving" and "the very poor"—are floundering. The metaphor designed, no doubt, to capture the urgency of the problem ("the multitude struggle and sink in the open-mouthed abyss" [ii]) signals at the same time that the poor are foreigners preparing, just off shore, for an invasion of England.

2

The Count's aristocratic status—he is, after all, a Transylvanian nobleman—has probably gone far to obfuscate his connections to the Victorian residuum. But the contiguity of social extremes was a familiar nineteenth century theme anatomized in the aristocrat disguised as a vagrant (from Pierce Egan's 1821 *Life in London* to A. Conan Doyle's 1892 "The Man With the Twisted Lip") and the vagrant disguised as an aristocrat (for Dickens, "the most vicious, by far, of all idle tramps is the tramp who pretends to have been a gentleman").[16] Given that by 1861 Henry Mayhew can treat "the close resemblance between many of the characteristics of a very high class, socially, and a very low class" (1:12) as a commonplace, the meeting of social extremes in Stoker's main character should come as no surprise. These extremes meet in the Transylvanian soil Dracula totes through England, for he can be land-owner (with its attendant security and power) and vagrant (with its spatial mobility) at the same time. Like the vagrant, he sleeps in his own dirt—but it is dirt owned by him.

Back at Dracula's castle social extremes also meet, for Dracula is driver, butler, and maid as well as master. Stoker structures the narrative in such a way that we suspect for several pages that the Count is performing household tasks before we actually see him making Jonathan's bed and setting his table (27). And the latter Jonathan discovers (and readers discover) surreptitiously, "through the chink of the hinges of the door" (27). This minor secret acts as synecdoche for the Count's larger secret: he is a lumpen dressed in aristocratic clothing.

In *The Eighteenth Brumaire of Louis Bonaparte* (1853), Marx, like Mayhew, links "the characteristics of a very high class, socially, and a very low class." Marx conceives of Bonaparte as just such a "princely lumpenproletarian."[17] Like Dracula, he is high and low, nobleman and nomad. And Bonaparte's role as "chief of the lumpenproletariat," like Dracula's, is a secret to be uncovered. The scandal Marx discloses in *The Eighteenth Brumaire* is that Bonaparte's allies include

> ... discharged soldiers, discharged jailbirds, escaped galley slaves, swindlers, mountebanks, lazzaroni, pickpockets, tricksters, gamblers, maquereaus, brothel keepers, porters, literati, organ-grinders, ragpickers, knife grinders, tinkers, beggars—in short, the whole indefinite, disintegrated mass, thrown hither and thither, which the French term la bohème. (75)

Fascinating and distressing for Marx, Bonaparte manages to ally the lumpenproletariat with the bourgeoisie *against* the respectable proletariat. The lumpenproletariat are allied, then, with "the bourgeois order ... a vampire that sucks [the peasantry's] blood and brains and throws it into the alchemistic cauldron of capital" (128).

Marx's linking of vampirism and the bourgeoisie supports Franco Moretti's thesis that Dracula represents monopoly capital and the bourgeoisie. Dracula certainly has some middle-class traits: his library includes the London Directory, the "Red" and "Blue" books, Whitaker's Almanack, the Army and Navy Lists, and the Law List (19); he reads a Bradshaw's Guide (mirroring Mina's knowledge of train schedules) (22); and, according to Jonathan, he "would have made a wonderful solicitor, for there was nothing that he did not think of or foresee" (31). But the Count's reference books and keen sense of detail do not advance the goals of the Crew of Light, including successful careers, the protection of female virtue, and generally "useful" lives (53). Instead, the Count uses these middle-class tools precisely to upset middle-class norms. Middle- and upper-class characteristics only cloak the Count's lumpen body—his coarse hands (18) and noxious smell—and allow him the latitude to maneuver in England as he chooses, better able to carry out his invasion.[18]

Like the aristocrat/begger nexus embedded in late Victorian culture, Dracula's network of lower-class allies which extends from Transylvania to England signals his ties to the lumpenproletariat. These allies aid in his battle against the Crew of Light and, at the same time, share a telling family resemblance. The Szgany gypsies are Dracula's closest allies and protectors who "call themselves by his name" (41). Their loyalty frames the narrative, for in the first chapter they hand over Jonathan's desperate shorthand letter explaining his imprisonment in Castle Dracula (an act without which the Count might have been prevented from entering England), and in the last chapter stab Quincy Morris, the Crew of Light's only casualty, as he attempts to charge the Count's carriage. With his uncanny mastery of the animal kingdom (especially the London Zoo's best-behaved wolf) and his proclivity for animal transformation, the Count himself fits contemporary descriptions of the gypsy, a skillful animal tamer and, to many English citizens, disgustingly animal-like in demeanor and disposition.[19] In his ability to hypnotize and cast the "evil eye" upon his enemies Dracula also resembles a gypsy. He hypnotizes Lucy and Mina before biting them, and even Jonathan, after Mina's gruesome exchange of blood with Dracula, must be awakened from "a stupor such as we know the Vampire can produce" (283). And en route to Dracula's castle, the crowd at the door of Jonathan's inn makes the sign of the cross and points two fingers toward him upon his departure, a gesture one of Jonathan's fellow passengers identifies as "a charm or guard against the evil eye" (6).[20]

The dock attendants at Whitby (where the Count begins his invasion) and at Doolittle Wharf (where he begins his escape) also contribute to the Count's mission by transporting his dirt boxes. In fact, the dockhands at Doolittle Wharf speak Dracula's language, generously sprinkling their language with the oath "bloody" (or "with blood," as Van Helsing records it). And they are all hesitant to tell the Crew of Light what they know about Dracula; only alcohol, or money for alcohol, will loosen their tongues. In this way they are parasites like Dracula, cadging "drinks" off of the upper-classes. The pairing of working men's drinking and vampirism earlier in the century, in an 1858 temperance tract entitled "The Vampyre, by the Wife of a Medical Man," indicates that Dracula's allies' drinking may be more than incidental.[21] In that tract, the "Vampyre Inn" sucks in the working class, turning them from industrious teetotalers to spend-thrift lushes—and moving them, in Victorian terms, from the respectable working class to the residuum. Vampirism even before Stoker's novel, then, can represent the temptation to acquire the vices of the lumpenproletariat.

If the dockhands appear at first glance to be the "industrious" poor (they are working, after all), undermining the argument that Dracula only allies himself with the wandering and dissolute, it is because dock work had a very different social valence for the Victorians. Dock work was itinerant labor, and the London quays were the socially and racially charged space of the Lascar and the vagrant. In fact, the Vagrancy Act of 1824 which, with a few amendments, dictated the legal treatment of vagrants throughout the nineteenth century, treated as a particular category of vagrant those "suspected persons or reputed thieves frequenting or loitering about a ... dock, or basin, or quay or wharf."[22]

In England, Dracula also allies himself with Renfield. In addition to his status as "madman," which places him squarely in the Victorian residuum, Renfield is, according to Seward, a "selfish old beggar," his straitjacket one from which "Jack Sheppard himself couldn't get free" (102). In these off-hand remarks, Seward reinstates the class hierarchy Renfield so flagrantly dismisses—a dismissal that deeply troubles Seward. When Renfield treats a mere asylum attendant and Doctor Seward in the same manner, Seward attributes this to Renfield's "sublime self-feeling" (100). "It looks like religious mania," Seward conjectures, "and he will soon think that he himself is God" (10). Similarly, when Renfield acts the part of a gentleman—speaking in a "courtly" (244) manner of "seconding [the former Lord Godalming] at the Windham," and praising suavely Arthur, Quincy, Van Helsing, and Seward in turn—Seward calls this "yet another form or phase of his madness" (245). Seward's indignation regarding the madman disguised as an aristocrat recalls Dickens's disdain for the "idle tramp who pretends to have been a gentleman." Like Dracula, Renfield has an uncanny ability to mask his place in the social residuum, and this ability frustrates and confuses the Crew of Light, for whom class status is crucial. It is important to them, for instance, that Jonathan is a "solicitor," not a "solicitor's clerk" (15), and that Arthur is a gentleman with "blood so pure" (122). Seward himself finds it "soothing" on the rare occasion that Renfield treats him with more respect than the asylum attendants (107).

Above all, Renfield's assistance in the vamping of Madame Mina allies him to the Count. His earlier dealings with the Count have, of course, empowered the latter to enter Renfield's window and to travel through the asylum to Mina's room (280). If unwittingly, Renfield assists in the novel's ultimate violation of bourgeois space and the ultimate—and most starkly depicted—spread of vampirism.

3

Having pointed out *Dracula*'s rhetoric of reform, and demonstrated the Count's resemblance to and alliance with the poorest of the Victorian poor, the most important questions still remain: Why would Stoker connect vampirism with extreme poverty in the first place, and what are the effects of that connection on our interpretation of Stoker's text?

Behind Stoker's use of the residuum lies what seems to be a common *fin-de-siècle* anxiety: that the English as a nation will become, like the residuum, weak, sensual, and undisciplined, and that this transformation will bring about England's decline. Social commentators of the nineties counted among their worries—along with waning global influence, the questionable legitimacy of the colonial project, and the concept of British "civilization" itself—complex changes in the middle-class moral fabric. While moral norms shifted at all levels of society, commentators focused on the poorest of the poor, since they offered the most striking portrait of domesticity, motherhood, female sexual purity, and masculinity gone awry. The vagrant and the slum-dweller lacked the orderly, comfortable home Victorian domestic ideology designated as source of family values and general moral health—and they lacked the supposed center of that home, the virtuous mother, who was often absent or, according to some, herself depraved. In the slums and "on the tramp," women did not always observe the rules of middle-class sexual virtue—be chaste, or, if married, be monogamous. Nor did men observe the rules of middle-class masculinity—be decisive, be earnest, and be a reliable provider.

Some commentators actually considered the lumpenproletariat, more than merely a portrait of deteriorating norms, a source of the nation's moral deterioration. If the disregard of motherhood, domesticity, masculinity, and female sexual purity had been part of representations of lower-class culture for decades, that disregard seemed in the nineties for the first time to be "spreading" to the middle- and upper-classes. The infamous Wilde trial of 1895 and the Cleveland Street scandal of 1889 (which uncovered a homosexual brothel catering to gentlemen) (Spencer, 206) made it clear that alternative versions of masculinity were being imagined and even acted upon by the aristocracy. Moreover, the aesthetic movement's emphasis on male sensitivity and introspection provided evidence that the "virile" ethos, the hallmarks of which were decisive action and the absence of emotional expression (Walkowitz, 17), was coming into question—at least among a vocal minority. The largely middle-class New Women who valorized women's education and work outside the home, demonstrated that, like older versions of masculinity, the cult of domesticity and its idealized version of motherhood might not prevail. More radical New Women, professing that women were entitled to the same forms of sexual expression as men, illustrated that even female chastity was not an irresistibly permanent norm. Because the middle- and upper-classes began to sanction these views long after they were sanctioned among the lower-classes (or so, at least, it seemed), commentators conceived of these views as a moral malaise spreading from the lowest ranks of the social body upward.

To this end, many myths were created. First, some claimed that vagrancy and its attendant idleness, promiscuity, and disregard of domesticity were contagious, that "any contact between intractable vagrants and respectable workers posed the danger that [wandering] impulses might be activated."[23] Others claimed that the mentally ill could spread a "contagion of moral leprosy," "multiplying a progeny" of the morally and mentally diseased, if allowed to mix with the sane of any class (Booth, 205). Slum-dwellers too were said to imperil the moral health of England. Even if their vice were somehow spatially contained, they could "rear an undisciplined population" made up of "not ... exactly the most promising material for the making of the future citizens and rulers of the empire" (66). It almost goes without saying that, above all of these, the prostitute was believed to infect the women and men of the bourgeoisie. In addition to spreading venereal disease, the prostitute inspired "lust" in men and, in the mere spectacle of her vice, imperilled the chaste female observer.

Stoker imports this model of moral contagion into his own text, for moral depravity is there represented as spreading from the vampiric residuum to the respectable middle- and upper-classes. In fact, the central anxiety among the Crew of Light is precisely the sort of lumpen takeover imagined by social commentators. Just as the slum-dweller can produce an infirm ancestral line unfit to be the "future citizens and rulers of England," Dracula can produce "a new and ever widening circle of semi-demons" (51), an entire nation of morally depraved vampires. Significantly, the spread of vice in *Dracula* occurs among those explicitly named or curiously resembling lumpen types—vagrants, madmen, prostitutes. Following the nineties commentators who believed vagrancy was contagious, Stoker depicts Dracula, a spatial nomad, as tempting Lucy to stray in Whitby cemetery, she in turn tempting the children of Hampstead to "stray from home" (177). Following the commentators who considered madmen morally dangerous, Stoker makes Renfield responsible for Mina's assault. And following the commentators who treated prostitutes as morally infectious, Stoker casts Lucy as a prostitute of sorts. Before being vamped, Lucy's nocturnal walks, alone and scantily clad, at worst suggest prostitution, at best, as Mina remarks, a serious risk to Lucy's "reputation" (92). After being vamped, Lucy's publicly sexual behavior includes the aggressive gaze and provoking deportment reformers attributed to the prostitute (Walkowitz, 23): she gazes unabashedly at the Crew of Light, her eyes "blaz[ing] with an unholy light" (211), and openly propositions Arthur, "Come to me.... My arms are hungry for you."

In addition to casting lumpen types as the transmitters of vice, when Stoker specifies just what Dracula's "semi-demons" look like, he focuses on the same vices journalists and reformers associated with the lumpenproletariat. For example, some writers castigated the "bad mother" (or absent mother) of the slums, selfish and inattentive, for causing slum conditions (Walkowitz, 120). Far less accusatory than many, William Booth comments in this vein that the lumpen-proletariat "needs a great deal of mothering, much more than it gets" (219). Stoker similarly associates vampirism with deviant motherhood. The Count repeatedly separates mother from child: the pleading Transylvanian peasant woman from her vamped baby (45), Mrs. Westenra from Lucy (thanks to the shock occasioned by Dracula's appearance [143]), and a host of Hampstead mothers from their "straying children" intent on following the "bloofer-lady," Lucy (177–78).

The Weird Sisters at Castle Dracula vamp rather than nurture the "half-smothered child" (39) Dracula throws at their feet. And after being vamped, Lucy contracts their strain of bad motherhood. When Van Helsing and Seward spot her in the cemetery, the babe at her breast is not being suckled, but sucked for blood (211).

Like the journalists of the eighties and nineties who repeatedly lamented the dust, rags, and lack of furniture in the living quarters of the very poor, Stoker adds to his picture of bad mothers the perversion of domesticity. Most of the rooms at Castle Dracula are locked or in disarray, its one comfortable chamber only a snare laid for Jonathan (16); Carfax Abbey, as mentioned before, looks and smells like a slum dwelling; and the house at Piccadilly "smells vilely," containing a wash-basin of bloodied water (301). When Dracula invades England, filth and disorder seem to spread to the Crew of Light's dwellings. At the Westenra's, the air assumes the foul smell of Dracula's quarters (Van Helsing's garlic makes Lucy's room "awfully stuffy" [133]) and the servants become drugged and debilitated (one even grows disloyal, stealing the cross that her mistress wears in death). Similarly, at Seward's asylum, Renfield actively collects the vermin that plagued the slums (68–69, 115). Finally, though this raises eyebrows among neither the Crew of Light nor any of *Dracula*'s critics, Mina, Arthur, Jonathan, and Van Helsing have by mid-novel made an insane asylum their home—a compromise of blissful domesticity to say the least.

Vampirism also entails the compromised masculinity of the lumpenproletariat. Reformers depicted the male casual laborer, like the slum-mother, as an inadequate parent—lazy, ineffectual, incapable of supporting a family (Walkowitz, 44). According to Booth, the slum-dwelling male is "impotent," his surrondings "manhood destroying" (Booth, 24). "Would it not be more merciful to kill [the very poor] off at once," asks Booth, rather than, by letting them remain in the slums, "crushing out of them all semblance of honest manhood?" (61). Jonathan and the captain of the Demeter echo Booth's sentiment: the captain wants to "die like a man" (85) rather than suffer the Count's presence; Jonathan vows that he will jump from the castle even to his death for "at its foot man may sleep—as a man" (53). While Jonathan owes his gender anxiety in large part to the aggressively sexual behavior of the female vamps and his near-miss at penetration (38), he owes it also to Dracula's advances. Dracula has, after all, exclaimed within earshot of Jonathan, "This man belongs to me! ... Yes I too can love" (39). Van Helsing too suffers the erosion of his masculinity. Otherwise free of the taints of vampirism, he begins to laugh and cry "just as a woman does" when he reflects on the ironic events surrounding Lucy's vamping and death (174).

The lumpen vice Stoker most obviously attributes to vampirism is female sexual impurity. As I have mentioned, Lucy's vampirism resembles prostitution. Even Mina, whose changes are far less extensive than Lucy's, becomes more openly amorous with Jonathan after being vamped (267). Furthermore, after being vamped both Mina and Lucy reject monogamy, another norm supposedly disregarded by the lumpenproletariat woman (Mayhew, 1:20): Lucy receives blood transfusions from three men besides her husband-to-be, the sexual symbolism of this noted later by Van Helsing (176), and Jonathan is cuckolded by Mina, whose intimate exchange with the Count takes place only feet away from him.

Wrapped up in this idea that the residuum will contaminate the upper-classes—and the vampire will contaminate the virtuous—is a preoccupation with the transgression of spatial boundaries. In fact, transgressing spatial boundaries could be identified as the controlling metaphor of *Dracula*. When the Count comes around, virtuous English citizens discover strange red marks on their necks, but, more striking, they experience a whole host of spatial transgressions, including invasions, escapes, and re-openings. The Count slips through windows and cracks of doors; "King Laugh" enters Van Helsing's body uninvited (174). The zoo animals, Lucy, and the children who follow her as the "Bloofer Lady" all escape the enclosed space they previously inhabited. Both Seward and Mina must re-open diaries they have definitively closed, the former stating explicitly, "everything is ... now reopened" (190); even Jonathan's mind becomes "unhinged" (36) after his encounter with the vamps at Castle Dracula. And of course Stoker's choice of homeland for the Count—Transylvania, across or beyond the forest—signals his interest in the crossing of boundaries.

In the decade before Stoker wrote *Dracula*, perhaps not coincidentally, an intense interest in spatial boundaries crossed by the lumpenproletariat arose among social commentators and journalists. It concerned "the threatening appearance of the poor in the 'wrong' part of town, in the form of socialist-led demonstrations of the East End unemployed in the wealthy West End" (Walkowitz, 28). This motion from East to West seemed especially transgressive in a city that was, since the era of mid-Victorian slum clearance, spatially segregated according to class (Walkowitz, 26). (Journalistic exposes such as George Sims's *How the Poor Live* [1883] and Gustave Dore and Blanchard Jerrold's *London: A Pilgrimage* [1872], further rigidified class hierarchy into geographic separation.) The demonstrations included some violence (one ended, for instance, in sporadic looting and rioting in London's principle shopping district), and came to a head on "Bloody Sunday," 18 November 1887, with yet another attempt to transgress spatial boundaries: a group of itinerant laborers and unemployed attempted to enter Trafalgar Square and were brutally repressed by police.

Only with contemporary fears of lumpen invasion in mind do the spatial invasions of *Dracula* come fully into focus. The Count's movement from Transylvania in the East to England in the West shares the same trajectory of the lumpen "invasion" from the East End to the West End of London. But more remarkable, the Count invades London itself from East to West. Mr. Joseph Smollet—the only workman, incidentally, both employed by the Count and described as "decent ... a good, reliable type" (260)—divulges the Count's plan, later recorded by Jonathan: "... the Count was fixed on the far east of the northern shore, on the east of the southern shore, and on the south. The north and the west were surely never meant to be left out of his diabolical scheme—let alone the City itself and the very heart of fashionable London in the south-west and west" (261). When Quincy and Godalming destroy the dirt boxes at Bermondsey and Mile End, then wait with the rest of the Crew for Dracula's arrival in Piccadilly, they attempt to prevent an invasion of the "fashionable London" stormed by the lumpenproletariat a decade before. In fact, Van Helsing's enigmatic reference to "King Laugh" (whose invasion of Van Helsing's body roughly coincides with the Count's invasion of England) may very well allude to those demonstrators in the West End, whom contemporary journalists dubbed "King Mob."

Vampiric and lumpenproletariat invasion share a spatial parallel even more striking: windows and doors act as the locus of entry for both. The Count's reliance on the open window to access his victims may seem rather banal for a monster of his supernatural caliber; he can change shape, command animals, and summon the "strength of twenty men" and the "aids of necromancy" (237), but has trouble with closed windows. Stoker's focus on windows and doors makes more sense, however, in light of contemporary representations of the lumpenproletariat. An 1850 *Punch* cartoon entitled "A Retired Neighborhood" (Figure 1) provides a fairly early depiction of a vagrant kept from the drawing room (and the female observer) by one thin pane of glass.[24] Like Dracula, this vagrant seems to be warded off more by a young woman's attitude than any physical barrier—she looks more disdainful than frightened. Doors and windows were associated with the lumpenproletariat in the nineties as well: Booth notes that "it is customary in the slums to leave the house door open perpetually, which is convenient for tramps, who creep into the hallways to sleep at night" (162); slum neighborhoods were distinguished from respectable working-class neighborhoods by, among other things, their open doors and broken windows (Walkowitz, 35); and the demonstrations of 1887 included, significantly, the breaking of windows in the fashionable Pall Mall district (Walkowitz, 28).

As the latter suggests, physical violence was certainly a part of late-century anxieties about the "invading" residuum. But in a decade when, as Martin J. Wiener demonstrates, novelists and journalists represent the poor as debilitated and pathetic much more often than powerful and wicked,[25] it seems clear that the anxiety generated by lumpen invasion extends much further than material risks to, as I have argued thus far, their ability to represent a decline in respectability that portends the decline of a nation. Booth's vagrant in the doorway does not threaten harm as much as stigma to the house's inhabitants. *Punch*'s vagrant at the window is more embarrassing than menacing, the humor of the cartoon deriving in large part from the young lady's predicament—she cannot possibly include a tramp in her genteel description of aristocratic leisure. Even the shattering of Pall Mall windows, while threatening and costly, also suggests the disgrace of social discord—and this at a time when the products featured in those windows have newly entered into rigorous, discouraging competition with German and American products (Arata, 622). In *Dracula*, too, the fear that the vampiric residuum will compromise respectability at times eclipses the fear that they will physically harm anyone. When Jonathan cuts himself shaving and the Count lunges with "demoniac fury" at the blood on his neck, then smashes Jonathan's shaving mirror in a fit of rage, Jonathan immediately remarks: "It is very annoying, for I do not see how I am to shave, unless in my watch-case or the bottom of the shaving-pot, which is fortunately, of metal" (26).

4

Given the *fin-de-siècle* preoccupation with crossed boundaries and the transmission of lumpen vice, the solution seems simple: the respectable and the unrespectable must be separated spatially. To this end, reformers of the last decades of the nineteenth century hatched schemes to segregate the unrespectable poor from the rest of the working class (Walkowitz, 26). The plan outlined in William Booth's *In Darkest England and the Way Out* clearly illustrates this trend, and resonates suggestively with Stoker's solution for the Count seven years later. Booth opens his book analogizing the English poor to the African native for a full four pages, concluding that, since English soil "breeds its own barbarians," "pygmies" (11), and "savages" (12), attention should be focused not on colonization and conversion of foreign lands but on homegrown problems: "... think for a moment how close the parallel is, and how strange it is that so much interest should be excited by a narrative of human squalor and human heroism in a distant continent, while greater squalor and heroism not less magnificent may be observed at our very doors"

(12). While Booth may mean well, selecting this particular analogy for its potentially powerful rhetorical effect on an audience enthralled with faraway lands and the "savages" found there, the analogy transforms the poor into foreigners who, not born in England, have no right ultimately to settle in England.

As mentioned above, Booth's image of the poor floundering in the sea off the shore of Salvation Army benevolence has the same effect. The very poor are not of our soil, this image seems to argue, but constitute a nuisance sufficiently urgent and proximate that they must be rescued. Once rescued, Booth argues, the poor should be settled in one of three colonies: the City Colony, the Farm Colony, and the Colony Across the Sea (Figure 2). Booth's description of these programs makes it clear that the Colony Across the Sea is the final solution toward which the tripartite system moves. Some in the City Colony would be "sent home to friends happy to receive them on hearing of their reformation"—the respectable reformed, in other words, can stay—but the rest would be "passed on to the Colony of the second class" (92), the Farm Colony. Once there, some "would be restored to friends up and down the country"—again, the reformed remain in England—but the "*great bulk*, after trial and training, would be passed on to the Foreign Settlement, which would constitute our third class, namely The Over-Sea Colony" (93, emphasis added). The visual depiction of the colonies, included in the 1890 edition in an 11 x 17 color foldout, sets up this teleology along the axes of Christian salvation, from the depths of the dark sea to the heights of placid sky. Emigration provides, then, the final heavenly resting place of the lumpenproletariat.

The three major phases of Booth's plan—the invasion of the poor, their stay in English communities, and their ultimate emigration—parallel the three phases of Dracula's movement. And in its final expulsion of the Count, *Dracula*'s solution to vampirism bears a striking resemblance to Booth's. For purging England of the contagion of moral decay in the social residuum facilitates the restoration of middle-class virtue. Having sheared Dracula's throat and sired a child, Jonathan recovers his masculinity; Godalming and Seward each happily marry; even Van Helsing is drawn into the domestic circle, holding little Quincy on his knee in the novel's final tableau. And of course Mina redeems the bad mothers of the text, assuming her rightful position as the "brave and gallant ... mother" who raises Quincy with "sweetness and loving care" and, equally important, provides an opportunity for male rescue—the novel's final line reminds us that the men "did dare much for her sake."

But as some critics have noted, the conclusion of *Dracula* is not as tidy and resolved as it might first appear.[26] For, as much as the Crew closes their

windows permanently to the Count, and, as this reading suggests, as much as the late-century English close their windows to the corruption of the residuum, there seem to be complicated, somewhat inexplicable forces that let them in. Several critics have identified these forces with the unconscious, arguing that Dracula's victims—whatever their conscious professions and actions—unconsciously desire to be vamped[27]: Jonathan *wants* to cross the threshold at Castle Dracula and later enter the locked drawing room to be vamped; Lucy walks in Whitby cemetery and opens her bedroom window *hoping* to meet a handsome vampire. While there is some justification for the assertion that the unconscious motivates these acts (Jonathan is, after all, an engaged man with the fruits of marital union no doubt on his mind, and Lucy has professed a playful wish to marry all three of her suitors at once [59]), these readings tend to impose an enormous amount of order and predictability on a disease that spreads in a highly disorderly fashion. It is never clear, for instance, why the supposedly innocent children of Hampstead want to be vamped, or why they will not themselves become vampires.[28] Moreover, it is completely unclear what unconscious desires, if any, explain Mina's vamping. It is not even nominally her act, as it is with Jonathan and Lucy, that admits the vampire; instead, it is Renfield, several rooms away, who admits her attacker.

There is an alternative (or an addendum) to the theory that vampiric desires are unconscious desires, and this alternative wholly jibes with one of the most crucial developments of late-nineteenth-century thought. In the midst of new theories of biological and social determinism, Stoker's text demonstrates that resisting or admitting the vampire is not—or at least not solely—a matter of free will. As David Glover points out in reference to *Dracula*, "particularly after 1880, the liberal presumption of individual autonomy came increasingly to be compromised by ideas and findings thrown up by the rapid expansion of the natural and social sciences" (Glover, 999). This ambivalence about autonomy characterizes Stoker's work, "the spheres of freedom and determinism ... always cloudy, and even multi-accentual."

In this light, the unpredictability of vampirism's spread makes more sense; even a virtuous, middle-class woman like Madame Mina cannot completely control her fate. Indeed, if, as this reading has suggested, Stoker means the spread of vampirism to stand in for the spread of cultural decline occasioned by lumpenproletariat vice, the novel seems somewhat skeptical of the control any individual English citizen can have over the normative cultural changes occurring at every turn. The erosion of domesticity, female chastity, and traditional male sexuality cannot be halted as simply and irreversibly as Dracula seems to be; nor can tough questions about new ideas—homosexuality and women's independence certainly among them—be, like Booth's lumpenproletariat, simply exiled across the sea.

On the surface, Stoker's text celebrates through the expulsion of Dracula the efficacy of sheer human effort to stem the tide of cultural change; the human will emerges from *Dracula* more than unscathed, triumphant. But as Mina's predicament shows, stealthily and inexplicably the vampire will come, whether we will or no—even if the unconscious bids him stay away. With this understanding, when Bilder the zoo-keeper claims that the London Zoo's "nice, well-behaved" wolf "escaped simply because he wanted to get out" (139), we have the sneaking suspicion that he had no choice in the matter. When Van Helsing explains that King Laugh does not ask "May I come in?" but instead "I am here" (174), we might suspect that Stoker is really talking about cultural change.

Notes

I would like to thank Nina Auerbach and David J. DeLaura for helpful comments on earlier versions of this essay.

1. For recent attempts at historicizing *Dracula*, see: Stephen J. Arata, "The Occidental Tourist," *Victorian Studies* 33 (1990): 621–45; Christopher Craft, " 'Kiss Me With Those Red Lips': Gender and Inversion in Bram Stoker's *Dracula*," *Representations* 8 (1984): 107–33; Ernest Fontana, "Lombroso's Criminal Man and Stoker's *Dracula*," *Victorian Newsletter* 66 (1984): 25–27; David J. Glover, "Bram Stoker and the Crisis of the Liberal Subject," *New Literary History* 23 (1992): 983–1002; John L. Greenway, "Seward's Folly: *Dracula* as a Critique of 'Normal Science,' " *Stanford Literature Review* 3 (1986): 213–30; Marjorie Howes, "The Mediation of the Feminine: Bisexuality, Homoerotic Desire, and Self-expression in Bram Stoker's *Dracula*," *Texas Studies in Literature and Language* 30 (1988): 104–19; Daniel Pick, " 'Terror of the Night': *Dracula* and 'Degeneration' in the Late Nineteenth Century," *Critical Quarterly* 30.4 (1988): 71–87; Carol Senf, "*Dracula*: Stoker's Response to the New Woman," *Victorian Studies* 26 (1982): 33–49; Kathleen L. Spencer, "Purity and Danger: *Dracula*, the Urban Gothic, and the Late Victorian Degeneracy Crisis," *ELH* 59 (1992): 197–225; Jennifer Wicke, "Vampiric Typewriting: *Dracula* and its Media," *ELH* 59 1992): 467–93; Jules Zanger, "A Sympathetic Vibration: *Dracula* and the Jews," *English Literature in Transition* 34 (1991): 33–44. Further citations of these in text.

2. On criminality and degeneracy, see Fontana, Pick, and Spencer; on foreignness, Arata and Zanger; on homosexuality, Craft and Howes.

3. Kathleen Spencer, for instance, identifies the novel as part of the "urban gothic" and "romance" genres, both of which focus on the "preservation of boundaries," attempting to allay fears about cultural decline through "stabilizing certain key distinctions which seemed, in the last decades of the nineteenth century, to be eroding: between male and female, natural and unnatural, civilized and degenerate, human and nonhuman" (203).

4. While a few critics have explored the class dimensions of Stoker's novel, none has connected the Transylvanian nobleman with the lumpenproletariat, and none has explored in depth the Count's relationship to the poor in general. Franco Moretti identifies Stoker's Dracula solely with capital and the bourgeoisie, rightly emphasizing Dracula's parasitic nature, but ignoring his alliance (and the bourgeoisie's sometimes-alliance) with the lumpenproletariat. Burton Hatlen in the opposite vein rightly associates Dracula with the lower classes, identifying the threat of Dracula with "the threat of a revolutionary assault by the dark, foul-smelling, lustful lower classes upon the citadels of privilege." But Hatlen misses Dracula's distance from the so-called industrious classes, calling Dracula a "peasant" and a "worker." See Moretti, "The Dialectic of Fear," *New Left Review* 136 (1982): 67–85; and Hatlen, "The Return of the Repressed/Oppressed in Bram Stoker's *Dracula*," *Minnesota Review* 15 (1980): 80–97.

5. To date, I have not found better terms than "lumpenproletariat" and "residuum" (the two are used interchangeably here) under which to group individuals such as beggars, gypsies, petty thieves, vagrants, and casual laborers "on the tramp." On the "residuum," a Victorian term, see Gertrude Himmelfarb, *The Idea of Poverty: England in the Early Industrial Age* (New York: Alfred A. Knopf Inc., 1984), 356. On the particular stigma attached to casual labor during the latter half of the century, see generally Gareth Stedman Jones, *Outcast London, A Study in the Relationship between Classes in Victorian Society* (London: Oxford University Press, 1971).

6. William Booth, *In Darkest England and the Way Out* (London, 1890), 25. All future references to Booth are from this text.

7. Lionel Rose, *"Rogues and Vagabonds": Vagrant Underworld in Britain 1815–1985* (London: Routledge, 1988), 91. Further citations in text.

8. Henry Mayhew, *London Labour and the London Poor* (New York: Dover Publications, Inc., 1968), 1:1. Further citations in text.

9. Of course Godalming is an aristocrat, but he participates in the Crew of Light's mission to uphold middle-class norms—female chastity, monogamy, medicine, technology, and the written word, among others—against Dracula's invasion.

10. At times, Mayhew becomes quite adamant about the distinction: "I am anxious that the public should no longer confound the honest, independent working men, with the vagrant beggars and pilferers of the country; and that they should see that the one class is as respectable and worthy, as the other is degraded and vicious" (3:371).

11. Bram Stoker, *Dracula* (Oxford: Oxford University Press, 1983), 251. Further references to *Dracula* are from this edition.

12. Quoted in Judith R. Walkowitz, *City of Dreadful Delight: Narratives of Sexual Danger in Late-Victorian London* (Chicago: University of Chicago Press, 1992), 27. Further citations in text.

13. Reverend Andrew Mearns, "The Bitter Cry of Outcast London," in Peter Keating, ed., *Into Unknown England 1866–1913, Selections from the Social Explorers* (Manchester: Manchester University Press, 1976), 110.

14. Mearns compares animals' lairs favorably to slums: "We do not say the condition of their homes, for how can these places be called homes, compared with which the lair of a wild beast would be a comfortable and healthy spot?" (94).

15. Peter Stallybrass and Allon White, *The Politics and Poetics of Transgression* (Ithaca: Cornell University Press, 1986), 131–32.

16. Charles Dickens, "The Uncommercial Traveller—On Tramps," *All the Year Round*, June 1860, 232.

17. Karl Marx, *The Eighteenth Brumaire of Louis Bonaparte* (New York: International Publishers, 1963), 75.

18. Through Arthur, Stoker makes explicit the latitude accorded aristocrats based solely upon their social status, for only by using "Lord Godalming's" name can Jonathan gain information about Dracula's house in Piccadilly, and only by Arthur's request for a key can they enter the house—an invasion that mirrors Dracula's invasion of England. Social extremes meet in Arthur just as they do in Dracula—he is aristocrat and burglar, the former facilitating the latter.

19. While the English identified all vagrants and poor wanderers as somewhat animal-like, gypsies bore the brunt of this stigma for their supposed fondness of "unclean meat" and their willingness to live in close quarters with animals. J. Ribton Turner, *A History of Vagrants and Vagrancy and Beggars and Begging* (London, 1887), 496–97.

20. Even the history of the gypsies in Transylvania and England suggests connections with the Count. George Borrow's 1843 *The Zincali, or An Account of The Gypsies of Spain* explains that the first gypsies in Eastern Europe "made their appearance A.D. 1417 ... and settled in Moldavia.... a greater number of adventurers followed during the next succeeding years, making excursions into Wallachia, Transylvania, and Hungary." This entry

of Gypsies from India to Dracula's own region coincides roughly with the lifetime of prince Vlad V of Wallachia, upon whom the character of Dracula is based, who lived from 1431 to 1476. A conflation of the nobleman and the gypsies who came to serve him, between Dracula and his Szgany, seems highly possible given that the Count lived in the historical period during which his country first became racially "impure." While Dracula would never admit to or even suspect gypsy lineage ("I am noble; I am *boyar*; the common people know me, and I am master" [20]), he himself remarks that his people exist in "the whirlpool of European races," that his blood, while strong, is not like Lord Godalming's, "pure." George Borrow, *The Zincali, or An Account of The Gypsies of Spain* (London, 1843), 1:14.

21. This tract is mentioned in Brian J. Frost, *The Monster with a Thousand Faces: Guises of the Vampire in Myth and Literature* (Bowling Green: Bowling Green State University Press, 1989), 43; and in Christopher Frayling, ed., *The Vampyre: Lord Ruthven to Count Dracula* (London: Victor Gollancz, 1978), 40.

22. *Encyclopedia of the Laws of England With Forms and Precedents*, vol. 14 (London: Sweet & Maxwell, 1909), 418.

23. George K. Behlmer, "The Gypsy Problem in Victorian England" *Victorian Studies* 28 (1985): 231.

24. The vagrant is more than likely Irish, given that he holds a shillelagh, a wooden cudgel that was a traditional Irish weapon. Moreover, the cartoon runs just a few years after the Irish Potato Famine, which brought an enormous influx of Irish immigrants to England, many of whom were forced to take up a tramping lifestyle. At the same time, the cartoon seems to parody *Oliver Twist's* illustration of Sikes and Fagin gazing through a window at Oliver, safe with Mr. Brownlow in the suburbs. (I am indebted to David J. DeLaura and Donald Gray, respectively, for these suggestions.)

25. Martin J. Wiener, *Reconstructing the Criminal: Culture, Law, and Policy in England, 1830–1914* (Cambridge: Cambridge University Press, 1990), 215ff.

26. Daniel Pick argues, for instance, that "the text ... recognizes a certain sense of failure—an element of horror is always left over, uncontained" (71). Richard Wasson argues, "while on the surface Stoker's gothic political romance affirms the progressive aspects of English and Western society, its final effect is to warn the twentieth century of dangers which faced it.... It is Dracula's menace that is most memorable" ("The Politics of Dracula," *English Literature in Transition* 9 [1966]: 27). Christopher Craft argues that the "triple rhythm" of Stoker's novel (characterized by the Count's invasion of England, his involvement with English citizens, then expulsion) provides "aesthetic management" for the fears and anxieties raised by the Count, but does not ultimately allay them (217).

27. For example, according to Carol A. Senf, "*Dracula* reveals the unseen face in the mirror; and Stoker's message is similar to the passage from *Julius Caesar* which ... might be paraphrased in the following manner: 'The fault, dear reader, is not in our external enemies, but in ourselves'" ("*Dracula*: The Unseen Face in the Mirror," *Journal of Narrative Technique* 9 [1979]: 170). According to Burton Hatlen, Dracula is "the other that we cannot escape, because he is part of us" (125). Gail B. Griffin argues that "the roots of ... Harker's experiences in the castle are, of course, in himself: uneasiness and fear mingle with 'longing': the 'dark and dreadful things' are in his own 'wicked, burning desire'" ("*Dracula* and the Victorian Male Sexual Imagination," *International Journal of Women's Studies* 3 [1980]: 455).

28. Van Helsing suggests that the staking of Lucy will prevent the children's transformation (215), just as the staking of Dracula prevents Mina's, but why then does he insist that if Arthur had been bitten by Lucy he would certainly after death "have become *nosferatu*, as they call it in Eastern Europe" (214)?

NINA AUERBACH

Dracula: *A Vampire of Our Own*

DRACULA'S NEW ORDER

Dracula is so musty and foul-smelling, so encrusted with the corruption of ages, that it sounds perverse to call him "new." The up-to-date young people who hunt him dread his ancientness. To them, Dracula is not simply evil; he is an eruption from an evil antiquity that refuses to rest in its grave. The earnest Jonathan Harker, who visits Castle Dracula to his bane, fears that although his shorthand diary "is nineteenth century up-to-date with a vengeance," "the old centuries had, and have powers of their own which mere 'modernity' cannot kill."[1] Ruthven and Carmilla looked as young as their enthralled prey; Dracula flings his weight of ages against the acquired skills of a single generation. Surely this antediluvian leech has no role in their smart new century.

In his novel, Dracula awes because he is old, but within the vampire tradition, his very antiquity makes him new, detaching him from the progressive characters who track him. Ruthven was in some threatening sense a mirror of his schoolfellow Aubrey; Varney reflected his predatory society; Carmilla mirrored Laura's own lonely face. But in our first clue to Dracula's terrible nature, Jonathan Harker looks in his shaving mirror and sees no one beside him. In Jonathan's mirror, the vampire has no more face

---

than does Dickens's Spirit of Christmas Future. In his blankness, his impersonality, his emphasis on sweeping new orders rather than insinuating intimacy, Dracula *is* the twentieth century he still haunts. Not until the twentieth century was he reproduced, fetishized, besequeled, and obsessed over, though many of his descendants deny his lovelessness—and perhaps their own as well. Dracula's disjunction from earlier, friendlier vampires makes him less a specter of an undead past than a harbinger of a world to come, a world that is our own.[2]

Most critics who bother to study Dracula at all proceed on the lazy assumption that since all vampires are pretty much alike, his origins extend neatly back through the nineteenth century to Lord Ruthven, Varney, and, particularly, Carmilla.[3] Dracula, however, is less the culmination of a tradition than the destroyer of one. His indifference to the sort of intimacy Carmilla offered a lonely daughter is a curt denial of the chief vampire attribute up to his time.

Carmilla aspired to see herself in a friend. Dracula, in one of his few self-definitions, identifies only with a vanished conquering race whose token is not a mortal but an animal: "We Szekelys have a right to be proud, for in our veins flows the blood of many brave races who fought as the lion fights, for lordship" (p. 28). No human can share the mirror with a lord of lost races whose names Englishmen can't pronounce. Dracula's strangeness hurls to oblivion the Byronic vampire refrain, "Remember your oath." Earlier vampires insinuated themselves into a humanity Dracula reshapes, through magic and mesmerism, into his unrecognizable likeness.

Dracula's literary affinities lie less with vampires in earlier prose tales than with Keats's *Lamia* (1820), a poem that insists on the barriers between immortal predator and human prey. Lamia is a gorgeous serpent-woman whose influence flowers in vampire works of the 1890s; before that, she mattered less to vampire writers than did Geraldine, the serpent-woman of Coleridge's *Christabel*, who bequeathed human sympathies to the vampires she engendered.

Geraldine, we remember, diffused herself into Christabel's bleak household, exuding her identity into Christabel herself and half-becoming—as Le Fanu's Carmilla would do—the dead mother of her beloved female prey. Geraldine's potency rested in the breast that transfixed Christabel, a breast the reader never saw: the fountain of her expansive power was "a sight to dream of, not to tell."

Lamia dreams and tells; its serpent-woman is less sharer than spectacle. Like Lycius, the innocent young man she seduces, we watch Lamia's transformative gyrations from without. Some of us might have breasts, but none of us has Lamia's exotically endowed body, "Striped like a zebra, freckled like a pard, / Eyes like a peacock, and all crimson barr'd."[4] Like Dracula with his Szekelys and lions, Lamia transfixes spectators because she belongs to a world only exotic animals share; no human body can emulate hers. Like Dracula's, Lamia's main vampiric attribute is not interpenetration, but transformation.

Keats's poem, like Stoker's novel, is a tale of metamorphoses. Lamia mutates continually (from serpent to goddess to mortal woman to nullity), confirming as she does so the barriers between life forms; over and over, she defines herself by what she is not. The world of Keats's gods, to which she belongs, is as distinct from that of mortals as is the world of Stoker's vampires: "Into the green-recessed woods they flew; / Nor grew they pale, as mortal lovers do" (ll. 144–45). In Coleridge's poem, Christabel's father understandably mistook Geraldine for his friend's daughter, but Keats's Lycius never thinks Lamia is human, even after her transformation into a maiden: like Stoker's seemingly mad Renfield, Lycius worships another order of being and knows he does. Christabel's household absorbed the vampire, while Lamia is segregated from the society she intoxicates: Lycius abandons his own home for Lamia's "purple-lined palace of sweet sin," a retreat as distinct from an ordinary residence as Stoker's Castle Dracula.

As with Dracula, to know Lamia is to destroy her. In the spirit of Stoker's interdisciplinary expert Van Helsing, Lycius's tutor Apollonius recognizes Lamia for what she is; he eyes her piercingly at her wedding feast, forcing her to vanish. The lore—scientific, superstitious, theological, criminological, legal, and geographic—with which Van Helsing comes equipped similarly allows Dracula to be defined and thus dissipated. For Keats and Stoker, vampires are so distinct from humanity that to know them is to dispel them; they can be cataloged, defined, and destroyed. Scientific expertise supplants the oath with which Polidori bound vampire to mortal.

Expertise had little relevance to Dracula's ancestors in English prose. Weaving in and out of their human prey, mysteriously incorporating their nature into our own, they were not remote spectacles, but congenial fellow travelers who were scarcely separable from their victim or from us, their victim/reader. Dracula is on a journey that is not ours. With his advent, vampires cease to be sharers; instead, they become mesmerists, transforming human consciousness rather than entering it. When he rejected Coleridge's Geraldine for Keats's gorgeous Lamia, Bram Stoker created an uncongenial vampire for an obscure future.

Dracula is defined by repudiations and new beginnings. Conventional wisdom assumes its derivation from *Carmilla*, but Stoker's most significant revision excised from his manuscript the shadow of Carmilla and everything she represented. In a canceled, posthumously published opening chapter, frequently anthologized as "Dracula's Guest," Jonathan Harker is trapped in a blizzard on his way to Castle Dracula. He stumbles into the tomb of

COUNTESS DOLINGEN OF GRATZ
IN STYRIA

Terrorized by her sleeping, then shrieking, specter, he is trapped until a great wolf, which may be Dracula himself, shelters him from the storm and saves him from this terrible woman.[5]

Since Carmilla is also a female vampire from Gratz, in Styria, scholars take Countess Dolingen as proof of Le Fanu's influence on Stoker.[6] Actually, though, the shadowy Countess personifies an influence rejected: the spectacle of a "beautiful woman with rounded cheeks and red lips, seemingly sleeping on a bier" (p. 170) has little to do with Le Fanu's insinuating guest, who, infiltrating the dreams of her hostess, is most dangerous when awake. Moreover, if this chapter was ever part of *Dracula*,[7] Stoker wisely deleted it, thereby exorcising an imperial female vampire who drives Dracula into an alliance with Jonathan. The women Stoker retained—Dracula's three lascivious sister-brides; the vampirized Lucy and Mina—may writhe and threaten, but all are finally animated and destroyed by masterful men. A ruling woman has no place in the patriarchal hierarchy *Dracula* affirms, a hierarchy that earlier, more playful and sinuous vampires subverted.

Dracula is in love less with death or sexuality than with hierarchies, erecting barriers hitherto foreign to vampire literature; the gulf between male and female, antiquity and newness, class and class, England and non-England, vampire and mortal, homoerotic and heterosexual love, infuses its genre with a new fear: fear of the hated unknown. Earlier prey knew their vampires and often shared their gender: Carmilla introduces herself to Laura in a childhood dream. But Dracula is barred from the dream of Stoker's hero, which admits only three "ladies by their dress and manner," one of whose faces Jonathan, like Laura, "seemed somehow to know ... and to know it in connection with some dreamy fear" (p. 51). Jonathan's flash of recognition remains unresolved, tempting later vampire hunters to identify this fair predator with Lucy or Mina or both.[8] But whichever woman arouses his dreamy fear, Jonathan surely does *not* recognize his own face in the vampire's as Le Fanu's Laura did. Like the empty mirror, the face of the demon cannot reflect its prey, nor can Dracula participate in Jonathan's exclusively heterosexual vision of three laughing chomping women who are not only an alien species, but an alien gender. Stoker austerely expels from his tale of terror the "intimacy, or friendship" that had, since Byron's time, linked predator to prey.

Like Lord Ruthven, Dracula was a proud servant's offering of friendship to a great man: the actor Henry Irving, whose splendid Lyceum Theatre Stoker managed from its ascendancy in 1878 to its fall out of Irving's control in 1898. Like Byron, Irving became a hero for his age because he played damnation with flair; his celebrated Mephistopheles gave Dracula his contours, just as Byron's sexual predations, in verse and out of it, had flowed into Ruthven. Moreover, Irving, like Byron, could be turned into a vampire by an underling not simply because he posed as a demon, but because both men radiated the hero's simulated transparency. Though they were known by all, they were tantalizingly unattainable in private to the men they lured into fellowship.

But friendship with Irving was a tribute to exalted distance, not a spur to dreams of intimacy. Ellen Terry, Irving's partner at the Lyceum, wrote shrewdly about his almost inhuman remoteness:

> H.I. is odd when he says he hates meeting the company and "shaking their greasy paws." I think it is not quite right that he does not care for anybody much.... Quiet, patient, tolerant, impersonal, gentle, *close*, crafty! Crafty sounds unkind, but it is H.I. 'Crafty' fits him.... For years he has accepted favours, obligations to, etc., *through* Bram Stoker! Never will he acknowledge them himself, either by business-like receipt or by any word or sign. He 'lays low' like Brer Rabbit better than any one I have ever met.[9]

Accepting with pride the role of Irving's liaison with the outside world, Stoker was no Polidori, fantasizing class equality and impossible communion. Stoker knew his place, a mightier one than Polidori's. As Byron's personal physician, Polidori was hired to care for that famous body, but he ministered only to be mocked. Stoker had no access to Irving's body but he did run his empire, where his responsibilities were "heady and overwhelming. He oversaw the artistic and administrative aspects of the new theatre, and acted as Irving's buffer, goodwill ambassador, and hatchet man. He learned the pleasures of snobbery," admitting only the artistic and social elite to the glamorous openings and even more theatrical banquets over which Irving presided after the performance.[10] Like Jonathan in *Dracula*, Stoker deftly manipulated the business of modern empire—particularly the intricacies of money, travel, and human contact—that paralyzed his master. Onstage, Irving's power to mesmerize crowds was as superhuman as the vampire's, but he relied, as Byron never did, on the worldly dexterity of the servant who made him immortal.

Byron's dismissal was Polidori's mortal wound, but Irving never betrayed Stoker's faith in his master's protection. Even when Irving's theatrical fortunes began to decline, shortly after *Dracula* was published, Stoker continued to celebrate his master's benevolent omnipotence, writing glowingly about "the close friendship between us which only terminated with his life—if indeed friendship, like any other form of love, can ever terminate."[11] One doubts whether the friendship was "close" in Polidori's sense, but when that life did terminate, Stoker wrote a two-volume official memoir, *Personal Reminiscences of Henry Irving* (1906), that consecrated his subject with a reverence grànted only to dignitaries and authors—never, until then, to an actor. The Irving of *Personal Reminiscences* is as marmoreally undead as the more animated Dracula.

Polidori never recovered from the humiliation of his service to Byron, writing truculently that "I am not accustomed to have a master, & there fore my conduct was not free & easy"; Stoker grew stately in his master's shadow, feeding on hero worship while paying extravagant lip service to heterosexual love.[12] Polidori's "free & easy" vampire who subsists on mortal affinities yielded at the end of the century to Stoker's master, an impenetrable creature hungering for control.

Jonathan's Master

Dracula's protracted intercourse with Lucy and Mina, whom he transforms in foreplay so elaborate that few readers notice its narrative incoherence, made him a star in the twentieth century. Jonathan Harker, the only man who is Dracula's potential prey, is overshadowed by bitten women who, in Lord Ruthven's time, were mere shadowy counters in the game between the men. Jonathan, however, is no player. His relation to Dracula is defined solely by power and status, with none of the sympathetic fluctuations that characterized the intercourse between Ruthven and Aubrey.

Polidori's Aubrey was a "young gentleman" flattered to travel with Lord Ruthven; Stoker's Jonathan Harker is not a gregarious youth on a grand tour, but a lonely tourist on a disorienting business trip who enters Castle Dracula as an employee. Dracula's ritual greeting—"Welcome to my house. Come freely. Go safely. And leave something of the happiness you bring" (p. 16)—sheds on his plodding solicitor the aura of an earlier age when travelers were gentlemen whose freedom of motion could be assumed. Fussing about his itinerary and his comfort, Jonathan is a coerced and reluctant tourist who is never his own man even before he becomes the vampire's prisoner. Encompassed by wonders and horrors, he relinquishes all responsibility for his journey with the querulous exclamation, "Was this a customary incident in the life of a solicitor's clerk sent out to explain the purchase of a London estate to a foreigner?" (p. 13).

In fact, as Jonathan goes on to remind himself, he is no longer a clerk, but a full-fledged solicitor. By the same standard, Count Dracula surely would prefer to be referred to by his title, and he is no foreigner in his own country. The edgy civil servant diminishes everything he describes; Dracula inspires in him neither wonder nor curiosity. Because Jonathan withdraws from communion into petty professionalism, employee and employer have nothing in common. Dracula's initial orations about his own heroism are a self-obsessed public presentation far from the intimate confessions of Carmilla, which demanded a response in kind. Like the Irving of Stoker's *Personal Reminiscences*, Dracula requires only an audience onto whom he can exude his construction of himself. Like the Stoker of the *Reminiscences*, Jonathan is merely the intoning man's scribe: "I wish I could put down all he said exactly as he said it, for to me it was most fascinating" (*Dracula*, p. 28).

Even when Jonathan, spying, realizes that since there are no servants in the castle, Dracula has been cooking and serving his meals, making his bed, and driving him in the coach, he feels no affinity with his host in this menial role: the servant's proficiency only reinforces the master's intimidating omnipotence. From the beginning to the end, this vampire monotonously plays the role he has assigned himself—"I have been so long master that I would be master still" (p. 20)—relinquishing the versatility of his kind.

There are no more companionable journeys, only Jonathan's uncommunicative voyeurism.[13] Instead of sharing with Dracula or feeding him, Jonathan spies on him from distant sites. Critical ingenuity can detect various subtle affinities between the horrified young man and the horrible old vampire[14]—Jonathan, does, for instance, crawl out of the castle in the same lizardlike fashion that appalled him when he watched Dracula do it—but finally, both assume the rigid roles of master and servant, spectacle and spectator, tyrant and victim, monster and human, making no attempt to bridge the distance. Caste, not kinship, determines their relationship. It is impossible to imagine Dracula admonishing Jonathan to remember his oath, for though Jonathan is a scrupulously obedient employee and even, for a while, a courteous guest, he is incapable of the voluntary—and lordly—fealty an oath demands. "Sent out" to the vampire, he quickly becomes the vampire's possession, though since he is too pure and proper to be possessed, he fittingly remains unbitten.

According to Stoker's working notes, the heart of *Dracula* was not blood, but an assertion of ownership. "One incident and one alone remained constant [from 1890] right up to publication day [in 1897]": Dracula's occupation of Jonathan. One of Stoker's editors unearths the claim at the heart of his novel:

> In March 1890 Bram Stoker wrote on a piece of scrap paper, in handwriting which he always called "an extremely bad hand": "young man goes out—sees girls one tries—to kiss him not on the lips but throat. Old Count interferes—rage and fury diabolical. This man belongs to me I want him." Again, in February 1892, in one of the many "structures he scribbled down: 'Bistritz—Borgo Pass—Castle—Sortes Virgil—Belongs to me.'" And in shorthand, again and again, over the next few years: "& the visitors—is it a dream—women stoop to kiss him, terror of death. Suddenly the Count turns her away—'this man belongs to me'"; "May 15 Monday Women kissing"; "Book I Ch 8 Belongs to me."[15]

Belongs to me. These words define the vampire the twentieth century cannot leave alone. The shared Romantic journey in which nothing impedes two gentlemen's movements but the occult ends with a servant immobilized and imprisoned in a castle he never wanted to enter. Byron's "journey through countries not hitherto much frequented by travellers" terminates in a monomaniac's refrain: "Belongs to me."

Jonathan's Progress

Dracula's possession of vampire literature was so unremittingly bleak that his best-known progeny tried not to hear their master's words. Whether they are moviemakers or literary critics, twentieth-century acolytes want to turn this account of appropriation into a love story, as if invoking "love" and "sex" would save our culture from seeing its own unresponsive face in the mirror.[16] It goes against the grain to recast Stoker's novel as a love story, but the first (and still the best-known) film adaptations tried to return to a pre-*Dracula* tradition by restoring, even intensifying, the homoerotic bond between predator and prey: both discard Stoker's Jonathan, a loyal employee to his bones, for a self-determined protagonist who willfully abandons domesticity to embrace undiscovered countries. But restoring the mutuality between victim and vampire does not restore the half-human vampire of an earlier tradition; instead, it forces us to question the possibility of human men.

F.W. Murnau's silent *Nosferatu* (1922) and Tod Browning's stagy

Dracula (1931) feature the first male mortals in our tradition whom the vampire not only lures, but actually bites.[17] Both choose to go to his country; as penance for voluntarily crossing the border, both belong to the vampire not only in body, but in blood. The young traveler into the unknown is not an infatuated schoolmate, as Polidori's Aubrey was; he is not simply "sent out," like Stoker's Jonathan; he re-creates himself in his journey toward the vampire. These early cinematic pilgrims are infected by the vampire's hunger before they set off to meet him. Their restless willingness to abandon decorum adds psychological dimension to their relation with the vampire, but it softens Stoker's impersonal vision of dominion. Stoker's Dracula can subjugate the most stolidly reluctant mortal, while these movie Draculas cast their spell only over alienated, even tainted visitors.

Murnau's film features a sick city, not an invaded nation. Renfield,[18] Stoker's lone "zoophagous" madman who becomes Dracula's acolyte only after incarceration in Dr. Seward's asylum, is in *Nosferatu* Jonathan's mad employer, a secret enemy agent who chortles over the vampire's occult messages and gloats over his wish to buy a house "in our city."

Jonathan—who now represents only a real estate agency, not the lofty British law—is as receptive to the vampire's infection as is the city itself. Gustav von Wangenheim's performance is all preening and guffawing. He is delighted to abandon the embraces and mystic foreboding of Nina (not "Mina"; see n. 18 above)—to whom he is already married in Murnau's version—for a stint in the land of the phantoms. Cautionary expertise, here embodied in the *Book of Vampires* he finds at his inn, only makes him guffaw further; with his instinctive respect for authority, Stoker's Jonathan wore the cross the worried peasant gave him, while Murnau's Jonathan tosses the book, and all authorities, aside with a blasphemous self-delighted laugh.

Unlike Stoker's traveler, who waits with impatient helplessness for various and increasingly sinister vehicles, Murnau's *walks* across the border. His coachman refuses to pass over the bridge into the land of phantoms, and so Jonathan crosses it on foot, accompanied by the portentous title: "And when he had crossed the bridge, the phantoms came to meet him."

This momentous transition is far from the nervous docility of Stoker's Jonathan: "I feared to go very far from the station, as we had arrived late and would start as near the correct time as possible. The impression I had was that we were leaving the West and entering the East" (p. 1). In Murnau's film, at the moment of Jonathan's crossing, the world changes: beyond the bridge, the film is photographed in negative, reversing the phantasmal country to black-on-white rather than conventional white-on-black.

Max Schreck's Dracula is closer to the ghostly Ruthven of the Victorian stage than to the heavily material creatures of Stoker's novel. Murnau's looking-glass photography and Schreck's luminous makeup, with his radiantly obtruding bald dome, fingers, ears, nose, and ratlike teeth (which, unlike the familiar dripping canines, he never seems to use), function like the Victorian vampire trap to dematerialize the creature's hunger. Like those of the Victorian actor disembodied in the vampire trap, his movements are ostentatiously unnatural: on the ship, he doesn't climb out of his coffin, but is miraculously elevated from it; in Bremen, he dissolves (with his coffin!) through a solid door.

Moreover, while Stoker gets his first big effect by revealing that his corporeal Dracula has no soul and therefore casts no shadow, Schreck *becomes* his shadow in the climactic episodes when he stalks Jonathan and Nina, a shadow even more elongated than his body, its interminable fingers seeming to slide through matter as it glides toward his prey. This vampire is scarcely bounded by matter, expanding into the shadow, or looking-glass image, of the madly chortling community that courted him, of which Jonathan is the representative.

Murnau not only has Dracula bite Jonathan at least once (Nina's somnambulistic powers prevent a second attack); his crosscutting emphasizes the parallel rhythms of the vampire's and Jonathan's journeys back to Bremen—a suggestive convergence that Stoker's narrative chronology suppresses—so that when the invasion finally comes, we are never sure whether Dracula or Jonathan (or both in collusion) unleashes the rats that carry the plague that wastes the city.

Like his vulnerable agents (Renfield is lynched for his collaboration with the vampire, and Jonathan is ambiguously debilitated for the rest of the movie), Murnau's Dracula is more carrier than master. His ghostliness makes him as fragile as he is agile. Isolated by his clownlike makeup and by immobilizing compositions that confine him within closed spaces or behind bars, he is no more than a shadow of the community he infects. As the first vampire to be destroyed by the sun under which Stoker's Dracula paraded vigorously,[19] he inaugurates an important twentieth-century tradition; but when Nina sacrifices herself to family and community by keeping Dracula with her after daybreak, Schreck merely vanishes. Unlike the more seductive vampires of the 1960s and '70s, he is not fleshly enough to burn.

The final title—"as the shadow of the vampire vanishes with the morning sun"—presumably heals the stricken community and Jonathan as well, allowing us to forget the ominous fact that the sun usually *creates* shadows rather than dissipating them. But Bremen has already infected itself from within. It was Jonathan's wanton walk across the bridge that desecrated his family and city, thereby fusing the domestic and the foreign, the mortal and the monster, the victim and the tyrant, all of whom Stoker kept carefully apart. By making Dracula a shadow of the good men of Bremen, Murnau also crosses the bridge between men and women that Stoker scrupulously erects: Stoker's Dracula possesses only females, while Murnau's uses no lustful, animalistic women as his agents, but only respectable men. According to the *Book of Vampires* that Jonathan discovers, "Nosferatu drinks the blood of the young." Indifferent to gender, Nosferatu unleashes mass death, not individual sexuality. Anyone, under Murnau's rules, will satisfy a vampire.

But only a pure woman can destroy one. Nina accordingly becomes the final, crucial bridge between town and invader, humanity and the monster. By luring the vampire to her bed so that he will vanish with daybreak, Nina both dies for humanity and, more knowingly than her husband, crosses the bridge beyond it. Nina's ambiguous sacrifice abolishes Stoker's polarization between pure and carnal women, for Nina is less a victim than a link between shadow and substance, life and death, corruption and respectability. She may dispel Max Schreck, but she also marries him to the civil domesticity she represents.[20]

Murnau's film is, of course, admonitory, not, as Stoker wanted to be, congratulatory: Stoker quarantined his vampire from British civilization, while Murnau's was a shadow of his own diseased Germany.[21] Thus, *Nosferatu* itself crosses the bridge between classes, genders, and orders of being that *Dracula* erected so carefully. But in bringing Jonathan and Dracula together, as sinister collaborators if not friends (Murnau's Dracula reads with silent disdain as Jonathan wolfs down his meals, while Stoker's declaims about himself at length as Jonathan nibbles delicately), Murnau does not restore the vampire's mortal sympathies; instead, he intensifies Stoker's vision of impersonal power. Max Schreck is dispelled, but he was only the city's shadow. *Nosferatu* seems to begin where *Dracula* might have ended, in a community that has been transformed into something savage and rampant. An image of the picturesque antihuman, Bremen survives its citizens, whether they are mortals or vampires.

Tod Browning's American *Dracula* is famous now only for Bela Lugosi's performance, but in one sense this commercial American movie, inexpertly adapted from a popular if quite un-Stokeresque Broadway play, is more daring than the masterpiece of German Expressionism serious audiences revere. Following Murnau's lead, Browning transforms Jonathan from a dutiful servant with corporate loyalties to an eccentric trespasser who courts transformation, but Browning's defiant explorer, the wild and maddened Renfield, is no prospective husband; he is scarcely even a man of business. Dracula's visitor is no longer Stoker's stolid, if fragile, emissary of Western civilization; as Dwight Frye plays him, Renfield is so effete and overbred that he is more bizarre than Lugosi's impeccably mannered vampire.[22]

Renfield has nothing of the employee about him: florid and faintly effeminate, he is a Hollywood version of a decadent English gentleman. Stoker's Jonathan was infallibly, if condescendingly, courteous to his Transylvanian hosts; Browning's Renfield orders them around like a stock American tourist, even calling imperiously to his unholy coachman, "Hi, Driver! What do you mean by going at this—." His disapproval is squelched only when he sees that his coach is being led by a bat (not, in this version, by Lugosi himself, whose Dracula is too stately to make a good servant). Renfield's white hat and cane make him an oddly dapper figure among the hefty Transylvanians; he floats through his coarse surroundings with a demeanor of dreamy rapture that anticipates Fred Astaire's until, to his horror, the ghostly vampire women swarm around him and he faints, only to be swooped upon by Dracula.

This Dracula never affirms "This man belongs to me," for Dwight Frye's Renfield belongs to nobody. He does claim that his journey is "a matter of business," later muttering something to Dracula about the lease on Carfax Abbey, but he represents no organization, nor is he tied to the domestic characters we will meet later. "I trust you have kept your coming here secret," Dracula intones. Renfield indicates that a secret journey posed no problem, thereby breaking the social web that bound Stoker's Jonathan to the mighty institutions of British law and marriage and implicated Murnau's Jonathan in civic corruption and domestic hypocrisy.

The doomed traveler in the American *Dracula* floats beyond ties, so it is safe for him to become Dracula's servant. Once bitten, he turns extravagantly mad, but unlike the women, he isn't quite a vampire. In the long, dull domestic portion of the film, Dwight Frye's pyrotechnics provide a counterpoint to the stolidity of humans and vampire alike, just as his character—the vampire's servant who can't shake off human sympathies—links human to inhuman by belonging to neither. Renfield is as alien and irritating to Dracula, who finally tosses him down a huge staircase, as he is to his mortal and supposedly sane caretakers. In the American 1930s, the corrupt traveler, not the vampire, is the movie's authentic alien. Sucking blood is less sinful than is Renfield's mercurial desire to leave home.

The Transylvanian beginning, the most compelling portion of the movie, hints at the old Byronic fellowship between dandy and vampire. Renfield is not Dracula's property as Stoker's Jonathan was, but neither is he Dracula's friend. The film establishes an identification between these two overdressed creatures—Lugosi wears cloak, tuxedo, and medals even indoors—that in 1931 America whispered of perversity. Bela Lugosi is not the phantom Max Schreck was; he is corpulent, clothes-conscious, and, in close-up, clearly wearing lipstick and eye makeup, the only male character who does. In the "dinner" scene that follows Jonathan's arrival, no food is served; this Dracula avoids the indignity of cooking for his guest and the awkwardness of watching him eat.[23] There is no coziness in this Castle Dracula, only the covertly titillating effect of two baroque men eyeing each other in a grotesque set freighted with cobwebs, candelabra, and suits of armor. Renfield gets only a glass of wine, and that only so Lugosi can intone his deathless "I never drink—*vine*," an archly self-aware aside that Browning's movie originates: Stoker's growling Count was no ironist.

The wine also allows Renfield to cut himself so that Dracula can eye him hungrily and then shy away from his crucifix. But even before he sees blood, Dracula has been leaning lewdly toward Renfield; when Renfield sucks the blood from his own finger, Dracula grins knowingly, presumably savoring their affinities. When, in a silent, gracefully choreographed sequence, he banishes the vampire women and stretches toward Renfield's throat, he communicates less pride of ownership than the embrace of kinship. Browning's Renfield is so clearly beyond the pale of any human community that the bond between vampire and mortal Stoker did his best to break is, however briefly and perversely, renewed.

But once they leave Transylvania and the domestic story begins, this faint communion of dandies is over: power and mastery prevail.[24] Renfield mutates from fop into madman who is always trying vainly to elude his many keepers; Lugosi also drops his foppishness, becoming so dependent on commanding attitudes and penetrating stares that he practically turns into a monument. His affinities are no longer with the mercurial Renfield, but with Edward Van Sloan's marmoreal Van Helsing, who is even more autocratic than the vampire. Whatever intensity the movie retains comes less from Dracula's predations among sketchily characterized women than from Van Helsing's and Dracula's battle of wills.

Humanity triumphs when Van Helsing becomes a more overbearing patriarch than the vampire. He disposes of the other human men almost as easily as he stakes Dracula, for Seward is a cipher and Jonathan a fool. Unable to imagine a heroic human lover, Browning's adaptation consigns Jonathan to romantic parody, breathing such lines as "My, what a big bat!" and (to Mina as she is manifesting vampiric tendencies) "You're so—like a changed girl. You look wonderful!" Such a silly man might become a husband when the vampire is dead, but he is no use to heroes. Browning drops the corporate ethos that makes the vampire hunt possible in Stoker's novel.[25] Van Helsing brooks no collaborators; he saves humanity by barking out the Dracula-like demand, "I must be master here or I can do nothing." The affinities of Transylvania fall away; the question of Browning's film is which is to be master. Once the movie concludes that humanity needs a leader, Dracula becomes surprisingly vulnerable, allowing himself to be staked with scarcely an offscreen grunt. Does he refuse to fight for his life because he misses home and Renfield?

Immediate descendants of Stoker's novel, Murnau's *Nosferatu* and Browning's *Dracula* struggle to reunite the vampire to his mortal friend. In both cases, though, apparent affinity yields to that more vulnerable bond, perversity.[26] Finally, both films acquiesce in the emphasis on power they inherit from Stoker: Murnau's stricken Jonathan languishes into the civic corruption both he and the vampire represent; Browning's Dracula abandons Renfield to his keepers to engage in an authoritarian duel with Van Helsing. Both movies finally succumb to the coldness at the heart of Stoker's novel, the requiem of a tradition of intimacy.

Dracula is a desolate inheritance for Murnau's *Nosferatu* and Browning's *Dracula*, which become more joyless as they proceed, concluding in images of ineffable loss. Both are more doleful than the novel they adapt because both banish Stoker's Lucy Westenra, whose kaleidoscopic transformations are Stoker's substitute for the affection that had been the primary vampire endowment. Lucy's transformations, the most memorable spectacles of the novel and of most movies after the 1960s, leaven the heterosexual hierarchies that deform the creatures vampires had been. By relegating Lucy to the role of an incidental off-screen victim, Murnau and Browning cast off Stoker's sadism as well as his spectacle; by focusing instead on a restless man who travels beyond boundaries toward the vampire, both apparently look back with some yearning toward the homoerotic phase of vampire literature. Finally, though, their stories are trapped in the weary decorum with which Stoker made vampires palatable in the 1890s.

Vampire Propriety

Critics unfamiliar with vampire evolution fail to notice the relative respectability of Stoker's predators, especially his women. Bram Dijkstra, for example, deplores *Dracula*'s legacy in terms quite different from mine. Disapproving of vampires in general rather than these particular vampires, he laments that after Stoker, "Female vampires were now everywhere.... By 1900 the vampire had come to represent woman as the personification of everything negative that linked sex, ownership, and money."[27] But Stoker cleaned up more than he degraded. Above all, he gentrified female vampires, who, for the first time, are monogamously heterosexual. Van Helsing even seems to doubt whether Lucy can digest female blood, at least from the veins of servants. According to his diagnosis, "A brave man's blood is the best thing on this earth when a woman is in trouble" (p. 149), and also, presumably, when she needs nourishment.

Not only do Lucy and the sister-brides in Castle Dracula prowl exclusively at men;[28] Lucy, at least, becomes more virtuous after death than she was in life. Far from personifying a reversion to woman-hating in late Victorian men, Lucy raises the tone of female vampirism by avoiding messy entanglements with mortals, directing her "voluptuous wantonness" to her fiancé alone.

"Come to me, Arthur. Leave those others and come to me. My arms are hungry for you. Come, and we can rest together. Come, my husband, come!" (p. 257). As a vampire, Lucy the flirt is purified into Lucy the wife. The restless pet who had collected marriage proposals and complained, "Why can't they let a girl marry three men, or as many as want her, and save all this trouble?" (p. 78), the enticing invalid who had "married," through blood transfusions, those very three men (plus the smitten Van Helsing), ignores, as a vampire, "those others" who bled into her adoringly: for the first time she wants her prospective husband and no one else.

Vampirism in *Dracula* does not challenge marriage, as it did earlier; it inculcates the restraints of marriage in a reluctant girl. Even before Arthur celebrates their wedding night with hammer and stake, thumping away unfalteringly while her "body shook and quivered and twisted in wild contortions" (p. 262), Dracula had baptized Lucy into wifely fidelity.

Lucy is more monogamous than the promiscuous vampires she inspired. Two representative vampire women from 1900 have no loyalties left; both are indiscriminate incarnations of female hunger. Hume Nesbit's story "The Vampire Maid" reduces its Ariadne to a biting thing: "I had a ghastly dream this night. I thought I saw a monster bat, with the face and tresses of Ariadne, fly into the open window and fasten its white teeth and scarlet lips on my arm. I tried to beat the horror away, but could not, for I seemed chained down and thralled also with drowsy delight as the beast sucked my blood with a gruesome rapture."[29] When church restorers disinter an ancient demon in F. G. Loring's story "The Tomb of Sarah," scientific reality is more ghastly than any dream: "There lay the vampire, but how changed from the starved and shrunken corpse we saw two days ago for the first time! The wrinkles had almost disappeared, the flesh was firm and full, the crimson lips grinned horribly over the long pointed teeth, and a distinct smear of blood had trickled down one corner of the mouth."[30]

Lucy's progeny, Ariadne and Sarah, do not, like her, mature through vampirism into true womanhood: they are closer to the will-less killing machines who dominate later twentieth-century vampire literature. These dreadful female mouths that feed on popular culture at the turn of the century do personify unleashed female energy in the fear-mongering way Dijkstra suggests, but this energy is not as anarchic as it looks. Since these indiscriminate biters are heterosexual, their raging desire aggrandizes men as well as depleting them.

Moreover, their men are immune from female demonism: Ariadne and Sarah offer not Carmilla's dangerous empathy, but oblivion. Ariadne induces "drowsy delight"; Sarah lures a young man by murmuring, "I give sleep and peace—sleep and peace—sleep and peace" (p. 103). These fin-de-siècle vampires do not arouse unclassified sensations; they induce postcoital fatigue. Their horror springs from their propriety. As good women, they want only men; in approved motherly fashion, they do not stimulate, but lull. The vampires Lucy spawned may be more promiscuous than she, but they are, like her, sexually orthodox. A model of wifeliness, as much a true woman as a new one, Lucy infused womanliness into her kind. Her innovative propriety is a testament to the heterosexuality of her twin creators, Dracula and Bram Stoker.

Perhaps because he is so normal, Dracula is the most solitary vampire we have met. He is, as far as we see, the only male vampire in the world: there is no suggestion that the sailors he kills on his voyage to England will join the ranks of the Undead. Moreover, he can anticipate no companionship, for Stoker's rules allow only humans to unite. "We have on our side power of combination—a power denied to the vampire kind" (p. 238), Van Helsing assures his vigilante community. Ruthven, Varney, Carmilla, and their ilk flourished because of their "power of combination": gregariousness was their lethal talent.

Innovative in his isolation, Dracula can do nothing more than catalyze homoerotic friendship among the humans who hunt him. His story abounds in overwrought protestations of friendship among the men, who testify breathlessly to each other's manhood. In fact, Van Helsing should thank the vampire for introducing him to such lovable companions. Borrowing the idiom of Oscar Wilde's letters to Lord Alfred Douglas, he declares himself to Lucy's former fiancé "I have grown to love you—yes, my dear boy, to love you—as Arthur" (p. 169). For Dracula and his acolyte Renfield, blood is the life, but the men who combine against him find life by drinking in each other's "stalwart manhood" (p. 168).

Dracula forges this male community of passionate mutual admiration, but he cannot join it. Only indirectly, by drinking Lucy's blood after the four men have "married" her (and each other) in a series of transfusions, can Dracula infiltrate the heroic brotherhood. Turning women into vampires does nothing to mitigate his solitude: his mindless creations have too little in common with him to be friends. Many twentieth-century adaptations soften Dracula's contempt for women by making him fall in love with Mina, aiming to promote her to his co-ruler, but in Stoker's original, Mina is only a pawn in his battle against the men. Stripped of his power of combination, catalyzing homoerotic friendships in which he cannot participate, this vampire loses his story, for he has no confidante willing to hear it.

Dracula begins the novel by telling an unresponsive Jonathan Harker his history in almost flawless English, but thereafter he is silent. In the massive, impeccably collated testimony that comprises the long English portion of the novel, Dracula has no voice: he leaps in and out to make occasional florid boasts, but his nature and aspirations are entirely constructed—and diminished—by others, especially Van Helsing.

As Van Helsing gains authority, Dracula's fluency evaporates into the dimensions of a case history. The lordly host who began the novel was, according to Jonathan, a master of civilized skills: "He would have made a wonderful solicitor, for there was nothing that he did not think of or foresee. For a man who was never in the country, and who did not evidently do much in the way of business, his knowledge and acumen were wonderful" (p. 44). In England, though, Jonathan and the rest turn their judgment over to Van Helsing, whose floundering English somehow confirms his authority, as that of psychiatrists will do in 1930s popular culture. Van Helsing assures his followers that the vampire is still precivilized, "a great child-brain" growing only slowly into the position of "the father or furtherer of a new order of beings" (pp. 302–3). Having devolved, under Van Helsing's authority, from magus to embryonic patriarch, Dracula is easily immobilized and trapped. As a presence, he is extinguished so early that at the end, a mere bowie knife kills him: his death requires neither Bible nor stake. Dracula is so easily, even inevitably, obliterated that all concerned forget the elaborate rituals needed to still the writhing Lucy.[31]

Dracula is dissipated less by science or the occult than by the clamor of experts that gave form to his decade. His responsiveness to his enemies' classifications sets him apart from the other great monsters of his century. Frankenstein's creature galvanized his book with an eloquent apologia halfway through. Even monsters who had not read Milton defined themselves with ease: Lord Ruthven in his various incarnations, Varney, Carmilla, all renewed themselves through compelling and compulsive self-presentations. Varney dissociated himself easily from the ignorant mob that pursued him, whose superstitious violence threw the vampire's superior humanity into relief. Dracula has no mob to tower over, but only the constraining categories of professional men. His relative silence has, of course, fed his life in the twentieth century: as we shall see, he is so suggestively amorphous in Stoker's novel that he is free to shift his shape with each new twentieth-century trend.[32] In 1897, though, Dracula was, despite his occult powers, so comparatively docile a vampire, so amenable to others' definitions, that he stifled the tradition that preceded him.

As the first vampire who conforms to social precepts, fading into experts' definitions rather than affirming his unnatural life, Dracula is a consummate creation of the late 1890s, dutifully transmitting its legacy to our own expert-hounded century. The British 1890s were haunted not only by the Undead, but by a monster of its own clinical making, the homosexual.[33] In constructing an absolute category that isolated "the homosexual" from "normal" men and women, medical theory confined sexuality as narrowly as Van Helsing does the vampire. More in conformity than in ferocity, Dracula takes definition from a decade shaped by medical experts.

I suspect that Dracula's primary progenitor is not Lord Ruthven, Varney, or Carmilla, but Oscar Wilde in the dock.[34] The Labouchère Amendment of 1885, which criminalized homosexuality among men, not only authorized Wilde's conviction: it restricted sexuality in the next decade "by shifting emphasis from sexual acts between men, especially sodomy, the traditional focus of legislation, to sexual sentiment or thought, and in this way to an abstract entity soon to be widely referred to as 'homosexuality'" (Dellamora, *Masculine Desire*, p. 200). The Wilde trials of 1895 put a judicial seal on the category the Labouchère Amendment had fostered. As a result of the trials, affinity between men lost its fluidity. Its tainted embodiment, the homosexual, was imprisoned in a fixed nature, re-created as a man alone, like Dracula, and, like Dracula, one hunted and immobilized by the "stalwart manliness" of normal citizens. Now unnatural and illegal, the oath that bound vampire to mortal was annulled.

Before the Wilde trials, vampires felt free to languish in overtly homoerotic adoration of their mortal prey: in "The True Story of a Vampire" by Eric, Count Stenbock, published the year before Wilde's incarceration, Count Vardalek madly plays Chopin to a faunlike young man, kisses him on the lips, and weeps over his "darling's" diminishing "superabundance of life."[35] Dracula was born in reaction to Vardalek's devouring love: new rules imposed on his alien kind forbid him to love anyone on earth. The only music that moves him is the music of the wolves, and he cannot participate even in that.

Dracula's silence recalls the silence forced on the voluble Wilde after his trials. The foreigner who had poured out irresistible words in flawless English tried vainly to speak after the judge had sentenced him to prison. "'And I?' he began. 'May I say nothing, my lord?' But Mr. Justice Wills made no reply beyond a wave of the hand to the warders in attendance, who touched the prisoners on the shoulder and hurried them out of sight to the cells below."[36] As in the London books of *Dracula*, the versatile and florid performer disappears under institutional regulation.

The ghostliness of earlier vampires had deflected improper intercourse with mortals: when a vampire walked through walls or turned for life to the moon, audiences remembered that he was another order of being, one whose body (as opposed to his teeth) could not quite penetrate a human's. Dracula, fully corporeal, has no sheltering spirituality, and so he is as vulnerable as Oscar Wilde to opprobrium and incarceration. Unlike Wilde, however, Dracula is careful.

His intensifying silence, his increasing acquiescence in what experts say he is, reflect the caution of Stoker's master, Henry Irving. In 1895, just after the Wilde trials—which subdued English manhood in general and the English theater in particular—Stoker began in earnest to write *Dracula*, which had haunted him for five years. Irving had spent 1895 lobbying for his knighthood (the first ever awarded to an actor) by petrifying himself and his Lyceum into attitudes of patriotic grandeur, although his imperial postures had been assaulted by two wicked Irishmen: Shaw, whose savage reviews exposed, in the person of Irving, all British heroes to terrible laughter; and the seductively rude Wilde, whose comedies mocked everything that was supposed to inspire Irving's audiences. Bram Stoker, a third Irishman but a loyal one, protected Irving against potentially lethal laughter. His *Dracula* was fed by Wilde's fall, but its taboos were those of his master, whose reward came on May 24, 1895: on that day Irving's knighthood and Wilde's conviction were announced, ending the comedy. As a martyr, though, Wilde had won, for he drained the vitality of Stoker's vampire as consummately as he had deflated Irving's heroics in his glory days.

When Irving died ten years later, the *Daily Telegraph* praised him for rescuing England from the "cult" of Oscar Wilde (quoted in Skal, *Hollywood Gothic*, p. 36). But he never rose again. Irving and all heroes were forced to define themselves in opposition to the devastating figure of Wilde, whose fate became an actual vampire that drained the vitality of future theatrical generations.[37] Irving held the stage for a few more years because of what he was not; he turned from player to exemplary façade. Oscar Wilde in prison constricted actors as well as vampires, forcing expansive figures into self-protecting silence. The Wilde trials, and the new taboos that made them possible, drained the generosity from vampires, forcing them to turn away from friendship and to expend their energies on becoming someone else.[38]

Transformations

Adhering to more taboos than he breaks, Dracula inhibits future vampires in major ways. Varney and his ilk reached outward to take their essential life from the moon; Dracula takes his from his coffin. His existence is hedged by absolute if arbitrary rules vampires fear to break even now. His need to travel with hampering boxes of native earth; his enfeebling inability to form alliances; his allergies to crucifixes, communion wafers, and garlic;

his vulnerability to daylight—all defined vampires by the many things they could not do.

In Transylvania, his fixed role of master blocks his infiltration of human lives; in London, his helpless responsiveness to expert definition depletes him long before his actual death. The creature who insists on playing master is forced to take the shape of human fears. But despite these impediments, Dracula has one gift that inaugurates a new dispensation for vampires: his transforming powers, the sole compensation for his hedged-in life.

Before *Dracula*, vampires were incessantly, aggressively, themselves, though some, like Varney, had a predilection for disguise, while others, like the stage Ruthven, faded in and out of materiality. The midcentury moon, the source of their occult powers, turned them on and off like a light switch without altering their natures. Early film Draculas share these intact egos, scarcely evoking Stoker's mutable monster. Max Schreck's and Bela Lugosi's define themselves by florid, reiterated mannerisms and extravagant makeup that immobilizes their expressiveness. "I *am* Dracula," Lugosi announces with ponderous relish. Surely he will never be anyone else.

Stoker's Dracula, on the other hand, is many creatures, not all of whom have titles or even names. Not only does he go from a steely old man to a frisky young one in the course of his novel, stealing the youth from a Jonathan grown white-haired and tired; he becomes at need a wolf, a bat, a dog, as well as fog and mist. Animals flee Max Schreck's phantasmal Dracula, the enemy of vitality, but animals become Stoker's Dracula, who inaugurated the shape-shifting vampire we live with today. Barred from union with mortals or with other vampires, Dracula diffuses his solitary nature into other orders of being.

But his transformations are more convenient than spectacular. After reaching London, he is so indirect a presence in his story that his metamorphoses are muffled. We never see him changing shape; his ability to slide in and out of human form makes him a wily antagonist, not a source of awe. His changes are modestly presented compared to those of Lucy and Mina, his female victims. Once again, women perform on behalf of withheld males the extreme implications of vampirism. Just as Carmilla played out the erotic implications of Ruthven's forbidden friendship, Lucy and Mina exhibit the new metamorphic prowess of vampirism in the 1890s.

One of Stoker's great chills is Van Helsing's tolling line: "Madam Mina, our poor, dear, Madam Mina, is changing" (p. 382). The line is authentically frightening because it is uncharacteristically subtle, reminding us that we have no fixed idea what Mina is changing into. We know what Lucy, the pampered belle, became when she changed, but how can Mina become a fleshly predator, a "bloofer [beautiful] lady" who offers children dangerous kisses?

For Mina, unlike Lucy, is an earnest wife and unwavering motherly beacon inspiring brave men. Even before she is bitten, her almost occult secretarial competence endows her with the metamorphic potential of the New Woman; she repeatedly saves the day by knowing some bit of mystic lore about office work. Accordingly, once Mina begins to be a vampire, she is no bloofer lady, but a medium whose mind forces itself into Dracula's until, immobilized in his coffin, he virtually becomes her creature. Lucy is transformed into a ravenous animal, Mina into a clair-voyant; neither is like their progenitor Dracula (both lack his shape-shifting ability, hairy palms, red eyes, and veneer of civility), nor do they have the ironic tinkling laughs of Dracula's Transylvanian sister-brides. No vampire, it seems, is like any other. In fact, as vampires, Lucy and Mina have less in common with each other than they did when they were alive. The discrepancy between the women's transformations hints at the range of a vampire's possible selves.

Sexually, Stoker's vampires are dutifully conventional; personally, they lack flair, craving only power and possession. They are striking only in their transformative potential. Like all respectable creatures, they suggest more selves than they let us see. Most particularly, their animal affinities, which may seem the ultimate constraint in their already constrained lives, point toward an expanded being new to vampires.

> Hitherto I had noticed the backs of his hands as they lay on his knees in the firelight, and they had seemed rather white and fine; but seeing them now close to me, I could not but notice that they were rather coarse—broad, with squat fingers. Strange to say, there were hairs in the centre of the palm. The nails were long and fine, and cut to a sharp point. As the Count leaned over me and his hands touched me, I could not repress a shudder. It may have been that his breath was rank, but a horrible feeling of nausea came over me, which, do what I would, I could not conceal. (Pp. 25–26)

In Jonathan's first extended view of Dracula, he is fine (aristocratic) in dim light, coarse (animal) when he comes close. His civilized and his brutal sides seem as rigidly differentiated as were Dr. Jekyll and Mr. Hyde's. No one but Jonathan suggests that his breath may be rank; Lucy and Mina, who know his mouth, never admit to smelling it; thus it is likely that it is not his bad breath, but his hairy palm, or animal potential, that brings on Jonathan's "horrible feeling of nausea." On this first meeting, Dracula flaunts his animalism more than he will do later. His sly touch is a prelude to his lyrical response to the howling of the wolves: "Listen to them—the children of the night. What music they make!" (p. 26). His wolfish affinity repels Jonathan, but in this suggestive tribute, Dracula expands beyond hierarchical categories to appropriate an inhuman art that goes beyond the mere brutality of a Mr. Hyde.[39]

Apart from his trademark bloody fangs, Dracula loses his expansive animalism in most twentieth-century films. Actors like Lugosi, Christopher Lee, and Louis Jourdan may be sexier on the surface, but they are so self-consciously irresistible that it is hard to picture them howling with wolves. In most vampire films, animalism is less metamorphosis than coded eroticism, but in late Victorian England, animals were not represented as notably sexual. Instead, they generated a lonely awe human beings were too socialized to inspire.

"'I wonder,' [Seward asks Renfield, his zoophagous lunatic] reflectively, 'what an elephant's soul is like!'" (p. 324). The question torments Renfield, leading Seward to conclude that "he has assurance of some kind that he will acquire some higher life. He dreads the consequence—the burden of a soul" (p. 325). In his assumption that only "higher life" has a soul, Dr. Seward shrinks into humanity just as Jonathan Harker did when Dracula's hairy palm touched him. The zoophagous maniac knows better. The resonant question of animal souls, or some purely animal principle of existence, lends intimations of transfiguration to Stoker's bleak portrait of vampires.[40]

It is not Dracula rampant or Dracula in his coffin that inspires Jonathan's half-despairing, half-awed cry: "What manner of man is this, or what manner of creature is it in the semblance of man?" (p. 48). At the climax of his Transylvanian visit, Jonathan is stricken with holy terror at his host's elusive animalism: "What I saw was the Count's head coming out from the window. I did not see the face, but ... I could not mistake the hands which I had had so many opportunities of studying.... But my very feelings changed to revulsion and terror when I saw the whole man slowly emerge from the window and begin to crawl down the castle wall over that dreadful abyss, *face down*, with his cloak spreading out around him like great wings" (pp. 47–48).

Since he can turn into a bat, Dracula has more efficient means of transportation than crawling down his castle walls; perhaps he does so here only for exercise, but his sport devastates Jonathan with a vision of otherness in human shape. It also teaches Jonathan his own metamorphic potential; with the deftness of Kipling's Mowgli picking up animal skills in the jungle, he will escape from the castle by similarly crawling down the wall: "Where his body has gone why may not another body go?" (p. 62). Jonathan's chaste emulation of his master's body is as close as he comes to turning into a vampire. He is never as hungry as Lucy or as clairvoyant as Mina, but when he emulates Dracula, he does briefly expand his awareness of his own potential elasticity.

In its time, Dracula's descent, not the three weird women who captivate Jonathan in the next scene, was the heart of the novel's horror; Skal (*Hollywood Gothic*, p. 39) reproduces the cover of the first paperback edition, in which Dracula, a dignified old man, crawls down his castle wall. His short cloak does not begin to cover his agile body; his sleeves and trousers are hiked up to emphasize the recognizably human hands and bare feet with which he propels his descent. This Dracula has no fangs, long nails, blazing eyes, or other vampire accoutrements familiar from later illustrations and films: his horror is his human body, a horror that lived beyond the turn of the century. In a draft of *The Waste Land*, T. S. Eliot amplifies his "bats with baby faces in the violet light" with the *Dracula*-derived line, "I saw him creep head downward down a wall."[41]

Attracted as our own century is to the three slavering sisters, with a relish we insist is Victorian, these lustful fiends decorate neither the original paperback nor T. S. Eliot's Modernist Gothic. In its time, *Dracula*'s most resonant image was that of a lone human body doing a supposedly nonhuman thing associated with neither sexuality nor predation. As in his paean to the music of the wolves, he is exhibiting, for no particular reason, his animal affinities.

Dracula was not the first Victorian monster to flaunt his transfiguring animal potential. In 1884, a young surgeon with some of the compassionate curiosity of Stoker's Dr. Seward was transfixed by a poster advertising the spectacle of an Elephant Man. The actual Joseph Merrick, whose patron Frederick Treves became, was a tragic example of false advertising: a small man weighted down by deforming epidermal growths, the frail Merrick had little in common with an elephant. Nevertheless, when Treves wrote his memoir forty years later, he described the poster more vividly than he did his patient:

> Painted on the canvas in primitive colours was a life-size portrait of the Elephant Man. This very crude production depicted a frightful creature that could only have been possible in a nightmare. It was the figure of a man with the characteristics of an elephant. The transfiguration was not far advanced. There was still more of the man than of the beast. This fact—that it was still human—was the most repellent attribute of the creature. There was nothing about it of the pitiableness of the misshapen or the deformed, nothing of the grotesqueness of the freak, but merely the loathing insinuation of a man being changed into an animal. Some palm trees in the background of the picture suggested a jungle and might have led the imaginative to assume that it was in this wild that the perverted object had roamed.[42]

Responding to the "transfiguration" of the poster rather than the pathos of the man, Treves could be describing the crawling Dracula: "There was still more of the man than of the beast. This fact—that it was still human—was the most repellent attribute of the creature." Like Dracula crawling down his battlements or Kafka's Gregor Samsa waking from uneasy dreams, the poster of the Elephant Man reveals the creaturely capacities of an apparent human whose "repellent" animalism may endow him with holy terror: Leslie Fielder associates the Elephant Man with such un-Christian divinities as "the elephant-headed Ganesh from the Great Temple at Karnak, awesome but somehow neither loathsome nor grotesque."[43] The image of a monster who may also be a god forces on Treves Dr. Seward's perplexed question: "I wonder ... what an elephant's soul is like!"

After Merrick died, Treves convinced himself that this elephant at least had a soul, one that cast off the beast to assume a perfect manly body: "As a specimen of humanity, Merrick was ignoble and repulsive; but the spirit of Merrick, if it could be seen in the form of the living, would assume the figure of an upstanding and heroic man, smooth browed and clean of limb, and with eyes that flashed undaunted courage." Dracula brings no such assurance to the professional men who study him. Dracula, like Merrick, is a dandy who lives without mirrors, an essential celibate with embarrassingly "amorous" proclivities,[44] a charismatic isolate who is helpless before the human community. As with Merrick, his one source of stature is his propinquity to animals.

The nineteenth-century Development Hypothesis, most famously demonstrated in Darwin's revelations of humanity's animal origins, revised Victorian faith in humanism—and thus in heroism—in ways that involved both denial and abashed embrace. Throughout the century, guardians of powerful institutions affirmed their shaky humanity by cataloging and thus controlling animals as Van Helsing does Dracula: as Harriet Ritvo demonstrates, "Animals were uniquely suitable subjects for a rhetoric that both celebrated human power and extended its sway, especially because they concealed this theme at the same time that they expressed it."[45] Accordingly, at midcentury, Tennyson became Poet Laureate after his *In Memoriam A. H.* exhorted struggling readers to evolve beyond their animal inheritance by "working out the beast, / And let the ape and tiger die."

But animals were not so easily killed: their new genealogical intimacy with humans raised them, in the eyes of compassionate reformers, to moral and spiritual exempli whose life shared human sacredness. In 1847, the *Christian Remembrancer* forbade pious readers to let apes and tigers die: "There is a growing feeling of reverence for the lower creation.... We regard them as sharers in one quality, and that the most tangible portion of our inheritance—they share in life, they are living creatures."[46] Like Renfield's biblical "the blood is the life," philanthropic reverence undermined human-centered hierarchies on behalf of a vital fellowship whose sacred essence was pagan. As literary rhetoric became increasingly weary and pessimistic, this fellowship became covert salvation: union with animals beatified a declining humanity. By the 1890s, man himself seemed so depleted that, in fiction at least, the ape and tiger might have been all that kept his vitality alive.

Kipling's *Jungle Books* (1894) feature a boy-hero fitting for a shrunken decade who, far from working out the beast, takes his power from beasts: raised by wolves and schooled by a wise panther and a tender bear, Mowgli relishes the ontological fluidity and heroic skill instilled by his jungle teachers. Though Kipling's narrator ranks the animals in incessant if arbitrary fashion, assuring us, like the guardian of culture he wants to be, that they all defer to Mowgli's human superiority, these hierarchical protestations fall away when Mowgli graduates into a human society more brutish than the jungle. In his first foray to his kind, he is banished for being a "wolf-child," "a sorcerer [like Dracula] who can turn himself into a beast at will."[47] When, indisputably a man, he leaves the jungle for the last time, his life as an Indian civil servant will surely lack the perpetual transfiguration of a jungle existence where he spoke every animal's language. Kipling tempts us to picture a colonized Mowgli sighing nostalgically for the wolves and his wolf-self: "Listen to them—the children of the night. What music they make!"

Only his animal affinities make Mowgli worth writing about at all. Like the Elephant Man who preceded him and the vampire that followed, Mowgli is a hero because he can become an animal. The animals that glorify the boy have little to do with eroticism, which, in the *Jungle Books*, is virtually a human trait: Mowgli knows he must leave the jungle when he reaches puberty and finds himself drawn to a woman. The loving and potent community he leaves behind—the snake Kaa, the bear Baloo, the panther Bagheera, and his tutelary brother wolves—is composed of aging male celibates. In most 1890s representations, animals are grand because they scarcely couple. Like that of the Elephant Man, their allure is their singularity.

Dracula crawling down his castle walls is not as winsome as the Elephant Man or Mowgli, but he is like these late-Victorian hybrids in that his creaturely alienation from humanity makes him the center of a cult, one that in Dracula's case is thriving today. Monotonously asserting a dominion that isolates him from humans and other vampires; so alone that, like most tyrants, he is vulnerable to anything that is said about him; hedged by the arbitrary rules that have come to define his vampireness: Dracula steals power from awe-inspiring animals.

This power is muted compared to Mowgli's; aside from a few nostalgic remarks and his one solitary crawl, we never see him changing. In England, his one gesture of animal kinship—apart from commanding a swarm of rats to frighten the vampire-hunters away—is his release of the wolf Bersicker from the zoo, a perplexing gesture described so indirectly that we never see Dracula and the wolf together. Does he need Bersicker to let him into Lucy Westenra's bedroom, to which he always had access before? Or does he, like Mowgli, come into his powers in the company of wolves? Like his crawl, his release of the wolf makes little narrative sense,[48] but it does provide this vampire with the one bond his author does not taboo.

Though Stoker only sketches Dracula's animal metamorphoses, awe at animals underlies his story. Van Helsing demonstrates wonders to his skeptical hearers by summoning a pageant of immortal beasts: "Can you tell me why, when other spiders die small and soon, that one great spider lived on for centuries in the tower of the old Spanish church and grew and grew, till, on descending, he could drink the oil of all the church lamps? ... Can you tell me why the tortoise lives more long than generations of men; why the elephant goes on and on till he have seen dynasties; and why the parrot never die only of bite of cat or dog or other complaint?" (p. 237).

Dracula's association with these vigorous creatures gives him a subterranean vitality new to his kind: it is less his autocratic assertions than his unbounded identity and his ability to expand the identities of others beyond human limits that give Dracula the aura of power his plot, in fact, denies him. Succeeding Draculas would not know what to make of the metamorphic power that had such intensity in the 1890s. While Max Schreck's teeth are ratlike, he never turns into a rat, seeming most alive when he is half-disembodied or swelling into a shadow. Bela Lugosi is occasionally replaced with a rubbery bat, but Lugosi himself is so statuesque that one cannot imagine him changing into anything.[49] Wolf aficionados in the first half of the twentieth century took the more pathetic form of were-wolves. I suspect, though, that without his furtive animalism, Dracula would never have survived to metamorphose on film. His empathy with "children of the night" rather than with humans released a dimension of fear: the fear, not of death and the dead, but of being alive.

The Blood Is the Life

Earlier vampires may not have been mortal, but they could pass as human. Despite his corpse-like pallor, Ruthven was a popular party guest, while even with his protruding teeth Varney was a far better neighbor than Dracula would be. Only his eyes reveal his malevolence, but there is nothing characteristically animal about "a lurking and suspicious look," which could characterize any number of human villains and paranoid heroes.

Carmilla appears to be winsomely human. She becomes an animal only fitfully and ambiguously, and only when she is feeding. Laura perceives "a sooty black animal that resembled a monstrous cat. It appeared to me about four or five feet long, for it measured fully the length of the hearth-rug as it passed over it; and it continued to-ing and fro-ing with the lithe sinister restlessness of a beast in a cage.... I felt it spring lightly on the bed," but in Laura's kaleidoscopic perception the cat quickly mutates into "a female figure standing at the foot of the bed, a little at the right side." When the General replaces her as narrator, he describes the feeding creature as less animal than thing, "a large black object, very ill-defined, crawl[ed], as it seemed to me, over the foot of the bed, and swiftly spread itself up to the poor girl's throat, where it swelled, in a moment, into a great, palpitating mass."[50] Compared to Dracula, whose first appearance reeks of animalism, Carmilla is at best "very ill-defined." We know her only as a passionate friend who in her hunger becomes something else.

Dracula's blatant animal affinities are new to vampires; they alone lend vitality to this constricted, life-denying tyrant. Dracula is not only unprecedentedly animal-like; he is the first vampire we have met who is not visibly a corpse. Like the vampires he makes, he is alive even in his coffin: "It seemed as if the whole awful creature were simply gorged with blood; he lay like a filthy leech, exhausted with his repletion" (p. 67). Ruthven was notable for "the deadly hue of his face, which never gained a warmer tint" (Polidori, *The Vampyre*, in *Penguin*, p. 7), but Dracula is hideously ruddy. Ruthven was dead; Dracula, in Stoker's suggestive coinage, is *un*dead.

This coinage was central to Stoker's image of his book, which, as late as a month before publication, was titled not *Dracula* but *The Un-Dead* (Frayling, *Vampyres*, p. 300). The original title may be less striking than the weird name, but it points toward the essential gift of Stoker's vampires to the twentieth century: a reminder, not of the dreadfulness of death, but of the innate horror of vitality.

"The blood is the life! The blood is the life!" Renfield cries for them all (p. 181). But this paean to bodily fluids entered our imaginations only with Bram Stoker's Undead. Earlier vampires enfeebled their prey; Dracula energizes his, reminding his victims—and us—that they have life in them. Just as he makes Jonathan aware of his animal potential, he executes transformations that are less purely erotic, in the sense of something shared, than they are sensory: the women he transforms come to apprehend the vibrancy of their world. Le Fanu's Laura was aware under Carmilla's ministrations only of Carmilla and her own sensations, but Stoker's Lucy describes her initiation as a breathtaking awareness of newly vivid surroundings. Despite our own critical infatuation with Dracula's sexuality, Lucy's awe at her expanded world is as solitary as Jonathan's crawl down the castle:

> I remember, though I suppose I was asleep, passing through the streets and over the bridge. A fish leaped as I went by, and I leaned over to look at it, and I heard a lot of dogs howling—the whole town seemed as if it must be full of dogs all howling at once—as I went up the steps. Then I have a vague memory of something long and dark with red eyes, just as we saw in the sunset, and something very sweet and very bitter all around me at once; and then I seemed sinking into deep green water, and there was a singing in my ears, as I have heard there is to drowning men; and then everything seemed passing away from me; my soul seemed to go out from my body and float about the air. I seemed to remember that once the West Lighthouse was right under me, and then there was a sort of agonising feeling, as if I were in an earthquake, and I came back and found you shaking my body. I saw you do it before I felt you. (P. 130)

Stoker's Undead do not drain vitality; they bestow it. Anne Rice will glorify this sensory reincarnation as quasi-angelic "vampire sight," but in the 1890s Stoker associates it with the unabashed blood-awareness only animals enjoy.

A pageant of wounded women illustrates vampires' progress, at the turn of the twentieth century, from death to heightened life. In Polidori's *Vampyre*, Aubrey is entranced by the "lifeless corpse" of his beloved, on whom Ruthven has fed: "He shut his eyes, hoping that it was but a vision arising from his disturbed imagination; but he again saw the same form, when he unclosed them, stretched by his side. There was no colour upon her cheek, not even upon her lips; yet there was a stillness about her face that seemed almost as attaching as the life that once dwelt there" (*Penguin*, p. 15). Aubrey's Ianthe is doubly still because there is no suggestion that Ruthven has transformed her; the vampire's animating powers affect no one but his splendid self. Like Wordsworth's mountains or Keats's urn, Ianthe lures the poetic viewer because she is utterly without life. The vampire bestows a stillness no mortal can emulate.

Varney's supine Flora is more ambiguous. As a potential vampire, she is "more beautiful than death" not because she is livelier—like Ianthe, she is irresistibly immobile—but because death's proximity turns her into art.

> She looked almost the shadow of what she had been a few weeks before. She was beautiful, but she almost realized the poet's description of one who had suffered much, and was sinking into an early grave, the victim of a broken heart:
>
> "She was more beautiful than death,
>
> And yet as sad to look upon."
>
> Her face was of a marble paleness, and as she clasped her hands, and glanced from face to face ... she might have been taken for some exquisite statue of despair. (Rymer, *Varney*, p. 134)

Death clings to Flora while she lives, making her desirable. When Stoker's Lucy is a corpse, she is desirable because she is not dead at all: "There lay Lucy, seemingly just as we had seen her the night before her funeral. She was, if possible, more radiantly beautiful than ever; and I could not believe that she was dead. The lips were red, nay redder than before; and on the cheeks was a delicate bloom" (p. 245).

Once again, women display the powers male vampires are too respectable to release.[51] "She was more beautiful than death"; "I could not believe that she was dead." It is not only that Lucy changes; she embodies the change in the vampire's powers. Earlier female victims were seductive because stilled. Through them, death immobilized life, while in *Dracula*, life engorges death. Lucy enthralls spectators because she is *not* stilled. After death, she continues to writhe and foam, prowl and shriek, turning not to marble, but to blood.

It is easy and obvious to condemn out of hand the sexist sexuality of her staking, in which her fiancé "looked like a figure of Thor as his untrembling arm rose and fell, driving deeper and deeper the mercy-bearing stake, while the blood from the pierced heart welled and spurted up around it" (p. 262), but its erotic vitalism is, for better or worse, vampires' new medium. The parallel scene of Clara's staking in *Varney* is all bloodless, loveless horror. The blacksmith, a more efficient executor than the vampire's stricken fiancé, does the staking with dispatch, after which Clara's father goes mad and the family collapses. We last see the benevolent patriarch Sir George Crofton gibbering about his own transformation: "I am a vampyre, and this is my tomb—you should see me in the rays of the cold moon gliding 'twixt earth and heaven, and panting for a victim. I am a vampyre" (p. 839).

When Clara is staked, her father's authority dissolves into vampiric babble, while Lucy's staking confirms the authority of an armed community of fathers. Granted that her wedding is a rape; vampires who appreciate only power and possession participate only in ceremonies of coercion. But for all the violence she ignites, Lucy is the first dead girl we have met who is in her heart alive. Inflexibly conventional, recoiling from intimacy, she and her bloody kind have survived decades of disapproval because they have no love of death and no sympathy with stillness. We may not like these vampires, but we continue to believe in them. Perhaps our century has made it impossible for us to believe in wiser fiends or better friends.

Notes

1. Bram Stoker, *The Essential Dracula*, ed. Leonard Wolf (1897; reprint, New York: Penguin, 1993), pp. 49–50.

2. Recent critics assiduously confine Dracula in his century; New Historicism or blindness to Dracula's role in shaping our present inhumanity inspires ingenious readings that see in him the spirit of 1897, Victoria's Diamond Jubilee year. Dracula has never been recognized as Stoker's bequest to a future that includes ourselves. Franco Moretti, for instance, sees in *Dracula* an allegory of 1897 capitalism; Christopher Craft brilliantly exposes its homoerotic undercurrents, "a pivotal anxiety of late Victorian culture," without acknowledging the more compelling and explicit homoeroticism of a tradition Stoker does his best to purge from *Dracula;* Stephen D. Arata reads *Dracula* as a late-Victorian nightmare of "reverse colonization," whereby "primitive" races supplant enervated Anglo-Saxons; Judith Halberstam analyzes Dracula's convergence with late-nineteenth-century anti-Semitic constructions of the smelly, parasitical Jew. See Franco Moretti, *Signs Taken for Wonders*, trans. Susan Fischer, David Forgacs, and David Miller, 2d ed. (New York: Verso, 1988), pp. 83–108; Christopher Craft, " 'Kiss Me with Those Red Lips': Gender and Inversion in Bram Stoker's *Dracula*," *Representations* 8 (Fall 1984): 107–33; Stephen D. Arata, "The Occidental Tourist: *Dracula* and the Anxiety of Reverse Colonization," *Victorian Studies* 33 (Summer 1990): 621–45; and Judith Halberstam, "Technologies of Monstrosity: Bram Stoker's *Dracula*," *Victorian Studies* 36 (Spring 1993): 333–52.

3. See, for instance, Christopher Frayling's tidy genealogy in *Vampyres: Lord Byron to Count Dracula* (London: Faber and Faber, 1992), pp. 3–84.

4. *The Poems of John Keats* (London: Oxford University Press, 1961), p. 162, ll. 49–50.

5. Bram Stoker, "Dracula's Guest" (1897; first published 1914), reprinted in *Penguin*, pp. 163–74.

6. See, for instance, Robert Tracy, "Loving You All Ways: Vamps, Vampires, Necrophiles and Necrofilles in Nineteenth-Century Fiction," in

Sex and Death in Victorian Literature, ed. Regina Barreca (Bloomington and Indianapolis: Indiana University Press, 1990), p. 42. William Veeder assumes that Van Helsing derives from Le Fanu's Dr. Hesselius and Baron Vordenburg, but long before Le Fanu's time, the vampire expert was a stock character in the theater: Planché's helpful chorus of spirits tells us what the vampire is, as does Boucicault's more accessible Dr. Rees. Keats's nasty expert Apollonius in *Lamia* is the most canonical example of the vampire hunter who kills by expertise. See William Veeder, Foreword, *Dracula: The Vampire and the Critics*, ed. Margaret L. Carter (Ann Arbor: UMI Research Press, 1988), p. xvi.

7. An assumption I, like Frayling (p. 351), find implausible.

8. In Stoker's *Essential Dracula*, p. 51, editor Leonard Wolf suggests that the blond vampire "may have something in common with Lucy"; Gerold Savory's thoughtful 1977 adaptation, starring Louis Jourdan and directed by Philip Saville, superimposes on the slavering vampire a memory of Mina's face as she demurely brushes her hair.

9. Ellen Terry's "About H. I.," her diary during the 1890s, which her daughter appended to the final edition of her autobiography. See *Ellen Terry's Memoirs*, with a preface, notes, and additional biographical material by Edith Craig and Christopher St. John (1932; reprint, New York: Benjamin Blom, 1969), pp. 270–71.

10. David J. Skal, *Hollywood Gothic: The Tangled Web of Dracula from Novel to Stage to Screen* (New York and London: W. W. Norton, 1990), pp. 26–27. Also see my *Ellen Terry, Player in Her Time* (New York: W. W. Norton, 1987), esp. pp. 190–200.

11. Quoted in Phyllis A. Roth, *Bram Stoker* (Boston: Twayne, 1982), p. 5. Roth goes on to claim "that Stoker's friendship with Irving was the most important love relationship of his adult life" (p. 136), though she suggests shrewdly (p. 14) that *Dracula* somehow sapped Irving's imperial potency.

12. His great-nephew claims that Stoker died of syphilis caught from the prostitutes to whom he turned when his chilly wife refused further sexual relations after the birth of their son. See Daniel Farson, *The Man Who Wrote* Dracula: *A Biography of Bram Stoker* (New York: St. Martin's Press, 1975).

This rehearsal for Ibsen's *Ghosts* is a suggestive genesis of the most theatrical vampire ever created, but the rigidly polarized roles—frigid wife and contaminating whore—allotted to the women of this biographical script are probably the consequence, not the cause, of Stoker's consuming hero worship of Irving. We should not condescend to Stoker's supposedly "Victorian" definitions of women without remembering their entanglement in Irving's theater and Irving's own emotional and imperial magnetism. Many Victorian men reduced their women to labels; few had their imaginations aroused by a compensating Irving.

13. In Fred Saberhagen's wonderfully witty and astute novel *The Dracula Tape*, in which Dracula gets to tell the story Stoker refuses to include, the vampire complains sardonically about his doltish guest: "He misinterpreted these oddities, but never asked openly for any explanation, whilst I, wisely or unwisely, never volunteered one.... My little Englishman was tolerant of it all, but he was dull, dull, dull. A brooder, but no dreamer. There was no imagination in him to be fired." *The Dracula Tape* (1975; reprint, New York: Ace, 1980), pp. 16, 31. Saberhagen's Dracula wants to restore the communion with mortals that was the birthright of earlier vampires.

14. Christopher Craft, "'Kiss Me with Those Red Lips,'" pp. 110–16, is particularly ingenious in describing, and thereby authorizing, the homoerotic contact that does *not* take place in *Dracula*.

15. Stoker's "original Foundation Notes and Data for his *Dracula*" in the Rosenbach Library in Philadelphia, quoted in Frayling, p. 301; reprinted by permission (see n. 40 below).

16. Two of the most stylized *Dracula* films, directed by Tod Browning (1931) and Francis Ford Coppola (1992), advertised themselves as love stories: Browning's was billed as "the strangest love story ever told," while Coppola's ads reassured us that "love never dies." In both, though, the vampire performs on a plane so remote from the other characters that one can scarcely imagine vampire and mortal touching or even conversing, much less biting or loving.

17. These Jonathans are presumably uninfected at the redemptive endings of their movies, but later film Jonathans amplify Murnau's suggestive variation by actually becoming vampires. See especially Terence Fisher's *Horror of Dracula* (1957), the first of the brightly colored Hammer films that illuminated the 1960s, in which Jonathan, here a susceptible vampire-hunter, is easily seduced by a chesty vampire woman who wears a tunic; Dan Curtis's TV movie (*Bram Stoker's Dracula*, 1973), starring Jack Palance, which follows the Hammer tradition by abandoning Jonathan to the three ravenous vampire women so that he can become a snarling monster Van Helsing must stake at the end; and, most dramatically, Werner Herzog's *Nosferatu the Vampyre* (1979), a searing remake of Murnau's film. In Herzog's revision, a grinning, fanged Jonathan ends the movie by galloping off to become king of the vampires after his wife has sacrificed herself in vain. Only Herzog follows Murnau by discarding the three intermediary female vampires, allowing Dracula himself to transform his vulnerable guest.

These later Jonathans are all oafish revisions of Stoker's supposedly heroic civil servant, who obeys a paternalistic employer by bringing to a wild country the light of British law. In the 1960s and 1970s, movie Jonathans, like the imperial mission they represent, are corrupt and vulnerable. Although, unlike Stoker's pure survivor, they become vampires with scarcely a whimper of protest, they resemble Stoker's character, who exists to belong to someone in power, more than they do the passionate friends of the generous Byronic gentry.

18. I use Stoker's names here for the reader's convenience. *Nosferatu* was a pirated adaptation of *Dracula* whose original titles muffle its debt to Stoker by renaming the characters; Dracula, for example, becomes Graf Orlok. Some later prints revert to the Stoker names, though "Mina" mutates into the more powerful and euphonious "Nina." Skal, *Hollywood Gothic*, esp. pp. 43–63, provides a thorough and witty account of Florence Stoker's Van Helsing–like pursuit of Murnau's elusive film.

19. Stoker's Van Helsing affirms that the vampire's "power ceases, as does that of all evil things, at the coming of day" (p. 290), but the sun is no threat to Dracula's life: it merely limits his shape-shifting capacity.

20. Gregory A. Waller writes eloquently about the wives in Murnau's original *Nosferatu* and Werner Herzog's remake, whom he sees as solitary warriors, independent of traditional weapons and of the wise directing father figures who contained Stoker's women. According to Waller, *Nosferatu*'s women are as isolated in bourgeois society as the vampire, sacrificing themselves ironically—and, ultimately, tragically—to institutions that ignore and silence them; see Gregory A. Waller, *The Living and the Undead: From Stoker's Dracula to Romero's Dawn of the Dead* (Urbana and Chicago: University of Illinois Press, 1986), p. 225.

Waller's excellent account of mutating vampire representations is sometimes sentimental about victimized women, who, in both versions of *Nosferatu*, seem to release through self-sacrifice their own rebellious vampiric allegiance, though they refrain from snarling and growing fangs.

21. Siegfried Kracauer's *From Caligari to Hitler: A Psychological History of German Film* (Princeton: Princeton University Press, 1947) reads *Nosferatu* prophetically, as an allegorical warning against the plague of Hitlerism. Kracauer's influential reading is truer, perhaps, to the coldly imperial Dracula than it is to Murnau's ravished ghost.

22. Waller, *The Living and the Undead*, p. 92, notes astutely that in the American film, Renfield is maddened by Dracula, while in Stoker's novel the vampire manipulates a madness, embodied in Renfield, that lurked in England before his coming. This contrast holds if one reads the screenplay alone, but Dwight Frye's performance is so bacchanalian from the beginning that it is difficult to call the pre-Dracula Renfield "sane."

23. In the so-called "Spanish *Dracula*" (1931, dir. George Melford)—a Spanish-language adaptation for Mexican distribution that was filmed at

night, on the same set and from the same shooting script as the Hollywood version—Dracula feeds Renfield generously, but Pablo Alvarez Rubio's affable chicken-chewing dispels any erotic tension between himself and Carlos Villarias's vampire. Accordingly, Villarias's Dracula leaves Renfield's prone body to his sister-brides.

The Spanish *Dracula* is technically superior to the Hollywood original: its photography is more sophisticated, its women are sexier, and its narrative is slightly more logical. It ignores, however, the subterranean attraction between the vampire and his guest that invigorates Browning's version.

24. The jarring shift of rhythm and focus after the movie leaves Transylvania is due in part to the producer's squeamishness; on the final shooting script, Carl Laemmle, Jr., wrote the Van Helsing–like rule, "Dracula should only go for women and not men!" David J. Skal, *The Monster Show: A Cultural History of Horror* (New York: W. W. Norton, 1993), p. 126. Early Hollywood movies allow emotional complexity to spill out in improbable countries like Transylvania or King Kong's Africa or Oz, but it is barred from home.

25. This shift of authority from an egalitarian vampire-hunting community to Van Helsing's autocratic leadership is the thesis of Waller's analysis of *Dracula*'s immediate descendants in film (*The Living and the Undead*, pp. 77–109).

26. Jonathan Dollimore writes compellingly about the rise of perversity as a creed in the 1890s, a decade in which the rigid categories erected by new experts in sexology came to restrain the play of affection. Because of Oscar Wilde's imprisonment and its aftermath, the willful evasion of categories that the creed of perversity proclaims is at best fragile, at worst doomed: "So in creating a politics of the perverse we should never forget the cost: death, mutilation, and incarceration have been, and remain, the fate of those who are deemed to have perverted nature." *Sexual Dissidence: Augustine to Wilde, Freud to Foucault* (Oxford: Clarendon Press, 1991), p. 230.

27. Bram Dijkstra, *Idols of Perversity: Fantasies of Feminine Evil in Fin-desiècle Culture* (New York and Oxford: Oxford University Press, 1986), p. 351.

28. Judith Weissman notes that in *Dracula*, "the one group of people that [female vampires] never attack is other women." Weissman, "Women and Vampires: *Dracula* as a Victorian Novel" (1977), reprinted in Carter, ed., *Dracula: The Vampire and the Critics*, p. 75.

29. Hume Nesbit, "The Vampire Maid" (1900), reprinted in *Dracula's Brood: Rare Vampire Stories by Friends and Contemporaries of Bram Stoker*, ed. Richard Dalby (London: Crucible, 1987), p. 221.

30. F. G. Loring, "The Tomb of Sarah" (1900), reprinted in *The Undead: Vampire Masterpieces*, ed. James Dickie (London: Pan, 1971), p. 100.

31. Phyllis A. Roth suggests plausibly that since Dracula is not staked, but only stabbed with a bowie knife, he does not die at all: he simply turns himself into mist after sending his captors a last look of triumph. See her "Suddenly Sexual Women in *Dracula*" (1977), in Carter, ed., *Dracula: The Vampire and the Critics*, p. 67, n. 27.

By so flagrantly ignoring his own elaborate rules, Stoker was probably leaving room for a sequel he lacked the heart or energy to write. Dracula's anticlimactic death, if it is a death, reminds the reader that once he has been silenced, even a vampire is easy to kill.

32. Many critics and novelists, even more loyal to the vampire, perhaps, than Renfield, have reconstructed Dracula's suppressed narrative. The most persuasive critic to do so is Carol A. Senf, "*Dracula:* The Unseen Face in the Mirror" (1979), reprinted in Carter, ed., *Dracula: The Vampire and the Critics*. Senf claims that *Dracula* is dominated by a series of unreliable, even criminal narrators who suppress their vampire/victim: "Dracula is *never* seen objectively and never permitted to speak for himself while his actions are recorded by people who have determined to destroy him and who, moreover, repeatedly question the sanity of their quest" (p. 95).

Senf's persuasive essay could be a gloss on Saberhagen's *Dracula Tape* (1975), whose urbane Dracula reinserts himself into Stoker's narrative, exposing with relish the incompetent dolts who persecuted him in the 1890s. This Dracula plays Van Helsing by telling Van Helsing's story: "When I have made you understand the depths of the idiocy of that man, Van Helsing, and confess at the same time that he managed to hound me nearly to my death, you will be forced to agree that among all famous perils to the world I must be ranked as one of the least consequential." Fred Saberhagen, *The Dracula Tape* (1975; reprint, New York: Ace, 1980), p. 101. Like Senf, Saberhagen accuses Van Helsing of murdering Lucy with incompetent blood transfusions, then exploiting vampire superstition to cover up his own malpractice. Like most Draculas in the 1970s, Saberhagen's is, emotionally and intellectually, a superior being who genuinely loves Mina. He transforms her to save her from the mortal idiots who bully and adore her.

Saberhagen's iconoclastic Dracula paved the way for garrulous and glamorous vampires like Anne Rice's Armand and Lestat, who not only tell their own stories, but initiate them, thus becoming culture heroes in a manner impossible to Stoker's compliant Count.

33. The word *homosexual* had been part of medical jargon since the 1870s, but it began to infiltrate popular discourse in the 1890s. The first reference to it in the *Oxford English Dictionary* is dated 1897—*Dracula*'s year—in which Havelock Ellis apologizes for using this "barbarously hybrid word." There is an abundance of studies exploring the emergence of homosexuality as a new clinical category in the late nineteenth century. All

acknowledge their debt to Michel Foucault's pioneering *History of Sexuality*, 2 vols., trans. Robert Hurley (New York: Vintage, 1980, 1986). In writing about nineteenth-century constructions of homosexuality as a clinical monster, I am especially indebted to Lillian Faderman, *Surpassing the Love of Men: Romantic Friendship and Love between Women from the Renaissance to the Present* (New York: Morrow, 1981), and Richard Dellamora, *Masculine Desire: The Sexual Politics of Victorian Aestheticism* (Chapel Hill: University of North Carolina Press, 1990).

34. Eve Sedgwick claims that in literature, 1891 was a watershed year in the construction of "a modern homosexual identity and a modern problematic of sexual orientation." Eve Kosofsky Sedgwick, *Epistemology of the Closet* (Berkeley and Los Angeles: University of California Press, 1990), p. 91. For most nonliterary observers, however, 1895—in which homosexuality was publicly, even theatrically, defined, isolated, and punished in the famous person of Oscar Wilde—was surely the year in which the public learned what writers had sensed four years earlier. Talia Schaffer's essay "A Wilde Desire Took Me': The Homoerotic History of *Dracula*" (*ELH: A Journal of English Literary History* 61 [1994]: 381–415) demonstrates in persuasive detail the association between *Dracula* and the Wilde trials.

35. Eric, Count Stenbock, "The True Story of a Vampire" (1894), reprinted in *The Undead*, p. 169.

36. H. Montgomery Hyde, *Oscar Wilde* (London: Methuen, 1975), p. 374.

37. In the theater at least, Wilde's disgrace seems to have had, if anything, a freeing impact on the next generation of women, in part because the Labouchère Amendment ignored lesbianism: the new constraints on men freed women to experiment with new theatrical idioms. As they did when they were vampires, women acted uninhibited roles that were taboo for men. See, for instance, my account of Edith Craig's unabashed—if admittedly professionally marginal—community of homosocial and homosexual women in *Ellen Terry, Player in Her Time*, esp. pp. 364–436.

38. Skal, *Hollywood Gothic*, pp. 34–38, discusses the affinities between Stoker and Wilde, two Irishmen who adored Whitman and loved the same woman: Wilde proposed to Florence Balcombe, whom Stoker later married. Skal does suggest that Wilde's trials motivated the strident antisex rhetoric of Stoker's later career, but he ignores the power of the trials over Stoker's imagination of Dracula, a conjunction Schaffer analyzes with depth and thoroughness.

39. This aesthetic animalism evokes Henry Irving's famous performance in *The Bells*, in which, during his reenactment of murder, he is said to have thrown back his head and howled when he reached the line: "

'How the dogs howl at Daniel's farm—like me they are hungry, searching for prey.' And then [continues the enthralled observer] he howled. It makes my hair stand on end when I think of it." Like Irving, Dracula turns animalism into a compelling art form. Quoted in Marius Goring, Foreword to *Henry Irving and* The Bells, ed. David Mayer (Manchester: Manchester University Press, 1980), p. xv.

40. Stoker's working notes include typed excerpts from a "Goldon Chersonese" by "Miss Bond," many of which deal with transfiguration and animal worship: "The Malays have many queer notions about tigers, and usually only speak of them in whispers, because they think that certain souls of human beings who have departed this life have taken up their abode in these beasts, and in some places for this reason, they will not kill a tiger unless he commits some specially bad aggression. They also believe that some men are tigers by night and men by day!" Stoker's own commentary makes clear that this animal possession generates not degradation, but awe: "It almost seems as if the severe monotheism to which they have been converted compels them to create a gigantic demonology." Quoted by permission of the Rosenbach Museum and Library, Philadelphia, Pa. (Stoker, Bram, *Dracula: ms. notes and outlines* [ca. 1890–ca. 1896], EL4/f.s874d/MS).

41. Leonard Wolf makes this connection in *The Essential Dracula*, p. 47.

42. Sir Frederick Treves, "The Elephant Man" (1923); reprinted in Michael Howell and Peter Ford, *The True History of the Elephant Man* (Middlesex: Penguin, 1980), p. 190.

43. Leslie Fiedler, *Freaks: Myths and Images of the Secret Self* (1978; reprint, New York: Anchor, 1993), p. 174.

44. Howell and Ford, pp. 210, 110, 206. On p. 35, Howell and Ford make explicit what Treves's memoir discreetly implies: that Merrick's "penis and scrotum were perfectly normal."

45. Harriet Ritvo, *The Animal Estate: The English and Other Creatures in the Victorian Age* (Cambridge, Mass.: Harvard University Press, 1987), p. 6.

46. Quoted in James Turner, *Reckoning with the Beast: Animals, Pain, and Humanity in the Victorian Mind* (Baltimore: Johns Hopkins University Press, 1980), p. 133.

47. Rudyard Kipling, *Jungle Books* (1894–95; reprint [*The Jungle Book*], Middlesex: Penguin, 1987), pp. 81, 93.

48. Adaptations that use the release of the wolf feel the need to rationalize it more clearly than Stoker does. In Dan Curtis's 1973 TV movie (*Bram Stoker's Dracula*), for example, Jack Palance's Dracula uses the wolf to attack and distract the vigilant *Arthur*, his primary antagonist, while the vampire finishes off Lucy. Stoker's Bersicker only frightens to death Lucy's innocent mother, which Dracula surely could have done himself.

49. In the exuberantly revisionary 1970s, vampires regained hints of their animal powers. Louis Jourdan, in Philip Saville's BBC *Dracula* of 1977, was the first cinematic Dracula to crawl down his castle walls in the lizardlike manner Stoker described. Saville, however, insulates his human characters from vampiric transformations more chivalrously than Stoker did: his Jonathan never attempts to emulate Dracula's crawl, but instead jumps awkwardly, feet first, out of the castle window, retaining his humanity at the cost, one imagines, of a painful fall.

50. J. Sheridan Le Fanu, *Carmilla* (1872; reprinted in *The Penguin Book of Vampire Stories*, ed. Alan Ryan [New York: Penguin, 1988]), pp. 102, 130.

51. Elisabeth Bronfen claims that dead women are powerful artistic subjects because of their otherness: "Because the feminine body is culturally constructed as the superlative site of alterity," it both expresses death and deflects it from the artist and viewer, who are inevitably male. *Over Her Dead Body: Death, Femininity and the Aesthetic* (New York: Routledge, 1992), p. xi. I doubt whether, even in the most patriarchal societies, men have a premium on seeing. I suggest instead that women are culturally constructed vehicles of intimacy rather than otherness, and thus—in art, at least—are freer than men to act out embarrassments like desire or death.

Chronology

1847 Born Abraham Stoker on November 8 to Abraham Stoker, who works in the Civil Service at Dublin Castle, and Charlotte Matilda Blake Thornley, his wife. Sickly as a child, Bram remains in the care of his uncle, Dr. William Stoker, until the age of seven.

1859 Begins at Reverend William Wood's preparatory school in Dublin.

1868 Graduates from Trinity College with honors in science. Following in his father's footsteps, enters the Civil Service at Dublin Castle.

1871 Father moves the family to Europe following his retirement. Bram stays on in Dublin, writing theater reviews for the *Evening Mail.*

1872 Completes a master's degree in mathematics at Trinity. Delivers an address entitled "The Necessity for Political Honesty," which is later published.

1875 Publishes short fiction in *The Shamrock.*

1876 Father dies in Italy. Meets actor Henry Irving.

1877 Resigns his position with the *Evening Mail* to travel in Ireland and research his first book, *The Duties of Clerks of Petty Sessions in Ireland.*

1878	Hired by Henry Irving to serve as business manager at the Lyceum Theater. Marries Florence Anne Lemon Balcombe, who had been courted previously by Oscar Wilde, on December 4.
1879	Publishes *The Duties of Clerks*, his first book. Florence gives birth to Irving Noel Thornley Stoker, their only child, on December 31.
1882	Publishes *Under the Sunset*, a book of short stories. Receives the Bronze Medal of the Royal Humane Society for his attempted rescue of a suicide.
1886	Takes up the study of law and publishes *A Glimpse of America*, based on lectures on the United States delivered at the London Institution.
1889	*The Snake's Pass*, a work that draws on his experiences as Inspector of Petty Sessions, appears serially in *People*.
1890	Finishes legal studies and is called to the bar, though he never practices law. Publishes *The Snake's Pass* in book form and starts preliminary work on *Dracula*.
1897	Publishes *Dracula*. Produces a play based on the novel in order to widen the scope of his rights to the story.
1898	Publishes *Miss Betty*, an historical novel, which he dramatizes soon after.
1899	Publishes *Snowbound: The Record of a Theatrical Touring Party*.
1901	Mother dies.
1902	Publishes *The Mystery of the Sea* and presents a dramatic version at the Lyceum in the spring, shortly before the theater closes.
1903	Publishes *The Jewel of Seven Stars*.
1905	Henry Irving dies in October and is buried in Westminster Abbey. Publishes *The Man*.
1908	Publishes *Lady Athlyne*.
1909	Publishes *The Lady of the Shroud*.
1910	Publishes *Famous Impostors*.
1911	Receives a grant from the Royal Literary Fund. Publishes his last novel, *The Lair of the White Worm*.
1912	Dies April 20, with his wife and son at his bedside.

Contributors

HAROLD BLOOM is Sterling Professor of the Humanities at Yale University and Henry W. and Albert A. Berg Professor of English at the New York University Graduate School. He is the author of over 20 books, including *Shelly's Mythmaking* (1959), *The Visionary Company* (1961), *Blake's Apocalypse* (1963), *Yeats* (1970), *A Map of Misreading* (1975), *Kabbalah and Criticism* (1975), *Agon: Toward a Theory of Revisionism* (1982), *The American Religion* (1992), *The Western Canon* (1994), and *Omens of Millennium: The Gnosis of Angels, Dreams, and Resurrection* (1996). *The Anxiety of Influence* (1973) sets forth Professor Bloom's provocative theory of the literary relationships between the great writers and their predecessors. His most recent books include *Shakespeare: The Invention of the Human*, a 1998 National Book Award finalist, and *How to Read and Why*, which was published in 2000. In 1999, Professor Bloom received the prestigious American Academy of Arts and Letters Gold Medal for Criticism.

PHYLLIS A. ROTH is Professor of English at Skidmore College. Her publications include *Bram Stoker*, *The Writer's Mind: Writing as a Mode of Thinking*, and *Critical Essays on Vladimir Nabokov*.

CAROL A. SENF is an Associate Professor in the School of Literature, Communication, and Culture at the Georgia Institute of Technology. A specialist in 19th century literature, she is the author of *The Vampire in Nineteenth-Century British Fiction* and *The Critical Response to Bram Stoker*.

GEOFFREY WALL is Senior Lecturer in the Department of English and Related Literatures at the University of York. He has published translations of *Madame Bovary* and Flaubert's *Selected Letters*, and is currently at work on a biography of Flaubert.

CHRISTOPHER CRAFT teaches English at the University of California, Santa Barbara, and has written *Another Kind of Love: Male Homosexual Desire in English Discourse, 1850-1920.*

JOHN ALLEN STEVENSON is Associate Professor of English at the University of Colorado, Boulder. He specializes in 18th century literature and cultural studies and has published *The British Novel, Defoe to Austen: A Critical History* as well as essays on Fielding, Richardson, Sterne, and Emily Brontë.

DANIEL PICK is Professor of Cultural History at the Queen Mary University of London. His publications include *Face of Degeneration: A European Disorder*, *Svengali's Web: the Alien Enchanter in Modern Culture*, and *War Machine: the Rationalization of Slaughter in the Modern Age*.

KATHLEEN L. SPENCER teaches in the Humanities Division at Cincinnati State Technical and Community College and specializes in 19th and 20th century literature and science fiction.

JENNIFER WICKE is Professor of English at the University of Virginia. A specialist in modernism, critical theory, and media studies, she has published *Advertising Fictions: Literature, Advertisement, and Social Reading*.

LAURA SAGOLLA CROLEY teaches English at the University of Pennsylvania and specializes in 19th century British literature.

NINA AUERBACH is Professor of English at the University of Pennsylvania. Co-editor of the Norton edition of *Dracula*, her publications include *Women and the Demon: The Life of a Victorian Myth*, *Romantic Imprisonment: Women and Other Glorified Outcasts*, *Private Theatricals: The Lives of the Victorians*, and *Our Vampires, Ourselves*.

Bibliography

Arata, Stephen. "The Occidental Tourist: *Dracula* and the Anxiety of Reverse Colonization." *Victorian Studies* 33, no. 4 (Summer 1990): 621-45.

Astle, Richard. "Dracula as Totemic Monster: Lacan, Freud, Oedipus, and History." *Sub-stance* 25 (1980): 98-105.

Auerbach, Nina. *Our Vampires, Ourselves*. Chicago: Chicago University Press, 1995.

———, and David J. Skal, eds. *Dracula*. New York: W. W. Norton, 1997.

Belford, Barbara. *Bram Stoker*. New York: Knopf, 1996.

Bentley, C.F. "The Monster in the Bedroom: Sexual Symbolism in Bram Stoker's *Dracula*." *Literature and Psychology* 22, no. 1 (1972): 27-34.

Carter, Margaret, ed. *Dracula: The Vampire and the Critics*. Ann Arbor: University of Michigan Press, 1988.

Case, Alison. "Tasting the Original Apple: Gender and the Struggle for Narrative Authority in *Dracula*." *Narrative* 1, no. 3 (1993): 223-43.

Craft, Christopher. "'Kiss me with those red lips': Gender and Inversion in Bram Stoker's *Dracula*." *Representations* 8 (Fall 1984): 107-33.

Croley, Laura Sagolla. "The Rhetoric of Reform in Stoker's *Dracula*: Depravity, Decline, and the Fin-de-Siècle 'Residuum.'" *Criticism* 37, no. 1 (Winter 1995): 85-108.

Davison, Carol M., ed. *Bram Stoker's* Dracula*: Sucking Through the Century*. Toronto: Dundurn Press, 1997.

Demetrakopoulos, Stephanie. "Feminism, Sex Role Exchanges, and Other Subliminal Fantasies in Bram Stoker's *Dracula*." *Frontiers: A Journal of Women Studies* 2 (1977): 104-113.

Dijkstra, Bram. *Idols of Perversity: Fantasies of Evil in Fin-de-Siecle Culture*. NewYork: Oxford University Press, 1986.

Ellman, Maud, ed. *Dracula*. Oxford: Oxford University Press, 1997.

Farson, Daniel. *The Man Who Wrote Dracula: A Biography of Bram Stoker*. London: Michael Joseph, 1975.

Florescu, Radu and Raymond McNalley. *In Search of Dracula*. Boston: Houghton Mifflin, 1994.

Gelder, Ken. *Reading the Vampire*. London: Routledge, 1994.

Glover, David. *Vampires, Mummies, and Liberals*. Durham: Duke University Press, 1966.

Greenway, John. "*Dracula* as a Critique of Normal Science." *Stanford Literary Review* 3, no. 2 (1986): 213-30.

Halberstam, Judith. "Technologies of Monstrosity: Bram Stoker's *Dracula*." *Victorian Studies* 36 (Spring 1993): 333-352.

Hatlen, Burton. "The Return of the Repressed/Oppressed in Bram Stoker's *Dracula*." *Minnesota Review* 15 (1980): 80-97.

Hindle, Maurice, ed. *Dracula*. Harmondsworth: Penguin, 1993.

Howes, Marjorie. "The Mediation of the Feminine: Bisexuality, Homoerotic Desire and Self-Expression in Bram Stoker's *Dracula*." *Texas Studies in Language and Literature* 30 (1988): 4-19.

Hughes, William and Andrew Smith, eds. *Bram Stoker: History Psychoanalysis, and the Gothic*. London: Macmillan, 1998.

Johnson, Alan. "Bent and Broken Necks: Signs of Design in Stoker's *Dracula*." *Victorian Newsletter* 72 (1987): 17-24.

Leatherdale, Clive. *Dracula: The Novel and the Legend*. Westcliff-on-Sea: Desert Island Books, 1993.

Ludlum, Harry. *A Biography of Dracula: The Life Story of Bram Stoker*. London: Foulsham, 1962.

McWhir, Anne. "Pollution and Redemption in *Dracula*." *Modern Language Studies* 17, no. 3 (1987): 31-40.

Miller, Elizabeth, ed. *Dracula: The Shade and the Shadow*. Westcliff-on-Sea: Desert Island Books, 1998.

Pick, Daniel. "'Terrors of the Night': *Dracula* and 'Degeneration' in the Late Nineteenth Century." *Critical Quarterly* 30, no. 4 (1988): 71-87.

Richardson, Maurice. "The Psychoanalysis of Ghost Stories." *Twentieth Century* 166 (1959): 419-431.

Roth, Phyllis. "Suddenly Sexual Women in Bram Stoker's *Dracula.*" *Literature and Psychology* 27 (1977): 113-121.

Schaffer, Talia. "'A Wild Desire Took Me': The Homoerotic History of *Dracula.*" *ELH* 61 (1994): 381-425.

Seed, David. *Bram Stoker*. Boston: Twayne, 1982.

———. "The Narrative Method in *Dracula.*" *Nineteenth—Century Fiction* 40, no. 1 (1985): 61-75.

Senf, Carol. "*Dracula*: The Unseen Face in the Mirror." *Journal of Narrative Technique* 9, no. 3 (1977): 160-178.

———. *Dracula: Between Tradition and Modernism*. Boston: Twayne, 1998.

Showalter, Elaine, ed. *Sexual Anarchy: Gender and Culture at the Fin-de-Siecle* (New York: Viking Penguin, 1990.)

Skal, David. *Hollywood Gothic*. New York: W. W. Norton, 1990.

Spencer, Kathleen L. "Purity and Danger: *Dracula*, the Urban Gothic, and the Late Victorian Degeneracy Crisis." *ELH* 59 (1992): 197-225.

Stevenson, John Allen. "A Vampire in the Mirror: the Sexuality of *Dracula.*" *PMLA* 103, no. 2 (March 1988): 139-149.

Wall, Geoffrey. "'Different from Writing': *Dracula* in 1897." *Literature and History* 10, no. 1 (1984): 15-23.

Wicke, Jennifer. "Vampiric Typewriting: *Dracula* and its Media." *ELH* 59, no. 2 (1992): 467-93.

Wolf, Leonard, ed. *The Essential Dracula*. New York: Penguin, 1993.

———. *A Dream of Dracula*. Boston: Little, Brown, 1972.

Wood, Robin. "Burying the Undead: The Use and Obsolescence of Count Dracula." *Mosaic* 16 (1983): 175-187.

Acknowledgments

"Introduction" from *How to Read and Why* © 2000 by Scribner. Reprinted by permission.

"Suddenly Sexual Women in Bram Stoker's *Dracula*," by Phyllis Roth. From *Literature and Psychology* 27, no. 3 (1977): 113-121. © 1977 by Phyllis Roth. Reprinted by permission.

"*Dracula*: The Unseen Face in the Mirror," by Carol A. Senf. From *The Journal of Narrative Technique* 9, no. 3 (1979): 160-170. © 1979 by The Journal of Narrative Technique. Reprinted by permission.

"'Different from Writing': *Dracula* in 1897," by Geoffrey Wall. From *Literature and History* 10, no. 1 (Spring 1984): 15-23. © 1984 by Thames Polytechnic. Reprinted by permission.

"'Kiss Me with Those Red Lips': Gender and Inversion in Bram Stoker's *Dracula*," by Christopher Craft. From *Representations* 8 (Fall 1984): 107-133. © 1984 by the Regents of the University of California. Reprinted by permission.

"A Vampire in the Mirror: The Sexuality of *Dracula*," by John Allen Stevenson. From *PMLA* 103, no. 2 (March 1988): 139-149. © 1988 by The Modern Language Association of America. Reprinted by permission of the Modern Language Association of America.

"'Terrors of the night': *Dracula* and 'degeneration' in the late nineteenth century," by Daniel Pick. From *Critical Quarterly* 30, no. 4 (Winter 1988): 71-87. © 1988 by Manchester University Press. Reprinted by permission of Blackwell Publishing.

"Purity and Danger: *Dracula*, the Urban Gothic, and the Late Victorian Degeneracy Crisis," by Kathleen Spencer. From *ELH* 59 (1992): 197-225. © 1992 by The Johns Hopkins University Press. Reprinted by permission of the Johns Hopkins University Press.

"Vampiric Typewriting: *Dracula* and its Media," by Jennifer Wicke. From *ELH* 59 (1992): 467-493. © 1992 by The Johns Hopkins University Press. Reprinted by permission of the Johns Hopkins University Press.

"The Rhetoric of Reform in Stoker's *Dracula*: Depravity, Decline, and the Fin-de Siècle 'Residuum'," by Laura Sagolla Croley. From *Criticism* 37, no. 1 (Winter 1995): 85-108. © 1995 by Wayne State University Press. Reprinted by permission of the Wayne State University Press.

"Dracula: A Vampire of Our Own," by Nina Auerbach. From *Our Vampires, Ourselves*: 63-98 © 1995 by The University of Chicago. Reprinted by permission of the University of Chicago Press and the author.

Index